DESTROYERS OF THE LIGHT

THE BROKEN PROPHECY: BOOK TWO

DESTROYERS OF THE LIGHT

THE BROKEN PROPHECY: BOOK TWO

By
S.A. McClure

Not even embers shall remain

Destroyers of the Light
The Broken Prophecies Book Two

Written by S.A. McClure

Edited by Linda Sullivan
Cover Art by Katelin Kinney
Character Art by Stephanie Brown
Formatted by Red Umbrella Graphic Designs

Lunameed Publishing
lunameed@gmail.com
Indianapolis, Indiana
ISBN: 978-0-9992642-1-8

Printed in the United States of America.

First Edition.

For Michael.
Epic battle scenes forever. Thank you for spending countless
hours mapping out my war campaigns with me. You are the best
tactician a girl could ask for. This one's for you.

Nikailus Sindarthian

Starla

Amaleah Bluefischer

Colin Stormbearer

Chapter One

Kiela Rainforest, Smiel, The Second Darkness

Luminescent slime dripped onto Rhaelend's arm as he huddled beneath a giant kinella tree. Cursing beneath his breath, Rhaelend quickly brushed the slime from his body. A thin layer of lime colored residue clung to his skin. It smelled faintly of rotten eggs and Rhaelend had the distinct urge to use the last of his tiger lily oil to remove the stench. Instead, Rhaelend poured a small amount of water onto the glowing residue and began scrubbing at his skin. Sweat streamed down his brow.

Whispered voices caught his attention and Rhaelend instantly stilled. As slowly as he could, he gently tugged his sleeve over the still glowing streak on his arm. The whispers grew closer.

"These trees give me the creeps," a masculine voice with a slight drawl said.

"It's too hot in here," said another voice.

"We should turn back. You know what…"

"You know what, exactly?" a fourth person said. Rhaelend heard the scrape of metal as a sword was drawn from its sheath. "I'll not be havin' dissenters from the cause," the voice continued.

Rhaelend sucked in a sharp breath. *Of course*, he thought. *They're searching for deserters*. This, of course, did nothing to assuage his concerns. He was a deserter, after all.

"Yes, sir," one of the soldiers stammered. "We weren't talking about desertin', sir. I'm sorry, sir."

The way the soldier said 'sir' made Rhaelend smirk. Despite the words being spoken, it was clear to him that the soldier did not, in fact, believe in the cause. *None of us should*, Rhaelend thought as he deftly pulled his black cloak up and over his head in one, swift motion. He prayed to the Light that none of the soldiers had noticed.

The smell of smoke and the flicker of fire passed by the tree where Rhaelend was hiding. He tried counting the shadows but the soldiers moved too quickly. Rhaelend held his breath as the soldiers passed. They were a loud bunch and he hoped that any other deserters hiding in the forest would be able to evade capture the way he had. Rhaelend leaned his head back against the kinella tree and sighed.

A loud crunching noise above his head interrupted his sense of relief. Peering upwards, Rhaelend's stomach dropped. There, right above his head, was a shrieking monkey. He held a rock in his hand and seemed to be pounding the tree that Rhaelend was using for shelter.

No, no, no! he thought as the monkey seemed to notice him for the first time. With a trembling hand, Rhaelend raised one finger to his lips. In the dim glow of the tree's slime, Rhaelend saw the monkey cock its head at him. It hung by its tail and leaned in such that its face was mere inches away from Rhaelend's.

Rhaelend shivered as the monkey sniffed at him. It stared

into Rhaelend's eyes and poked a slim finger at his forehead. The monkey's fur tickled Rhaelend's skin and he let out a small snort. The monkey immediately drew back, baring its teeth.

And then the monkey shrieked.

"What was that?" He heard one of the soldiers yell.

"Dunno, came from over there."

Rhaelend heard clanking metal and ragged breathing as the soldiers advanced on his location. Still, the monkey continued to shriek. He tried to remember everything his father had taught him about the strange creatures who lived in the Kiela Rainforest. A single memory sprang to the forefront of his mind.

Rhaelend reached out his hand and muzzled the monkey's mouth. It didn't try to bite him but rather went entirely limp. The monkey's arms dropped to either side of Rhaelend's hand and its core sagged heavily. It reminded Rhaelend of the stuffed dolls his sister used to play with as a child. The memory did not quell Rhaelend's worries. Drawing the monkey close to his chest, he waited for signs of the soldiers.

Within moments, the soldiers' torchlight filled the forest. Rhaelend slowly sunk to the ground, his back still pressed against the tall tree. The kinella's roots were thick and tangled, but they provided ample locations in which Rhaelend could hide. Still cradling the limp monkey in his arms, Rhaelend slid between two roots.

Just as he slid his head beneath the root of the massive tree, Rhaelend heard rustling leaves from overhead. Boots, covered in the luminescent forest slime, stomped before his hiding spot. Holding his breath, Rhaelend peered up at the man above him. The soldier was large with a balding head and a bulging stomach. He wiped his nose with the back of his hand as he gurgled on his own mucus. Rhaelend wrinkled his nose in disgust. *They really don't have high standards for their soldiers nowadays, do they?* he thought as he continued to stare up at the man. He prayed the soldier didn't look down.

"I think I found something!"

The soldier turned his head toward the shout. He wavered a moment longer before grunting and heading away from Rhaelend's position.

"Look at this bit o'cloth I found. It's got the king's insignia on it."

Rhaelend's heart hammered in his chest. He tried to remember if he had snagged his uniform on one of the trees, but he had been in such a rush to escape that he couldn't remember.

"Let me see," the voice Rhaelend knew to be the captain's grumbled.

Chancing it, Rhaelend peeked over the side of the root. A cluster of soldiers circled around the captain. He sniffed at a small strip of yellow cloth. Rhaelend tightened his grip on the limp monkey. It didn't make a peep as it was pressed against Rhaelend's chest. For this, Rhaelend was thankful.

"You can smell the cowardice," the captain murmured as he spat on the cloth and dropped it to the forest floor. "The princess wants 'im alive, boys," he rubbed his hands together as he spoke. "He can't be too far away. Let's go find the pig."

The soldiers pulled curved blades from their belts. The metal gleamed in the torchlight as the men began whacking at the underbrush. Rhaelend knew that before long they would reach his hideaway.

He stared at the little monkey clutched in his arms. Its green eyes peered up at him. They seemed to be telling him something, though Rhaelend couldn't decide what it was. *It doesn't matter,* he thought as he stared down at the monkey. *They'll catch me one way or another.* Shaking his head, Rhaelend shoved the little guy into the folds of his cloak. As he withdrew his hand, the monkey instantly began shrieking again.

Rhaelend rolled out of his hiding spot to the sound of soldiers shouting. He knew they would be right behind him. He knew they would follow the sounds of the monkey's shrieks. He knew that he would most likely die. In that moment, Rhaelend didn't care. All he wanted was to be free.

Chapter Two

Faer Forest, Lunameed, 325 years later

Cool air blasted into Amaleah's back as she plummeted into the well. The imprint of Thadius's push burned her skin. *Did he really just shove me to my death?* she thought. *I'm not ready to die. Not now!* she tried to scream but the air caught in her throat the way a mouse is caught in a trap. Her skin was so numb from the cold that she barely felt the pain when her leg scraped against the rough stone wall of the well. Icy wind pressed into her face, sending shivers down her spine. She whimpered as she imagined what was waiting for her at the bottom on of the well. The longer she fell, the slower time seemed to slip by.

Amaleah bit her bottom lip until she tasted the hot copper of her own blood. As she flicked her tongue across her bleeding wound, Amaleah realized that she was no longer afraid. She had seen her nursemaid murdered before her; she had witnessed the demise of her father's senses; she had escaped. *I'm stronger than this*, she told herself. *I've come too far to let a little fear stop me know.*

The well narrowed and her shoulders scraped against the stone. Amaleah screamed as her skin were peeled away from her muscle.

Tears streamed from her eyes, leaving trails of ice in their wake. Closing her eyes, Amaleah pled with the Light to let her live. Her head knocked against an outlying rock and Amaleah saw bursts of red light. Her body squeezed through a narrow opening before plunging into freezing water. The impact of the water hitting her body so unexpectedly caused a momentary sense of being paralyzed. The water felt like ice melting against her skin as her body sunk deeper into the depths of the pool. Stretching out her arms, Amaleah could only feel the weightlessness of nothing. No sound traveled through the water, but a dull thudding echoed in her head. Opening her eyes, Amaleah peered out into the depths of the water. There was only darkness.

Amaleah gasped as she realized that she couldn't even see her hand in front of her face. Water filled her mouth. Amaleah coughed and more water rushed in. Panicking, she clutched at her throat. The water was so dark she didn't know which way was up.

Thrusting her arms and legs downward, Amaleah wildly propelled herself upwards. Her mind grew fuzzy and her muscles felt weak. She stretched her hand skyward, grasping for any sign of the water's surface. There was nothing except water.

Something soft and feathery brushed against her foot. Amaleah twirled around in the water, her mind suddenly much clearer than it had been before. She could see nothing. Her heart hammered in her chest as she tried to see in the dark water. The feathery touch stroked her skin again and Amaleah screamed. She inhaled water as soon as her mouth opened.

The water was sweet, almost like a fruit cider, yet it carried an acid taste to it that left her wanting to gag. *Why didn't I notice before?* she thought as she tried to swim upwards. Kicking rapidly now, she could feel the water create currents around her. She pushed with all her might against the weight of the water, thrusting herself up through its darkness. *I'm almost there*, she told herself. *Just a little further*. Her muscles burned. Her thoughts jumbled. *I can't give up*, she thought weakly. *I can't…*

Amaleah's thoughts faded as the water consumed her.

As if in a dream, Amaleah felt the feathery touch slide up her leg at a rapid pace. If she had been on land, she knew the sensation would have caused the hairs on the back of her neck to stand on-end. As it was, her mind replayed all the stories her tutor had told her as a child. Her favorites had been about the mermaids. She smiled faintly as the memory of Cordelia filled her mind.

Cordelia, she thought dimly, *blessed me*. Amaleah's chest swelled. *My meeting with Cordelia was so long ago*, she thought. She tried to concentrate on the memory she'd forged in her mind, but she couldn't remember.

Bubbles burst on her arm, startling her.

Opening her eyes, Amaleah saw two bright yellow lights shining in the darkness mere inches from her face. Their brightness blinded her. She blinked. And the lights blinked back.

Transfixed by the lights, Amaleah numbly bobbed in the water. They were unlike anything she had ever seen before. Dark gold lines crisscrossed through the lights and narrow black slits ran their full length. Her air-deprived mind tried to reconcile the light with the darkness but utterly failed. Fuzzy thoughts crept through her. Her weightless body somehow felt separate from herself. Lethargically, Amaleah made one last attempt to swim away from the lights.

Without warning, the feathery tendril wrapped itself around Amaleah's waist and tightened like a noose. Although she was weak and her lungs burned for want of air, Amaleah struggled against the tendril.

The tendril drug her through the water. Her ears popped and

her lungs burned. She weakly clawed at the tendril. To no avail. Amaleah's head lulled and her limbs went weak. Without warning, the creature whipped her upwards, unraveling its tendril as it went. Her head broke the surface of the pool and Amaleah sucked in a deep breath of air.

Panting, she tread water as her chest relaxed and her mind began to clear. She peered around her. The walls of the small cavern glowed a dim green. They shimmered as if they were in constant motion. A massive stone formation hung from the cavern's ceiling. It whirled with a brilliant white light. The air around Amaleah turned pleasantly warm. The dull ache in her muscles receded and her thoughts became crisp.

"Where am I?" she asked. She tried to keep her voice calm, but she knew that it trembled as she spoke.

A deep rumbling sound shook the cavern walls in response. Sparkling rocks cascaded into the water all around her. In the distance, Amaleah could hear the roar of wind as it passed through a tight corridor. She shivered as the sound reminded her of abandoned wings in Maravra's Tower. Lifting her chin, she called out, "I am Amaleah Bluefischer, Princess Heir of Lunameed, and I demand a response."

She waited, her heart hammering in her chest. Each second seemed to be an eternity. Without warning, the cavern's walls began to rattle the way a child shakes its first toy. Pebbles no larger than the tip of her fingernail pounded into her body. *At least I can still feel pain*, she thought as she swam to the pool's edge.

Then, as suddenly as it had begun, the cavern's walls settled as if releasing a long-held breath. Swirling mist seeped from between Amaleah's fingers as she clung to the hard stone. It wrapped itself around her body. It clung to her as she quickly shoved herself away from the rock. All around her, glimmering mist filled the cavern. It undulated between bright white and a dim green. Frantically, Amaleah twirled around in the water. She was trapped.

"Tell me what you want from me," she whispered as the mist swept across her face. "I need to know," she pled.

The mist reared back as if a snake ready to attack. It swayed before her. The mist was so dense and moved in such precise motions that Amaleah almost believed it was corporeal. *Stupid*, she thought as she thrust herself to the side.

The mist rushed at her so quickly Amaleah had no time to react before it seeped into her mouth and nose. Clutching her hands to her throat, Amaleah tried to hold her breath. Still, the mist pressed against her. Although the mist did not speak, it called to her.

Her mind immediately stilled as the mist encircled her exposed skin and soaked into her body. Slowly, she began to rise from the water. Her fingertips were the first to cast a bright light from them. Her toes, nose, and chest followed. In an immense burst of light, Amaleah shone as bright as any star in the sky. In that moment, she did not feel the cold. She did not hear the voices frantically calling her name from above. She did not know the pain of her broken body. All she knew was that she was one with the light.

She was fearless.

Amaleah sighed heavily and shimmering mist gushed from her mouth. She clamped her hand over her lips and pressed her palm so firmly into her skin that she felt bruises blossom across her flesh. Her brilliance began to dim as more mist escaped her with every breath.

Staring upwards, Amaleah realized that she was now scant inches from the glowing gemstone. It hummed softly as she reached one trembling hand towards it. Amaleah delicately placed a single finger upon the stone's smooth surface. It was surprisingly hot and she quickly withdrew her hand. Lyrical notes reverberated through the cavern as Amaleah timidly caressed the stone once more. It vibrated beneath her touch.

"I don't understand," she said as she stroked a silver-toned vein in the stone's surface. Mist swirled before her face as she spoke and her light dimmed just a tad more. "What does this mean?" she quailed.

The stone pulsed with light. The air became dense and Amaleah felt an urgency she hadn't before. She stared, transfixed at the pulsating light. Strange patterns, full of symbols Amaleah had never seen before, scrolled across the smooth stone. Entranced, she pressed her palm against the stone once more. It radiated heat so scorching that tears welled in her eyes the longer she maintained contact with the stone. At last, the final line of symbols flashed beneath her palm and a searing pain coursed through her. She ripped her hand away from the rock.

Amaleah's light instantly dimmed and she plummeted into the water. Kicking wildly, Amaleah broke the pool's surface and heaved in a breath as if it would be her last. The massive stone above her still glowed faintly, yet even its brilliance had faded when Amaleah withdrew her hand. She stared up at the stone, contemplating the mist, the vibrating patterns, and the light that had surged through her body.

The sound of plopping water drew her attention.

"Who's there?" she called out, her voice trembling.

Water droplets splashed her face in the wake of a massive dark shape slapping the water in front of her. She let out a shriek of fear before propelling herself backwards. Colliding with smooth stone, Amaleah scanned the cavern for any sign of escape. There was none.

The same yellow lights from before surfaced from across the

length of the cavern. *Too close*, Amaleah thought. She estimated that the distance between them was a mere twenty paces. The eyes did not move and neither did Amaleah. Holding her breath, Amaleah waited for the creature to make its next move.

As if on cue, the feathery touch of the creature's tendrils caressed Amaleah's leg. She winced and the tendril instantly withdrew. Amaleah sighed in relief and a puff of vapor followed. Her teeth chattered and Amaleah realized just how cold the cavern had gotten since she'd communed with the mist and light. Wrapping her arms tightly around her shoulders, she tried to stop herself from shivering. She closed her eyes and clenched her teeth.

When she opened them once more, the eyes from across the cavern were now directly in front of her.

Amaleah squealed. It was not a dignified sound and, had she been in her father's court, she would have been highly embarrassed by the noise that escaped her lips. As it was, she blushed as the creature cocked its head at her. Her heart still hammering, Amaleah regarded the terrifying creature with interest rather than fear. As she studied it, she found the creature less frightening than even moments before.

It had a massive beak with a sharp looking point at its center. Its body was a blob that was covered in thick tentacles. The creature stared steadfastly at Amaleah. It was so close that she could feel its hot, sticky breath on her cheeks.

"Amaleah Bluefischer, you have arrived at last," the creature squawked. Amaleah could smell decay on the creature's breath. *I'm about to die*, she thought as she resisted the urge to cover her nose with her hand.

"It appears that I have," she replied, her voice quivering slightly. A sharp pain flashed through her head as she spoke and she cradled her forehead in her hands.

When next she looked at the creature, it had cocked its head at her once more. There seemed to be an expression of concern embedded in those yellow eyes. Amaleah attempted to smile, but failed miserably as another spike of pain flashed through her.

"You are unwell, My Lady?" the creature asked in a gravelly tone.

"Yes," she stuttered.

Without warning the creature pressed one of its tendrils across her forehead. Water trailed down her brow and pooled on her chin before dripping off her face. The tentacle was warm, although not unpleasantly so. Amaleah found herself leaning into the creature's touch.

"You are not accustomed to harnessing the Light."

It was not a question. Amaleah found the creature's statement unnerving. A voice in the back of her mind echoed her father's words. *Burn, burn them all.* She shivered as she remembered the smell that still lingered in the abandoned wing. She wasn't sure why the Baron and his daughter popped into her mind now. They had never demonstrated any sign of possessing magic.

"I'm not sure what you mean," Amaleah responded after a pause. "I can use magic, if that's what you're implying."

The creature let out a dry, raspy sound that could be nothing other than a laugh.

Amaleah wrinkled her nose in dismay.

"Oh, don't look like that, child," the creature responded. "We all know what you are."

Amaleah stiffened. "I'm a person, not a thing, and I would take kindly to you addressing me as such."

"All who possess the Light are things in the eyes of our kings," the creature hissed. The venom it held in its voice gave Amaleah pause as she considered her next words.

13

"I would like to change that, if I can."

Silence filled the cavern. The sound of small, glowing fish popping up from the water filled all Amaleah's senses.

"It matters naught what you wish you could do, Amaleah Bluefischer, but what you achieve with your gifts."

Amaleah sat in silence for several moments. She had never considered the difference between intention and impact. *How many unsung heroes throughout the ages had worked towards a better world, only to be thwarted in the end?* she pondered. She presumed it was many.

"What am I?" she finally asked the creature.

"You are the Harbinger."

Amaleah sighed in frustration. "Yes, I knew that. But," she began, pinching the flesh between her thumb and forefinger to stop herself from showing her frustration, "what does that mean?"

"It means," the creature said, "that you are the Light's chosen savior. You alone will bring balance back to our world. You alone will fight the darkness that invades our lands and succeed. We have waited millennia for you. And now you are here."

The creature's voice came out in a rushed rasp that Amaleah found difficult to understand. Still, she comprehended enough. She was the 'chosen one,' for all that was worth. *I'll probably have to sacrifice my life or something in the end*, she thought, annoyance flicking across her face.

"And what if I refuse?" she asked, her voice a mixture of sincerity and contempt.

Light burst from the stone hanging above them so brightly that Amaleah saw ghosts flash through her eyes even after she closed them. Despite the cavern being beneath ground, a great gust of wind pommeled into her. Through the popping in her ears, Amaleah heard the creature speak.

"There is only one choice, Harbinger."

The wind died and the bright light dimmed. Tears leaked from the corners of Amaleah's eyes as she slowly opened them. The creature's beak rested a hair's breadth away from her nose.

"We make our own destiny," Amaleah responded defiantly. She had worked too hard to escape her father just to fall into the trap of another arranged future.

"We shall see," the creature replied.

Amaleah could smell the rancid odor of decay upon its breath. The creature frightened her, yet she saw a deep melancholy within the creature's glowing eyes. Hesitantly, Amaleah placed her hand upon the creature's brow. Its skin was surprisingly dry and smooth. She gently massaged her thumb across the creature's face. It quietly purred as she traced the slope of the creature's nose. She laughed as it closed its eyes and nuzzled against her palm.

"It has been too long since anyone has dared touch me the way you are right now," the creature croaked. Although it did not shed tears, Amaleah heard the catch in its voice. Her own heart constricted as she imagined how lonely this creature must be.

"Shh," she said softly. She rubbed her thumb across what she could only assume was the creature's cheek. It hummed and leaned into the warmth of her palm. It remained like that for several moments before pulling back and peering into her eyes once more.

"I can see the Light within you, child," the creature's voice came out in a hiss as it backed away from her. "You radiate the Light like none I have ever seen before, not since the Creators themselves." The creature slid through the water until its beak nearly touched Amaleah's nose. Amaleah resisted the urge to pull away from it. Somehow, she sensed that doing so now would be a mistake.

"Yes," the creature whispered. "I see it in you." The creature's tendrils splayed wildly as it spoke. "You have been blessed."

Its golden eyes narrowed and one of its tendrils pulled the long silver chain out from beneath Amaleah's wet tunic. The conch shell shimmered a bright silver that reflected on the dark water. The creature twisted the shell all around before finally letting the necklace drop back onto Amaleah's chest. "My cousins, the sirens, have blessed you as well. Do not deny that you have been chosen." The creature's voice sounded sad as it wrapped a thick, muscled tendril around Amaleah's waist. "It is time I returned you."

With that, the creature jerked Amaleah beneath the surface of the pool and pulled her into its depths. Amaleah barely had time to suck in a shallow breath as her nostrils were filled with the cold water. She fought against the creature, certain that its aim was to drown her and then eat her. *It had all been a ruse*, she told herself.

But then, as if by some miracle Amaleah couldn't yet explain, the creature flung her from the water and into the flickering, dim light filtering from the hole she'd been shoved into. Pebbles cascaded into the water all around them, making tiny plopping sounds as they slipped beneath the surface. Muffled voices echoed from above. All she could make out was the faint sound of her name.

Blinking, Amaleah turned to face the creature who had not eaten her.

"Why?" she asked. The single word hung in the space between them. It felt heavy and burdensome.

The clear film coating the creature's eyes narrowed as

Amaleah leaned in closer to the creature.

"I said, tell me why."

"I never did care for the flesh of humans, even the magical ones. You're too stringy."

Never, in all her life, had Amaleah thought humans would taste stringy. Marbled, yes. Or even tough. But never stringy.

"Stringy?" she asked, with amusement.

The creature began to respond when a large pebble fell into the water between them. Dark water splashed Amaleah in the eye, causing her to blink rapidly.

"I'm coming, Amaleah," a gruff voice echoed from above. "Just stay where you are. I'll find you."

More pebbles plummeted into the water as her rescuer rappelled down the stone wall. Amaleah turned to look at the creature again. A lingering sensation of warmth and light and hope passed through her as she peered into its golden eyes and she somehow knew that this was only the beginning of their journey together. She didn't even know the creature's name

"What should I call you, the next time we meet," she asked.

"I am no one," the creature hissed as it began backing away. When it reached the farthest wall away from her, it said, "We haven't the time to discuss this, Harbinger. There is much to be said, much for you to understand."

"You're not no one," Amaleah murmured as more rocks thudded into the water and the faltering light from above cast shadows all around them.

The creature hissed at her. "Foolish. That's what you're being. Listen to me, Harbinger, and listen well. You are the one spoken of in old. I can sense it upon you. I have witnessed the light claiming you as its own. I know this to be true."

Amaleah opened her mouth to speak, but the creature wrapped a feathery tendril around her face so quickly that she barely uttered the first syllable.

"You alone can save us. There will be those who test you, who try to steal you away from the Light. Do not be tempted, Amaleah. Do not let the Darkness win."

"I'm almost there," the voice from above shouted at an ear-splitting volume. Amaleah cupped her hands over her ears as the man's voice boomed around the cavern. The creature curled its tentacles around her arm and slowly pried her hands from her head.

"Trust none but Thadius," the creature whispered in a rush. "He will guide you when the others are blinded by their lust for your power. Remember this, Harbinger, even the hearts of the purest among you may become corrupted. When the Darkness pervades our world, let not your heart waiver."

Amaleah's eyes burned as dust and rock flooded their air space. She sneezed, then coughed, then sneezed again as she inhaled the dust. Ducking her head beneath the surface, Amaleah let the chilled water wash away the grime from her eyes. She scrubbed at her face. Her hands were like ice on an already chilly day as her fingers raked across her skin. Her head pounding, Amaleah raised her head once more only to discover that the creature had disappeared.

"Amaleah?" the voice called from above. In the dim light seeping through the crevices, Amaleah saw an outstretched hand.

"Take my hand, Amaleah. Just take my hand."

Feeling dizzy, Amaleah pushed herself through the water until she was directly below the outstretched hand. She trembled as she reached upwards. *If I am the Harbinger*, she thought, *then I need to learn to rid myself of my fears*. She shivered as a voice echoed in the back of her mind, *even the hearts of the purest among you may become corrupted by the darkness*.

Her rescuer wrapped an arm around Amaleah's waist and

lifted her from the water. "Hold on, Amaleah," he whispered.

The cavern was too dark and Amaleah's vision was too blurry for her to see his face. Still, she clung to him. Her head spun and dancing lights floated before her. Images of people dying flashed through her vision as the last of her body left the water. She felt weightless, as if her body and her spirit were separate. Her legs scraped against the jagged edges of stones as they were heaved upwards. Biting her tongue, she stopped herself from screaming out in pain.

"It's alright," the council member whispered. "I've got you."

It was too dark to see who had retrieved her from the well. Silent tears streaming from her eyes, Amaleah pressed her cheek against the council member's back. She didn't know what to believe anymore. Images of the chaos she'd witnessed flashed through her. She felt the agony and smelled the stench of death as her home burned. Her father's face filled her mind as she'd stabbed him. The images twisted and reformed into ones of which Amaleah had no memory. She saw entire races destroyed. She heard the whimper of children as they watched their parents being slaughtered. She felt cold steel slide across her skin as a figure in red held a sword to her throat. Amaleah shook her head to rid herself of the images. *I survived,* she reminded herself. *I will always survive.*

Chapter Three

"What happened to you down there?" Castinil demanded.

Her shoulders shuddered as a cool wind whipped through the trees. Amaleah swore she saw silver in the older woman's eyes as she clamored from Beo's grasp.

"Thank you," she murmured to the wolf-man as he quickly backed away from her. His nostrils flared as a gust of wind sent her scent in his direction. As discreetly as she could, Amaleah smelt herself. The hint of decay and old water wafted from her. Shrugging her shoulders, Amaleah took a step towards Castinil.

"Do you know what's down there?" she asked. She looked around the circle and noticed that Yosef held a blade to Thadius's bare chest. The centaur smiled at her, merriment still dancing in his eyes. She did not return the smile as she drew her gaze back to Castinil.

"It is a shrine to the Light," the old woman began.

"Let me stop you right there," Amaleah cut in. Her voice remained steady as she spoke. She caught a glimmer of movement from the corner of her eye and saw Helena rest her hand on Armos's arm. Castinil scowled at her, but paused. Amaleah didn't care if she was being impertinent. She didn't care if they found her to be a spoiled, insolent child. She wasn't. Not anymore. "I can tell from your expression that you're not used to being interrupted." She swept her arm around the circle, "I can tell that all of you have been at this for a long, long time," she emphasized the second 'long' as she held Castinil's gaze. "But, let me tell you something about what is going to happen next."

Amaleah crossed her arms over her chest to hide the shuddering as she spoke. She knew what she was doing was risky, but she was tired of being ordered around. Exhausted from the constant secrets being tossed around her, she wanted answers.

"If, and I mean IF, I am going to serve as your 'Harbinger,' then I expect for you to tell me things about the prophecy. I expect for you to treat me like the princess I am. I demand that you include me in decisions that affect me," she sucked in a breath as she considered her next words. *I have nothing to lose,* she reminded herself. "I make my own destiny. You do not choose for me."

Laughter. Laughter was what followed her monologue. Amaleah seethed as she peered around the gathering. Helena clutched at her chest as if the very words Amaleah had spoken had been a blow to her heart. Gren, the enormous tree-creature bellowed a low chuckle while Beo released a series of harsh barks. The yet unnamed creature who stood amidst the tree tops chortled in a surprisingly high-pitched tone. Amaleah felt her cheeks flush.

Only Thadius and Yosef remained silent as they stared at her. The centaur's expression was one of genuine surprise. She supposed they had identified her as an insipid fool of a princess who needed their guidance to grow into a warrior. It was all another label to place upon her. Amaleah was tired of labels.

Castinil clapped her hands twice and the laughter instantly died. "You think you can tell us, the Keepers of the Light and the constables of prophecy, what to do? You may be the Harbinger, Princess, but you are far from holding the importance you seem so eager to thrust upon this order."

Amaleah gulped, but stood with her back straight and her chin up. Still, she felt the icy gaze of Castinil as the older woman strode towards her with an elegance Amaleah would not have expected from such an old woman.

"Tell me, Princess, do you yet know how to wield the Light that so clearly emanates from you? Do you understand the gravity of what an error while using magic could cause?" she gripped Amaleah's chin in her icy hand. Purple veins pulsed beneath the woman's wrinkled skin, the familiar scent of snow and cinnamon somehow comforting.

She jerked her head out of the woman's grasp and glared at her as she said, "I can learn."

Her words sounded weak. She knew they were weak. She was weak. She shook her head and vowed to herself that she would get stronger.

Castinil surveyed her face. Amaleah thought she saw a glint of approval in the older woman's expression, but it was so fleeting that she couldn't be sure.

"Tell us what happened in the caverns beneath the well, Princess, and we will determine our next steps," Castinil whispered.

Amaleah weighed her options. The way she saw it, she only had one route to take.

"I met the creature that lives within the well. I do not know its name," Amaleah paused. The thought of revealing how the light had warmed her and coursed through her body made her cringe.

"It told me that I had been blessed, for I am destined to become the Harbinger spoken of in old."

Silence. Amaleah didn't know what she had been expecting, but it certainly had not been silence.

"So, Glenda actually told you that you were the Chosen One?" Castinil asked incredulously. Her cheeks paled as she spoke. "But you are so untrained."

Amaleah laughed nervously at the woman's words. "Glenda, as you called it, made it clear that I, and I alone, will be the one to rescue all of Mitier from destruction." She forced herself to stare down each of the Keepers. Their faces were a mixture of awe and contempt. Amaleah promised herself that she would remember those who looked upon her with anything but admiration.

Amaleah could feel Castinil's hot breath on her face. She could smell the woman's scent and hear the creaking of her bones as she swayed slightly in the wind. The older woman's eyes glazed over as she stared just past the top of Amaleah's head. Amaleah chewed on her bottom lip as she waited for Castinil to respond. The clearing was deathly silent. Birds did not chirp and squirrels did not hop from branch to branch as the entire gathering waited.

Amaleah found herself holding her breath as she waited for Castinil to say or do something. She shifted from one foot to the other. A shiver ran up her spine as her still wet shoe squished in the mud. The sound of it rippled through the air like a tidal wave. Her shoulders tensed and the hair on her arms stood on end as she felt multiple eyes upon her. Still, Castinil did not speak. Not even her eyes shifted towards Amaleah. Abashed, she forced herself to remain steady, though her body still swayed in the breeze.

Finally, Castinil clucked her tongue and motioned for Amaleah to sit upon the cool, damp grass of the forest floor. She sneered at the idea of sitting on the muddy ground. She knew she was already covered in blood and grime, but the idea of sitting on the ground seemed wholly undignified to her. She opened her mouth to say as much when she caught Thadius's eye. He held her gaze, his expression a plea. Amaleah chewed on her bottom lip, but proceeded to sit as requested.

"If you are to be our Harbinger, then you must learn to control your powers."

"I know…"

Castinil silenced her with a single look that spoke every curse Amaleah had ever heard. She felt the heat rise in her cheeks as she hunched her shoulders and silently waited for Castinil to continue.

"What you take on is a great responsibility, Amaleah. If you are, indeed, the one spoken of in old, then there will be a great number of sacrifices you will need to make for the good of our people. Magic must remain in this world." Castinil's shoulders shuddered as she peered around the clearing. When her gaze finally fell upon Amaleah again, her eyes were blazing. Amaleah gulped at the fire held within that gaze. "We must protect the Light's will," Castinil whispered, her voice barely more than a sigh upon the wind.

Coldness filled the clearing. Amaleah's breaths appeared in mist as she forced herself to peer into Castinil's eyes. She curled her fingers into fists as she heard the other Keepers rustling all around her. She knew they thought her nothing more than an insipid princess, too young and naïve to be of much use to them. *I will not be afraid*, she promised herself. *I will never be afraid.*

"I willingly accept the challenge, Castinil," Amaleah said. A warm breeze caressed her cheek as she spoke. It smelled of wildflowers and sunshine. It was a scent she knew better than any other. Her father had plied her with bottles of the perfume her mother used to wear during his courtship of her. A small smile played across as her lips as she looked straight into Castinil's eyes without flinching. Her voice did not shake as she continued, "I believe that my mother, Lady Orianna, would have chosen this path for me, if she were still alive to give counsel."

A collective sigh filled the clearing at the use of her mother's name. To Amaleah's satisfaction, the older woman's eyes softened at the mention of Orianna. Just as quickly, they hardened again as she looked down the bridge of her nose at Amaleah and sneered, "You are insolent, immature, and pigheaded."

Amaleah's stomach dropped at the words. Yet still, she clenched her teeth and forced herself to hold Castinil's gaze.

"I may be immature and naïve, Castinil, but I am no fool. I have seen the horrors of this world; I have seen the role my father has played in the terrors that fill the night. I will not be a part of his darkness. If I am the Harbinger that you keep talking about, then train me to be stronger. I can handle anything you throw my way."

Castinil glared at Amaleah. The wrinkles in her cheeks crinkled as she stooped so that her nose met Amaleah's. Amaleah cringed at the pungent scent of the moist air from her breath. Still, she did not pull away from the woman.

"Bah," Castinil finally grumbled as she pulled away from Amaleah. She turned her back to the princess in a movement so quick Amaleah thought she had imagined it. But, there the older woman was, speaking to the rest of the Keepers as Amaleah remained shrouded by the woman's shadow.

Amaleah glanced in Thadius's direction. Iron shackles cut into the centaur's skin as he pulled against them. She could already see the pink of his flesh as his body was ripped by the cold metal. Yosef still clenched a dagger in his hand. Its sharp tip glimmered in the flickering light of the torches. Amaleah gulped as she saw, as if for the first time, the thin trails of blood running down his chest.

Trust none but Thadius. The thought rang through Amaleah like lightning in a winter storm. Standing, she took a timid step towards the chained centaur. As if anticipating her intentions, Thadius caught her gaze and shook his head. It was such a slight motion that Amaleah almost thought that she had imagined it. That is, until Thadius let his body sag against the chains and his head fall against his chest.

"You have heard the arguments from both sides of this dispute. You all know and understand the stakes. If we make the wrong choice now, it could mean the destruction of our entire world." Castinil's voice was strong and smooth. It flowed over Amaleah and chilled her very heart. Amaleah found herself shivering as she waited for what was to come.

"Let us vote," the woman said at last.

Chapter Four

"It is done."

Silence hung in the air, oppressive. Amaleah wrapped her arms around herself as she shivered in the coldness that swept across the clearing at Castinil's words. For better or worse, the Keepers had made their decision.

"What of Thadius?" Helena chirped from where she stood next to Armos. Amaleah turned to face the woman as she straightened her shoulders and raised her chin perceptively higher. "What will we be doin' with him?"

All eyes turned towards the centaur, who bucked against the iron chains that held him in place. Yosef still held his blade to the centaur's throat.

"We should kill him and be done with it," Beo snarled. His pointed teeth clicked viciously as he spoke. Helena gasped at his words and opened her mouth to speak just as Gren spoke in his slow, steady speech.

"We would not have received Glenda's insight had it not been for his actions."

Amaleah caught herself thinking the words the tree-man was going to say before he even got close to saying them.

"He's a danger to us all," Beo growled through clenched teeth. He pointed a single finger in Thadius's direction. His claw sparkled in the flickering torchlight. "That," he paused before uttering the greatest insult a centaur could receive, "horse is barely capable of thinking beyond the present. He makes rash decisions that put us all in danger."

"He is also our representative from their ancient line," Armos broke in. "I do not think that Queen Nadine will take kindly to her cousin being disposed of by us. He is their emissary, after all."

Amaleah's heart hammered in her chest. Glenda's words reverberated in her mind as the Keepers continued to argue like children before her. Beads of sweat formed on her neck the longer she waited for the others to make a decision. With clammy hands, vomit creeping up her throat, and quaking knees Amaleah stepped forward.

"Excuse me," she stammered. When none of the Keepers turned her way, she said again, only louder, "Excuse me!"

Castinil cast a glare her way as the rest of the Keepers quieted down enough to hear what Amaleah had to say.

"I know you might not believe me, but when I was down in the well Glenda told me that I could trust Thadius." It wasn't entirely a lie. The strange river creature had also told her that the rest of the Keepers could not be trusted.

"And?" Castinil reported, her voice cold as ice.

"And," Amaleah began, "you just voted to train me as the Harbinger." She pointed a squat finger in Thadius's direction. "I want him to be my trainer."

Laughter filled the clearing.

"No," Castinil chortled. "He cannot be your trainer. He barely possesses the knowledge and skills to be a member of our order."

Thadius hung his head at Castinil's words. Amaleah could see his entire body shudder as he sucked in a breath at her words.

"Your order just voted me into your ranks, Castinil," Amaleah hissed, her voice a warning. "You need me. And I," she waved her hand in Thadius's direction, "need him."

"Choose another to train you, Harbinger," Castinil barked the last word as if it were a poison on her tongue.

"No," Amaleah said flatly. For too long had she been cooped away, shuttered from the world. For too long had she been the subject of others' whims and decisions. *No more*, she promised herself. *I am no one's pawn.*

Castinil's eyebrows rose until they nearly touched the line of her wispy white hair.

"No?" she purred. Her voice was like nails on metal in Amaleah's ears.

"No," Amaleah said again. This time she took a timid step towards Castinil as she spoke. "No, you cannot tell me what I can and cannot do. No, you will not hinder my training by denying my choice in trainer. No…"

"We get the point, Princess," Castinil snarled. Her face was taunt and cold as she spoke. She clucked her tongue as she peered down at Amaleah before sighing loudly. "Thadius may serve as your trainer as long as you allow me to choose a second."

The Keepers released a collective breath. Amaleah almost laughed at the sound of their breaths.

"Fine," she said.

"Fine," Castinil responded.

Amaleah watched as Yosef unlocked the chains clamped around Thadius's body. The centaur's otherwise unmarred skin bore blisters and scrapes where the iron had bit into his flesh. He limped as he strode towards her, gratitude etched on his face. He winked at her as he took his place at her right-hand side. A smile spread across her face, but Amaleah only turned to face Castinil as she said, "And who would be your choice, Castinil?"

The older woman bared her teeth in what Amaleah couldn't take as anything but a sneer. She turned away from Amaleah as she walked around the clearing. Helena bowed her head, her lips trembling. As she passed by the torches, still barely smoldering, they snuffed out. Smoke curled in an array of shapes as one-by-one the lights went out.

"There is only one whom I would trust to train you," Castinil said softly. Her voice carried notes so vicious that a shiver spider-walked down Amaleah's spine. The older woman stopped before Yosef and Amaleah groaned internally.

"He has been loyal to the Keepers for some time now," Castinil continued. "He is a true hero to the magical realm."

"He has fought many of our battles and always succeeded in his tasks. Yes," she said, almost absent-mindedly, "You will do."

She stopped before Yosef.

"It would be a great honor to serve the Lady Orianna's daughter, Castinil," Yosef growled. His voice was so naturally gruff that Amaleah found it difficult to determine when he was being cruel and when he was attempting to hold back his true emotions.

Before Castinil could respond the sound of crunching twigs filled the forest. Amaleah heard Thadius hiss as an arrow sped past his head, nicking his ear in the process.

"Your Father," he said as he practically dragged her to the stone well. He shoved her to the ground, his muscles flexing before her face. If they hadn't been in near mortal danger, Amaleah might have swooned because of the centaur's muscular body. As it was, she was simply grateful that the Keepers all seemed to be trained in the art of battle.

Dozens of soldiers, all clad in Lunameedian greens and blues flooded the clearing. Arrows flew through the sky, blotting out the stars and moons far above. The Keepers, though many of them appeared frail and at the end of their days, drew weapons Amaleah had not noticed before. Even Helena wielded a heavy-looking ax. Amaleah's jaw dropped as she saw the kindly old woman sink the blade into a soldier's skull with a sickening crunch. She spun on the soldiers surrounding her from behind, blades already firmly in hand. Amaleah watched as the woman sliced through her opponents with apparent ease. She swiped away a trail of her wispy hair, smearing blood across her brow in the process. She and Castinil pressed their backs together as they fought against the onslaught of soldiers.

Thadius bucked and sent two men flying through the air as they neared where Amaleah knelt. He yelled a war cry as he drew twin blades from a leather pouch tied to his back. He lodged them in the neck and chest of an oncoming assailant. The man fell directly in front of Amaleah, his eyes still open. Her stomach roiling, Amaleah crawled away from the body. Her hands slid over the blood-slick ground.

In the chaos, Amaleah didn't notice as a shadow crept towards her until it was too late. A meaty hand clamped over her mouth and yanked her from the ground. She tried to bite his hand. His stiff leather gloves protected him against her teeth. She thrashed wildly, her elbow narrowly missing his eye. Cursing beneath her breath, Amaleah attempted to kick her assailant in the groin. He evaded her attack in a swift motion that made Amaleah's head spin.

She pissed herself. The hot liquid soaked her leggings as she dragged her feet in the ground. Her captor hissed as the smell of ammonia slammed into them both. The sound of breathless curses followed. Amaleah took advantage of her assailant's moment of distraction.

She stomped on his foot.

The man released a loud yelp of pain as he loosened his grip on Amaleah's body. Using his lapse of judgement to her advantage, Amaleah swung her knee straight into the man's groin. Without pausing Amaleah brought her arm up and slammed her elbow into her captor's nose. She heard the distinctive sound of crunching bones as his head snapped back. She didn't wait to see if he recovered as she bolted towards the woods.

Amaleah leapt onto a low hanging branch. She could feel the pressure building inside of her. It pressed against every inch of her, begging to be released. She couldn't think about that now, not when her father's men had found her. She did the only thing she could think to do. She began climbing. Her nails bled as she clawed her way higher. She climbed and she climbed until the roar of battle was distant and a gentle breeze caressed her skin. Her back was soaked from sweat and her hands ached from finding hand holds in the sparser sections of the tree, but at least she had escaped.

She knew that she wasn't safe. She wasn't sure that she would ever be safe again, at least not as long as her father was alive. Or was it Namadus who had scouted her out? In some ways it didn't matter. There was a sickness corrupting her court and Amaleah would be damned if she allowed it to continue spreading. She had seen what her father was capable of doing— what Namadus allowed her father to do. As she perched high above the battle, shielded by the trees, she vowed to herself that she would save her people. Even if it meant sacrificing everything she had in the process.

I will not be afraid, she whispered to herself as the pressure within her made her head ache and her vision bleary. *I am the Harbinger, and I will not be afraid.* Spreading her arms wide, Amaleah released the power that had been building within her.

Chapter Five

There was only silence. And darkness. And emptiness. Amaleah coughed and a cloud of dust billowed before her as her eyes adjusted to the dark. Her ears began ringing as she sat up. She slumped back to the ground. Her entire body ached. She peered around her, trying to determine where she was, what had happened. Barren trees surrounded her. She could see their broken forms bowing in the wind. Fog moved through their bones, creating shadowing images in the faint light of the sister moons. Amaleah lifted her head to peer at them and a heavy pain shot through her. Gripping her head with both hands, she closed her eyes and counted to five. The hair on her arms stood on end and the wind seemed to be whispering to her to run, to get away, to escape. Amaleah's eyes flew open.

Figures moved through the mist and shadow. They moved quickly through the broken bows of the trees. Amaleah wasn't sure if she were too far away, if the ringing in her ears blocked it out, or if they simply weren't making any sound, but she heard nothing as they approached her.

The wind became more insistent. She swallowed hard before pushing herself up onto her elbows. Her arms quivered and she collapsed back into the mud.

Footsteps. Amaleah heard footsteps sinking into the mud close by. She looked in the direction of the figures in time to see that one of them was lumbering towards her. She knew she couldn't run, not in her current condition anyway. She felt around herself, searching for something—anything—with which to defend herself. Her hand found the boney hand of a fallen soldier. His tunic was stained dark with blood that still ran warm beneath her fingers. She flinched, but pushed through the nausea that swept through her. There was no time for squeamishness if she was to be the Harbinger. She felt her away cross his chest and to his belt. She found nothing.

Cursing softly to herself, Amaleah forced herself to get on her knees and crawl. She'd barely moved a foot before her knees buckled beneath her and she fell into the mud. She scooted backwards as the figure drew closer. The distinct outline of a long sword rose above his head.

Amaleah's heart hammered in her chest as she desperately swept her hands across the ground.

"We were supposed to take you back to the palace alive," the soldier coughed. He stepped into a swath of moonlight, his features finally illuminated. Blood seeped from a deep wound in his chest. He coughed again and more blood dribbled down his chin. "You're an evil thing, aren't ya?" he spat. His eyes narrowed on her. "Murderer," be bellowed as took another step towards her. His arms quivered slightly as he brought down the sword.

Amaleah rolled. She felt the slice of the blade graze her arm, but ignored the flicker of pain as it spread its way across her. Her body was fatigued and weak. She tried to stand, tried to run away as she saw the soldier wrench the sword from the mud.

"Wait," she said, holding her hand before her. "I don't understand. I haven't killed anyone." she said. *That's not true*, a voice whispered in the recesses of her mind. *It was your actions that killed Mr. Sweets*. She shook her head. *No*, she told herself. *It had been my father*.

He laughed hoarsely. "I'm all that's left." His voice was devoid of all emotion. Amaleah had never heard a voice so empty before. Not even her father had sounded this despondent.

"Please," she whispered, her strength failing her as she tried to stand once more. "I just wanted…"

"You just wanted to save yourself," the soldier coughed. Warm blood splattered across Amaleah's face as he spoke. She resisted the urge to wipe the blood from her skin. "All of you royals are the same. None of you care about the people."

"That's not true," Amaleah whimpered.

A low laugh filled the space between them. "Oh yes, it is. You could have stayed in the capital. You could have returned with us without a fight. You could have…"

He coughed again. It was a wet, wheezy thing. Amaleah could tell that his arms were trembling as he pointed his sword at her.

"How can you say that?" she asked. She would have thought that her people would have wanted her to escape. "You know what my father wanted from me. Please, you have to understand."

"Understand?" he asked, his voice low and barely audible. "I understand that you murdered a hundred men tonight whose families will never see them again. I understand that you chose yourself over your people." The sword fell to the ground with a loud squishing noise as he collapsed to the ground. "You're nothing," he whispered.

"You're wrong," Amaleah said. She crawled closer to him. His breathing was ragged as she grasped his hand. She needed to make him understand, needed him to know the truth. "I'm the Harbinger. I can…"

"You can die, before it's too late," the soldier said as he fell forwards.

"I'm sorry," Amaleah whispered, tears streaming from her eyes as she grasped his blood-slick hand in her own. He did not try to pull away from her as she squeezed his hand tightly. "I'm so, so sorry," she whispered as she heard the soldier take a long, shuddering breath before going completely still.

She held his hand until the darkness claimed her once more.

"Amaleah?" a purely masculine voice asked as warm hands shook her shoulders. Someone lightly slapped her cheeks. "Amaleah!"

Her eyes shuddered open. Harsh white light filled her vision and she instantly closed her eyes again.

"Thank the Light," another voice—this one feminine—said.

"Amaleah, can you hear me?"

She cracked her eyes, filtering out the harsh white light.

"Take her to the safe house," a voice that sounded like Castinil's said. "There's no way King Magnus could have known we were here without the help of a traitor. Our home may be compromised." She paused and Amaleah could have sworn she heard a soft sob escape Castinil before the older woman said, "And, we need to find Helena."

Yosef's shadowy face loomed over her. She squirmed as he wrapped his cold, hard arms around her body. He smelled of battle, blood, and death. Amaleah clawed at her own hand to keep herself from attacking him. Castinil had said something about Helena. She needed to help. She needed to find the kind old woman.

Yosef strode across the clearing. Bones crunched beneath his heavy walk.

"Let me go!" Amaleah yelled. "I can take care of myself."

Instead of responding, Yosef increased the pace of his walk.

"I said: Let. Me. Go!" Amaleah shouted as she beat against Yosef's solid chest with her small fist. He gave no sign of even noticing her attack.

Amaleah tried to draw upon the pressure—the magic—she had felt earlier, but she found only an empty reserve. Limply, her arm fell to her side as darkness consumed her.

———◆———

Voices echoed all around her. Dim shapes. A whir of color. Smoke. Amaleah couldn't focus on any of them. Soft fabric beneath her fingertips. She shivered. Cold. So cold. "She's gone."

Amaleah tried to concentrate on that voice, tried to place where she knew it from, but she didn't.

"We have to tell her," another voice said.

"Not now."

A warm, wet cloth pressed against Amaleah's brow. She wrinkled her forehead as water dripped down her cheeks. The sound of a crackling fire captured her attention right before she felt the heat and firmness of someone sitting next to her on the bed. She cracked an eye and saw Armos looking down at her.

"Welcome back," he said. His brow furrowed as he pressed two fingers against the spot on her wrist.

Her lips were chapped and her throat dry. "Water," she managed to croak.

"Ah, yes," Armos said as he hobbled over to where a pitcher of water and fresh fruit stood on a stand. He poured a tall glass of water and held it to her lips.

She gulped the water down until the cup was entirely dry and still her throat felt rough.

"You should try to sleep more," Armos said as he felt her brow with the back of his hand. "Your fever is still rampant."

Amaleah shook her head. Despite the pain covering her whole body, she needed to know what happened to Helena. She needed to know what she'd done when she'd released her magic.

"There will be plenty of time for us to discuss what happened once you've recovered," Armos said as he patted her hand. "For now, you need to sleep." With that, he blew a handful of herbs into her face. Her nose tickled and Amaleah thought she'd sneeze, but instead she felt her muscles relax and her body go limp.

Amaleah jerked awake. Sweat covered her body, soaking through the soft linen underclothes she still wore. They were stained a brownish-red color that Amaleah knew was blood. She choked back a sob at the thought. A fire roared in the hearth and Amaleah could smell the distinct scent of jasmine wafting through the air. Her throat was still dry as Amaleah groped for the glass she assumed would be arm's reach from the bed. She sent it crashing to the ground in a spray of glass. Tiny shards skidded across the floor, causing rainbows to dance upon the floor as the fire roared on. She half-smiled at the beauty of it.

Thundering feet echoed down the hall as someone approached her room. A terse knock followed by the squat form of a young woman drew Amaleah's attention away from the glass.

"Who are you?" Amaleah asked when she realized she didn't recognize the woman.

"Beatrice, at your service, miss," the woman said as she fetched a broom and pan from the corner. "But most of the ones who stay here call me Bee." She blushed as she spoke, her porcelain cheeks turning a rosy pink color. Despite the woman's girth, she really was quite pretty.

"Bee," Amaleah said, "Can you tell me where we are?" Her throat scratched as she spoke and she wished she hadn't broken her glass of water, but she forced herself to continue. "It's very important that I understand where I am. Do you think you could help me with that?"

"Well, of course, miss." The woman paused, "It's just that Miss Castinil made me promise I'd fetch 'er the moment you woke."

Amaleah sighed loudly. Her head still ached and her lips were so chapped they were actually bleeding. "Bee," she said softly as she stretched out a hand towards her, "Please, you must understand. I'm the future queen of Lunameed and I need you to tell me where we are."

"That will be all, Beatrice," Castinil snarled from the

doorway. The maid quickly brushed the remaining shards of glass into her pan before bobbing her head once and dashing from the room.

"You are in the Keeper's safe house, but we can't stay here for long," Castinil said dryly as she entered the room.

Amaleah did not respond to her. Rather, she began picking at the dirt beneath her nails and hoping that it wasn't blood. She knew it was. It was too black to be anything else.

Castinil sat on the edge of Amaleah's bed without asking. She patted Amaleah's leg before saying in such a monotone voice that Amaleah had difficulty understanding her words.

"Helena died in the blast."

The blood in Amaleah's veins turned to ice. "But I created that blast," she began. Tears leaked from the corners of her eyes. She hadn't intended to kill anyone. She'd just wanted the fighting to stop, to stop the pressure from continuing to build in her mind.

"We know," Castinil cut in. "And we understand. We know Helena, had she survived, would have understood. You're too raw with your powers, Amaleah. You have more strength in you than any we have ever seen before, but it is untamed. If you want to stop yourself from ever doing something like this again, then you must learn how to control your abilities."

Amaleah wrung her hands in her lap. She looked everywhere around the room, except at Castinil. Everything and everyone she trusted had turned to ash. It was as if it were an illness that could not be cured. Those who followed her had no chance at survival.

"I'm sorry," she managed to say.

"Hush," Castinil said sharply. "There is no time or room for such sentimental ideals, Harbinger." She stood and began pacing the small room. "We will not let Helena's loss hinder your progress. In one day's time, you will leave this place to train with the elves. Yosef and Thadius will travel with you."

Amaleah opened her mouth to respond but stopped herself when Castinil raised a single hand. "You will not fight against our methods. You will not argue with what you must learn if we are all to survive. We will only have one chance, Amaleah."

"I understand," the princess replied. Despite the ache in her body, she stood and clamored towards Castinil. The older woman did not object as Amaleah drew one of the many daggers strapped to her waist. Nor did Castinil utter a word in disapproval as Amaleah quietly sliced the palm of her hand open.

Amaleah winced as pain slid through her, but she didn't let that stop her. "I promise, Castinil. I swear it." She let her blood fall into the fire as she spoke. "Let this be a symbol of my commitment to discovering the true meaning of my prophecy."

The fire sizzled as her blood fell into its depths. When the last droplet had fallen, Amaleah closed her hand into a fist and returned to her bed.

Amaleah thought about what little time she'd had with Helena. A part of her wished Castinil to be wrong. She wanted to take back her weakness, to stop herself from using her magic to end the battle. But, she couldn't. She would never be able to take back the lives she had taken. For a moment, she could almost feel the heat of her father's blood on her hand as she'd stabbed him. *Am I any different than my father?* she thought as she waited for Castinil to respond. In many ways, she wasn't sure that she was.

"Amaleah," Castinil said, her voice tight. She strode over to where Amaleah sat and took a seat next to her. Her silver hair fluttered around her like snow on a crisp winter morning. The thought almost made Amaleah smile, almost. "We will be hard on you. And you will have to make sacrifices that no one of your age should have to face."

Amaleah looked at Castinil as she spoke. Her eyes filled with unbidden tears that she couldn't control. Suddenly, the older woman grasped her hand with her own.

"Many of us have waited so long for your arrival that we aren't sure what the correct course of action is anymore. We've lost sight of the Light. There are some that even believe we have been abandoned to the darkness," she squeezed Amaleah's hand as she spoke. "But, be that as it may, we cannot lose hope."

Amaleah sat in silence, tears still streaming down her cheeks. Castinil did not continue speaking. She just held Amaleah's hand. There was a comfort there that Amaleah had never before experienced.

Castinil patted Amaleah's hand, her bony fingers hard against the soft spots of Amaleah's palm. "Listen to me child. I know that you have not truly had rest since you left Estrellala, perhaps even since you left Maravra's Tower. But, we believe there is a traitor among our ranks."

"But who?" Amaleah asked.

Castinil raised an eyebrow at the insolence of Amaleah's question, but continued as if Amaleah had not spoken. "Based on what happened tonight, we no longer believe that the safest place for you is among our council."

Amaleah ripped her hand out of Castinil's. "What?" she exclaimed.

"We've made arrangements for the elvish clans to take you in as one of their own. They already know of the circumstances surrounding you."

"But…" Amaleah began.

"No buts, Harbinger," Castinil clucked. "They will get you nowhere." She patted Amaleah's cheek as she spoke.

Amaleah resisted the urge to scratch the woman's eyes out. *Who is she to tell me where I go and what I do?* Amaleah thought, her cheeks flushing with anger. "You're not my mother, Castinil," she said in short, deliberate breaths. "And you will not treat me as such."

The woman scoffed at her. "No, Harbinger, I am not your mother. I'm sure she would have done a much better job discussing sacrifice with you, seeing as how she gave her life for yours."

Her words hit harder than any ever had before. Amaleah's stomach roiled as she blinked once then twice in Castinil's direction. She couldn't see, couldn't think. Everything was a haze of her father's words to her time and time again. He oscillated from loving her like his long-lost bride and hating her for not being the dead queen. Her mother.

She felt the power building within her once more. Felt her anger and grief fill the center of that pressure.

"I'm sorry I took her from you," Amaleah said quietly. "I'm sorry I'm not as pretty as she was or as graceful. I'm sorry I can't think strategically like she could or make plans that rallied the people behind my words. I'm sorry that I am such a complete failure, Castinil." Her words were bitter and she knew it. She was just so tired of being compared to her mother that she no longer cared what other people thought. And, she was angry. She was angry because she had never gotten to know her mother the way so many others had. She had never gotten the chance to talk to her mother about her dreams, or boys, or what decisions to make in tough situations. She had been robbed of that chance. So no, she didn't care what Castinil thought about her.

"And those are the words of our next great hero," Castinil responded. There was no compassion in her tone.

Amaleah shrugged her shoulders. "I'm not the one who chose this path, Castinil. Think what you will, but I promise you this: I will save the Lunameedian people from my father."

Castinil laughed. It was a harsh and resentful laugh that made Amaleah's skin crawl.

"You really are just a naïve little princess, aren't you?" Castinil asked, no longer laughing.

Amaleah peered down at her hands. She didn't know how to respond to Castinil. She might have been young and naïve once, but she had seen and been through so much since then. She could barely remember the girl she'd been when she'd first returned to Estrellala.

"You honestly believe that this is just about saving Lunameed?" Castinil continued. Venom coated each of her words. "This isn't just about your kingdom, girl. This is about the whole of Mitier."

"I know that, but…"

"Clearly, you don't."

Amaleah glared at the older woman but said nothing. She no longer believed there was anything she could say, not anyway. Castinil's mind was already decided.

"Perhaps tonight's events will help you understand the mistakes you make will negatively affect us all. Perhaps it is a good thing that you will be sent to Encartia. Perhaps there you will be able to grow."

Amaleah snorted. She hadn't intended to, but it just came out. Castinil cocked an eyebrow at her, but Amaleah was already responding to Castinil's thoughts.

"I'm sorry you don't think I was the proper choice. Maybe I'm not. Maybe I'll fail in the end. All I can say is that I haven't seen the world beyond Lunameed, but I love my country and I want to save it from the likes of my father. Of course, I understand that what I do affects the entire tapestry of our world, but I can't focus on that, Castinil. Thinking about the whole of Mitier is too much. But, if I break that down into smaller steps, the task before me doesn't seem so daunting."

Castinil searched Amaleah's face before decidedly lifting herself from her chair and striding towards the door.

"You may think you have it all figured out, Amaleah, but understand this: you don't."

With that, Castinil flung the door open and strode from the room. Amaleah sat, slack-jawed and wide-eyed, on her bed for several moments before pouring herself a cup of tea and sinking back onto her bed. Despite the warmth from her cup, she still felt icy cold. It had been her fault. She'd killed Helena and all those other men and women. Her men and women. Lunameedians.

Tears streamed down her cheeks at the realization that these would not be the last. She would use her powers again. She would kill again.

Chapter Six
The Second Darkness, 333 Years Before

Kilian clutched Her to his chest. Her caramel skin glowed faintly in the darkness. He could see the swirls of her veins forming dark rivers in the sea of her body. He lightly traced one of those swirls with his finger. Her skin was smooth and warm beneath his touch. Nestling his face into her hair, Kilian breathed in the scent of her. The smell of chocolate and pine needles, and salty air filled his senses. A small moan escaped her lips as she leaned into him and Kilian smiled. He was glad that he could still have that effect on her.

"You seem troubled, Kilian Clearwater," she murmured. She didn't look at him as she ran her hands over his bare chest. Her touch left ripples of warmth in their wake. He shivered slightly as her hand lingered on the soft spot between his abdomen and his groin. She nipped at his ear as she commanded, "Tell me what troubles you."

Kilian felt the swell of her power wash over him. It had been thirty years since she'd first gifted him with his powers and still the weight of her magic on him was intoxicating. Instead of answering, Kilian left a trail of kisses along her jaw before finally placing his lips on hers. She ran her tongue over the length of his bottom lip before quickly nipping him and pulling back.

"Answer me," she demanded.

Kilian's body went rigid at the tone of her voice. She so rarely commanded him in this way that Kilian could almost forget the sense of powerlessness he felt at her demands.

He toyed with a stray strand of her hair as he said casually, "I just thought that the fighting would be over by now."

She pushed herself up so that her face rested on her hands as she peered into his eyes. The purple starbursts at the center of her eyes made Kilian's blood sizzle. She was the most beautiful woman he had ever seen. He leaned in to kiss her once more.

She stopped him with the touch of her fingers on his lips. "That simply won't do, Kilian," she said.

"I'm sorry," he responded, though he wasn't sure if she meant that kissing her wouldn't appease her or if his disinterest in fighting was the real cause of concern.

"You are the Light's Hero, Kilian. With that comes certain responsibilities."

"I understand that," Kilian began.

"And your responsibility is to complete the assignments we give you," she continued, speaking over him.

Kilian sighed, his shoulders sagging. "It's just that, you know what Ula Una means to me."

She ran her fingers through his hair and he purred at her touch.

"Yes, all of us understand, Kilian."

"Then why…"

"Why send you to eliminate the threat Bluebeard and his warriors pose to the Light's work?" she raised an eyebrow at him as she spoke. "You already know the answer to that, Kilian."

Her words were not the ones he had hoped to hear. Bluebeard, for all his faults, had been his friend. In his formative years, Bluebeard had been the man who took him under his wing. He'd been the one to rescue him from his village and set him on the right path. He'd met Her because of him. Kilian could not stomach the thought of harming him. Worse than the idea of hurting the current merking, was harming his niece, Cordelia. She had been so patient with Kilian during his time in Ula Una. She was the sweetest, most endearing little girl Kilian had ever met.

"There has to be another way," Kilian pressed. He knew he was pushing her past her breaking point, but he didn't care. Not this time.

"Because of you, Clara has been reunited with her sword, Kilian," She said. Her words were clipped and hard.

Kilian pouted at her as he said, "I didn't know he would choose her over us."

"You poor, unfortunate fool," She murmured as she cupped his chin in her hand. "It's sad, but true." She sliced his battle-worn cheek with one of her sharp nails as she continued, "If you truly believe that the remaining six of us will be safe with Bluebeard and Clara continuing to wage war against us, then I think it best that you tell me that now." The violet starburst in her eyes shimmered as she stared at him. Kilian felt the warmth leave his body as he peered into those hard eyes.

"I would never do anything to put you in danger," he stroked her hair with his hand as he spoke. "I love you, Tavia."

Her caramel skin turned black as wisps of ash lifted from her face. She narrowed her eyes at him. He so rarely saw her glare at him the way she was now.

"You know you are never to call me by that name, Kilian Clearwater. I am your queen and you shall refer to me as such." Ribbons of black and gold light flowed around her as she spoke. They twirled around Kilian's neck and hands, binding him.

"I'm sorry," he managed to whisper as the ribbon of light around his throat cut off his airway.

She squeezed him to the point where deep bruises formed on his flesh before finally releasing her hold on him. His entire body sagged as he fell into her arms and silently wept. She offered no words of encouragement to him as she held him in her arms.

"My queen," he whispered over and over again in his hoarse voice. He barely sounded like himself. He placed kisses along the tops of her breasts and cradled her in his arms as he spoke to her. Still, she offered no sign of recognition towards him.

"I swear to you that I will rid Mitier of your foes. I will fight for you until I can fight no more. Please, my queen, please." His lips dry and chapped, he pled with her until she finally regarded him with a deathly scowl.

"And what of Bluebeard and his wretched court? What of the rogue Creator who has been corrupted by the Darkness, Kilian? What of them?"

Kilian shuddered slightly as he forced himself to imagine what it would be like to kill Reginald Bluebeard. He had dreamed of it during those early months of his training. He had planned it when he'd been stuck with a drunkard on a nearly forgotten island. He had left those notions behind when he'd finally been blessed by the Creators.

"As you wish, my love."

She smiled at him then. Her perfectly pouted lips were full and lush and Kilian knew they would be soft as he leaned towards her and kissed her passionately on the lips. She kissed him back just as passionately. These were the moments Kilian lived for. He cherished every moment he spent with Her. He thought about her constantly. She was his everything.

She pulled away from him and said in a deep, husky voice, "you will leave on the morrow to fulfill your promise to me."

It was not a question. Nothing she ever required of him was a question. Just an indisputable command. Kilian nodded into her chest as she held him tightly against her. She moaned as he kissed his way down her neck and breasts before finding the hot wet spot between her legs.

"I will return to you," he said as he lay beside her after the candles had melted into darkness. "I will always return to you."

She said nothing as she released his hand and rolled over so that her back was to him. Kilian contained the sob that swelled within him as he heard her breathing deepen into the steady purr of her muffled snores. He knew she loved him. There was no other option but their love. It was the singular most important thing in the whole of Mitier and Kilian was determined to protect her.

Even if it means killing Bluebeard? A nagging voice hissed in the recesses of his mind. An image of Cordelia's young face flashed through his mind. She had grown during the many years of battle between Lunameed and Szarmi. She had matured into a strong-willed, intelligent, and stunning young siren. Kilian couldn't imagine being the one to end her life, but he knew that, as the Light's Hero, he would need to be the one to take their lives.

Silent tears ran down his cheeks as he wrapped his arm around Her and fitfully drifted off to sleep.

Chapter Seven

Near Sueria Tower, Arcadi Forest, Lunameed

The massive grandfather clock next to the mantle chimed the evening hour. Nikailus watched as the figure of the gray father peered at the stars from within his castle. His tiny silver telescope reflected even smaller stars. As the clock struck eleven, the man slipped back into his chambers to chart what he had discovered and reflect on the variety of life. This depiction had been created for each of the clocks given to the brethren. Just like the other eleven stories held within the timepieces, the story of the gray father was seminal to one of the pillars of the order. The pursuit of knowledge and understanding—at all costs—was the most valued trait among his order.

Nikailus twiddled his thumbs as he waited. He had always thought that the story of the gray father was a tad overplayed. Yes, the pursuit of knowledge was important; however, Nikailus had always been drawn to the ninth hour. This one told the story of how power is passed from one generation to the next. It told of how the brethren had increased their powers over the centuries that had passed since the Creators left the whole of Mitier to rot in their wake. Nikailus was one of the few who believed that the Creators would return one day. They would not be the gracious bringers of light they were so often displayed as. No, Nikailus

51

knew the truth of the Creators. They embodied two sides of the same coin. It was Nikailus's role to ensure that the Creators chose the path that would lead to power.

Indeed, this was why Nikailus continued to sit in the cramped, drafty room in a building that was little more than a hovel near Sueria Tower. His greasy, stringy hair fell into his eyes as he dug the dirt from beneath his nails. Black clumps fell onto his lap. He grimaced as a nail sliced through the flesh beneath his middle finger. A deep purple bruise spread across his once pink nail. Growling softly to himself, Nikailus continued onto the next finger.

"You never did learn your lesson on cleanliness," a smooth voice said as Jonathan finally entered the room. His white curls glistened like silver in the small amount of moonlight that seeped in through the window. Nikailus ignored the older man as he dug out a particularly deep bit of grime. He heard Jonathan sigh and heard the squeal of the over-stuffed chair as the man sank into it.

"I see that you are determined to disregard my lessons," Jonathan began. Nikailus steadfastly ignored the older man. When he had cleaned out the remaining trail of dirt beneath his nails, Nikailus stretched his arms far behind him. His muscles ached as he held this position for several seconds. He stood and took a different stance by bringing his arms high above his head and peering upwards. He slowly bent down so that his hands touched the ground. His lower back stretched as he knelt.

"Nikailus, I did not ask you to meet with me so that you could practice yoga," Jonathan drawled. "We have much to discuss." He snapped his fingers at Nikailus.

Nikailus detested being snapped at. In fact, he hated it so much that he turned his back on Jonathan and took another stance.

"Nikailus," Jonathan hissed. Nikailus knew it was a warning.

He knew that his mentor, even in his old age, would be able to disable him within moments. He was the best fighter in his class, but Jonathan continued to outperform him in every fight.

Huffing, Nikailus took a seat opposite the older man.

"I have news," Jonathan began. Nikailus yawned widely. His mentor's words were ones he had heard on multiple occasions. He did not trust that whatever news Jonathan had to share with him would be 'great' or exciting.

"It has begun!" Jonathan stated emphatically. "The Harbinger has arrived." His eyes gleamed as he spoke and his words came in such a rush that Nikailus barely had time to register them. He clasped his hands before him. "We would like you to be her escort to the promised land."

"Me?" Nikailus asked incredulously. "Don't mistake my words for reluctance, Jonathan. I am very honored and humbled by your selection." He paused as he considered his next words.

"But?" Jonathan prodded.

"But," Nikailus continued, "why would the Light choose me above all others? I am nobody."

"You are spoken of," Jonathan responded vaguely.

Nikailus clutched at the small, embroidered pillow nesting between him and the arm of the chair in which he sat. Its frayed edges reminded him why he had chosen to join the Order in the first place. Shaking his head, Nikailus lifted his face towards Jonathan.

"What does that mean?" he asked.

Jonathan sighed. "We do not speak of the prophecies or their meanings." Nikailus could see that Jonathan's hands shook as he spoke. "But, I believe that it is time that you learned the truth."

"I hope this isn't going to turn into one of those vague stories you're always telling me," Nikailus retorted. "I really am in no mood to hear your meanderings, Jonathan."

The older man chortled. "I do not meander," he said, a small smile twisting his expression. "It was no coincidence that we found you as a small child, Nikailus. We had been searching for you for decades. And, when the Harbinger was born, we knew that a boy of about your age would be present as well. You are to seduce her, to make her believe that the Light has forsaken us to the ruin of this world. It will only be through the purity of the Blessed that we shall prevail."

Jonathan's voice was emphatic and passionate. Nikailus hung on the man's every word as his mentor finished his speech, "You shall be our king."

King. The word reverberated through every fiber of Nikailus's being. He had never imagined himself as a king before. He knew he was powerful. He was certainly more powerful than all the other initiates he'd faced over the years. Many of his peers already looked to him for guidance. Yet, he had always imagined himself taking command of the Order in the wake of the Supreme's demise. Never had he ever visualized himself as a king.

"No," he whispered.

"Yes," Jonathan responded. "You are ready for this task, Nikailus. I promise you this."

Nikailus breathed in slowly. It was difficult to do, considering the rapid thundering of his heart. "What must I do?" he asked.

Jonathan held his hands before him in a prayer-like pose. He lightly tapped his fingers as he considered Nikailus.

"I am sure you have heard the rumors about the Princess Amaleah?"

Nikailus nodded.

"Excellent, excellent," his mentor responded absentmindedly. "Then you know that the King propositioned to wed her. You know that she fled the palace, perhaps even the whole of Lunameed. War is upon us, my son. This is our chance."

Nikailus silently watched as his mentor pulled on tight-fitting leather gloves and reached into his breast pocket. Carefully, Jonathan unrolled a long piece of parchment. Its faded ink sprawled across the page in a tight, elaborate script.

"This is one of the few copies left. Too many were destroyed during the Wars of Darkness. But, we were able to rescue this one."

Bits of the parchment crumbled and fell to the floor in a heap of dust. Nikailus reached out to trail his fingers along the text, but Jonathan slapped his hand away.

"If you must touch the scroll, then you must wear gloves and be as gentle as possible. This is the only copy we have."

"If it's so precious, why didn't you make copies of it?" Nikailus asked incredulously. He found it difficult to believe that the Order would have kept something so precious without making a copy.

"We tried," Jonathan explained. "Each time one of our scholars transcribed the text onto a new piece of parchment, the paper would turn to flame and ash. We believe that the Creators intended for the prophecies of old to be destroyed. They never intended for us to fulfill the demands the Darkness and the Light have placed upon us."

"Perhaps," Nikailus said as he drummed his fingers on his knees. "But it is also possible that they intended to protect us."

"This is why I always chose you as my top apprentice. You question the way the world is. You hunger for more."

At this, Nikailus peered out the window. The sky had turned dark and he could see, even from this distance, that the tower had turned an ashen grey in the dim light. He drummed his fingers on the window sill. He was dimly aware that Jonathan was talking in the background. Nikailus did not differentiate between the words, rather, he analyzed the land leading to Sueria Tower.

The trees had begun to change color. They formed a patchwork of golds, maroons, and browns. Leaves drifted on errant winds. Nikailus sighed loudly as he turned to face his mentor.

"Enough," he said softly.

A shocked expression passed over Jonathan's face before he leaned towards Nikailus, a smile curling across his face.

"And what would your bargain be," Jonathan asked.

Nikailus smiled. "You know me so well," he said. "If I accept your argument that I am destined to be the next Lunameedian king, then I will need to know what the Blackflame Order needs from me in return."

"That's an easy one," Jonathan responded quickly. "When you successfully seduce the Harbinger, we expect that you will remember who provided for you all these years. We expect," he said as he leaned towards Nikailus, "that you will seek guidance from the Order when you have the power to influence the entirety of Mitier."

"Is that all?" Nikailus asked sardonically.

Jonathan tapped his fingers together as he regarded his apprentice. "Let me ask you a question, son," he said as he continued to glare at Nikailus. "What do you envision for your future? What is it that makes you crave for more?"

"Honestly," Nikailus responded, "I always thought that I would one day leave the Order of the Blackflame."

"You're lying," the older man said through clenched teeth. "None have every yearned for a life outside of our order."

"And what if I did?" Nikailus retorted. "What then?"

"You would be laid to rest," Jonathan responded

automatically. "Like all before you have been."

Nikailus's breath caught in his chest at his master's words. "And you would do this to me?"

Jonathan sighed. "I must admit, you have been a favorite among our order since you were a child. Your power knows no bounds. You have surpassed even some of the most ancient in our ranks. Still, if this conversation does nothing else, you have proven yourself to be impatient and entirely without ambition. Perhaps we should reconsider our offer to make you our king."

"No," Nikailus whispered. His voice was so soft that, for a moment, he thought he had imagined responding at all.

Jonathan smiled slyly at him before saying, "Ah, I see. You want control over our order but you do not want to pay your dues. This is not how the world works, Nikailus."

"It will be when I'm done with it."

Jonathan barked a harsh laugh. "How the young are naïve," he said. "Too bad, you're also insipid."

"Too bad you spent your whole life in an order that will never give you the respect that you so desperately crave."

"Nikailus," Jonathan said in warning.

"Thank you, teacher, for telling me exactly where to find the girl. Once I've won her over to me, how likely do you think it is that she will follow the Blackflame?"

Jonathan spluttered slightly. That was all the response Nikailus needed. "Goodbye Jonathan," he said as he trod towards the door. "Thank you again for your lessons. They were quite enlightening." He opened the door and strode from the room. He did not look back.

Chapter Eight

Faer Forest at the River Estrell Crossing, Lunameed

Amaleah's already muddy boots sank into even deeper mud as she stepped into the river bed. She shivered as water soaked into the hem of her leggings. She never knew the water of the River Estrell could be so frigid.

"Watch your step," Thadius said as he slid down a small crest in the mud. He was now chest deep in the rushing water.

She couldn't be sure, but she thought Yosef chortled at Thadius's fall. They had been on the road to Encartia for nigh on four days. During that time, she had heard Yosef and Thadius bicker with each other nearly the entire time.

"Aren't centaurs supposed to be sure of foot?" Yosef said as he bounded across the river. Amaleah couldn't see any sign that the reaper had gotten the least bit wet as he'd crossed the river.

Thadius could not respond, as the water had now completely covered his mouth. His nose barely crested the rushing water. Amaleah watched as the centaur drifted downriver several feet before finally popping up on the other side. Water droplets ran down his bare chest. They glistened in the sunlight as they trailed across his flesh. Amaleah felt her cheeks flush as she watched him climb the riverbank on the other side.

"It's not so bad," he called back to her as he whipped his tail in a spray of glistening water droplets.

"It's freezing," Amaleah chattered.

"Just keep swimming; you'll be fine."

Holding her hand over her nose, Amaleah plunged into the icy water. In that moment, she decided that the water was decidedly not fine. Still, she remembered what Thadius had told her to do. She kept swimming against the current. She knew she was drifting. Her leggings and leather jerkin became water logged and heavy. Her muscles ached as she fought against the current. She kept repeating Thadius's phrase to herself. She would keep going. She would keep swimming.

And then her head burst above water as her feet met the thick mud of the other embankment.

"I've got you," Yosef hissed before she felt his skeletal hand latch onto her arm. He heaved her out of the water like she weighed little more than a newborn kitten.

"Thank you," she whispered when she'd finally caught her breath again.

"T'was nothing," Yosef murmured as he helped her climb the steep bank of the river.

Amaleah shivered as she leaned into the reaper. It was still chilly and being soaked through did nothing to alleviate the ice that seeped into her bones. Yosef pulled the fur cloak her father had made for her from her pack and wrapped it around her shoulders.

"You should get some use out of this," he said. "There's no reason to let Sylvia's sacrifice go to waste."

Amaleah's teeth quit chattering as the cloak flowed around her. Somehow, even though her entire pack had been submerged within the water, the cloak had remained dry. She knew it was fae magic. She knew the fae queen had aligned herself with her father, the mad king of Lunameed. She vowed to herself that she would have no qualms about eliminating the fae for what they had allowed to happen to all those people.

She still hadn't forgiven herself for bringing the poor baker into the mix. Mr. Sweets had had a family. It was because of her that he was dead.

"T-thank you," she said again. Tears swam in her eyes as she remembered, just vaguely what Sylvia's voice had sounded like. She chided herself on forgetting these details, but still, it became more and more difficult for her to remember as the days continued to pass.

Yosef nodded but said nothing as he scanned the trees before them. She thought she heard him sniff at the air before growling softly. Thadius, in his usual fashion, continued chatting away, seemingly unaware of Yosef's change in behavior.

"What is it?" Amaleah asked as she came to stand next to Yosef.

The wraith did not answer. Instead, he marched to the tree line and peered into their depths. Still, Thadius yammered on. He spoke animatedly about how he had once fought a dozen spindrels on his own. Amaleah found this difficult to believe since she'd seen him yelp at a tiny spider that had crawled across his leg. Since spindrels were supposed to be three times the size of a human and abnormally vicious, there was no way he was telling the truth.

"Quiet," Yosef said, his voice brittle.

Amaleah crept up to where he stood. She felt him tense as she drew her dagger from her belt. Despite their training, Amaleah still had not mastered the art of hand-to-hand combat. She was progressing, just slowly.

He held an arm out and pushed her back slightly. His black robe slipped from his head, revealing his burned-out eyes. Although Amaleah had seen his face on multiple occasions now, the shock of the hollow, black holes where his eyes should have been never ceased to send a chill down her spine.

Wordlessly, for once, Thadius trod up next to them. He notched an arrow in his long bow and drew it. His arm muscles bulged as he strained them. Amaleah never did get tired of watching him flex. The thought made her cheeks flare with warmth before she forced herself to remember that they were in danger.

The wind whistled through the dead leaves of the forest. It seemed to whisper her name as it rushed past her in a whip of cold air. Parting her lips, Amaleah almost responded to the question she thought she heard.

An arrow whizzed by her face, mere inches from striking her, before lodging in the mud behind her. Startled, Amaleah released a yelp of surprise just as Yosef shoved her behind him. His cloak fluttered all around him as he raised a mighty staff. She was completely concealed behind him as another arrow narrowly missed striking him in the chest.

Thadius released his arrow a second too late. Amaleah heard him curse as she heard the resounding thud of the arrow lodging itself into a tree.

Yosef used one hand to push Amaleah towards a tree. He never left his position in front of her, not even when a spray of arrows sank into the ground all around them.

"Who are they?" she hissed when they'd finally made it to one of the trees.

"I don't know," Yosef replied. His voice was unusually raspy as he continued, "I've never smelled anything like them before. Amaleah now knew what made Yosef's voice sound as strange as it did. He was worried. "Stay here," he commanded as he fluttered away in a heap of black of cloth.

Amaleah's heart hammered in her chest and she struggled to

control her breathing. Her head throbbed as she realized that her magic was once again building within her. Closing her eyes, Amaleah tried to focus on her breathing. She tried counting backwards from three thousand, but was unsuccessful in controlling the influx of magic that coursed through her. A single scream escaped her lips as it erupted from her in a torrent of flames.

She did not blister. She couldn't even feel the heat as the flames soared past her, lighting everything around her on fire. Her coat of many furs shimmered slightly as the flames licked at it. Her entire body felt like it was being ripped apart as more energy burst from her. To no avail, she grasped for any thread she could find in a desperate attempt to rein in her magic.

"What's all this about now?" a gruff voice bellowed as a large man with curly red hair and an even curlier red beard walked past Thadius and Yosef with little fanfare. They stood, slack-jawed as he emerged from the flames. Only his face, which was covered in black soot, appeared to have any effects of the fire.

"Who are you?" she asked, raising one eyebrow.

"Redbeard at your service, miss," the man said with surprising civility. He clutched a worn axe in one hand and a jewel encrusted dagger in the other.

"Redbeard," a voice called from beyond the wall of flames. "A little help here," it continued plaintively.

"Listen, girl, I need you to remove that there wall of flame, if you know what'll be good for you."

Amaleah clenched and unclenched her fist as she listened to him speak. "Redbeard seems like a strange name. Who are you, really?"

"Jorah Ansel, if you must know," the man said as he shot a look over his shoulder at the thick wall of smoke separating him from his remaining men. "Please," he said, "At least let them out of the burning forest."

She squeezed her fists tightly as she attempted to bring her magic back to a controllable level.

"Please," he pled again. "Most of 'em have families that rely upon them."

Amaleah sucked in a sharp breath as she imagined stripping the flames from the world. Her skin prickled and an icy breeze grazed her back as she continued to take her magic back. With a flash of blinding blue light, the flames disappeared. Her knees buckling, Amaleah fell to the ground.

A ringing filled her ears as she tried, unsuccessfully, to see what was happening around her. She saw fuzzy images of men rushing forwards. A lone figure walked towards her. She thought she screamed 'no,' but she didn't hear her voice. The ringing persisted. Her heart hammered. Sweat rolled down her brow. She cringed as she saw a ribbon of darkness streak past her. Men scattered. They ran before her as it were a game to confuse her. A warm hand grasped her own. Rough calluses scraped against her palms. Her magic flared once more. She couldn't see his face.

"Amaleah," a warm voice whispered near her ear. "Please, you have to wake up."

She knew that voice. A stab of pain shot through as she tried to remember. Frustrated, she attempted to slam her fists into the ground. Her muscles wouldn't respond. Fear oozed through her. If she couldn't control her own body, she had no way to defend herself. More vague shadows circled around them. She watched as their fuzzy outlines drew ever closer.

"Just hold on," he whispered again. She could hear him say other things. She knew he was trying to reason with the man who followed them.

"Drop the girl," a gruff voice cut through the ringing in her ears.

"Never," her captor replied.

Something fast and small zipped through the air. She assumed it was an arrow, though she couldn't see to be certain.

"I said, drop the girl," the man repeated.

Amaleah held her breath as she waited for her captor to decide. She knew he would have a better chance at escape without her. She was deadweight. She coughed as she swallowed a lump of ash. She couldn't stop coughing. She clutched at her throat. She tried to remember what it felt like to breathe.

A firm hand slammed into her back. A puff of grimy air escaped her lips. She hiccupped before breathing normally.

"That'a girl," someone said. She wasn't sure who.

A face became clearer as she turned her head in the direction of the voice. A red beard grew in curls around a plump, round face. He had long hair. Amaleah didn't know if she had ever met a man with as long of hair as he had.

"We've already claimed her, Redbeard," the voice she knew to be Thadius's said. Relief washed over her. He hadn't died in the fight. She hadn't killed him.

"Oh, come off it, Thadius. She's a human being. She can't be claimed," Redbeard replied defiantly. He released his hold on her, as if to prove his point. Amaleah smiled slightly at the man's tone, even if she was at a loss as to who he was.

Amaleah looked between the two men as they stared each other down. Her arms were covered in gooseflesh and the hair on the back of her neck prickled as she waited for the tension to break. Her thoughts raced. Her vision cleared. And still, the men continued to glare at each other. If Amaleah didn't know better, she would have thought they were having a silent conversation between themselves.

Thadius shuffled his hooves and stepped closer to Amaleah. He smelled of wet horse and ash. She crinkled her nose in disgust and was about to step away from him, when he lifted her from the ground and swung her onto his back.

"Duck low," he hissed. She didn't hesitate to comply. The men surrounding the area broke into a charge. Amaleah quivered as she felt her magic respond to the threat they posed.

"Concentrate on your breathing," Thadius huffed as he surveyed the oncoming onslaught. She sensed that he was looking for any break in their guard, any chance to escape. She couldn't focus on that now. Her magic continued to rise within her. Her muscles cramped. Her head pounded. She needed a release.

A cold hand pressed firmly upon her back.

"Yosef," she whispered in surprise as the reaper whipped the reins of his horse across its flanks. A Szarmian banner lay on the horse's back, causing Amaleah to hiss in repulsion as she stared down at the red insignia.

Yosef tilted his head at her in what she assumed was acknowledgment before racing ahead of Thadius. The mare he rode staggered on the unfamiliar ground. Amaleah watched in horror as one of the mare's legs caught in a rut between two rocks and she went tumbling to the ground. Yosef pitched, falling beneath his steed.

Amaleah screamed. It was earsplitting and brittle, even to her own ears.

"Enough," she heard a gruff voice yell across the field. Thadius did not stop running.

The air shimmered. Amaleah felt the air cool as a wicked fast breeze swept past them. The air seemed to crystalize in its wake. Amaleah could see what appeared to be ice grow up from the ground. Instinctively, she dug her knees into Thadius's ribcage and closed her eyes. His hooves scraped across the rocky, muddy terrain before they slammed into the crystalized wall.

Her shoulders ached and she could taste the copper of her own blood as she ran her tongue over a split lip. Cautiously, she prodded at her arms, legs, and abdomen. Nothing seemed to be broken, just sore and bruised. She was disoriented and had the peculiar sensation of not knowing up from down. She vomited before rolling onto her back.

"The girl in the yellow dress," the man staring down at her said when she finally felt well enough to open her eyes. "I'm so glad that we had the chance to meet again."

Amaleah blinked up at the figure standing over her. His face was shrouded in shadow, but she somehow knew him.

"Prince Colin of Szarmi," she croaked, "how nice to see you again."

He stretched out a hand to help her from the ground.

"You two know each other?" Thadius hissed as he kicked out with his legs. Colin backed away lest he receive a kick to the gut. Amaleah chuckled at his fear of her companion.

"Well, not exactly," she said. "His actions the night of that fatal ball helped me escape though. He was quite daring," she said as she stared at the prince.

"Yes, well…" Colin stammered. His cheeks were flushed and Amaleah could see a swath of sweat on his brow. "I just wanted…"

"Of course, I knocked him out before I had a chance to thank him for his services," Amaleah said, a hint of humor in her voice. "It was quite easy; I was shocked."

"It wasn't that easy," Colin replied plaintively.

"Yes, it was," she teased.

"Uh hem," a voice coughed from behind Amaleah. She spun

to see the large redheaded man standing directly behind her. Soot and other grime covered his face as Amaleah peered up at the beast of a man. The air around him seemed to shimmer as she stared up at him, and, for a moment, she saw an entirely different person. The image faded quickly, but it left her with a jarring sensation she had difficulty shaking as the man began to speak.

"My name's Jorah Ansel, but most of me men call me Redbeard," he said as he stuck out his hand towards her. "I know that you've just faced quite an ordeal. So has that lad over there," he nodded towards Colin. "But, I'm here to offer me services to you in the hopes that we can bring about some change to Mitier."

Amaleah stared past Redbeard and into the woods beyond. Charred remnants of her outburst smoldered in the background and Amaleah cringed. She hoped that Yosef and Thadius were correct in their estimation that the elves would be able to help her learn to control her abilities. Secretly, she had her doubts, but still, she never voiced her concerns to either of her two companions. However, she also recognized that she needed allies if she was to win the war.

"Perhaps, we can work together in this endeavor," she said coolly as she accepted the man's outstretched hand. She looked over to where Colin stood sheepishly behind her and smiled. "And you, Colin of Szarmi? Shall we be friends?"

He smiled back at her. "I thought you'd never ask," he responded.

"Wait," Thadius said. "You're telling me that we just had this whole kerfuffle over nothing? You had an outburst of your magic for nothing? And now we're just going to stand here and shake hands and be friends?"

"Well," Amaleah said, "it certainly appears that way."

Thadius stomped his hoof and glared at her, but Amaleah simply smiled up at him. She knew her crusade to win the

Lunameedian throne would be a treacherous one. She would need all the help she could get, even if it did come in the puny form of the Szarmian prince.

Redbeard bellowed an enormous laugh at Thadius's tantrum. "And here I thought all centaurs were supposed to be regal and poised," he chortled.

"I have truly never understood why that was the conception," Thadius said. "We centaurs are known for our brute force and wild ways. Well, that is, in my tribe we are."

"And you're humble, too," Redbeard sniffed as he turned to face Amaleah. He whistled softly as he peered into her face. "You're a pretty one, if I ever saw one."

Amaleah smiled up at him. "Thank you," she murmured.

The giant man looped his ax to his belt. "You're the spittin' image of yer mother."

"You knew my mother?" Amaleah asked, her voice piqued.

"Well o'course I did," Redbeard roared. "She was part of the rebellion."

Amaleah had never heard about a rebellion in Lunameed and she certainly had never heard a story about her mother joining one. She scrunched her lips as she looked him in the eyes and said, "My mother never fought in a rebellion."

"Well ho!" Redbeard said. "For a child who never personally knew Orianna you seem to be quite defensive over her."

A shiver of silence crawled over the gathering at Redbeard's words. His cheeks paled when he saw the look in Amaleah's eye. She tried to hide the tears that welled there, but couldn't stop them from sliding down her cheeks as she stammered, "Yes, I never knew my mother. But I can promise you this: her loss made my life more terrible than you can ever imagine. It was her death that made my father lose his mind. It was her death that forced me into exile. You may have known the Lady Orianna, but you do not know me."

Redbeard stepped forward, his legs shaking slightly. "Child, I didn't mean to give offense. It's just…" he paused as he fumbled with the fringe of his jerkin. "It's just that your mother was a very special lady to me and she is someone that I have thought about these past seventeen years nigh on constantly. She was a true unsung hero, Amaleah."

Amaleah shrugged her shoulders.

"But, I must tell you, yer wrong about the rebellion. Yer mother was one of the leaders before yer father found her."

"What?" Amaleah asked, incredulously.

"It's true!" Redbeard stated emphatically. "I wouldn't lie to you, princess."

"I don't believe you," she said.

It was Redbeard's turn to shrug. "No matter," he said as he peered up at the sun. His shoulders slumped as he realized just how far the sun had fallen in the sky. "Listen, Princess, we're on a mission here that can't be stopped. So, either you believe me when I tell you that what we're trying to do here is of the utmost importance or we'll have to continue fighting until we get past ya."

"But," she began.

"No buts, Princess," he paused as he stared down at her. Despite his ruddy cheeks and laugh lines, Amaleah could see the reprimand in his eyes. "This is the only choice."

"You won't hurt her," the Szarmian prince bleated.

Amaleah turned to face the prince. He was exactly as she remembered him, only not. She couldn't quite place her finger on it, but he seemed less naïve than he had just a few short weeks before. She knew she was. She found herself hoping that whatever the prince had faced had been nothing compared to what she'd endured.

"No," Redbeard said, "we won't be hurting her."

The prince sighed. "Good," he said after a moment of silence. "Princess Amaleah," he said as he took a step towards her. "It is very good to be formally introduced to you at last." He smiled at her.

Amaleah liked the way the corners of his eyes crinkled as he smiled and the sincerity she found in his words. She nodded her head to him in acknowledgment before staring Redbeard down.

"Tell me, Mr. Ansel, what are you hoping to accomplish in Lunameed in the company of our foreign prince?" she smiled up at him. "I must say, I find it quite strange that the future king of Szarmi just happened to be wandering the Arcadi on the eastern side of the Seppiet River at the exact same time that I was." She poked a single finger in the air towards the large man. "What are you doing here?" she demanded.

"I can answer that one," Colin replied before Redbeard had a chance to speak. "Much has happened to me since the ball, Princess. I think it would be best if we put aside the desire to fight one another and focus on the task at hand: winning back our respective kingdoms."

Amaleah raised an eyebrow at Colin's assertion that they both had a kingdom to win, but she said nothing as Yosef deftly stepped in front of her.

"We accept your offer for a truce," he said. As usual, there was no hint of emotion in his voice as he spoke. Amaleah found his inability to emote entirely frustrating. She knew of no other way to get him to tell her his thoughts.

Thadius huffed behind her, his breath warm on her back. Amaleah spun to face her chosen mentor. "What's wrong?" she asked in a low hiss.

"I don't know yet," he said. Something just seems strange to me."

"It's fine, Thadius," she cooed. "Honestly, the Szarmian prince helped me escape from Estrellala," she paused, considering his facial expression. He still appeared hesitant so she placed her hand upon his forearm. "Please, you have to trust me on this one. I don't believe he means us any harm."

"That was before you killed and wounded some of his men," the centaur sniffed.

"Oh, come now, Thadius. What would it take for you to trust me enough on this one?" Redbeard asked.

"For starters, you could work on NOT attacking us," Thadius fumed as he crossed his arms over his muscled chest.

"I'm sorry," Redbeard responded. "We have the Szarmian prince with us. We have to be more careful than usual."

They glared at each other until Yosef finally said, "It's settled. We'll travel with you to Encartia. Beyond that, I guarantee nothing."

"Done," Redbeard said as he stuck out his hand.

Amaleah sighed in relief as her little band followed Redbeard's crew back to their small camp. Dusk was settling and the fading light would make trekking through the Arcadi Forest treacherous.

"Seems like we'll be spending more time together, Princess," Colin murmured as he fell into step beside her.

The corners of her mouth pulled into a sly smile as she responded, "Seems like."

Chapter Nine

Miliom, Szarmi

"Captain Conrad," Queen Vista said, her voice low and cool. "I am to understand that your soldiers at Ford Pelid have yet to declare for my daughter, Coraleen, as the Princess Heir." She eyed him over the brim of an eyeglass she used to read important documents. "Instead," she sighed, "they have continued to proclaim Colin as the rightful heir to the throne. Surley you know that my son is dead."

She shuffled the papers on her large wooden desk as she waited for the captain to respond. She knew he had a soft spot for her son. Colin had implied as such in his letters to her over the years.

The captain cleared his throat before saying, "I can't control what my men believe in their hearts, Your Majesty." She scowled at him. A lesser man would have quaked at that stare, but Captain Conrad stood, his back straight and his head held high as he waited for his queen to respond.

"Their oaths were not to Colin!" she screeched. Her voice was so shrill that it made Conrad's ears ache. "They were to the Szarmian throne." She tapped her long, razor-like nails on her desk. "Fix this," she said. "That's an order."

Captain Conrad stood motionless before her for several

moments.

"Your Majesty, I…"

"You dare defy me?" she asked, her voice cold. "Do you know what happened to the last man to defy me?" her voice was soft and she glanced around her as she spoke.

"No, My Queen," Conrad spoke quickly. He averted his gaze from her face as he spoke.

She raised her eyebrows as she considered him. He had risen quickly within the ranks. He was a tall man, with broad shoulders and thick muscular arms. He was considered one of the most honorable men within the armies and had been given a place of honor among the instructors at Ford Pelid. Queen Vista had always been led to believe that the captain loved Szarmi more than he did the crown. Still, he had yet to declare for her daughter following the announcement of Colin's death.

"Conrad," she sneered, "I believe you have been given ample amounts of time to understand that my son, the Light keep him, has passed from this earth. The bastard king to the north murdered him in cold blood." She pointed towards the glass case she kept with the wax mold of Colin's decapitated head. "Do you see that, Captain? That is what the Lunameedians will do to us all should we allow it. They are barbarians."

Conrad stared at the replica of Colin's head. His eyes seemed to glisten but not a single tear slid down his cheeks as Vista continued to stare at him.

"We cannot dilly dally as we have in the past. The time for action is now, Captain. We need you. The crown needs you to declare for Princess Coraleen so that we can begin to heal from the loss of my son."

The captain's back went rigid. Vista reveled in the pain that crossed his face the longer he stared at the severed head. She knew it matched Colin's features perfectly.

"I agree, Your Majesty," he said, his voice stilted.

Vista raised an eyebrow at him and clicked her nails on the arm of the throne.

"Yes, well, you best get your men in line. We cannot afford any more time to be wasted in searching for a prince that no longer lives," she spoke softly. She knew her words would have a greater impact with the less force she put behind them. The captain was cunning enough to understand what she meant, the threat laced within her words.

"I will see to it directly, My Queen," he said. He blinked when he said, 'my queen,' but Vista forgave him this error in judgment. She needed him. Clapping her hands twice, two servants scurried to the front of the room.

"Bring the good captain pen and parchment. We will send the record post haste."

The servants dipped their heads to the queen before scampering away. She waved her hand at the captain before turning back to the papers the Borgandians had sent her. Her father had passed and her sister had taken the throne. Well, that is to say, her sister's husband sat on the throne and she pulled the strings behind it. Vista's lips curled into a smile as she read her sister's hand.

"Uh hem," a voice interrupted her.

She looked up. There, still standing at the foot of the stairs leading to her small dais, stood Captain Conrad. She blanched.

"What is it?" she hissed.

He didn't even flinch from the tone in her voice. She listened in awe as he said, "Your Majesty, there is one other topic I must discuss with you before I can, in good conscious, sign any papers stating my pledge to the Princess Coraleen."

Anger boiled within her. She would not let this bull-headed, bear of a man dictate what she or her daughter would do. Vista had waited for years to be released from the burden of being chained to a man. She had the power now and she was not about to lose it.

"Yes?" she said.

If Conrad was perturbed by her response, he didn't let on. His lack of fear infuriated her. Everyone was meant to be afraid of her and Coraleen. They were meant to obey. She continued to click her nails on the golden arm of the throne as she waited for Conrad to explain himself.

He cleared his throat loudly. Vista smiled at this. *Yes,* she thought, *let him be nervous about my reaction.* Jeering down at him, she said, "Please, continue."

"Szarmi has a long history of training our monarchs to rule with power and military strength. It is my understanding that Princess Coraleen has received private training in these matters from tutors chosen by your royal highness."

"Get to the point, Conrad," Vista snarled. Of course, she had made Coraleen study the art of war. The girl was Szarmian. She was meant to rule.

"I believe that the armies would fall into line more swiftly if she were to undergo training at Fort Pelid, Your Highness." He did not stutter as he spoke. Nor did he quake when she leaned forward and barred her teeth.

"You think that the tutors I hand-picked to train the Princess did not provide her with the necessary skills?" She smiled sourly at him. "Choose your next words carefully, Captain."

To her surprise, Captain Conrad didn't even hesitate to respond to her. "It is not about the excellence of her tutors or her abilities, Highness. It is just that, in every generation, the ruler of Szarmi has trained at Fort Pelid. If the Princess is to take her place among the rulers of our great nation, then she will need to take this rite of passage."

"Nonsense," she murmured. "I can see no reason for Coraleen to degrade herself at that place. Do not think for a second that I didn't know the conditions you put Colin in during his time on the training grounds. He told me…"

"Forgive me, Your Majesty, but I believe you have failed to understand me."

Her lips trembled at his insolence. Never, in all her days in Szarmi, had anyone dared defy her the way this man was now. She had made a vow to herself and to her daughter that they would never be ruled by a man again. Clenching her fists, she stood from the throne.

"No, Conrad, it is you who does not understand. Coraleen will be Queen. She will command the armies. She will garner your respect and loyalty. Choose to disgrace her now and you will live to regret it."

She snapped her fingers and a row of heavily armed men stepped from the shadows. Their hands clutched the pommels of their swords as they stared ahead of them.

"I only want what's best for our nation, Your Majesty. And for the Princess Coraleen."

She clucked her tongue at him. "If that were true then you would ensure that Coraleen is placed on the throne."

The captain audibly sighed. She smirked down at him. *Pity he's so loyal to Colin*, she thought. *He would have made an excellent playmate*. "You will obey me," she snarled at him after a moment's hesitation.

"I have served the crown faithfully these past forty-nine years, Your Majesty. I would do nothing to derail the process we've made. Please understand me when I say that the personal training you provided for Coraleen made her tough enough to compete with men who have been training their entire lives to serve at the crown's whim. She will be a great queen. But," he continued as he held up a single finger and pointed it at the queen, "I will not break the tradition that has held this country together for centuries."

Queen Vista considered the soldier standing before her. He was rugged, his face weather-beaten from traversing the whole of the realm. Yet, he bore no signs of weakness. His beard was neatly trimmed and his clothes were well-maintained. Yes, she considered him in the way she considered all men that were her prey.

She opened her mouth to respond to the captain but was interrupted by the entrance of her servants bearing the ink and parchment she'd ordered only moments before.

"Your answer?" Conrad asked as the servants placed a small writing desk before him.

Her lips curled into a smile. No one had dared defy her since King Henry had died. No one. It filled her with a sense of excitement as she peered down at the man before her. Waving her hands, the servants silently crept into the shadows before leaving them in the room alone.

Conrad's eyebrows rose but he made not a sound as she gracefully walked towards him. She still smiled at him as she trailed a long, sharp nail across his cheek. She admired his ability to remain stoic as she trailed her nails across the soft spot of his throat. She'd had the tips of her nails coated in molted gold to hide the shard of metal adhered to her skin. A momentary desire to slit his throat filled her. She imagined what his warm blood would feel like as it spilled over her hand.

But then, she noticed, he breathed normally. There was no sense of fear within him. To her delight, she realized that there was also no hint of defiance either. He was a true soldier of the crown, hers to command.

"I will send my daughter to your training grounds, Captain," she acquiesced. "But she will be accompanied by her personal trainers to ensure that you do not overstep."

"Highness," he whispered, "it would be an insult to my men. Surely you must see that we are still renowned for our military. She would be in the best of hands."

"Be that as it may, Captain," she said his title in a hiss of breath, "I prefer for her to be guarded and trained by my personal picks."

He glared at her. *A challenge*, she thought as she squeezed her fingers. He didn't even flinch as one or her nails sliced a thin line across his skin.

"They are all female," she snarled at him, "her trainers and guards."

"I know that," Conrad began.

"I made it my vow that Coraleen would never know the horrors of being a woman in a world ruled by men, Captain. I will not start letting her idealism for this world fade because of the pride of a few men."

"Good men," the captain responded. "They are good men, all of them."

She dropped her hand from his face. "Yes, well, be that as it may, Coraleen will still train with her personal guard. You may provide additional lessons to her and she will be allowed to spar against the cadets. But, she will not be completely under your command. No king would allow his captains to rule him."

"This may be true, Highness, but a good ruler knows when to listen to the counsel of his—or her—advisors. I'm telling you, the training she will undergo at Fort Pelid is a time-honored tradition that is about more than just strategic planning and battle tactics. We shape them into the rulers they were meant to be."

She shrugged. "And still you have not swayed me," she said. "I grow tired of this back and forth banter, Conrad. Sign the papers. Declare Coraleen as the rightful heir and I shall send her to your precious Fort Pelid to train."

He sighed. She assumed it was in relief before he snarled back at her, "She will need to stay there for a minimum of six months."

"One," she interjected.

"Three," he said, his voice soft and sharp. "And that is the final offer. She needs time to build rapport with the soldiers. Even Colin, despite his obvious lack of talent when it came to fighting, was able to garner their respect. She will need to do the same if she ever hopes for the army to give up hope of the prince returning."

He must have known that he'd misspoken when he saw her face because, for the first time since arriving to meet with her, he blanched. His face paled and she could see him flexing his hand in rapid succession.

"I'm sorry," he murmured. "I know it is too soon," he trailed off as Vista turned her back on him.

Fool, she thought as she added a tremor to her voice. "It is too soon, Captain, and I will thank you to remember to whom you are speaking. I am the Queen of Szarmi. I am the one who rules this kingdom. Not you. And you would do well to heed my requests."

He bowed his head to her.

Men are so easy to control when you know the right maneuvers, she smiled to herself at the thought. "I will make arrangements. She will stay for three months. It will be good for her to get out of the palace."

He bowed once more towards her before bending down and scribbling his name on the parchment. Her lips curled into a smile at the sound of her victory.

Chapter Ten

Estrellala, Lunameed

Starla threw her dagger at the target and smiled as the blade dug itself into the red circle at its center for the fifth time in a row. She moved to retrieve the blade when she heard the creak of her door swing open. Not for the first time, she was thankful she'd scoured the iron until it squeaked at even the slightest provocation.

"You really should have that oiled," her uncle's voice sneered as he strode into the room. His black robes billowed around him, giving him the appearance of a bat in flight. Starla hated bats almost as much as she despised her uncle. It took all her will power not to gag at the stench of decay. He always smelled of rot.

"But then, how would I know when to expect you?" she asked as she gave him a sanguine smile.

Ever the courtier, her uncle merely nodded at her in response. But she had seen his eyes. She knew how to sense when he was a threat and when he was in good spirits. Today was most assuredly one of the former.

"I have a mission for you," he began.

"Oh?" she said.

His eyes narrowed at the interruption, but he continued, "I

want you to seek out the princess. I don't care what it costs or the lengths you must take to retrieve her, but you must bring her back to the capital."

"And if I refuse?" she asked, a purr in her voice.

"We both know you won't do that," her uncle responded.

She shrugged her shoulders.

"You know the cost of your insolence," he hissed at her. It took all of Starla's willpower to keep herself from lodging her dagger in her uncle's throat. She breathed in deeply, her nostrils flaring. "It would be a pity if Viola befell some great tragedy," he continued.

Starla rolled her eyes at him. "We both know that you would never actually harm my sister, Uncle," she barred her teeth at him. "We just mean so much to you," she said sarcastically.

He chuckled at her. The sound of his laughter roiled her stomach, but Starla forced herself to stare him down. A smile slid across his face the way she imagined a wolf smiles before pouncing on its prey.

"I have heard rumors about how Viola spends her idle time," he said casually. "I know that she seeks the company of other ladies."

Starla's heart beat more rapidly in her chest. No one could have known about her sister's proclivity for other women. They had been so careful to hide her dalliances from the court. Starla had ensured that Viola could see her consort without prying eyes and rumors.

Her uncle stroked his chin as he considered her. Starla knew the color had drained from her face. She knew that, even if her uncle had guessed about Viola that her silence was answer enough.

"Viola is a very vivacious woman. Yes," he said, "and it was high time that she wed for the favor of our family."

"No!" Starla shouted.

"Oh?" her uncle murmured as he took a step closer to her.

Her dagger felt slick in her hand as she flexed her fingers. Instinct told her to ram the blade into his heart, to get away, to warn her sister. Her sister, who had consoled Starla when they been punished by their governess during childhood. Her sister, who had taught Starla the art of lying without really lying. Her sister, who had learned to love again in a way Starla knew she never would.

"Harm her and I swear that I will never serve you again," she whispered. Her voice came in a low, husky rasp that barely registered, even in her own ears. Still, she flung herself at her uncle and shoved him against the wall. The blade of her small dagger pressed firmly into the soft spot between his Adam's apple and his chin.

"Hmm," he said as he smiled down at her. He barely seemed to notice the blade as he asked, "Is that so?" When she did not immediately answer, he gently shoved her hand away from his throat and said, "You forget that I am the one who raised you, Starla. I am the one who has trained you for all these years. I know when you make an empty threat," he said impassively.

"You don't know everything, Uncle," she said as her shoulders fell even as she continued to stare him in the eye.

"Ah, but I know enough to know when you are lying."

They stared at each other. Starla could not shake the feeling that she was at the precipice of a great decision that she did not fully understand. A memory of her sister filled her mind. It had been yuletide and Viola had been radiant in her ice blue gown. Shimming snowflakes had been stitched over the entire bodice. Starla knew the amount of tears, sweat, and blood that had gone into the making of that gown. All day, her sister had talked about the pastries and the dancing and the men she'd kiss. Her cheeks had been rosy with happiness. Starla had not been invited. She had never been invited to those types of parties. When Viola realized that Starla wouldn't be joining her, she sent her carriage away and spent the evening with her. Her sister was many things, but she had always been there for Starla.

"Fine," she muttered quietly. "I will seek out the simpering princess for you." She was about to continue with her conditions when her uncle cut in.

"You will leave at dawn," he snarled as he turned to leave her quarters.

"And Viola?" Starla couldn't help herself from asking. She could hear the catch in her voice as she spoke. The vulnerability that small catch revealed in her made her want to gag.

"Will be married off to the highest bidder," her uncle responded, "as she always would have been." His sneer did nothing to assuage the anger welling within her.

"You can't!" she hissed at him.

"Consider it a show of my kindness that I will allow her to choose her husband from an acceptable list of bachelors. Let us not forget, Starla, that you were trained to assassinate and your sister was trained to spy. You each have your own... specific talents. It would serve you well to remember this."

Starla said nothing as her uncle vacated her quarters. She seethed. It wasn't just that he believed he could order her around like a dog, it was that he was determined to enslave her sister as well. Viola deserved more than a petty life spent mooning over a greasy lard of a man. She knew her uncle. She knew his list of suitable bachelors would be full of rich men twice her sister's age. She also knew that any man would be repulsive to her sister. They always had been.

She paced around her small sitting room. The carpet was threadbare and faded from the months of footsteps she'd spent roaming her suite. It was the only way she knew how to ease her heavy heart and find clarity in the jumbled mess of her thoughts. Tonight, it didn't help.

"Starla?" her sister's cool voice said as she entered the room. Her face was pale and her usually perfectly styled hair was disheveled.

"Sister, what is it?" Starla asked as she rushed to Viola's side. She was surprised to find that Viola's cheeks were sunken and beads of sweat coated her brow.

"It's finally happening, Starla," she whispered. "He's finally determined that it's my time." Her voice shook, Starla could tell that her sister's happiness at finally being of use to the family was slowly fading at the realization that she would have to give up Nefta.

"What did you say?" Starla asked, though her heart ached to do so.

"I said yes, of course. If Mother were still alive…" she started.

"But she's not," Starla interrupted. She had never met their mother but she couldn't believe she had wanted her daughters to be her brother's political pawns.

Viola ignored Starla's interjection as she continued, "…she would want this for me. She would want me to give up my selfish pursuits."

Starla watched as Viola tried to convince herself that marrying a man for political gain was what she actually wanted.

"Please," she said, as Viola turned to hug her. "Please don't let this happen."

Viola clicked her tongue. "You don't understand, Star. Uncle wants me marry someone rich and I feel as though I have to comply. Please," she whispered, "you have to understand."

Starla didn't understand. She couldn't. She knew her sister

had hungered to be chosen by their uncle for special tasks. So far, he had always chosen Starla to complete his projects. It was Starla who had attacked the crown prince of Szarmi. It was Starla who had been sent to retrieve the Princess Amaleah.

"I love you, Viola, and I understand why it's important to you that Uncle has finally asked you to secure power for our family. But," she said as she lifted her sister's chin until their eyes met, "I can't believe this is what you want. What about Nefta? What will you tell her?"

She laughed a harsh, bitter laugh. Starla's cheeks paled at the sound of her sister's bark. "In so many ways, you're still so young, Starla."

Her ears felt hot and she knew they had turned their tell-tale shade of bright red. She despised being called young.

"You still don't understand the world. Not really.""Yes, I do!" Starla responded, too defensively. "I've killed people and done things that you can't even imagine."

"And yet, you're too young to know what it means to be responsible for something more than yourself."

Starla's stomach did flips at her sister's words. If only she knew what Starla had done to protect her from a worse fate. She thought about telling her sister about the deal she'd struck with their uncle, but thought better of it. Instead she said, "You have no idea about the things I've done."

"Oh?" Viola sighed. She shrugged her shoulders and took a step away from her. "And what things have you done to protect anyone but yourself?"

Again, Starla wanted to tell her sister what she had attempted to do—what she had succeeded in doing. "I can't tell you that," she said in a rasp.

"Pity," Viola said. "And here I thought that you would finally open up to me about the horrible things Uncle has made you do."

They stood in silence. Starla breathed heavily. She couldn't seem to control her thoughts. Her heart pounding, she finally said, "I wish you would trust me when I say that everything I've done has been for you and this family."

"IF that were true," Viola scoffed, "then the mad king would be dead and Uncle would be the one sitting on the throne." Her eyes blazed as she spoke and Starla knew her sister was telling the truth. "Didn't Uncle order you to stop the princess before she was able to escape the palace? It must be such a disappointment to him that you let her slip from your fingers."

"Now you're just being mean," Starla murmured.

"Harsh is the world, Starla. Yet again you've proven that you barely understand anything outside of court life. I'm sorry, pet, but you're in no position to give me advice. I will marry whomever Uncle chooses. I will bear an heir to the throne. I will do my duty to our house." She panted as she spoke, but she continued nonetheless. "I will give up Nefta."

"I just think there has to be another way," Starla responded.

"There isn't."

A tear trailed down her sister's cheek and Starla quickly reached a hand to wipe it away. Her fingers lingered on a curl of her sister's hair. She tucked it behind Viola's ear before saying, "I will find a way to save you."

"You're sweet, sister, but this is just the way the world is. Women are meant to serve as pawns for their family's gain. We are the subjects of men."

"I will never allow myself to be ruled by a man," Starla responded vehemently. "Never." Her eyes blazed as she spoke and her lips trembled. She knew she must look half-mad, but she continued, "There will come a time when women will rule this world, Viola. I intend to be there when that happens."

Her sister sighed and patted her hand gently. "If only that were true."

Viola squeezed Starla's fingers gently before letting herself out of the room. Starla could still feel the warmth of her sister's touch when she turned to face the target behind her. Puckered holes from where her daggers had struck true gaped in its cloth covering. Each one marked a spot where Starla imagined striking her uncle.

She wiped the single tear that freed itself from her eye as she thought of her sister's reaction to the news that she would be wed. Bile rose the back of her throat as she imagined the conversation she was sure Viola was having with Nefta at that very moment. It wasn't fair. It wasn't fair that men decided when and how women could operate. It wasn't fair that women were traded like goods at market.

She had meant what she said. She intended to be there when there was an uprising. She hoped she would have the courage to be a part of it.

Chapter Eleven
Arcadi Forest, Lunameed

Colin's hands felt heavy and sweaty as he clamped them over the reins of his horse. He stole a sideways glance at the woman riding next to him. She was a far cry from the princess he'd seen in the yellow dress all those months ago. Her face was smudged with dirt and her hair was a tangled mass of chocolate brown curls. Every so often, when a ray of sun struck her hair in just the right place, he had seen strands of golden red coursing through her hair.

Shaking his head, Colin silently chided himself for paying any heed to the princess at all. He reminded himself that there were more important things to attend to: like the fact that he needed to win his kingdom back. The memory of his sister's betrayal continued to wake him in the dead of night. He had seen his men fall. He heard her whispered words as she'd denounced him as an imposter. He had felt the cold blackness of the Arcadi River wash over him.

"We'll reach Encartia by sunset if we maintain this pace," Thadius called over his shoulder. He peered at the sun as he spoke and compared measurements on his map. Colin had decided that he didn't like the foppish persona the centaur put on, but he was intrigued by the hints he saw behind the mask. At times, Colin believed that he could almost befriend the centaur. At others, he knew the princess's companion would never trust him.

"Perhaps we should break for a small bite t'eat," Redbeard huffed. The massive man walked alongside his horse. He'd claimed it was for the exercise, but Colin knew that Redbeard suffered from saddle sores.

"We should push through till we arrive at the city," Thadius responded. He rolled the map until it was a tight tube of parchment. "These woods are not what they seem, now that we've entered elvish country."

"Bah!" Redbeard muttered as he yanked on his horse's reins. "The elves know me in these parts. They won't be bothering our party."

"You can't guarantee that, friend," Thadius responded, his voice dangerous.

"Please," Amaleah cooed as she urged her horse forward. "Stop."

Thadius glared at the princess. Colin cocked an eyebrow when he noticed how Redbeard's expression softened as he regarded her. He and Colin had only been traveling with the princess and her companions for two days now, but he doted on her the way a father does his own daughter.

"We cannot risk stopping again, Amaleah," Thadius whispered. He glanced around the party before leaning down close to Amaleah's ear and whispering so softly that Colin couldn't hear the centaur's words.

Colin thought about all the scenarios they could encounter during the remainder of their journey. Captain Conrad's words filled his mind as he tried to calculate their chances of success. He knew the odds weren't great. He knew that his ability to reclaim the Szarmian throne was slim. Still, he clutched at the tiny wisps of hope that his men would still follow him.

It's not enough to simply develop a strategy, Colin. You must study the great strategists of the Wars and adapt to our new technologies. The words zipped through Colin's mind, calling him to act. The hair on his arms raised as he remembered how the mad king—the princess's father—had impaled dozens of people on pikes leading into Estrellala. The scent had been sickening. He remembered his panic at having to leave Jameston and his men behind. The thought of Jameston clouded his thoughts. *He can't be dead*, he told himself. *He can't be.* In his heart, he wasn't sure what he believed.

A meaty hand clamped down on his shoulder, sending Colin into the air about three inches before he realized that the hand belonged to Redbeard.

"You're sure your contact will be there?" Colin whispered as he eyeballed the other man. Sure enough, the old barkeep was sucking on a long, thin pipe. Tendrils of smoke floated around the man's massive beard as he nodded his head.

"'Course she'll be there. She's always there this time o'year for the solstice," the older man replied. "I know she'll help us, me boy, if that's what yer worried about. She's a pro at sneaking people across the border."

"And you're positive she won't refuse us because I'm the King of Szarmi."

"Ah, she won't care about that, son. She knows what it's like to be one of the forsaken."

Colin mulled over the word 'forsaken.' He wasn't convinced he liked being tied to that word. Somehow it felt too definite, as if he would be unable to escape from it. He swallowed hard.

"Did you know that one of the elven tribes goes without clothes on a permanent basis," Redbeard asked as he continued to puff on his pipe. He was seemingly unaware of how his use of the label 'forsaken' had affected Colin.

"Really?" Colin asked, intrigued. He'd never met someone who forwent clothes by choice before. "Don't they, you know, get cold?"

"Not at all," Redbeard said. "In fact, I have it on good authority from one of them that they feel more connected to the earth when going without attire."

"I suppose that could be possible," Colin said, though he still couldn't fathom going every day without clothing.

They continued in silence for several moments, until Colin caught himself stealing glances at the princess again.

"You should just talk to her," Redbeard huffed.

"Talk to who?" Colin replied defensively.

The barkeep chuckled at him before saying, "I'd be mighty afraid of her power if I was you. But that ain't no reason to be this shy of her." He shoved Colin in the back as he spoke. "Go on now."

Colin grumbled beneath his breath as he guided his horse towards Amaleah. Thadius still strode beside her, his face grim. He glowered at Colin as he approached. Colin almost turned tail and rode away, but Amaleah smiled broadly at him and motioned for him to join her.

They marched their horses, side-by-side for several paces before Colin stole another glance at her. Her cheeks were flushed and her green eyes glistened as she stared ahead of her. They did not say anything, as if breaking the silence between them would break the spell. Nothing would change the history between their kingdoms or the fact that her father had almost killed him. Nothing changed the fact that she had agreed to marry her own father.

"So," he said, his voice crumbly and uncomfortable, "I hear that the weather in Encartia is always warm and sunny."

She looked at him then, her smile turning into a slight frown. "Yes," she responded, her voice monotone. "I have read the same."

"You've never been there?" he asked, surprised.

"No," she said simply. "My father never took me before…" she paused for a moment before saying, "before Lord Blodruth left and he sent me to the tower shortly after."

"Oh," he said. He had forgotten that she'd been imprisoned in her own kingdom, by her own father. He'd heard rumors, of course. And, he had read the dispositions from his father's spies. Yet, he had never imagined that the accounts were true.

The hands clutching her reins were bitter white and shaking when Colin looked at her again. All the rosy color had drained from her cheeks.

"I'm sorry, you know," he said, "for what your father did to you."

She sighed and looked away from him. Instinctively, Colin knew that the princess shed tears she didn't wish for anyone to see. "Yes, well, it's not your fault that he went mad and banished me to a nearly forgotten tower before deciding that he wanted to marry me."

Colin resisted the urge to lean away from her. Her voice was filled with wrath and he saw in the quiver of her lips and the sharpness in her eyes that she would do anything to protect herself from King Magnus. He tentatively reached out a hand and squeezed her shaking one.

"There is no more reason to fear, Princess," he said in his most cavalier style. "Once I have reclaimed my throne, I will help you to win your own."

She smiled sadly at him and said, "We shall see."

She nimbly pulled her hand out from under his and turned in her saddle to face Thadius. Colin's heart sank. He had never been rejected by a woman before. Never. He thought about pulling her back to face him again, but somehow knew she wouldn't take kindly to his pressure.

A bird called loudly in the tree beside him. Colin jerked his head up as he tried to identify where the sound had come from. It sounded like none of the birds he'd read about in his research into Lunameed.

The bird called again and this time, several more birds called in agreement. Colin's grip on his reins tightened as he stared at the place he'd just heard the birdcall. There was no tell-tale flutter of leaves as a bird flapped its wings nor was there the sound of squabbling from among the treetops.

"Do you hear that?" he asked.

"What?" she asked just an arrow whizzed past her ear. At first Colin thought that it had not grazed her, but as he continued to look upon her face he noticed the small trickle of blood slipping down her neck. She ran a finger through the red liquid and stared intently at her finger. It was as if she couldn't believe that she'd just been injured.

Colin reached an arm out and shoved her flat against her horse. Another arrow lodged itself in the mud directly in front of Colin's horse. A long, teal and white feather fluttered in the breeze from its tail. Tied to its shaft was a small slip of parchment. Without waiting, he leapt from his mount and slipped the mud-covered arrow from the ground. Carefully, he unbound the tendril of leather that held the note closed and peered down at the single symbol written on the parchment.

He couldn't read it. He knew it was an elvish word, but he had never been taught to read the ancient writing by his tutors. They had told him that it was the language of the darkness and mystery.

"Do you know how to read Elvish?" he asked from the

corner of his mouth. His voice was so low that he wasn't confident that Amaleah had heard him.

"Only some," she responded. She did not tear her gaze from the trees before them. Her eyes were wide, wider than he had ever seen them. White circles surrounded her pupils and Colin noticed how she flexed and unflexed her hand. He had the urge to clasp her hand in his own, to tell her that she would be safe as long as they were together. Instead, he offered the slip of paper to her and bowed his head and he waited for her to read the symbol.

"It's much more intricate than I've ever seen before," she began. "But," she said as she tapped a curlicue at the top of the symbol, "this indicates a question." She bent over the parchment, nearly pressing her nose to it. "And this," she said, "means savior... or friend... I'm not sure which." She pursed her lips. "This!" she exclaimed as she traced the pattern of six lines, "is an offer of peace."

Redbeard strode to the front of the line. His massive shoulders shook as he stepped past Colin's horse and his booming laughter filled the forest.

"Come on out, you old fool," he shouted. He crossed his arms across his chest and waited.

Colin glanced up at Amaleah. She clutched the slip of paper between her fingers before slipping it into the folds of her gown. He willed her look at him, to let him know that they were on the same page, but she stared steadfastly ahead of them.

Without a sound, seven shadows appeared within the tree line.

"Castor, I know you're a member of the scouting party. I can smell ya from here," Redbeard continued. "Is this any way to treat an old friend?"

One of the shadows—the largest among them—stepped

forward. He was a massive man. If Colin didn't know better, he would have thought the man had been cross-bred with the giants. His long, blue hair flowed over his shoulders in thick braids. He wore a leather tunic and leggings with a thick belt strapped to his waist. Colin counted seventeen weapons on the man, but he assumed there were more strapped to him in places Colin couldn't see.

"The only friends I see here are the men standing at my back," the giant responded.

"Too bad," Redbeard responded as he plucked a wooden box from the folds of his coat. "And here I was going to offer ya some of the best mureechi I've ever had."

Castor's eyes narrowed as he took another step forwards. "You brought an army with you." It was not a question. The elf sniffed at the air before notching another arrow and aiming it straight at Colin's heart. "And you brought a Szarmian."

Redbeard held up his hands. "Guilty as charged," he said as he proffered the box of mureechi towards the large elf.

"You brought him to our sacred grounds," the elf said, his arrow still pointed at Colin.

Blood pounded in his ears as he waited for the elf to loose his arrow upon him. As Redbeard waited to respond, his bowels turned to water.

"And can you detect who this Szarmian is?" he asked. His voice was nonchalant, but Colin could see the tension in Redbeard's shoulders as he spoke.

Castor nodded and two more figures emerged from the shadows. They passed by Redbeard without a glance as they approached Colin. He stretched his hand up and grazed the side of Amaleah's hand. He smiled when she didn't flinch away from him.

The figures stood on either side of him, their faces

impassive. They both had purple-veined porcelain skin that seemed almost translucent when light struck it. They had the same black hair and eyes. In one, smooth motion, the first of the elves grasped him by the shoulders and yanked him towards Castor.

The giant of an elf sniffed at the air again. "You reek of royal blood," the man growled, baring his teeth in the process. Colin went rigid. The soldier leaned in closer and raised his eyebrows. "You're sure this is the heir to the Szarmian throne?" he snarled.

To Colin's dismay, Redbeard shrugged his shoulders. He gaped at the barkeep and silently begged him to catch his eye. Redbeard didn't even glance at him as he said, "He's the best ruler Szarmi will ever know."

To Colin's surprise, Amaleah stepped forward and said, "I know him to be the true Szarmian heir." Her voice was strong and clear and beautiful. Colin swung his head towards her, but she was looking straight at Castor. "He was introduced at court as Colin Stormbearer. He is who he claims to be."

Again, the elven soldier sniffed at him. Colin gritted his teeth as Castor gripped his face hard between his fingers and peered into his eyes.

"We will see what Elaria has to say about this," Castor said.

"Elaria?" Redbeard asked, surprised etched in his voice. "Not Kileigh?"

Colin tried to remember what Redbeard had told him of the Elven world. Unlike the rest of Lunameed, the elves had maintained their sovereignty. Traditionally, they had aligned themselves with the Lunameedian rulers, but they had the ability to choose.

"Elaria is my matron. She will decide what to do with the whelp," Castor said.

Redbeard bowed and began backing away from Castor and his men. The sentries holding Colin in place released him and began following their leader. Colin released the breath he had been holding as their icy fingers left his skin.

A delicate touch caressed his hand, jolting Colin. He spun around to see that Amaleah had crept to where he stood and taken his hand. She jerked her head towards the small band of soldiers behind them. Colin glanced back to where Castor and his men had stood only moments before. The only thing before him were trees, mist, and shadow. Rolling his shoulders, Colin allowed Amaleah to lead him back to their group.

Redbeard gave no explanation as he silently led the troupe through the woods. Every so often, Colin would hear the snap of twig or the call of an owl as they passed through the night shrouded forest. The roar of a far-off waterfall filled the air, muffling out any hope of conversation.

And so, the not-so-merry band of scrounged up soldiers and Amaleah's escort trudged onwards. Colin's hand continued to tingle with the warmth of Amaleah's touch as they passed through the dense mist that cloaked the foot paths and underbrush. Following the interaction with Castor and his men, Yosef had insisted that Amaleah walk beside him. Not even Redbeard had questioned the wraith's demand.

Golden light flickered ahead of them. Colin counted at least a dozen torches lining a winding path through the forest. Redbeard raised his left fist and the entire party stopped their progression as the barkeep stepped forward. The scent of mureechi filled the air. Colin opened his mouth to reprimand Redbeard for his choice in timing when he heard a voice call through the darkness.

"You old fool."

"Is that you, you ol' scoundrel?" Redbeard called out,

amusement in his voice.

"Who else would be waiting for you on the side of the road at this time of night?"

Redbeard laughed as he confidently stepped forward. Colin gasped as a Szarmian woman strode from behind a tall tree lining the path. Her features were cast in shadow, but he could tell that she carried a long staff with her.

Redbeard embraced the woman in a mighty bear hug. Her feet lifted from the ground as the barkeep tugged her tightly against his chest. She laughed merrily and swung her one free arm around his neck. Smoke of her pipe swirled around the pair of them.

Thadius coughed loudly and Redbeard slowly released the woman.

"Friends, let me introduce you to the woman who is gonna save the world."

"Redbeard," the woman chided as she walloped him on the arm. "That is no way to introduce me to the future king of Szarmi."

She walked into the light, her hand extended. Colin gasped again at the sight of her face. An eyepatch covered her left eye. Mounds of scar tissue exploded from the eyepatch in a starburst. Her dark, chocolatey skin puckered into purplish masses as the scar extended down her cheek. Her jawline clenched the longer Colin stared at her face without extending his own hand.

Amaleah nudged him forward and Colin finally took the woman's hand in his own.

"Name's Rikyah of the Silver Moon. My grandmother has been waiting for you," she said. Her voice was strong yet contained a hint of humor in it. She smiled at Colin. "It is good to have another outsider among us."

Colin pulled his hand from her grasp and wiped his sweaty

palm upon the leg of his pants.

"Yes," was all he said in response. His eyes trailed over her scar once more before landing on her hair. Purple and red streaks had been dyed into her short locks. It was then that he noticed the delicate curve of her ears and the slight point at their tips.

"You're part elf!" he exclaimed. "But… how?" Never, in all his years, had he ever met someone of mixed heritage from his kingdom, at least, not with the magical world.

"I am," she said, though her voice was sad. "I will explain at breakfast. But first, I think it is time that you and the rest of your party join me in the Silver Moon outpost. We have prepared baths and food for you for the night. Elaria will meet with you in the morning."

She motioned for them all to follow her as she turned down one of the side paths leading in a different direction. Redbeard followed her without hesitation. Yosef was the next to follow. His cloak billowed behind him in a writhing twist of blackness. A hint of cold brushed against Colin's skin as he stared after the wraith.

Thadius led Amaleah down the path as well. She smiled at Colin as she passed. Colin wondered if the Lunameedian princess ever doubted herself. She certainly seemed more confident than he was.

With a sigh, Colin followed behind the crowd. He knew the rest of the soldiers Redbeard had gathered would follow him from behind, but their presence did nothing to alleviate the feeling that something sinister lingered in the trees all around them.

Chapter Twelve

Droplets of water trailed down her breasts as she rose from the water. Her skin was nearly iridescent as ripples of color ran down her shoulders, her navel, and then lower. Colin's eyes roamed over her body, memorizing every inch of her. The curve of her breast, the bend of her elbow as she interlaced her delicate fingers. A fire burned within Colin, so blistering that he could barely contain himself.

She rose further from the water, her golden blonde hair clinging to her body in all the places Colin most wanted to see. Starlight cast a shimmering glow upon the water's surface that rippled as she bobbed up and down. She laughed as she lifted her heart-shaped face to the sky and raised her arms up. The mirth on her face was the most glorious thing Colin had ever seen. Her sensuous lips curled into a smile as she beckoned him closer. He sucked in a breath as her cerulean blue eyes met his.

He waded deeper into the water.

"Colin," she cooed. His body responded to the sound of her voice. He could barely hear her now. *Glorious*, he thought. *She is a goddess. My goddess*. He claimed her. He would always claim her. She stretched out a hand towards him and Colin found himself doing the same. Their fingertips met and electricity flowed through him.

Without thinking, without pausing to consider, Colin gripped her hand and tugged her towards him. Their bodies collided in a spray of star-illuminated water droplets. Colin moaned as he felt the curves of her body press into him. She hooked one leg around his back, stabilizing her against him.

Trailing kisses down her slender neck, Colin whispered her name over and over and over again.

"Vanessa."

Her fingers wrapped themselves in his hair. He felt the warmth of her breath against his neck. He heard her sigh as he slid his hands down her back until they rested lightly on her hips. He longed to delve lower, to see the expression in her eyes as he gently slid into her.

"Vanessa," he whispered again.

A cold wind rustled the spring trees. Danger, they seemed to scream. Colin ignored their warning as he buried his face in the soft spot between her neck and shoulder. She moaned softly in his ear.

He felt her shift, felt her fumble for the pouch tied to her ankle. He already knew, had already lived this dream before. Opening his eyes, Colin saw, through the mist and shadow, Vanessa hold a slender dagger above her head. It was aimed directly at the center of his back.

Growling, Colin lunged forward at the same moment she began to let her hand fall. The jolt of being sent backwards loosened her grip on the dagger's hilt long enough for Colin to knock it from her grasp. It skidded across the water's surface before sinking into its depths. Vanessa snarled at him as she drew yet another dagger from a strap on her upper thigh.

Anxiety coursed through Colin's veins.

"No," he whispered. "Please."

Vanessa laughed at him as he begged her to stop, begged her

to change course.

He knew how this story would end.

Her blood on his hands. The scent of her vanilla perfume as she fell away from him. The sound of her last breath upon his cheek.

"No," he whispered again.

She threw the dagger.

For once, Colin almost let the blade sink deep into his chest. He almost let himself fade into the night like a lullaby on the wind. He almost let her win.

But, he caught the dagger, just as he had always done before. Its tip grazed his nose as it quivered in his hand. Her eyes widened, her lips parting as if to communicate her shock at his newfound abilities. Her blue eyes were calculating and cold, colder than Colin had ever seen them before.

She did not beg him as he returned the dagger to her. She did not cower as it found its home in her heart.

Cold hands gripped Colin's shoulders. Death had finally come to claim him; he was sure of it.

"Colin," a feminine voice said. Strong hands shook him. "Colin, are you alright?"

He clutched at the hands.

"You were screaming so we decided to wake you," the voice said, as if to explain their intrusion into his dreams.

"Get away from me," he grumbled. His shirt was soaked in sweat and he had a sour taste in his mouth.

"Are you sure you're alright?" the voice was pleading, weak. Colin detested that voice the moment he heard it.

"I said, go away!" he nearly shouted.

"Well now, there's no reason for that," a gruff male voice said.

Colin knew that voice. Redbeard. The name came to him the

way all his memories came to him as he faded out of sleep.

"I promise, I am quite alright," Colin said as calmly as he could. The hands on his shoulders squeezed him tightly before releasing him.

"Sounds ta me like you could use a tap of my mureechi pipe," Redbeard said. Colin heard him lumber across the room and begin rummaging through his pack in the dark.

"Colin?" the female voice asked, her voice plaintive.

He knew that voice. Yet, in the darkness, he could not remember to whom it belonged.

"I'm fine," he reiterated.

She didn't respond, but he could sense her standing over him. He thought of what to say to her, but he only found the void he always found after dreaming of Vanessa. It was as if a piece of him had shattered the night that her body had lain broken upon the courtyard grounds. He had done that to her. He had destroyed her.

Perhaps he deserved the damnation he faced in his dreams, the never-ending purgatory of what he had done to her. Never mind the fact that Vanessa had attacked first, that she had been sent there to assassinate him.

The girl gripped his hand and it was as if shooting stars suddenly shot through his body.

"I know what it is to face the darkness lurking behind the curtain," she said, her voice soft and soothing. "I know the horrors of this world."

Her voice broke. Warm tears cascaded onto their intertwined hands. Colin gripped her hand more firmly in his own.

"There is no shame in letting yourself feel the loss of this world. But," she continued, "do not let it consume you."

Colin breathed in deeply as hidden tears filled his eyes. For once, he didn't feel alone.

A match struck, creating a halo of golden-red light across the room from them. In its glow, Colin watched Redbeard pack a pipe full of the putrid-smelling herb and light it. The barkeep quietly crossed the room and held the pipe out to Colin.

"This will help you sleep," he said, his voice gruff.

"No, thank you," Colin replied.

Amaleah squeezed his hand again. Amaleah—that was her name; he knew it. He trailed his thumb across her skin. She was soft and warm and delicate. Until she tugged her hand out of his grasp, each movement felt like a current passing through him. The moment her touch left him, Colin felt ice seep into his veins.

Redbeard shoved the pipe in the hand Amaleah had just released.

"I insist," was all the man said as he sauntered back over to his mat on the floor.

Amaleah remained. Her features were slightly illuminated by the faint glow of the pipe, but he could not see her eyes. They were emerald green. He remembered them now. Not cerulean blue. Not *her* eyes. Colin sucked in another breath and slowly released it, calming his still rapidly-beating heart.

"You should try to get some more rest, Colin," the Lunameedian princess whispered. "From what Redbeard said tonight, our trials here have just begun."

Colin heard her take a step backwards.

"Wait," he whispered, his voice a hoarse rasp. "Please… don't go."

He couldn't see her face or hear her heartbeat, but he knew his words had somehow struck her. She lingered between where his cot was and the refuge of her own bedroll.

"I promise I won't bite," he said. His voice was little more than a plea.

She hesitated a moment longer. Colin slammed the pipe into

his mouth and reached out a hand towards her. His fingers met cold, empty air as he realized that she had slipped away.

***

Redbeard woke Colin before the first rays of morning light. The chill air sent shivers down his spine as he followed Redbeard down a wide, dirt path. A mixture of wooden and fur structures lined the path and stretched into the woods beyond. Gossamer fabric fluttered from the trees as birds hopped from one branch to the next. As the first rays of light struck the encampment, each of the structures sparkled like the jewels in Szarmi's treasury. Colin sucked in a breath at the radiance surrounding him.

"Glass and crystal are added to each of the dwellings here. It is a symbol of the beauty of the Light," Redbeard whispered to him from the corner of his mouth. Colin looked up at the man, but Redbeard continued walking forward as if he had said nothing.

Shadows darted between the trees above them. They leapt from branch to branch so quickly that Colin almost believed that he was imagining it. But no, a young elf, no more than eight years of age, hung from one of the lower-hanging branches and peered down at them. Colin spied her and smiled. Her sea green eyes appraised him. He waved and her cheeks reddened. Her long, ebony hair dangled as she swung her body back up and disappeared into the trees. Colin smiled to himself. He remembered Coraleen acting much the same way as a child.

He had not thought of her betrayal in several days. Now, it felt as if a thousand tiny blades were pricking his skin as the weight of her disloyalty sank in. She had sentenced him to die, in a foreign kingdom, alone. His shoulders shook as he bowed his head to quickly wipe away the tears that had sprung, unbidden, into his eyes.

"Are you alright, son?" Redbeard asked. He placed a meaty palm onto Colin's shoulder, but it did not ease Colin's trembling.

Colin flexed and unflexed his hand. *This is why I've come here*, he reminded himself. *I will right this wrong. I will reclaim my throne, even if it destroys me in the process.*

"Yes," he whispered hoarsely. "Yes, I am alright, Redbeard."

Redbeard left his hand upon Colin's back. Colin stole a glance at the older man. The man eyed him with concern and a frown on his lips.

"I'm fine," he reiterated. "Really, Redbeard, there is nothing to worry about."

Redbeard looked him up and down before releasing his grip on Colin's shoulder. "Then let's be on with it," he said.

Colin shrugged his shoulders as the warmth of Redbeard's touch evaporated. He continued to watch the trees as they made their way to what he presumed was the center of the encampment. He did not see the adventurous young girl again. For this, Colin heaved a sigh of relief.

The simplicity of the encampment contrasted the elegance of the city's center. A large, circular building loomed before them. Its walls were made from a type of stone Colin had never seen before. They glittered like the stars. The building reminded Colin of a cold winter night staring up at a starfall with his father. They had stayed up all night as brilliant balls of white and blue light had streaked across the sky. It was one of the few times King Henry had expressed his admiration for the unknown to Colin. He had always been in pursuit of more. More knowledge. More might. More power to rule over Szarmi. But, Colin had been given opportunities to see his father outside of the context of 'the king.' That night, his father had simply been a man hypothesizing about life beyond Mitier.

"It's absolutely beautiful," Amaleah exclaimed as she rushed forwards. Tendrils of her hair streamed behind her as the breeze caught her. Colin found himself staring after her, all thoughts of his father dissipating as she stared up at the massive wall. She laughed joyfully as she placed a single hand upon the stone wall closest to them. It pulsed with light beneath her touch.

"We cut the hands off those who dare to touch our most sacred building," a sly voice said from the shadows lurking inside the structure. "Even the future queen of Lunameed's hand is not safe from our vengeance."

Amaleah let out a yelp of surprise as the dark-skinned woman from the previous night emerged from the building. Colin was surprised the woman wore billowing pants sewn with metallic thread and beads. She wore a set of jewel-crusted daggers at her waist, but she had ditched the tall staff from her repertoire of weapons. She clutched a long blade in her hand. It gleamed in the morning light. Amaleah took a step back, her eyes wide.

"Really, Princess, what did you think was going to happen?" the woman asked. Her face was placid as she twirled the blade in her hand in a menacing fashion.

"I didn't know," Amaleah whispered. Her entire body trembled.

"Ah, Rikyah," Redbeard said as he stepped forward, subtly placing himself between Colin and Amaleah. "Why do you always play this joke on the new ones?"

Amaleah's cheeks turned a startling shade of red as she

looked between Rikyah and Redbeard.

"You always ruin my fun," Rikyah said with a pout as she whipped the blade in an arch before slipping it into a hidden pocket of her trousers.

"So, there's not a rule about touching the stone?" Amaleah asked, still wide-eyed.

Redbeard placed a hand on the princess's shoulder and said, "None except for the one this here cur creates to scare away visitors."

Rikyah smiled and bowed. The scar covering her left eye shimmered as she stared straight into Colin's eyes.

"So, you are the prince everyone keeps telling me about, eh?" she asked.

"And you're the Szarmian elf that never was before," Colin retorted.

"Just so," she replied, her eyes flashing with mischief.

"Come on ya love birds, we have a job to do," Redbeard said as he strode towards the entrance of the building. "Elaria will be waiting for us."

Yosef followed close behind Redbeard. Dark shadows seemed to whisper to him as his black cape fluttered of its own accord. Colin audibly gulped as he took his place after the wraith. Amaleah and Thadius fell into step behind Colin. He heard the centaur whisper comforting words to the princess. Colin glanced over his shoulder. Amaleah's cheeks were flushed and she looked up at the centaur with so much adoration that Colin had to stop himself from lunging at the beast.

An arm hooked around his neck and squeezed just as he took a step backwards. Soft fabric and hard muscle abraded his skin.

"Listen here, you Szarmian scum, I may look like your people, but I am loyal to Lunameed and Encartia."

Colin twisted around enough to look Rikyah square in the eyes. Unlike the brown he had been expecting, her eyes were green flecked with golden amber. They were like a spring meadow aglow with light. He smiled at the thought.

"Don't smile at me, you pig," Rikyah hissed, though her eyes contained none of the malice her voice did. "I've seen enough of what your people do to those they believe are traitors to their cause."

There was a trace, however small, of pain in her voice as she spoke. She released him as they entered the stone building. Colin wondered why she hated the Szarmians so much.

Crystal constellations covered the ceiling. The glittering stones provided the only light to the chamber. Fur rugs covered the floor, providing warmth. An assortment of books and strange contraptions littered the various tables crowded into the small space. Aromatic herbs hung before each of the windows, causing Colin to sneeze as their scents struck him all at once.

Redbeard kneeled before a woman sitting on a wooden chair. Her silver hair was curled with stones woven into braids about her crown. Each of the stones shimmered with different hues, one each to depict the seasons. She appeared old, with wrinkles to match. She clutched a long staff in her hand and, like Rikyah, a set of daggers hung from a belt at her slender waist. She murmured to Redbeard in a voice so low Colin could not hear what she said. Yosef stood behind the barkeep, his face turned towards the woman. Colin still wasn't sure how the wraith saw through his hollowed-out eyes.

"Sit here," Rikyah said abruptly as she pushed a wooden chair to Colin. It looked as it would collapse at even the slightest amount of weight, but, not wanting to be rude, Colin complied. She did the same for Amaleah, who interlaced her fingers and assumed a slack, immovable expression on her face as she regarded the woman in the chair.

"That must be Elaria," Colin murmured as he leaned in close to Amaleah's ear.

"Uh hem," Thadius grumbled as his face suddenly appeared between Colin and Amaleah. "No talking," he whispered, his eyes darting around the room.

Of course, Colin realized, *there could be danger here*.

He scanned the room, but saw nothing strange save for a contraption he knew to be invented in Szarmi. At first glance, it appeared to be a simple box. But, Colin knew, if you simply twisted the box in the correct way a hidden drawer would pop out from the side. Only one who knew the box's secret would be able to unlock its mysteries. Colin kept several to keep his keys and documents in. He vaguely wondered what his mother and sister had done to the boxes once he'd been presumed dead.

"And these are the future rulers of Lunameed and Szarmi," a soft, feminine voice said. It was not a question. Colin jerked his head up and peered at the tallest woman he had ever seen before. She stood at least two inches taller than Redbeard. Colin whistled in awe.

"You," she said, pointing at Colin, "come here."

Even if Colin had wanted to, he wasn't sure he could have ignored that request. He nearly ran to the woman's side. "I am Elaria of the Silver Moon," she said in that simple, melodic voice. "My granddaughter tells me that I should attempt to form a truce with you. She claims you have proclaimed your desire for the slaughter of the magical realm to end. She says you wish to educate the misguided among your people and forge a new world unsullied by the blood of war. She has told me much of your plans to rebuild Szarmi's farmlands, to provide employment in the factories for those who cannot grow food. She also tells me of the colorful lights you intend to install throughout the entirety of the kingdom that can be turned on with the single push of a lever."

A smile played across her lips. "What she had not told me, is why you are here." The smile disappeared from her mouth, leaving her with a dark scowl that sent shivers down his spine. Her eyes met his. Despite the youth of her face and voice, her eyes appeared older than Colin could possibly imagine.

She turned to regard Amaleah next.

"Princess Amaleah of Lunameed," she said as she dipped her head to the princess. "So, you have come at last." Her eyes glinted as she uttered a final word, "Harbinger."

Amaleah rose from her seat, despite the hands Thadius pressed down upon her shoulders. "I seek your people's wisdom, knowledge, and training," Amaleah said. "Please consider my appeal for asylum here until I am ready to fulfil my destiny."

"Your destiny is your own," Elaria said delicately. "But, you may stay with us here, in the Silver Moon camp, for as long as is needed. We can supply trainers for you and provide access to any number of books so that you may begin to learn the histories of our people."

The matriarch of the Silver Moon clan raised a single finger and pressed it to her lips, "But," she said, her eyes flashing, "if you betray us to your father, if you succumb to the darkness I feel roiling in my bones, you will forever be forsaken by all who dwell here."

Amaleah bowed deeply. "I understand," she whispered.

Elaria turned her attention back to Colin. A gentle breeze scuttled through the room, sending tendrils of the woman's hair fluttering across her face. She didn't even flinch as a piece of her hair flicked her in the eye. No, her entire focus was now on Colin.

Raising two fingers, Elaria motioned for Colin to step forward. When he took his first steps, she jerked her head towards Rikyah. Colin watched in dismay as Rikyah nodded and then began ushering everyone from the room. Even Redbeard followed her directives as he silently slipped through the open door. Colin willed him to look back at him, but Redbeard left without even so much as a glance in his direction. Fuming, Colin turned for face Elaria head-on.

"Come here, princeling," she said, cocking her head to one side. She inhaled deeply as he came to stand mere inches from her. She patted a chair next to hers. Colin followed her command without hesitation.

"Do you know who you are?" she asked, her voice sanguine.

"Of course, I do," Colin replied. "I am the crown prince of Szarmi."

"Ah," the matriarch said. "I see." She paused as she suddenly clutched his hand in her own and pulled his fingers out of his clinched fist. Her fingers traced across the palm of his hand. Her touch was light and fleeting, like a butterfly's kiss. She tapped at a spot in the middle of his palm. "And do you have a kingdom to show for your title?"

Colin opened his mouth to say that Szarmi had one of the largest land masses in the whole of Mitier. He was proud of his kingdom's holdings and took pleasure in ensuring that his people continued to thrive. But then, the cold reality of what his sister had done to him struck him once more. His blood turned to ice in his veins as he regarded the matriarch sitting beside him.

"No," he whispered, his voice shallow and hoarse. "Not at present anyway."

Elaria raised an eyebrow at that but continued her line of questioning. She asked him questions about his training as a Szarmian royal. She questioned him on the political climate within his kingdom. She asked him about his convictions about relations between the magical and nonmagical people. When Colin had sufficiently bared his soul to the matriarch, she merely nodded at him. A smile played across her lips as she leaned forward and clutched his hand.

"If you were to be returned to your kingdom—given a second chance at ruling—what would you do for your people and your nation?" her voice was gentle and soft, like a spring flower tickling his skin. Colin returned her smile. It was not the court face he normally reserved for meetings like this. No, it was genuine, and real, and terrifying.

"It has always been my greatest ambition to unite the bonds that tie our people together," Colin began. "My father used to encourage me to seek out truth above all else. He was convinced that we had made a grave error." He paused as he remembered how his father would take him on rides through the countryside.

Outside the city, Szarmi was awash with hills covered in the widest array of color Colin had ever seen. Flowers and crops and forests were arranged in neatly organized rows. Fields of yellow wheat and green stalks of corn dotted hills in the distance. In each of the towns he and his father visited, his father would tell him about the history of the land. Every town had its stories, its own foundation that needed to be understood. In every town, his father had told him to seek to understand first, and then to speak.

His father knew what his people were doing to the magical realm and yet he had done nothing. He had let them murder innocents. He had even rewarded some of the 'noblier' of his men. *All people need something to hope for, to believe that, if they just worked hard enough, they can achieve.*

"I see," Elaria said. The way she said it made Colin feel as if she had witnessed his memories and his thoughts. The idea was unnerving as she continued to peer into his eyes. He noticed for the first time how tiny shards of silver flashed in her eyes. Her teeth bared and shadows slithered around her head.

"Stay here," she commanded as she lithely rose from her chair and stalked to the structure's door. Her movements were feline and her pointed ears flicked as if she were hearing some distant, horrible sound.

The hair on the back of Colin's neck hackled as the sound of thundering hooves filled the room. The walls groaned and the sparkling stone pulsed in a ferocious rhythm. Colin jolted as Redbeard slipped into the room, his face paler than Colin had ever seen it.

"They've arrived," Elaria said. Her voice was quiet and firm. It held none of the curiosity Colin would have expected in this type of situation.

"Afraid so."

"The girl?"

"Safe."

Colin's knuckles turned white as he clenched them into tight fists. He was about to ask where Yosef, Thadius, and Amaleah were when the sound of a horn blasted through the air.

"Hide the boy," Elaria hissed as she straightened her back and strode from the room without so much as a glance in Colin's direction.

Soundlessly, Redbeard motioned for Colin to crouch below the windowsill. On his hands and knees, Redbeard crawled towards Colin. Dust swirled in the morning light streaming in through the windows. Colin's heart hammered so quickly in his chest that he thought for a moment that it would explode from the exertion. It didn't, thankfully, but still Colin fought against the fear that threatened to overtake him.

"Elaria," a high-pitched, cold voice snarled from outside. It was so shrill that Colin felt as if nails were raking down his back, leaving trails of crimson blood in their wake.

"It is a surprise to see you in the Silver Moon camp, Kileigh. To what do I owe this honor?"

Colin found himself surprised at the harshness in the matriarch's voice. He vowed to himself that he would never find himself on the receiving end of that tone.

Tinkling laughter. Whoever Elaria was speaking with laughed in the delicate, needy way of a complete fraud.

"You are too funny, Elaria. And, it has been too long since I made a visit to your home."

"I see," Elaria said. "And what would you like to inspect first, Matriarch?"

Matriarch? Colin thought as he attempted to rise up on his knees and peer out the window. *How old was this woman? She barely sounds older than thirty.* Redbeard's fingers dug into Colin's shoulder sending spikes of pain through his arm. Colin glared up at the man. Redbeard's gaze was hollow, as if he weren't really there at all.

"Redbeard?" Colin hissed, his voice so quiet he wasn't even sure the man would hear it. When his mentor didn't respond, Colin said again, in a louder voice, "Redbeard?"

"Who do you have lurking in your sanctuary?" the tinkling voice asked.

Gooseflesh spread across Colin's arms as he saw the glint of gold and heard the woman ask, "Whom do you attempt to hide here, Elaria?"

A burst of sunlight poured into the building as the main door was shoved open in a gusty breeze. Despite the golden rays of sunshine, Colin's teeth chattered. The sound of heels scraping against the stone floors of the building sent shivers down his spine. Redbeard, a dazed expression on his face, remained locked in place. For a moment, Colin wasn't even sure the man was breathing until he saw the mist form on the stone directly in front his mouth.

Rustling silk and crinkling tulle, these were the sounds Colin heard before the slight intake of breath as the most beautiful woman he'd ever seen entered the room.

She couldn't have been more than twenty years old. Her golden hair fell in curls about her heart-shaped face. Her bronzed skin seemed to glimmer as she stretched out a slender hand towards him. Colin dropped to his knees before her. He scanned her body from feet to head. Her lips formed a perfect pout when her eyes locked onto his.

Her eyes were the most vibrant shade of violet Colin had ever seen in a living creature before. Silver rings circled her pupils, making them appear to glow, even in the bright sunlight filtering in through the open door. Her long nails were painted and adorned with white diamonds. All thoughts of Vanessa and Amaleah fled his mind the longer he stared into the woman's eyes.

She scraped her nails across the length of his chin as she examined him. "You are a scrawny little thing," she said. Her nails bit into his skin. He smelled the coppery tang of his own blood and felt the hot liquid trail down his cheek. Yet, Colin barely registered the pain.

"But," she said as she tapped one of her nails on her golden cheek. "I have heard the rumors about you and would like to find out if they're true or not."

"They're true," Colin said the instant she released his chin from her grasp. "I want to bridge the differences between our nations. I want to see peace rule the whole of Mitier, not the fear, corruption, and suffering we currently have."

"You are a dreamer," the woman said, contemplatively. Her eyes roamed over his face, as if she could consume him. He shuddered slightly.

"Kileigh," Elaria said, stepping towards where Colin knelt before the matriarch. She held a long staff in her hand. And, although her voice was reprimanding, Colin noticed how Elaria's arm shook as she propped the staff on the floor. Sweat beaded on his brow. His nerves quivered as he considered Elaria's reaction to Kileigh. He knew he was ill-prepared for whatever the latter had in store for him.

The golden woman shifted her eyes towards Elaria. A scowl stretched across her face. Her violet eyes held a wisdom and a sadness in them that Colin found haunting. She was haunting.

"I tire of these constant games, Elaria," Kileigh sighed. She twirled a curl between two fingers so nonchalantly that Colin was mesmerized by the action. The golden strands glistened in the rays of sun streaming into the room.

"As do I, cousin," Elaria began.

Kileigh raised a single hand, instantly silencing whatever Elaria was about to say. Her eyes blazed as she looked down upon Colin.

"Your forefathers slaughtered thousands of our people. Your heroes desecrated our sacred grounds. Your actions speak louder than any word you have spoken." Pointed teeth that resembled fangs more than anything else flashed as she spoke. The brilliant glow that had surrounded her turned a molten purple. Through it all, Colin heard the splinter in her as she cried out in an earsplitting scream.

"We will not be broken by your ilk anymore."

Colin forced himself to not blink as he stared into Kileigh's eyes.

"My people remember," he whispered.

"What?" she asked, her voice full of venom.

"My people remember," he said more loudly. "They will always remember."

She hissed. Her golden hair seemed to slither across her skin as she glided towards him. Gooseflesh covered his arms, but still Colin continued to stare her down.

"Your people caused the atrocities. Your people continue to be consumed by hate when our people have sought peace for centuries. It is a wonder that the Princess Amaleah deigned to travel with you at all. She is the Light that will reignite this world. You are the filth that will mar her legacy."

She sniffed at him and scowled. "And you need a bath."

"A bath?" Never, in all his thoughts and imaginings, did he think that one of the matriarchs of the elven clans would request for him to bathe. His lips tugged upwards as he waited for her to respond.

She crinkled her nose at him, "Yes, scum, a bath."

"You're telling me that after all of that," he gestured around the room, "you're asking me to take a bath?"

She snorted. And not just a cute small snort, like the ones he'd heard from the miniature pigs the women of his court kept as pets. No, hers was the sound of a hog rooting for truffles in the forest. *Or*, he thought, *the blow of a horn from an untutored musician.*

And so, Colin burst into laughter.

Chapter Thirteen

Colin laughed until his sides ached and his lungs burned. Kileigh only smiled at him, her feline expression full of pointed teeth. She tapped her fingertips together, her nails clinking softly with each rap. With a final intake of breath, Colin stopped laughing as abruptly as he had started. When he realized that he had been the only one consumed by laughter, he knelt, self-consciously, before the matron and waited for her to continue.

"Such humility," she tutted as she continued to clink her nails. "You should have told me how amusing the boy is, Elaria. I would have come sooner."

The Silver Moon matriarch did not respond and Colin felt his insides quiver. He stole a quick glance at Kileigh's face and saw that she was watching Elaria with a cold smirk on her face.

"Well then," Kileigh said, "draw the water and prepare this boy a bath."

Elaria nodded and several other elves, none of whom Colin remembered noticing before, scurried from the room in a quiet frenzy. Kileigh examined her nails as servants hauled in an enormous wooden tub and buckets of steaming water. When the last of the elves brought in a chest of assorted jars and set it before Colin like a gift, Kileigh clapped her hands twice.

Rough hands yanked his shirt from his body, the threads

ripping. Colin knew his clothing was a little worse for wear, but he hadn't realized how bedraggled he must have appeared to everyone else.

"The girl?" the matriarch hissed as the servants began unbuttoning Colin's trousers. He swatted at their hands each time they attempted to pull his drawers down, but still they continued their chore.

"What girl?" Elaria asked. Her voice was soft and cold, yet there was no mistaking the quiet defiance in her tone. Colin glanced between the two women. Elaria, though beautiful, was an old crone. Kileigh was the exact opposite with her golden features. They glared at each other the way a pair of cats do right before a fight. Colin clawed at the palms of his hands as he waited to see what would transpire between the two matriarchs.

"What girl?" Kileigh scoffed. "What girl?" she repeated in a high-pitched squeal. "Are you mocking me, Elaria?"

"You asked, I clarified. But, if you don't have any specific questions regarding a specific female staying among my people, then I suggest that you ask your questions and be done with it."

Kileigh bared her teeth at Elaria, the whites of her eyes glowing in the dim light of the room.

"You know perfectly well that Amaleah Bluefischer walks among you." She glanced at Colin as she spoke and waved her hands at the servants, who promptly pushed him into the still-steaming water. They poured in mixtures of oils that made the water smell like exotic flowers and coconut. The servants dunked Colin's head underwater just as he heard Kileigh begin to speak again.

"You know what…"

He erupted from the water, gasping for air, just in time to hear the last of her words.

"When I return on the morrow, I expect to meet with her."

Elaria bowed to the matriarch, her shoulders sagging a bit as she did so. Colin swatted at the servants as they scrubbed at his body, including his nether regions. The once clear water had already turned a murky color when they dumped another bucket on top of his head. He shivered, as the water had cooled in the lae autumn air. Suds got into his eyes as soapy water streamed down his face. He groaned in pain as his eyes burned. The servants merely ducked his head under water once more before dumping the remaining water over his head.

"You have brought much strife to my people, Colin Stormbearer," Elaria said as the servants wrapped a thick cloth around his shoulders. It was soft and warm and smelled of cedar. Gooseflesh covered his skin as he stood in the open. Elaria sighed before lighting a fire in a small fireplace close to where she stood.

She motioned for Colin to take the seat opposite her and he did. Redbeard, whom Colin had assumed went to find the rest of their men, crept from the shadows and stood behind Colin's chair. Elaria ignored him as she turned her gaze fully upon Colin.

"You seek our help to reclaim your throne, yet you can give us no assurance that you will be successful in your pursuit. If you fail and we are implicated in your plans, your mother will stop at nothing to destroy us. You know this to be true, Colin." She pulled a thin pipe from her tunic and stuffed an herb Colin didn't recognize into its chamber. "But, if we do not help you and your sister is allowed to take the throne, she and your mother will destroy us anyway."

Redbeard squeezed Colin's shoulder in warning, but he ignored his friend as he said, "All I ask is that you help me cross the border between our lands."

Elaria held up a hand as he opened his mouth to continue.

Colin instantly fell silent.

"I understand that my granddaughter has already made a bargain with your friend." She glared at Redbeard from beneath her eyelashes. It was a fearsome look that sent a shiver down Colin's spine. "You should know that I have already granted her permission to take you, though I doubt that if I had denied her request she would have heeded my command."

Colin smiled up at Redbeard. Fire rushed through his veins at the thought of returning home. He knew, deep in his gut, that his people would support him. He knew the armies he'd trained with would recognize him as the true leader of Szarmi. He knew he would reclaim his throne. He nearly jumped from his seat for joy.

"But," Elaria continued, "I will not sanction any of my clan's people to accompany you, save for the ones in Rikyah's company. It will not be an easy task, this saving of your kingdom."

A servant quietly entered the room and laid a fresh set of clothes beside Colin, including a new set of boots and a coat. He stood behind his chair as he quickly dressed.

"I'll just have to take my chance," Colin replied as he laced his trousers on tight. "I have no other choice but to try."

Elaria nodded in understanding. She seemed frail, now that the golden matriarch had left and she was huddled near the fire. Colin wondered how long she had lived and if she could remember the Wars of Darkness. He was about to ask when Redbeard stepped forward, clearing his throat loudly.

"Elaria, if Kileigh is to return to your camp, I believe it would be best if Colin and me men were to leave with Rikyah tonight. 'Sides, the sooner we complete our mission, the sooner Colin here can send aid back to Lunameed when the time comes."

"When the time comes," Elaria whispered softly as she stared into the fire. "I would hope that you will do more than let an innocent boy and girl fight the final battle."

Wrinkles spread across her skin as she spoke and dark spots blotched her otherwise ivory skin. When she turned back to Colin, her eyes were glazed and her lips parched.

"What's happening to her?" Colin asked as he turned to Redbeard for answers.

Redbeard merely shook his head, his lips pursed.

"Tell me what's going on!" Colin shouted. Elaria's silver hair turned dull and her natural glow faded.

"Redbeard, you have to help her!" Colin pleaded. "Please!"

"I am fine, Colin Stormbearer," Elaria whispered, her voice hoarse and raspy. Her chapped lips bled as she spoke and a thin line of blood trailed down her chin.

"No, you're not," Colin said as he reached for her free hand. Her skin was so cold that he nearly dropped her hand in surprise.

"I just need some time by the fire is all," she said. Her voice was barely audible now.

Colin looked to Redbeard for answers. The older man merely shrugged his shoulders as he watched Elaria slowly fade into a shriveled old hag.

The fire crackled on. Colin's damp hair dripped water onto the wooden floor. And Elaria smoked her pipe in silence.

There was a light tap on the door before Rikyah entered the room. She took one glance at Elaria before she pulled a long staff from the wall and pressed it into the matriarch's hands. Colin could tell that the wood had been smoothed, not by rough cloth, but by hundreds of hours spent utilizing it.

The moment the wood touched Elaria's skin, color began to rise in her cheeks and the shadow creeping over slipped away with the morning light.

"Grandmother?" Rikyah asked as she continued to hold the staff in her grandmother's hands.

"Oh, lay off me, girl. You know I need to store as much of my strength as possible. War is upon us."

"Yes, Grandmother," Rikyah replied. Her voice was compliance, yet Colin saw her grip one of her jeweled blades as she spoke. He wondered what the relationship between them truly was.

Elaria gripped Rikyah's hand in her own. Her arm shook as she drew her granddaughter close enough to whisper in her ear. Colin desperately tried to hear what Elaria had to say to her granddaughter, but could hear nothing save for the heaviness of his own breathing.

Rikyah nodded as Elaria released her hold on her.

"I promise," she said as she ushered both Redbeard and Colin from the room. The doors and windows shut of their own accord the moment they set foot outside of its walls. Colin jumped as the door slammed shut on the tails of his coat as he rushed away from the building.

"We leave immediately," Rikyah said as she stalked over to a tall tree. Lights twinkled in its branches and, high above their heads, Colin could make out the dark lines of a house in the branches.

"Why?" Redbeard asked, "what's happened?"

Rikyah turned on him, her face pale. "The Darkness is coming, friend, and there isn't much time left to prepare."

"Yes, but what does that mean?" Colin asked as he followed Rikyah through a hidden door in the trunk of the tree. Elaborate iron stairs climbed as high as Colin could see through the hollow of the tree. Candles were lit and sparkling stones cast flashes of color all along the path upwards.

"It means, Colin of Szarmi, that there is much more at stake than just the future of your kingdom or ours. I will explain more once we're on the path to Szarmi. For now, understand this: we are only helping you reclaim your throne so that you will join us in the final battle. There is much left to settle from the wars of old."

She shared a glance with Redbeard that made the gooseflesh on Colin's skin reappear. He shivered.

"Can I at least say goodbye to Amaleah?" he asked.

"No time," Rikyah said as she sped up the stairs. "Gather your gear and your men. We leave when the sun marks the hour."

Redbeard nodded and pulled Colin behind him as he walked towards where the men were housed.

"I need to say goodbye to Amaleah," Colin said as he dug in his heels.

Redbeard released his arm and turned to look at him. His eyes darted around the small encampment before he leaned down and said, "I'm not sure where they spirited her away to."

"It doesn't matter. I'll find her."

"We don't have much time for that," Redbeard sighed."Please, Redbeard," Colin began.

"You really have fallen for her, haven't ya?" he asked, his voice gruff as he spoke. When Colin didn't reply, Redbeard continued, "She'll be a weakness for you. If you're going to reclaim your throne, there can't be any distractions. I'm sorry, Colin, but the answer is no."

Redbeard gripped his arm again and began pulling him towards their men.

"It's not a weakness to care about other people, Redbeard," Colin sniffed.

"It is," Redbeard said as he hoisted Colin onto the back of his horse. "She is."

"But we could help each other," Colin said.

Redbeard chuckled at that. "You could, if either of you were in a position to do it. But, you're not. All you'd be to one another is a distraction from the real goal, which is for you both to claim your thrones. Once that happens, and we once more push back the darkness, then—and only then—can you explore the possibility of what could be."

"I'm not a child, Jorah," Colin hissed. "I've loved before."

"Yeah? And how did that turn out for you?"

Colin knew Redbeard's words weren't meant to be spiteful or to hurt the way they did, but it was as if an anvil had been slammed into his chest. He could barely breath as he looked down at Redbeard from atop his horse.

"I killed her," was all he could say.

"And good riddance. Love is overrated, Colin. The sooner you learn that, the better off you'll be."

"What happened to you that made you like this?" Colin retorted. He clenched the reigns to his horse tightly in his hands as the rest of the men quickly packed their bags and saddled their horses.

Redbeard glowered at him as he said, "I loved a woman once, more than I think anyone had ever loved before. I did things for her… that I'm not proud of, Colin. I let myself become a slave to my lust for her. I became sidetracked from my true destiny."

"Sounds like you were someone awful important, if you had a destiny laid out before you."

"Heh," Redbeard huffed. "Everyone has a destiny, Colin, even if the elves and the sirens choose not to write about it in their fancy books and stories."

"You make it sound like all of the great stories are just that, stories."

"They are," he grumbled.

"I don't believe you. What about Sir Patrik or the Singing Seven? What about Bakwin and his defeat of the gruesome monster Swyvern? What about Kilian Clearwater?" He breathed in deeply. His mother had never approved of Colin's fascination with the Lunameedian warrior, but his father had encouraged him to explore all the Mitierian heroes. Kilian had always been his favorite, even if his awe of the warrior was mostly due to his mother's disapproval. "You know that the children in my kingdom aren't allowed to read about Kilian, right? He was the greatest hero the whole of Mitier has ever known. Perhaps the whole world has known and no one is allowed to know his stories."

Redbeard's expression tightened as he listened to Colin speak. "You idolize Kilian Clearwater?"

"Everyone should," Colin said resolutely. He stuffed his hands in his pockets and stared down at Redbeard. "He was the greatest hero I've ever read about, Redbeard."

"And what would you think if you found out that the great Kilian Clearwater was a total fraud?"

"He isn't," Colin said. He knew the hero would live up to his stories. He had to.

"But what if he was? What if all the stories told are dramatized events to make him seem like a much bigger hero than he actually was? What if his downfall was the same as what yours will be if you keep chasing after that princess?"

"Kilian didn't have any weaknesses. He was once shot a thousand times by arrows laced with poison and still he survived.

There's not a single thing that could stop him."

"Then what happened to him? Tell me, Colin, if this Kilian Clearwater was as strong and commanding as you're painting him to be, what befell him after the conclusion of the Wars of Darkness?"

Colin paused. No one knew what had become of the hero. He'd simply disappeared. His body was never found, nor his ax. His apprentice claimed he'd died during the Battle of Alnora, but there were no supporting accounts to back this claim. Few believed the apprentice's claim. Colin didn't.

"No one knows," Colin said, shrugging his shoulders. "Maybe he went off and married a beautiful woman and ended his days in peace. Maybe he's still at the Ruins of Alnora, waiting for the next hero to train. Maybe he's drunk and in a tavern somewhere singing about his triumphs as a warrior. Who knows? All I know is that he did great things for Lunameed and the magical realm. I can only hope to one day be as brave and heroic as he was."

Redbeard shook his head. "Every man has his own path, son."

"And every woman."

Colin spun his horse in surprise at the sound of Amaleah's voice. She had changed clothing since last he'd seen her. Her chocolate and auburn hair was pinned back with sparkling combs and she wore a silver-white gown that Colin couldn't quite decide was opaque or transparent. A dagger hung from the jeweled belt at her waist and, much to his surprise, she was barefoot.

He raised an eyebrow at her as she continued to walk towards them.

"It is not just men that get to have grand adventures and save the world, Redbeard." She patted the older man's arm but kept her gaze on Colin. "Women, too, have destinies and stories that sometimes outweigh those of their male compatriots."

"Yes, well," Redbeard stumbled over his words as he tried to recover from his error.

"Just remember who got the best of your dozens of men with only her two companions to help her," she said. She smiled, though the warmth did not meet her eyes. Not for the first time, Colin wondered if her magic were more of a burden to her than a blessing. Her expression darkened for the slightest of moments before she beamed up at Colin once more.

"I heard you were leaving," she said softly. "I thought I'd say goodbye and wish you blessings from the Light." She looked down at her hands as she spoke. "Perhaps we shall meet again one day."

"Perhaps," Colin said. He wanted to say more. He wanted to tell her all that he had been thinking and feeling for her the past several days they'd been traveling together. He wanted her to know his thoughts and dreams and desires. But, one glance at Redbeard told him that to speak now would be to ruin his forward momentum. He had a goal—one goal—to achieve. And, it had nothing to do with the princess standing before him.

She nodded, her eyes glistening slightly. "I pray that we both are able to reclaim our thrones, Colin, and that we will rule our respective kingdoms with grace and kindness. I hope that the feud between our people can finally be resolved."

He opened his mouth to speak, his resolve cracking, when Redbeard jumped in.

"Thank ya for yer kindness, Princess. I know I speak for us

both when I say that we have truly enjoyed traveling with you these past days. I, too, hope that one day you and the prince will be able to resolve yer differences and bring peace to the land. Truly, it's all I've ever wanted." He clutched her hand and began leading her away from Colin. She looked back at him, and Colin's heart skipped a beat. She really was beautiful. "But, the whelp won't be able to do this if yer here."

He shoved her firmly, yet gently, into the fray of elves walking between their homes in the trees.

She did not try to follow Redbeard back to where Colin sat on his horse. She seemed to glow faintly as Colin continued to look at her. Though it was day, the light seemed brighter all around her. He smiled at her and waved.

She lifted a single hand in response before turning her back on him and disappearing into the crowd.

Chapter Fourteen
Silver Moon Camp, Encartia

Nikailus breathed a sigh of relief as he watched the princess turn away from that swine from Szarmi. He had seen the way the prince had gazed at her. He had seen how the princess had responded to the prince's words. His clammy hands tossed his knife back and forth. He wanted nothing more than to slit the young prince's throat and be done with it. The girl was meant to be his. They were meant for each other.

He seethed as he watched the rest of Colin's men prepare to leave Encartia. He imagined how easy it would be to slip into his ranks, to pass himself off as one of Colin's supporters. It would be so easy. The grip on his blade went cold as he thought of the prince's hot, coppery blood soaking into the hems of his shirt.

The princess would never forgive him.

He was sure of it. He had seen the tenderness in her eyes as she bid the prince goodbye. He had seen the way she caressed his name with her breath. She cared for the swine, though it was beyond Nikailus to understand why.

And so, he waited in the cold, damp tree on the outskirts of the encampment. He watched as a stocky elf-woman with dark skin and multicolored hair strode towards the young prince. She was trailed by a rugged band of elves. One looked like a bear with his grizzly black beard and broad shoulders. A frying pan was belted at his waist and he carried a large staff with him. A young woman clung to his arm. Nikailus wondered if it was the man's wife or his daughter. He supposed it didn't matter. She didn't look anything like the man. Where he was portly and thick, she was pale and waifish. Neither of them looked like much of a threat to him.

The other two companions were a different story. The man, who was tall with silver hair and chiseled muscles, was nothing less than stunning. Well, he would have been, Nikailus decided, if it hadn't been for the twin scars that ran down the length of his cheeks. They were bulbous, pink, and puckered in the way that said they hadn't been properly treated. He wore all black clothing with little adornments. With a sword strapped to his back and a bow in his hand, he certainly looked as if he could attack and destroy anyone who got in his way. Nikailus instantly decided that he would be a worthy advisory if it ever came to it. Though, he hoped the man would fight on the side of magic rather than of the heathens to the south.

The last companion was interesting, to say the least. Her body rippled with muscles as she moved. She was fluid, like a river's water as she sauntered behind the dark elf. Her red hair was pulled into spunky pigtails that bounced as she moved. Nikailus's interest was piqued when he saw the slingshot clutched within her hand. His lips quirked as he saw her draw her weapon at the prince, a vicious expression on her lips.

The dark elf held up her hand and the pigtailed woman dropped her shot. Nikailus strained to hear what the dark elf— the leader—was saying to her companions. Stunned expressions crossed their faces, but they all nodded by the end of her speech. Nikailus found himself leaning forwards as he softly whispered a spell to increase his hearing.

"No time to waste," he heard the dark elf say as she patted the pigtailed elf on the shoulder.

"And you're sure we can trust him," she hissed in response, her hazel eyes flashing as she glared up at the prince.

The dark elf picked at a bit of hanging skin on her nail before responding. Her voice was nonchalant as she said, "I think that we have a real chance to make a difference here. Come if you agree. Or don't. Either way, I'm leaving."

"Are you sure that's wise?" the silver-haired man asked. His head inclined towards Nikailus's hiding spot, but he did not look in his direction. Still, Nikailus held his breath. Elves were notorious for having skills that superseded those of his brethren.

"Have I ever led you astray, Zeph?"

"Well, there was that one time," the silver-haired male responded.

The leader punched him lightly on the arm and smiled. "You know I would never ask you to do something unless I thought it would benefit our people in the end. Well gents, this is it."

"We should leave Kaila here. Perhaps Nylyla could care for her?" the bear-like man said.

"I don't need someone to care for me, Papa," the girl squeaked. "Besides, if I stay here, who will read all the maps and determine the best place to enter Szarmi?" She twirled a long silver chain between her fingers as she spoke. "No one, that's right. I'm the only one who can do this, Papa."

"You're too protective of her, Thomas," the red-headed elf said as she played with her slingshot. "She's been blooded,

Thomas. She has a right to claim her own choices."

"Say that when you only have one person left in the world," the man responded huffily.

"Uh hem," the dark elf said. "Now is not the time, gents." She raised her eyebrows at her companions before turning and bowing to the prince.

"My company would be honored to smuggle you back into your own kingdom, Highness."

Thomas snorted, but said nothing as the leader continued to bow.

"There's no reason for all that, Rikyah," Redbeard said. Even from the distance separating them, Nikailus could see that the ogrish man's jaw clenched as he spoke.

Rikyah turned back to her companions who shared a look amongst themselves before bowing to the prince as well. In unison, they pledged their mission to him. Safe passage across the border was all that the prince had asked for. Nikailus wondered if this was some trick the prince had concocted to discover how magical creatures had been crossing the border for centuries. He wouldn't put it past the swine.

"Thank you," the prince said. He looked genuinely pleased to have bodyguards for his journey. The stories about him must be true, Nikailus thought. He was nothing but a sniveling, weakling of a prince. There was no way the princess could have developed feelings for that pig.

The silver-haired man was looking in his direction. The breath caught in Nikailus's chest as he pulled the spell back in. It was not in his plans to alert the elves to his presence. Not yet, anyway.

"Zeph?" the leader shouted, loud enough for Nikailus to hear without using his spell.

The silver-haired man shook his head and turned his attention to the dark elf. His lips moved, but Nikailus was at a loss for what he said. He pointed in Nikailus's direction. Cursing beneath his breath, Nikailus gathered his small bundle of belongings and dashed deeper into the forest. He sent a tendril of magic behind him to cover his tracks and prayed that the elf wouldn't be able to detect his scent.

He ran for what felt like hours, though he knew he couldn't have gone more than a hundred meters before he ducked behind a fallen log. He waited. He listened. He forced himself to contain his magic as he tried to hear if anyone had followed him.

Birds chirped as they flitted from branch to branch. The trees themselves groaned as if being mowed down by a massive wind. Yet, there were no sounds of pursuit. Nikailus sighed heavily before cursing himself for his stupidity. He knew he should have reined in his magic before the elf caught on. He'd been over confident, just as Thomas had claimed he was.

A twig snapped nearby and Nikailus huddled deeper into the mud beneath the fallen tree. The spiny branches jutting out from the log pressed uncomfortably into his back, but Nikailus ignored the pain. No other sounds of footsteps passed through the forest. He counted to three and still nothing else happened. Still, it was better to be safe, than to be sorry. He snuggled in closer to the log and covered himself with his blanket. The mossy green and dark mahogany of the fabric blended in almost perfectly with his surroundings. He doubted that even he would have been able to find himself beneath the blanket.

His thoughts slowly turned to his plan. He needed to meet the princess. He needed to infiltrate her inner circle. She needed him. And he would be there to answer her call. He imagined how she would come to love him. He knew it would be true. It was what the Blackflame had prepared him for. It was everything he was meant to be. It was with this thought that Nikailus slowly faded into sleep.

Nikailus awoke to total darkness and the sound of beating drums. He couldn't remember where he had heard the music before, but it felt familiar to him. It called to him. Although the drums were faint from where he hid beneath the log, the sound reverberated through his very bones.

He stumbled through the forest. Twigs raked across his cheeks as he pushed forward, leaving thin cuts across his flesh. He barely noticed the sting of their whip. All he could think about was finding the source of the music. He tripped over fallen branches, lurching to the ground as his body continued to press forward when his feet couldn't carry him. Still, Nikailus picked himself back up and continued onward.

Bright lights flashed in the distance. A haze of smoke filled the forest, causing him to cough as he approached the light. Strange creatures hung from high branches and squawked at him as he crept beneath their perches. Their caws added a layer to the beating drums, only intensifying his sense of urgency to reach them.

Heat rose before him as he broke through a line of trees and found himself mere inches from a blazing stack of hay. He sneezed as the cinder-filled smoke filled his lungs and stung his eyes. Tears streamed from his eyes as he side-stepped the bonfire only to come face-to-face with one of the elves.

A long scar ran down the length of her otherwise stunning

face. Dark, chestnut curls framed her heart-shaped face. Her teal eyes sparkled from the blaze of the fire. Although Nikailus knew she must have been startled by his presence, she smiled at him and stretched out her hand in a welcoming gesture.

He stared down at her open hand, a look of utter disgust forming on his face. The elves had always been the enemies of his fellow sorcerers. There were countless tales of elves forming hunting parties to take down a rogue sorcerer, many of whom had been members of the Blackflame. He opened his mouth to scoff at her, to tell her that she could find her way to the Darkness, but stopped as his eyes fell on the ice blue pendant hung around her neck.

He had only ever heard stories of the pendant before. The opal had been smoothed and polished into a perfect circle before a curved line had been added to its center. Jonathan had told him about the importance of the stone to Elvish lore. It represented how the Light connected all things, the way the mighty rivers of Mitier did. Of course, he had also been taught about the betrayal of Szarmi. They had dammed off the only river running to Smiel during the Third Darkness. Everyone knew it had been a last-ditch effort to gain control of the territory. Unfortunately for Szarmi, they had been defeated during the Battle of Alnora months before their armies planned to invade Smiel. Now the lowly kingdom was little more than a desert filled with heathens. That pendant had more power in it than many of the objects the Blackflame had provided him with over the years. The drumming seemed to fade along with the brightness of the bonfire. All he could see was the pendant.

Her eyes darkened and she clutched at the pendant around her neck just as Nikailus reached for it. She swatted at his hand and released a loud yelping sound. Aq ripple of magic swept over him and Nikailus realized that he was no longer alone with the girl anymore. He glanced around the clearing, counting the shadowing figures as he went. There were twelve of them, all armed with long bows that seemed to shimmer. He assumed they represented the twelve Elvish clans, though they were not known for working together very often. He wondered what was so special about this girl before him, who bore the river pendant and could call members of the clans with a single cry.

In unison, the elves drew their arrows, all pointed straight at him. Nikailus imagined using the depth of his magic to shatter their minds. He could feel their agony as he crushed their bodies. He wanted to do that. His blood boiled with the anticipation of it.

But then, the girl pressed her hand onto his chest and Nikailus felt a deep calmness rush over him. It was as if all the anger, despair, and hatred he had been harboring his entire life disappeared with that single touch. He blinked up at the girl, his eyes wide. She smiled at him and once again held out her hand. This time, Nikailus took it.

Her hand was cold to the touch and bony. The elves surrounding them still held their bows taut, but allowed the girl to lead him through a series of bonfires. Other creatures Nikailus had heard about but never seen before milled about the clearing. They looked away from him as he passed. The sound of drumming swelled, drowning out all other sound. The girl squeezed his hand as they reached a circle of elves, all pounding on different types of drums.

Each and every one of them was shirtless. Symbols had been drawn on their shoulders, their chests, their backs, and their stomach. The designs swirled and seemed to slither with each thrust of their arms as they pounded on the drums. Nikailus was mesmerized by their movements. He watched in awe and didn't notice as the girl slipped her hand from his and joined a group of elves lining the clearing.

The drummers raised their mallets high above their heads and clacked them together twice before dropping their arms to their sides. A cool wind blew through the clearing, chilling Nikailus to the core. He shivered. The world seemed to become completely still. Not even the leaves in the trees rippled in the wind. Nikailus swept his gaze over the crowd. They stood, motionless. He wasn't even sure they were breathing. Even the elves who still aimed their arrows at his back were completely still.

Nikailus inhaled deeply and focused on his breathing the way the Order had always taught him to do. His heartbeat slowed as did his breathing. He knew what needed to be done. He flexed his shoulders as he prepared to release the full force of his magic on the armed elves behind him.

"Who are you?"

The voice cut through his thoughts. He balked, his eyes flashing open. Elaria stood before him, her face serene and her skin glowing.

Nikailus attempted to refocus his attack on her, but found that he couldn't muster any amount of force behind his thoughts. It was as if manacles had been bound around his powers. He struggled against them, to no avail. Chewing on the inside of his cheek, Nikailus twirled in a circle, noting where each of the elves stood. He caught the eye of the girl with the pendant before turning to face Elaria.

He knew who she was: matriarch of the Silver Moon clan. She had been a hero during the Second and Third Wars of Darkness. She was one of the oldest surviving elves in all twelve of the clans, yet she had never made a ploy to increase the power of her own clan. Instead, she had been content to help her clan thrive. And thrive they did. The Silver Moon elves were some of the best equipped, educated, and trained elves in the realm. But, they rarely became entangled in political plots. Nikailus saw this as a credit to Elaria and her leadership style.

He placed a coy smile on his lips as he regarded her.

"I am Nikailus Sindarthian, but you would not have heard of me." He cursed himself for using his real name. Now they would know who to look for. He clenched his fist in attempt to hide the nerves that plagued him.

"Is that so?" she asked, lifting an eyebrow.

The way she looked at him, it was almost as if she knew exactly who he was. His stomach tensed, but he forced himself to look her square in the eyes as he said, "Yes, it is."

"And tell us, Mr. Sindarthian, how did you come by our home here in Encartia? Many have tried to breach our borders, but so few have survived. You must be very powerful."

Nikailus coughed as he flexed his will against the restraints containing his magic. They held firm. He knew Elaria was the cause of the restraints and that she knew he had magic.

"Oh," he said, "is that where I am? I just heard the sound of the drums and followed it until I got here."

It wasn't entirely a lie. Jonathan had always taught him that to lie effectively you had to include an element of truth.

"I see," she said, taking a step closer to him.

He felt the elves surrounding them tense as she got within striking range of his sword. He didn't draw it, though he was tempted to use her as a shield. Instead, he shrugged and said, "You really ought to have better patrols on nights like tonight. You never know who could show up."

The matriarch smiled at him. Her expression darkened as she peered into his eyes. "Perhaps our lackadaisical patrols were intentional, Mr. Sindarthian."

His stomach dropped. Perhaps it had been too easy for him to sneak into their camp. His mind raced as he wondered how long they had known about his presence in the camp. He glanced around the clearing. The elves stared back him, their expressions grim.

"Tell me why you have come here," Elaria commanded. Her silver hair fluttered around her face as a shadow stretched over her body. Nikailus wanted to quiver, to show the fear lurking just beneath the surface, but he knew that to show his true feelings could mean his death. It is better to be seen as brave.

"I want to learn," he said as steadily as he could.

An intense pain pressed upon his mind. He ground his teeth and felt them shake as he bit back the scream that threatened to erupt from him. It felt like a thousand scorpion stings digging into his skin. He tried to fight back, to use his abilities to protect himself from the onslaught, but couldn't seem to gather his thoughts long enough to build a shield.

"Stop!" he managed to growl. He clenched his teeth again and heard a small crack before a dull ache shot through his bottom jaw. Blood drippled from his mouth as he opened his mouth in shock and pain.

"Tell me the real reason you're here, and all of this can stop." She took another step towards him.

Nikailus imagined reaching for his blade. He was quick, quicker than any man he had met. But he doubted he would be fast enough to outstrip an elf. They were physically better equipped to defeat him. Even with his copious amounts of training, Nikailus doubted he would be able to take on even one of the elves' children.

"You already know why I'm here," he managed to say between gulps of breath. He wheezed slightly as an invisible force slammed into him.

"True," Elaria said. "But, I still need to hear you say it."

Nikailus attempted one last feeble try to break through the shackles on his magic. His manacled mind remained suspended between freedom and imprisonment. He called for his powers and they fought against their restraints, but could not break free.

"What have you done to me?" Nikailus demanded. "Tell me what you have done."

"We had to be sure," was all Elaria said as she twisted her hand up and Nikailus slammed to the ground. He spat blood as he lifted his head to stare at her.

"How are you doing this?"

"When you're as old as I am, you pick up a few tricks along the way," she said, a smile curling on her lips. She flipped her hand again and Nikailus writhed in pain as his entire body lifted from the ground and slammed into a nearby tree.

"Elaria."

The voice cut through the night air, cold and firm. Nikailus lifted his gaze in time to see the girl with the pendant march towards the matriarch, her hands lifted high. She laid a single hand upon Elaria's arm and shook her head. Elaria unclenched the fist she had raised, her expression going slack.

Nikailus scrambled to feet. There isn't anything more pathetic than a sorcerer without his magic. He refused to be pathetic.

"I'm telling the truth," he said. "I just want to learn from you."

"For a trained sorcerer, I would have expected you to know

more about our customs, Mr. Sindarthian."

Nikailus's jaw dropped. This had not been what he was expecting.

"How did you…" he began.

"I know many things," Elaria said, her voice cold. "Just as I know you're not here to learn."

"But I am," Nikailus said, his voice pleading. He hated how weak she made him feel.

"If you were here to learn, then someone would feel your need and vouch for you."

"What?" he asked, incredulously. "You can't be serious."

"Oh, but I am. This is how it's done, Mr. Sindarthian. If you don't like it, we can simply kill you now and save ourselves the trouble."

"No," the girl said, her voice firm. She looked at him with keen eyes that made him feel as if she could see straight into the pits of his heart.

"Nylyla?" Elaria asked, her voice piqued.

"I will vouch for him," the girl said, blushing. Nikailus thought it was a strange thing to see the elf blush at saving his life, but what did he know.

"You're certain you want to take on this task?" Elaria asked. Her eyes flashed as she glanced in Nikailus's direction. "You do not know this sorcerer, Nylyla. You cannot know if his intentions are true."

The girl shrugged her shoulders. "I understand the risks."

Elaria looked back at him, her eyes hard. "You may learn from her," she hissed. "But, I will not release your powers until I am certain you can be trusted."

"What? Uh, no," Nikailus retorted. "You see, that simply

won't work for me. I need my magic."

"What you need," Elaria cut in, "is a hard lesson in what it takes to survive without magic. I can sense your power, Nikailus. There is no chance in the world that I would give you the opportunity to use that power against my people."

She motioned for her guards. They gagged him before he could utter another word. He did not struggle against them. He did not fight when they tied his hands and feet with rope nor when they placed a thick black cloth over his head. He didn't kick or try to jab them with his elbows when one of them swung him over his shoulder like a sack of potatoes. No, Nikailus simply went limp and let them do what they would. He had no power to defy them, not without his magic.

Without warning, the elves tossed him onto something soft that bounced as he rolled over. The sound of a squeaking door caught him off guard, but not the low click of a lock being slid into place. Nikailus tried to concentrate on the sounds of his surroundings, but he was breathing too hard to do so. Counting to twenty, he waited for any sign that one of the guards remained in the room with him. Not a cricket nor a bird chirped.

Wriggling his hands, Nikailus struggled against the rope binding his wrists. The thick rope bit into his flesh. Gritting his teeth, he forced himself to continue jerking against his bindings. Bit by bit, the ropes loosened. Until, at last, Nikailus could slip one of his hands free. The rope slipped from his skin, leaving him unbound.

Without hesitating, Nikailus removed the cloth over his eyes and peered around the room. He didn't know what, exactly, he had been expecting, but it certainly wasn't the ornately decorated room he was in. He lay on a plush bed with dozens of pillows and thick quilt. Each row of squares depicted a different Mitierian tale. The stitching made it seem like the characters from the story were moving. He shivered as he traced his finger over the depictions of the Creators at the bottom of the quilt.

In total, there were eight Creators: the Mother, the Warrior, the Gatekeeper, the Executioner, the Hunter, the Wanderer, the Blacksmith, and the Lover. Each had been given a different set of abilities and a different emblem to demonstrate their skill sets. Nikailus had been taught the lore, but he had always assumed that none still remained who actually believed in the nonsense that was religion of the Light. Like the rest of the Order, Nikailus believed that the only thing to worship was power. He didn't need to know where his strength had come from, just that he had it. He pushed the quilt away as he continued to search the room.

A fire crackled in the small hearth by the door. It cast shadows that danced along the walls as he admired the various pieces of artwork hung on the walls. They, too, depicted the ancient myths of Mitier, including the birth of the Creators and the world as he knew it. He would never understand how a people as old as the elves could put their faith in gods they could not touch or see or validate in any way.

A large bookcase filled the entirety of one wall. Leather-bound volumes protruded from its selves, beckoning to Nikailus. He had always loved to read and gotten through nearly a quarter of Jonathan's library before he'd begun his training in earnest. He stumbled as he took a step towards the bookcase and nearly fell flat on his face. Cursing himself for not untying the ropes around his feet, Nikailus sank onto the bed once more and hastily undid the knots. He trailed his fingers over the books, reading the titles as he went. There were books on the stars, the lore of the realm, even on the technological advances of Szarmi. He smiled as he selected a scrappy looking book that was tucked between two larger ones.

"The Widow's Tale," he read out loud as he scanned the cover.

It was little more than a children's book. Each chapter held illustrations of the events happening in the book. The pages were torn and, in some places, splotches of brownish-red drippled down the page. Nikailus didn't really want to know what kind of liquid had caused staining like that. Still, he pressed his nose deeply into the book's pages and breathed in deeply. And coughed as he inhaled a mountain of dust. To him, it was worth it to capture the musty scent of an old book that had been well-loved.

He had just finished reading the first two chapters of the book when the distant sound of drums drew his attention away from the words. Again, the beating called to him. It was as if his entire being was part of the music. It was layered and complex.

Nikailus found himself looking for tools, weapons, anything that would let him break the lock keeping him from joining the music. He banged against the door. Begged for whoever was guarding him to just let him out. He sank to his knees and recited prayers he hadn't even realized he still remembered. None of it worked. The door remained shut, locked, and completely unbreakable.

He crawled onto the bed, shoving the quilt to the floor as he did so. Who were the elves to keep him locked away from the music? They had no right to bar him from taking part in something that was so obviously a part of his very core. He thrashed as the rhythmic pounding of the drums continued. He bellowed his anger and fear.

A knock on the door startled him as he called out to the Light for the...he couldn't even remember how many times. Stumbling to the door, Nikailus pressed his eye to the small peep hole carved into its center. It was too dark on the other side for him to properly see who had come to visit him. It didn't matter; he couldn't open the door for his visitor anyway.

As if the person on the other side could read his thoughts, the door popped open soundlessly. Nikailus took several steps backwards as the door swung open, revealing a figure cloaked all in black with his hood drawn over his face. Nikailus almost screamed as a dagger whizzed past his face and sank into the wooden wall behind him. Jonathan would have been so disappointed in him; it was a good thing his mentor wasn't there to witness his cowardice.

"What are you doing here, Niko?" a feminine voice asked. Her voice was faint and reverberated around the small room as if they were standing in a stone cavern. Nikailus shivered as the sound of her voice swept through him.

"No one's called me Niko since I was eight. It's what my mother called me before she died," he said, avoiding answering her question. Another dagger slid through the air like a snake through water. This time, it sliced his cheek open in a long gash. Warm blood spurted from the wound, coating the hand he brought up to his cheek in red. She did not speak again as she drew yet another dagger from her belt.

It was then that Nikailus noticed the amount of metal that gleamed from her belt. She must have had nigh on thirty knives strapped to the thick leather cord around her waist. They shimmered slightly from the firelight.

"I know why I'm here, thanks," Nikailus said. He ripped the linen from his undershirt as he spoke and pressed it against the wound on his cheek. It soaked through within moments, but he knew he needed to continue applying pressure to the gash. "The better question is, why are you here?"

She clucked her tongue at him as she flipped the dagger in her hand up through the air before catching it, blade first between her thumb and index finger. The blade quivered lightly. Nikailus gulped. He never had been good at swordplay, much less knife throwing. In an instant, she had flipped the knife into her hand and thrown it at him. It nicked his ear before thudding into the wall behind him.

"Such childish games from a man-child barely capable enough to shield his mind from assault," the woman said, her voice like ice in his veins. Nikailus seethed at her words. He was not a 'man-child,' as she had called him. He was just a young man on a quest to rule the world.

"Unbind my powers and you'll see what I can do to you," he hissed.

The woman chuckled at him.

"Such arrogance from one who doesn't know how to defend himself without the use of magic." She flipped another blade into her hand, her face wan as she passed the knife from one hand to the other. "Do you know how to spot, just from someone's expression, where they will strike next?" She cocked her head at him before continuing without much pause, "No, of course you don't," she snapped. "I intend to change that."

"What?" Nikailus asked, incredulously. He took another step backwards. Two of the knives were dug deep into the wood mere inches from where he stood. If he could just reach them, then maybe—just maybe—he might be able to escape.

"Let me stop you right there," the woman said.

Nikailus instantly dropped the foot he'd raised to take another step backwards.

"I know what you're thinking, Niko, and it will never work."

"What are you talking about?" he began.

"You should know that all of my blades have been magicked to only work with blood of my line. Only I, and those I give my express consent to, can wield my knives without consequence. I would hate to have to scrape you off the floor like I did the last person who tried to use my knife against me."

Nikailus's jaw dropped. "You can't be serious."

"As serious as a wildfire on the southern border."

"So not that serious."

"Have you ever seen a wildfire on the southern border?"

"Well, no, but…"

"Then you should trust me when I say that it is one of the most serious things of all."

"Oh," he mouthed as he stole a quick glance at the knife closest to him. He sucked in a breath before gripping it firmly in his hand.

The moment his fingers wrapped around the hilt, the woman knocked it from his grasp. He barely registered her quick movement before he felt a sharp pain spread from his fingers to his elbow. He winced in pain.

"First lesson: never attack a stronger opponent unless you have a solid plan of action."

"You're here to train me?" he asked, his jaw dropping slightly.

"I am here," she said in clipped phrasing, "to measure your

worth."

"My worth?" he repeated. "How do you measure a person's worth?"

Instead of answering, she spun around in a blur of color before landing a blow to his abdomen. He doubled over, clutching at his aching middle. Before he could even think of taking on a defensive stance, she brought another dagger down and slid it across his throat. The cold metal sent a shiver down his spine.

"Why are you here, Niko?" she whispered in his ear. Her breath was like a gentle breeze on a spring day.

The blade pressed into his throat so tightly that he could barely breathe, much less speak. Nikailus yearned for his magic. With it, he would have been capable of disarming the elf with a single thought. She hugged him tighter against her body. He felt every curve beneath her cloak. Her taunt muscles hummed against his skin as she whispered, "Why are you really here?"

Her grip loosened just enough or him sink to the ground. Hot tears stung, but he forced himself to look her straight in the eyes.

"I want to learn," he said simply. It wasn't entirely untrue. He did want to learn. He wanted to learn everything about having faith in the Light, how to fight both with and without his magic, and how the elvish clans operated

"Well then," she said as she wiped away the small flecks of blood covering her blade, "you shall." She sheathed her dagger before pulling her hood down.

She was not what Nikailus had been expecting. He wasn't even sure what he had been expecting, but it certainly wasn't the ruddy skin marred by jagged scars spanning across her cheekbones. Pockmarks covered her forehead and her hair was slicked back with what looked like natural oil. Her lips were pulled back into a small smirk.

"Ugh," he murmured before saying loudly, "who are you?"

"Don't make me pull these daggers out again," she snarled.

Nikailus held his hands up, palms forward. "I'm sorry, he stammered. I meant no offense."

She shrugged at him. "You will learn to control your immediate reactions as well, Niko."

He looked down at his feet, fuming at himself for the misstep. Hearing the crunch of boots on the ground, he looked up to see the elf stride across the room until she was mere inches from him. She plucked both the daggers from the wall behind him. Sheathing one, she used the hilt of the other to lift Nikailus's chin until his eyes met hers. He grimaced at her glare.

"My name is Anno. I am of the Silver Moon Clan. I will teach you what you came here to learn."

Her words were stilted and Nikailus found it difficult to listen to the harsh cadence of her voice. The dagger's cold metal crushed into the soft spot of his jaw. He knew she could end him with just a bit more pressure applied to the hilt at his throat. She was skilled. She was strong. She was offering to teach him.

"I accept," he finally stammered.

She did not say another word as she quickly sheathed her remaining dagger and left him alone in the room. When he heard the click of the door's lock seconds after her departure he immediately knew three things: one, he was a prisoner; two, he had passed whatever test their little spat had been about; and three, he would have his shot at finally meeting Amaleah. It was exactly as he had planned.

Chapter Fifteen

Kiela Rainforest, Smiel, The Second Darkness

Rhaelend leapt across a small ravine. Dirt and rocks crunched beneath his feet as he landed heavily upon the opposite bank. The monkey, still screeching, wrapped its tail tightly around his arm and swung, shifting Rhaelend's balance. He tottered on the edge, the ground sinking under his weight.

"Heathen," he hissed as he put all his weight into jumping forward. The extra force of his push sent the dirt tumbling into the abyss just as his feet left the ground. He heard something crunch and felt pains shoot through his leg as he landed several paces away from where he had stood only moments before. Unable to apply any weight to his left leg, Rhaelend rolled through the underbrush. Brambles and thorns scratched his already mangled face. It was all he could to stop himself from shrieking just as loudly as the monkey.

Everywhere was smoke and shadow. Sweat dripped down his brow and into his eyes as he finally came to a stop a short distance from where he'd fallen. Gingerly, Rhaelend prodded at his injured leg. He could already feel swelling around his knee and his calf was tender to the touch. The monkey, thank the Light, had finally decided to stop its mad shrieking. Instead, it was now peering up at Rhaelend, its small face full of terror.

"You're just as afraid as I am, huh?" he said as he held out a hand towards it. His palm was bloody and bits of rock were embedded deep into his skin. A throbbing pain coursed through his leg, completely masking any discomfort he might have felt at the condition of his hand. He winced as he put weight on his knee and nearly fell. He caught himself on a tree, the bark scraping off the remaining skin that clung there. Stifling a scream, Rhaelend continued to present his hand to the monkey.

The monkey lifted his hand and peered at the bloody palm. It tapped softly on the oozing mess before licking at the wounds. Its tongue was warm and rough against his already mangled flesh. He winced again as the monkey pried a small rock from a tear at the base of his hand, close to his wrist. He bit his lip to smother the scream bubbling from his mouth.

Rhaelend shooed the monkey away, but it didn't budge. It proceeded to lick at his palm until the bleeding subsided and his dark skin could be seen beneath the muck. The monkey stared up at him with its too-big green eyes.

"I can't keep you, you know," Rhaelend whispered. "I am a man on the run now. After what the princess believes I did, there is not a chance in all of Mitier that she'll allow me to live."

The monkey continued to stare at him, its large eyes made larger by the flickering light routinely reflecting through the night sky. He had almost forgotten what tonight was. He used to love the Hero's Passage. As a child, his mother had always allowed him to stay up well past his usual bedtime so that he could watch the shooting stars pass through the night sky.

He had snuggled up tight against her. Although Smiel was never cool, it had been comforting to have his mother's arms wrapped tight around him. Sometimes he wished she stilled lived so that he could recapture that feeling of safety and warmth. Those days were long past.

She'd whisper in his ear, her warm breath gently caressing his cheek, "One day, you'll be among them."

He'd never believed her. Rhaelend was not a strong enough hero to save the world. He had no specialty skills. He wasn't brave. He was barely even kind. He was a nobody. As a teenager, he'd had grandiose ideas about unearthing his people's secrets from the past and future. He truly believed that all the creatures of the Mitierian realm had a chance to live in harmony. He had thought he might be worthy enough to make that happen.

The princess had not agreed, he reminded himself. She had not believed in his mission. A twinge of familiar sorrow swept through him. His family had served the Smielian royal family for generations. Rhaelend had been no different. Until tonight. Tonight, he had betrayed the family, betrayed her, in a way that could never be forgiven. Shaking his head, Rhaelend reminded himself that he had made the right choice for his people and the magical realm.

He knew he had to keep moving. He knew he had to survive the night. Everything depended on it. He tried to stand, but his leg gave out the moment he applied pressure. The monkey shrieked in warning as his already swollen knee landed on a large rock embedded in the mud. He cursed beneath his breath, the words making the pain seen somehow less than what it actually was. He had never believed his grandmother when she'd told him why she cursed so much during times of pain and stress. Never again would he doubt her.

The monkey squawked loudly and jumped rapidly up-and-down in front of Rhaelend's face. Dragging himself into a sitting position, Rhaelend peered into the dark jungle around him. He clapped a hand over the monkey's mouth, but still it continued to chatter.

The blasted monkey, he thought as he heard the distinct

sound of large men rummaging through the rainforest from just across the ravine. He held his breath, waiting for the men to pass. He could tell from the way the shadows from their torches grew that the men were closing in on him. All they had to do was cross the ravine and they'd find him. Rhaelend waited, hand clamped over the monkey's mouth, pressed tightly against the tree.

The torches passed.

Rhaelend sighed heavily in relief. He waited until the torches were well in the distance before releasing the monkey and staring into the foliage above him. From his vantage point, he could barely see the stars above. The treetops formed a dense canopy that blocked out the sky. Sighing, Rhaelend peered around the forest around him. He didn't recognize any of it. He had never before ventured so far from the path winding through the forest. He didn't know which way would lead him back to the city and which would lead him to the safe house.

He scanned the forest behind him. A short distance from his hiding spot, light shimmered on the forest floor and illuminated widow's bane and star flowers. Unlike the other flowers of the court, these two varieties were quite rare. Indeed, they were considered to be the most valuable of all the flowers for their lands.

"Poison," he whispered as he crawled towards the flowers on his hands and knees. He'd seen his mother do it, and her mother before her. Milking the flowers produced a toxin so quick acting that none had discovered a cure. Ever. The sale of even a drop of the flower's milk could feed an entire family for a year, maybe more. He considered all the things he could do with the fortune he'd gain from the six flowers growing in the small clearing. It would be enough to fund the rebellion.

And so, he crawled. Dark blood trailed behind him as he

drug his injured leg behind him. The monkey silently walked along beside him. For this, Rhaelend was grateful. There were still soldiers searching the forest. He knew he couldn't be too careful when it came to avoiding capture.

The pungent odor of the star flowers filled his senses. He'd only smelled the fresh scent once before, when his mother had purchased a live plant from a traveling merchant. She'd tried to spread its seeds, but they never took. Eventually, she'd milked the plant and set its dry husk ablaze. Star shadows danced in the night sky as the husk had burned and Rhaelend had wondered if it had been his mother's doing or if the shadows had been the flower's essence slowly fading into the abyss. He'd never asked his mother and now had no way of knowing, not since the king had ordered her hanged for treason against the crown.

Tears sprung, unbidden to his eyes as he drew closer to the flower patch containing the poisons. The widow's bane, unlike star flowers shimmered a translucent lilac color. Rhaelend breathed in deeply as he finally reached the widow's bane at the edge of the patch. It smelled of fresh strawberries and summer and an ocean breeze. Rhaelend knew that the flowers smelled differently, depending on what the person sniffing them most desired. Closing his eyes, Rhaelend breathed in again. This time, the flower smelled faintly of cinnamon and freshly baked bread.

He smiled faintly as the other scents associated with his mother flowed through him. He knew it was all a trick, that she wasn't really there. But, he could almost hear her voice and feel the touch of her hand on his as she taught him how to roll the dough more evenly. Without pausing a moment longer, Rhaelend plucked three of the flowers and gingerly placed them in his breast pocket.

"There he is!" a voice shouted from somewhere behind him.

Startled, Rhaelend peered behind him. His head spun from

what he knew was blood loss. The monkey screeched as the torches flew across the ravine, sending smoke in their wake. Rhaelend tried to crawl further into the flower patch, closer to where his mother's scent still lingered.

The monkey jumped on Rhaelend's back and began beating him with its miniature fists. If he hadn't been in such a dire situation, he most likely would have laughed at the notion of the tiny monkey scaring away the soldiers.

They didn't even pause as they clamored towards him.

"Be ready, men, he's a danger to himself and others."

At least they know some things about me, Rhaelend thought as he pulled himself forward.

The monkey leapt from his back. He heard it smack into one of the soldiers. It squawked loudly and a spurt of hot liquid slid down Rhaelend's face. He trailed a finger through the liquid and sniffed at it. *Blood*, Rhaelend realized. He wiped his hand on the thick foliage around him before launching himself at the feet of the soldier closest to him. Retrieving one of the flowers, Rhaelend squeezed its velveteen petals until a pearly white substance shot from its center straight into his assailant's eye, causing it to water. Where his tears trailed down his face, blisters followed.

The man howled in pain as he pressed a linen cloth to the already bursting pustules. Rhaelend didn't wait to see the man die before he bolted towards one of the other soldiers. He caught a glimpse of the monkey ripping the hair out of one of their heads as it squalled loudly. A brief smile pulled at Rhaelend's lips at the sight of the monkey leading the attack.

Fumbling for his dagger, Rhaelend dropped the half-used flower. His gloved hand was covered in the pearly-white poison and the slick metal of his blade slipped from his grasp as he tripped over an upturned root. He grimaced as he fell face first into what could only be described as a pile of dung. It tasted the way it smelled as he got a mouthful of the foul muck.

A sharp elbow slammed into his back, right between his shoulder blades. Rhaelend growled as he twisted around to face his assailant. A clump of dung dripped from his chin, landing on the soldier's boot.

The soldier scowled at him, a golden tooth gleaming in the light from his torch. "You'll pay for that," he hissed as he brought his sword down—hilt-first—towards Rhaelend.

Rhaelend rolled. He felt the filth squeeze into his nose and ears and he moved away from his attacker. He felt the dagger plunge into the ground beside his head. The air and ground reverberated from the impact of the thrown blade.

A whistle blew. Rhaelend knew the sound well. It was the call the soldiers used when a commanding officer was approaching.

No, he thought as he whipped his head around. *It can't be.*

Bushes and limbs rustled all around him. Rhaelend spun in a circle as he tried to determine where the attack would come from. There was no point in a believing that it would not come.

"Cease!" a woman called from the darkness.

Rhaelend tensed. He had not been anticipating this. She wasn't supposed to be here. She couldn't be. Breathing heavily, Rhaelend wiped his gloved hands on the ground before staggering towards the woman.

She rode on the white stallion her father had given her on her last name day. Its golden hooves glimmered in the flickering light of the torches. Her hood, though concealing her face, could not mask the beauty of her hair as it spilled out from it. She had the shimmering night hair of her family. None would fail to mistake her as anyone other than the Smielian heir.

She dismounted in one, swift motion before deftly drawing

her hood back. Her alabaster skin illuminated the night, it was so pale. Her playful, violet eyes searched his as she met his gaze. Rhaelend was the first to look away.

"What have you done?" she asked as she took a step towards him. Her voice was as cold as ice and Rhaelend shivered as her words flowed over him. "Tell me what you have done."

Even the monkey had stopped its babbling as Rhaelend stretched his hand out towards her, palm up. No trace of the poison was left behind. He waited, but she did not take his hand, did not offer understanding, or friendship. She didn't offer anything as she stood before Rhaelend. Her face was placid as she continued to stare at him. The air buzzed with what Rhaelend imagined was a thousand tiny bugs swarming his head. His lungs burned as he sucked in more breath. He could barely breath.

And still, she waited. Slowly, Rhaelend's hand dropped to his side. Squaring his shoulders, he met her gaze. And saw nothing of the girl he had dutifully served for the past thirteen years and been a playmate with before that. Her eyes narrowed and Rhaelend could see but the faintest trace of her violet eyes as she asked again, "What have you done, Rhaelend."

His breath caught in his chest. There was no forgiveness in her voice. He knew he shouldn't have wished for her to understand. He knew she would never love him as she had before tonight. He'd ruined any chance of maintaining what had been going on between them. Still, the anger, disbelief, and sadness in her eyes was almost more than he could bear.

"I'm sorry," he whispered. It was all he could muster as his chest continued to tighten.

Her hands clenched into fists at her sides and her jaw tightened. The wind picked up around them. Rhaelend heard the uneasy mutterings of the lesser known soldiers shuffling about in the shadows as the wind pressed into him with so much force that he was shoved backwards. The monkey cowered at his feet. He wasn't sure when it had returned to him, but he was thankful.

"My family gave you everything," she snarled. "I gave you everything."

It was true. The royal family had given him everything. They'd ensured that he'd received a solid education and training. They'd provided medical help to his mother after she'd contracted the blood virus. They'd treated him like family. They'd loved him.

"I'm sorry," he said again. And he was. He was sorry for the pain he had caused them. He was sorry for the way that their lives would be forever different now.

She held up her hand towards him, stilling the words already poised on his lips. Rhaelend clamped his mouth shut. She opened her own mouth to speak when the bell's tolling began.

Her face turned towards the city. Even in the faint light of the flickering torches, Rhaelend could see the concern etched in her features. *She should have stayed with him*, Rhaelend thought as he watched her lips curve downwards and a single, silvery tear roll down her cheek.

The soldiers began murmuring amongst themselves. Uneasy, Rhaelend began backing away. He needed to help the men and women who still fought for the Smielian people. He needed a way to get the ring—and his message—to the rebellion.

Slowly, Rhaelend slid the small package he'd been carrying out of his pocket. It hummed with power as he weighed it in his hand. Although no blood lingered on his hands, he felt its hot liquid flowing over his flesh. He knew he would always feel the life of the ones he'd killed on his hands. It was his curse for breaking the oath between servant and master.

In the smallest gesture he could manage, Rhaelend pressed the package into the monkey's hands. It cocked its head at the object but, thankfully, didn't chatter as it stared up at Rhaelend. He pressed a single finger to his lips and jerked his head towards the trees. The monkey lingered, looking between the parcel and Rhaelend's eyes. *Go*, Rhaelend thought, willing the command to reach the monkey. *Go*.

She strode towards him as the last of the bell's tolls echoed through the forest. Rhaelend didn't move, didn't fight against her as she gripped his chin between her fingers. The same energy he was so used to feeling between them continued to flow as she pulled his face upwards to meet her gaze.

"You did this," she hissed.

Rhaelend's stomach flipped. He had done it. And he knew that the guilt would forever haunt him. Still, he would do it again, if it meant saving his kingdom and his people.

"It was necessary," he whispered.

She squeezed and Rhaelend thought he heard a slight crack in his jaw. Pain shot through him, but still she maintained her grip on him.

"You betrayed us," she said. Her lips trembled slightly as she spoke. "You betrayed me."

"Yes," he said. There was no use in denying it. He knew she would probably never understand his reasons or forgive him for what he had done. He had hoped. He had dreamed that she would. But, he knew it was all folly.

"Why?" she asked, her voice pitching upwards. Rhaelend could see the shimmering tears filling her eyes as she regarded him and he wondered if she could feel the energy passing between them the way he could.

"We have to make a stand, Kiwanai."

Her name hung between them. He had not addressed her with her title. He had not used the formal names he'd been taught to use during his youth. He had chosen to use her real name—the one only her family was meant to use.

She slapped him. The sting of the blow reverberated through him, but still Rhaelend met her gaze as he spat blood. His entire left side ached and he was certain he had heard a louder crack in his bones when she'd struck him.

"And, I would do it again."

She raised her father's dagger to his neck. Rhaelend could feel the cool steel against his flesh. He did not fight against her. If she had been one of the soldiers, he would have fought. He would have done everything in his power to get away. But with her, he was powerless.

Her eyes roamed over his face. He knew she was searching for the lie, for anything that would allow her to believe that maybe he'd been lying. It was the only way he'd be safe, the only way she could save him. But, Rhaelend hadn't lied.

"Kiwanai," he whispered, though the blade scratched his neck and he could feel small traces of blood swell beneath the steel. "I am sorry."

She sliced his neck. Not deep enough to kill, but deep enough for his blood to flow. She backed away from him, shaking her head slowly. The blade dropped from her grip as she continued to gaze into his eyes. She trembled. Rhaelend instinctively wanted to reach out to her, to hold her as she processed through what he had done. He wanted to comfort her in her loss. He knew he couldn't.

So, he ran.

Branches struck his face, leaving scrapes across his skin. He ignored their sting as he fled through the forest. His jaw ached and the blood leaking from his throat made it difficult to breath.

She didn't kill me. The thought echoed through him as he continued to run through the forest. *She could have. I would have let her. But she didn't.* The thoughts kindled the smallest measure of hope within him, though he knew he had no claim to it.

He made as if to leap onto a boulder nesting between two trees when he felt a snap around his legs and he soared through the air before landing, face-first, on the ground. His head spun as he grappled with the pair of bolas wrapped tightly around his legs.

His hands, slick with blood, couldn't figure out how to unravel the cords of the bolas. He could see the soldiers approaching, could hear their mumbling as they drew closer. He pulled on one of the chords, willing it to loosen. It didn't. The soldiers were getting closer. He knew they would be upon him in an instant.

The monkey, he thought as he looked around him. He hadn't seen it run with the parcel, but it was nowhere to be found. He prayed to the Light that it had escaped, that it would find the rebels.

Twigs snapped behind him and Rhaelend jerked his head in the direction of the sound. All he saw was shadow as something heavy and cold slammed into his temple and darkness consumed him.

Chapter Sixteen

Port Verenis, Lunameed, 333 Years Before

Wraith Killer pulsed in his hand, its familiar heat flowing through him. Frost crunched beneath his boots as he strode through the fields. Remaining wheat stalks waved in the gentle winter breeze. Their fuzzy ends glimmered with a thousand diamonds as the mid-morning light passed through them. Kilian smiled at the sight. He had forgotten how beautiful winter could be, if you only stopped to notice it.

His smile slipped into a scowl as he saw the masts of the Dragon's Breath rising high into the clouds. They seemed to mix with the fluffy, white cotton balls suspended in the sky. It had been too long since he'd paid Bluebeard a visit. He wished it was under different circumstances now.

Despite the cold, sweat coated Kilian's brow as he crested the hill and peered down into the city of Port Verenis. He remembered the first time he'd crested this very hill and peered into the city. He'd been Bluebeard's companion then and they had just begun their quest to save the world. Wraith Killer vibrated in his hand at the memory. So much had happened since then. And, although not all of it was bad, the majority of it wasn't good either.

He envisioned his next moves. He knew the floor plan of the

Dragon's Breath by heart. He knew exactly where Bluebeard would be standing. He knew where all the new members of Bluebeard's new crew would be. He knew everything he needed to know to complete the mission She'd sent him on. Yet, here he was, smiling down at the ice diamonds caught on the left-over wheat from last harvest's crop.

He reminded himself that Tavia had trusted him enough to complete this mission. She believed in him, even if he was finding it difficult to believe in himself.

"What are ya doing here?" a voice hissed from behind him. He felt the point of a spear press into the small of his back as he turned his head to the voice. He sniffed at the air. Salt water and sea breeze. Merperson.

"I have business with Bluebeard," he responded stiffly. He did not take kindly to being treated like a villain.

"That's King Bluebeard to ya!" the merperson shouted. The spearhead pricked his flesh and Kilian felt the swell of blood waiting to spring from the wound once the scout removed pressure from it.

"What kinda business would tha'be?" the merperson asked, their voice sharp and tense. Kilian hunched his shoulders slightly as he swiftly spun until he was facing his assailant head-on.

"That's between me and *King* Bluebeard," Kilian said.

The scout shrugged. "You have to go through me to get the king. You best be answering me questions."

Kilian shrugged. It would be easy enough to cut through this idiot with little more than flick of his wrist. He'd killed far better warriors with Wraith Killer than the puny soldier standing before him now. But, he didn't want to alert Bluebeard to danger unnecessarily.

"Do you know who I am?" he asked. He puffed out his chest as he spoke and waited for the sentry to respond.

"Course I do," the soldier responded. "Yer Kilian Clearwater, the Light's Hero, and Killer of Creators."

"I would say more like Killer of Traitors than Creators," Kilian mumbled before saying clearly and loudly, "Then you can understand the importance of my meeting with Bluebeard."

The merperson huffed loudly as they motioned for Kilian to follow them down the hill. The closer they got to the city proper, the more Kilian noticed the change in the city's environment. There had always been peace keepers stationed at the port. Kilian had even been stopped by one during his first real visit. But now the streets were teeming with heavily armed soldiers. Some appeared to be more mercenary than soldier.

"Where did all these soldiers come from?" Kilian asked as he turned a corner too sharply and nearly collided with a rather burley looking soldier. The man grunted at Kilian before continuing on his way.

"The King hired em for security purposes, ya see. He always says you can't be too careful in these times."

"Right," Kilian responded as he scanned the streets of Port Verenis. He marked where bowmen stood on high rooftops. In total, he counted sixteen of them spread out in even intervals from the city center. He'd memorized the routes Bluebeard's men took as they patrolled the city streets. It was an easy task, since they seemed to be following a strict, circular pattern.

The soldier rambled on about the comings and goings of the townspeople as they led Kilian through the city gates. Despite the ravages of war, Port Verenis looked very much as it had all those years ago when Bluebeard had brought Kilian here. Smoke filled the city streets, almost to the point of snuffing out breathable air. The stench of humanity clouded his senses. Even with the fighting, the thousands of people who lived within the city limits hadn't fled. Kilian wondered if it was because they were brave, stupid, or simply didn't have the means to go anywhere else.

Beggars lined the city streets. Their handwritten signs spoke of the war. Many were missing limbs or claimed to be blind. A little girl, Kilian guessed she could be barely over the age of six, held up a rusted tin cup to him as he passed. She held no sign, but the dirt smudged on her forehead and the tatters she wore told him everything he needed to know. Her eyes held the clouded, distant look that all children bore when they were alone.

He had a memory of the nightmare that had plagued him for years following his defeat of Rhymaldis. His sister May, maggots crawling from her nose and pustules on her arms cradling his brother's dead body in her thin arms. Shaking his head, Kilian glanced back at the girl. Her belly was swollen from hunger. He remembered what it felt like to never know where your next meal was coming from.

Crouching beside the girl, Kilian lifted her chin with the back of his hand. The soldier continued walking down the street, but Kilian didn't mind. He knew where Bluebeard was.

"What's your name, girl?" he asked. His voice was gruff and almost callous. He didn't know when it had happened, but he had started to turn into his mentor. He grimaced slightly and jerked his hand away when the little girl didn't respond to him.

He began to walk to walk away.

"I'd pick wildflowers for you, sir. If you'd be willin' to pay me for them."

Her voice was frail and soft. Kilian spun around to face her once more.

"That'd be right nice," he said, smiling.

Her shoulders shook as she stood and Kilian realized just how slim she was. Her collarbone protruded through her tattered blouse and her skirt hung loosely from her waist. It only stayed up because she had tied a length of rope tightly around her middle. Still, she ran off more quickly than he would have thought possible. He waited in the street, the townspeople giving him a wide berth as they passed him by.

Eventually, the soldier wandered back to where Kilian stood. He squinted at Kilian and asked harshly, "What are ya doin'?"

"Waiting," Kilian responded, annoyed that the soldier was bothering him at all. He didn't need the soldier to gain an audience with Bluebeard. Even if he had to cut his way through the throng of soldiers to so, Kilian would meet with his mentor whether Bluebeard wanted to or not.

"For what?" the soldier asked. Kilian rolled his eyes at the soldier.

"Why don't you run on ahead and let Bluebeard know I'm here. I know how the old man hates surprises," Kilian said in way of response.

The soldier scratched his head and peered around the streets before shrugging. "Suit yourself," he said before walking down the path he'd just come from.

Kilian sighed in relief and looked at the sundial mounted to the center of the street's intersection. It was already past midday and he hadn't eaten since the night before. His stomach rumbled as the scent of freshly baked hot buns wafted through the intersection. He purchased a whole dozen from the baker before walking back to the girl's stoop and sinking to the ground.

He'd eaten seven of the buns by the time the girl reappeared at the end of the street, clutching a small bouquet of wildflowers in her grimy hands. She moved furtively, constantly looking over her shoulder as she moved, as if she were expecting to be attacked at any moment. Kilian smiled at her as she held out the bouquet, as if it was the most precious thing she owned in the world.

The bouquet was more weeds than flowers and the one rose that jutted up from the bouquet had a broken stem, but Kilian didn't mention it as he dug into his coat pocket and pulled a golden coin out. Her eyes turned into saucers as he offered it to her.

She looked between the coin and him and back to the coin before promptly snatching it from his hand and folded it into a dirty bit of cloth. She turned as if to leave him in peace again, but Kilian caught her arm.

"Are you hungry?" he asked, even though he already knew the answer.

She nodded, her eyes following her nose as she sniffed at the remaining hot buns nested on his lap.

"Here you go," he said, offering her all five of the remaining buns. She shook her head and tugged on her arm, trying to break away from him.

"It's alright," he said, coaxingly. "I promise, I'm not going to hurt you."

She began squirming in his grasp, her small body shaking violently. Kilian gripped her firmly, but was careful not to squeeze so tightly that he'd leave bruises. He drew her closer to him. She bit him; clawed at him; and then, she screamed.

The townspeople barely glanced in their direction at her screams. Even when he lifted her from the ground and began carrying her towards the edge of town, no one tried to help the girl. She began weeping, her tears leaving clean streaks on her otherwise dirty face. She didn't speak to him. She didn't plead. She just let him carry her through the town.

"Do you know who I am?" he asked as they reached the edge of the city and he finally put her down. She made as if to run, but Kilian held up an arm and she sank back into the grass.

She shook her head and a glob of snot dripped from her

nose. Kilian handed her a handkerchief from his pocket before continuing. "My name is Kilian Clearwater, and it wasn't so long ago that my family was as destitute as you are now."

Her lips trembled at his words.

"You've heard of me, then," he said. He knew it was true from the way she stared down at her clasped hands without speaking. Her tiny hands shook as she looked up at him. She had dark eyes that were nearly black. One of them, the left one, had a streak of yellow running down its center. *Odd*, Kilian thought as he reached for her hand.

"I'm not going to hurt you," he reiterated as he offered her one of the buns. After a moment's pause, she snatched it from his hand. She peered at him over the top of the bun before biting it into. She chewed slowly, as if savoring it before devouring the rest in two quick bites.

Kilian chuckled at her as he tossed her another of the rolls.

"Aisley," she said, her voice hoarse.

"Is that your name?" he asked.

She nodded as she took a bite out of the second roll. This time, she took her time eating the rest of the bun.

"That's a pretty name, Aisley," he said. "Are you from Port Verenis?" he asked.

She nodded.

"Do you have anyone waiting for you in the city?"

She dropped the last bite of her bun as she looked up at him, her eyes wide. Her lips trembled as Kilian scooted closer to her. He took her hand in his own.

"I'm not going to hurt them," he said. "I promise."

"There's no one," she said.

"I know that's not true."

She tried to pull away from him again. Kilian sighed. *So much for this being easy*, he thought as he tugged a small pouch from inside his coat pocket. It barely weighed anything, but it was one of the most precious things She had given him. It had no name, since so few people knew of its existence. He tugged the pouch open with his teeth and spilled an amount of the powder into his free hand.

Aisley began frantically pulling against him, as if she could sense what he was about to do.

"I'm sorry," he said and he blew the dust into her face. She scrunched up her nose and sneezed several times. Kilian released her hand and retied the pouch before placing it back into his coat pocket.

"Are you ready to talk now?" he asked.

"Yes," she said, her voice was monotone.

Kilian grimaced slightly, but continued, "How old are you Aisley?"

"Nine, ten next month."

He looked at her in surprise. She looked so much younger than nine with her birdlike features and timid voice. He handed her another roll, but she didn't even look at it as she sat with her back straight and her lips in a thin line. Although this wasn't the first time he'd used the dust to force people to answer his questions, he had never seen someone react the way the girl was. Her posture and movements were so unnatural.

"Who's waiting for you in the city?"

She didn't answer.

Kilian waited, drumming his fingers on his legs. He counted his heartbeats. He listened to the sounds of the city. He looked into her nearly black eyes.

Aisley blinked, but said nothing.

"Tell me who's waiting for you in the city," Kilian commanded, his patience running thin. No one had ever been able to resist the effects of the dust before. No one.

She opened her mouth. Kilian leaned forward, anticipating her response. Her cheeks flushed and a tear ran down her cheek. She bit her lip until a bubble of blood blossomed on her dirty lips.

"No," she whispered, hoarsely.

Kilian huffed, but then smiled.

"You will do nicely," he said before he lifted Wraith Killer and slammed it into the back of her head.

Chapter Seventeen

The Silver Moon Camp, Encartia, 333 years later

Amaleah paced around the room Rikyah had left her in. It was a simple room that was part of a large tree house on the outskirts of town. The room was small, but, with its pink and white décor and lace decorations, it felt cozy. It was close to the kitchen, so, although there was a fireplace, it was warm without a fire. Rikyah had left her almost immediately. She'd uttered a feeble excuse about needing to attend to business in town before slipping from the room. Amaleah had, of course, tried to open the door, but found it to be locked. And so, she began pacing.

She thought about Colin and what Elaria must be asking him. The Szarmians were known for their cruelty to the elves. For years upon years, they had murdered innocents who dared cross their border. And now the crown prince of Szarmi needed their help to reclaim his throne. She silently prayed to the Light for his protection as she walked across the wooden floor. Glass stained with multiple colors dangled in window. Although her room faced the wooded side of the treehouse, light spontaneously burst through windows, casting playful colors all around her. It did nothing to ease the queasiness in her stomach. She thought about slipping out one of the windows and shimmying down the tree to find out what was happening, but decided against it. She needed the elves' help just as much as Colin did, perhaps more so. She couldn't risk angering them by disobeying. Not yet, anyway.

When she heard the first sounds of the trumpet, the hair on her arms had risen and she'd felt the twinge of her magic blossom to life. Startled, she hung her head outside the largest of the windows and strained to see the clearing. There were too many trees and the clearing was too far away to see much. In fact, all she could see was the shimmer of golden halo bursting through the trees. The light was so bright it was nearly blinding.

Pulling herself back into the bedroom, Amaleah jiggled the door knob again. Still locked. She chewed on her thumb nail as she considered her options. She wished Thadius and Yosef had been allowed to stay with her, but Rikyah had taken them to a different room in the tree house. She thought about yelling for help, but was afraid one—or both—of them would let their wild side out and destroy the beautiful house in their quest to find her. Again, the risk wasn't worth the reward.

Sitting cross-legged on the floor, Amaleah rummaged through her small pack. The journal weighed heavily in her hands as she flipped through the pages until she found a blank one. Pulling out the small jar of ink and a stubby pen, Amaleah began writing out a plan. It was more a brainstorming bubble, but still, it was the making of a plan.

She twirled a finger through one of her curls as she contemplated what to do first. Her finger caught on one of the pins she'd used to keep her hair out of her face. *Of course*! she thought as she pulled the pin from her hair.

Jumping to her feet, Amaleah lunged at the door and shoved the tip of the pin into the lock. She had never picked a lock before, but she had seen countless others do it, including Sylvia. It couldn't be that difficult, could it?

She jiggled the pin in the lock. She twisted and shoved it. She tried to find the latch that would unlock the door. All to no avail. Curing beneath her breath, Amaleah yanked the pin out of the lock and threw it across the room. She should have asked Sylvia to teach her. The memory of her nursemaid made her breath catch in her throat, but didn't bring the onslaught of grief it had before. She didn't know if she was thankful or disappointed in herself for this. She didn't know what she should feel anymore.

A quick rap on the door tore her attention away from her thoughts.

"Yes?" she called, praying that whoever was on the other side of the door was a friend.

"Thank the Light!" She heard Thadius say before a loud pounding sound reverberated through the room.

"What are you doing?" she squealed as she backed away from the door. "Trying to kill me?"

"We figured you would take cover if you thought there was enough danger," he responded. She rolled her eyes at him.

"I know you're rolling your eyes, Amaleah. I can feel it."

"Nope," she called through the door. "Completely wrong. I'm just in here, patiently waiting for you to get me out."

There was another loud booming sound and the door shook violently. Dust fluttered through the air as the door shook again.

"Do you think they'll still teach me magic if we break down the door?" she asked.

"They better," Thadius responded. He sounded out of breath. She couldn't remember ever hearing him out of breath before.

There was another loud boom, this time followed by an earsplitting crack as the middle of the door exploded into hundreds of tiny wooden shards. Amaleah covered her head with her arms just in time to catch the bulk of the splinters in her arm instead of her face. She screamed in pain as a large shard wedged itself firmly in her forearm.

"So maybe this wasn't the best idea," Thadius said as he ambled into the room. His chest and arms were covered in bruises and Amaleah realized that he had been using himself as a battering ram to break into her room. She shook her head at him as she held out her arms for inspection.

It was Yosef who gently plucked the splinters from her arms. The deeper ones made her squirm as the wood slid from her flesh. But, it was the large one that nearly made her faint from the amount of blood that seeped from its hole once removed. She dry-heaved for several moments before allowing Yosef to inspect the wound for any smaller pieces that may have broken off during the extraction. Thankfully, none had. He spread a fowl smelling ointment on her wounds to keep them from festering before wrapping her entire arm in bandages from his pack.

"Thank you," she whispered, gingerly prodding at her arm when he'd completed his work.

He grunted in response, but, by now, Amaleah knew that was a good thing. She smiled at him.

"I take it no major injuries were obtained?" Thadius asked Yosef as he stomped over to her.

"She'll survive," Yosef growled.

Amaleah looked between them. "Oh no," she said. "You can't be arguing again. Not now."

Thadius looked at her abashedly.

"Uh uh. Nope. Not happening. Whatever it is, get over it. We're here now and I need to learn as much as possible before Elaria…"

"Elaria will let you stay until such a time as you either decide your training is complete or the situation in Lunameed becomes so dire you need to fight."

"Do you think it'll truly come to that?" she asked, even though she already knew the answer.

"Your father sent soldiers to kill anyone who had provided help to you after your escape from Estrellala. There's no going back from that, Amaleah."

She nodded. "What now?"

"Now, we find out what all that trumpeting was about. I had the strangest sensation that it wasn't a good thing."

Amaleah wrapped her cloak tightly around her shoulders and followed Yosef from the room. Wisps of black smoke trailed behind him as he strode down the stairs. Thadius took up the rear, his hooves clomping loudly on the wooden floor.

They had just reached the front entrance when a voice called from a side room, "Where are you going?"

Instead of running, Yosef pulled a pair of daggers from his belt and turned to face the voice. A waifish elf with a jagged scar running down her face emerged from the shadows. Her chestnut curls framed her otherwise stunning heart-shaped face. A smooth, blue pendant hung between her breasts. She held her hands up, no weapon in sight.

"I'll help you," she said, turning her palms up. Her clothes were simple, yet beautiful. The pale green of her outfit made her teal eyes even greener. She exuded peacefulness and calmness. Amaleah smiled at her.

"Who are you?" Thadius asked, stepping in front of Amaleah.

"Nylyla of the Opal River clan," she responded, still holding her hands out, palm up.

"What are you doing here then? I thought the clans remained separate, except on special occasions."

She cocked her head at him. "It would be a sad thing indeed if the twelve clans refused to interact between holidays," she said. Her voice held a firmness to it that Amaleah found unexpected. "There are many of us who choose to live in a different clan than the one we were born to."

"Don't insult her," Amaleah hissed beneath her breath.

Nylyla laughed, her voice a tinkling silver bell. "I am not insulted, Amaleah. Our customs are not well known among the other races within Mitier. Many among us would prefer to keep it that way."

"Oh," Amaleah mouthed before asking, "Where do you fall on that line of thinking?"

The elf smiled at her. "I believe that the more we know about one another the better. It is a shame that not more creatures celebrate the beauty of the other more often. There is much that we can teach one another, if we could just learn to put aside our differences. And our grievances."

"I agree," Amaleah said, though she had never really thought about it before.

"I think that we could become great friends," Nylyla said.

It was Amaleah's turn to smile. She didn't think she had ever had a real friend before. At least, not one that wasn't solely committed to her survival.

The elf turned her attention back to Thadius and said, "I am here because I live in this house, with Rikyah."

"Oh," Thadius said. "Sorry about the, uh ruckus, then."

She raised an eyebrow at him and the scar on her cheek stretched and puckered slightly as she said, "I'm sure Rikyah will fix the door before she leaves again."

"Does she do that often?" Amaleah asked. "Leave, that is."

"Yes, quite often. Indeed, she's normally only here for a few months out of the year to visit her grandmother."

"What was all the trumpeting about?" Thadius asked, his shoulders sagging slightly as he relaxed. Amaleah hadn't noticed how tense he'd been only moments before.

"All that trumpeting, as you call it, was the announcement that our matriarch has arrived."

"But I thought Elaria was the matriarch of the Silver Moon clan."

"Oh, she is," Nylyla said. "But, we elves are comprised of twelve clans, each with our own set of governance. The Encar clan is our ruling body and Kileigh is their matriarch. That makes her the leader and voice of the elves."

"I should meet her then," Amaleah said, turning to the door.

"No!" Nylyla nearly shouted. Amaleah looked back at her in surprise. The elf was blushing deeply and lowered her head. "It's just that, I don't think Elaria wanted you to meet our matriarch just yet. Though, since she's here, I doubt that your presence will be kept a secret for long. If one of our people doesn't speak of you, she'll sense your magic."

"Is that a bad thing?" Amaleah asked. She didn't understand why meeting the Elven matriarch would be a bad thing. Besides, she needed to build relationships with all the magical creatures in the realm if she were going to wage war on her father and win. She couldn't—wouldn't—let him stay on the throne as long as he remained a threat to their kingdom.

"It could be," Nylyla said. She took a step towards them and Yosef hissed, a dark mist drifting out of him. Nylyla, for her credit, barely flinched at the coldness as she walked right past Thadius and linked her arm in Amaleah's. "Come, let's wait for Rikyah to return and then you can decide your course of action."

Amaleah looked to Thadius for a reply, but the centaur merely motioned for Amaleah to speak. She chewed on her bottom lip before saying, "Alright."

Nylyla beamed as she led Amaleah into another section of the tree house. They entered a small kitchen at the back of the house. The elf pulled out a chair for Amaleah before filling a kettle with water and setting it on the fire.

"Do you prefer peppermint tea or chamomile?"

"Peppermint," Amaleah responded.

"Excellent choice."

"Do I get some tea as well?" Thadius asked as he forced himself into the small kitchen.

"If you like. Yosef, would you like some as well?"

"No, thank you."

Nylyla set a small plate of assorted cookies in front of Amaleah as she busied herself preparing the tea. It wasn't long before the kettle chirped and three cups of steaming hot peppermint tea rested on the kitchen table. Yosef stationed himself by the door. His black cloak billowed in a nonexistent wind. It was difficult to tell, but Amaleah chose to believe that he was scanning the windows for any sign of danger.

"When I first heard that you would be coming here, I was so excited to finally meet you, Amaleah," Nylyla said as she blew on her tea. "It was a very brave thing that you did, escaping your father's marriage proposal."

Amaleah nodded. She still didn't feel very brave. But, with her newfound abilities and her destiny weighing heavily on her, she knew she needed to at least fake confidence in herself.

"Rikyah told me about your father's madness. I am sorry to hear it. He was a good king…" her voice trailed off.

"Until my mother died," Amaleah finished for her. "Yes, I know. I've heard the stories."

Nylyla looked at her, a sad expression in her eyes. "I shouldn't have brought it up," she said. "I'm sorry."

"It is nothing," Amaleah said. "Tell me about Encartia," she continued, changing the subject.

Nylyla leaned in, a conspiratorial expression on her face as she said, "It would be better for me to show you." With that, she strode from the room.

Amaleah looked at Thadius, a confused expression on her face. The centaur just shrugged and sipped his tea. A moment later, Nylyla returned, a thick sheath of parchment in her hands.

"This is one of Rikyah's maps, but I'm sure she won't mind if I show you." She gingerly unfolded the parchment, revealing a highly detailed map of Encartia and the falls. Amaleah slid her gaze over the map until she found the words "Silver Moon Camp" etched across the paper in careful penmanship. The encampment was at the southernmost point of the region labeled Encartia.

"I had always thought the elves lived in the same city."

"A lie we spread ourselves."

"But why?" Amaleah pushed.

Nylyla shrugged her shoulders as she traced the outline of the Opal River borders. Slamming her finger into the center of the Encarti encampment, she said, "There are many among my people who believe that the elves are the dominant species. They think—they claim to know—that we are superior to all others." She trailed her fingers across the page until they landed on the Encartia Falls. "They think that because we were given dominion over the falls that the Light chose us. The Light didn't choose us. It didn't make us greater than other creatures."

Her cheeks flushed as she spoke and her words tumbled out of her so quickly that Amaleah almost didn't hear her say, "The lore we know is a sham meant to control us."

She glanced at Thadius, her eyes wide. What Nylyla had just said was sacrilege, punishable by death in Lunameed. She knew that Szarmi didn't follow the same traditions, but her kingdom did, even if their worship of the Light was superficial at best. Thadius shook his head at her. It was all Amaleah needed to know that they were treading on dangerous ground.

She cleared her throat before saying, "Does Rikyah believe as you do?"

Nylyla barked out a harsh laugh that didn't match her pleasant demeanor. "Rikyah goes her own way, in all things," was all she would say.

As if she had some supernatural ability to know when people were talking about her, Rikyah rushed into the house just as Amaleah opened her mouth to ask another question. Her eyes darted frantically around the room and her features, though dark had lost some of their luminous.

"Kileigh knows she's here," she said, jerking her head in Amaleah's direction.

Nylyla dropped her teacup on the ground, her hands trembling. It smashed into hundreds of pieces, but she barely seemed to notice as she strode towards Rikyah. "But how? And when?" she asked, her voice soft.

Rikyah shook her head, her eyes darting to Amaleah, who promptly stared down at her clasped hands. She tensed when she heard floorboards creak and then saw boots next to her slippered feet.

"Look at me, girl," Rikyah said, her voice firm. Amaleah glanced up at the woman and noticed how the puckered, starburst of a scar turned her dark skin into a mangled mess. She nearly gasped when the scoundrel leaned forward and whispered in her ear, "If you want to say goodbye to the boy, I suggest you do so before we leave."

Stunned, Amaleah watched as Rikyah drew Nylyla from the room. They were too far away for her to hear the words passed between them, but she hoped the smuggler wouldn't be too upset by the broken doors. Her skin buzzed with her magic. She sipped at her tea, but even it didn't help to calm her nerves.

"Tell me more about this Kileigh" she finally said.

"She's the matriarch of the Encartia clan," Thadius responded. "She's the youngest matriarch to ever have dominion over the twelve elvish clans. Besides that, I'm not sure what else to say about her."

"Oh," she murmured, tapping her fingers on her cup. "But then, why did Rikyah seem so afraid of her?"

Rikyah's words registered with her then. *If you want to say goodbye to the boy, I suggest you do it before we leave.* Colin was leaving. He was leaving to reclaim his kingdom and she might never see him again. Not if he failed.

Her mouth went dry. She couldn't let him go without saying goodbye.

Without saying a word, she bolted from the room and was out the door before either Thadius or Yosef could stop her.

Chapter Eighteen

"And every woman," Amaleah murmured as she stepped from behind a row of trees. She had listened to Colin and Redbeard discuss the prince's desire to save his kingdom. She smiled at Colin as he turned to face her. Her heart skipped a beat as he beamed at her. His golden-brown eyes held so much kindness in them that Amaleah hoped this wouldn't be the last time she'd see them. "It is not just men that get to have grand adventures and save the world, Redbeard." She continued.

Amaleah certainly had every intention of being a savior to her people. It was ludicrous to believe that only men could fulfill that role. She strode forward and patted Redbeard's arm. "Women, too, have destinies and stories that sometimes outweigh those of their male compatriots."

It was true. And yet, throughout history, men had notoriously received credit for the actions of her sex. She was determined not to let that be her story. Even if her magic destroyed her, she was unwavering in her desire to be remembered for saving her kingdom.

"Yes, well," Redbeard stammered.

Amaleah shrugged her shoulders. "Just remember who got thte best of your dozens of men with only her two companions to help her." The memory of the fire blazing before caused her insides to quiver. Her magic was still an uncontrollable force within her. Its fury scared her. She shook her head and peered up at Colin. His nearness left her feeling calm. This was why she had come.

"I heard you were leaving," she whispered. "I thought I'd say goodbye and wish you blessings from the Light." The thought of him leaving left her insides cold. "Perhaps we shall meet again one day."

"Perhaps," Colin replied.

Her heard stopped and she blinked down at her hands. She wanted nothing more than to spend more time with Colin, to learn more about him and his ideas of the future. He had so much optimism for the future that it was nearly infectious. In truth, she didn't want him to leave. She knew he needed to. She knew he had a duty to his own kingdom. But, she secretly wished that he could stay with her. Tears sprang to her eyes as she considered facing the challenges she knew she would encounter alone. Even though they had only spent a few days together, his presence filled her with comfort.

"I pray that we are both able to reclaim our thrones, Colin, and that we will rule our respective kingdoms with grace and kindness. I hope that the feud between our people can finally be resolved."

It was all she could think to say. It was better than wimpering like a small child and begging Colin to stay, that was for certain.

Redbeard clasped her hand in his and began leading her away from Colin before the prince could respond. He rambled on about how they must be going and that they couldn't do that with her present. She looked back at Colin to see him raise a tentative hand and wave at her in farewell. A smile spread across his face as she returned the gesture. She didn't know when or if she would ever see him again. All she knew was that she hoped their paths would cross in the future.

Tears slid down her face as she wandered aimlessly through the town. though many of the elves glanced at her with curiosity, none of them stopped her. None of them said a word to her as she wandered from street to street, if you could even call them that. They were really more paths through the trees. She had meant what she'd said to him. She did hope they could reclaim their kingdoms. And, she hoped that they could continue being friends. Their kingdoms needed peace, not animosity.

She was so lost in her own thoughts that she didn't see the elf coming around the corner until she had slammed right into her. Books and pens went flying through the air.

"I'm sorry," Amaleah murmured as she hurriedly shuffled the papers back into some small measure of order and shoved them into the elf's outstretched hand.

"Amaleah, is it?" the elf asked, her voice chipper.

Amaleah glanced at her and saw what she could only describe as an ugly elf. She didn't even know that was possible. Even with their scars, Rikyah and Nylyla could be considered nothing less than lovely. But the woman before her was anything but. She had buck teeth and a mop of fiery red hair. Unlike the rest of the elves living in the Silver Moon camp, this one was overly plump with rouge-red cheeks and puffy eyes.

When Amaleah didn't respond, the elf stuck her hand out to her and said, "Name's Wynona, but you can call me Wynna."

Only pausing for a heartbeat, Amaleah accepted the proffered hand. "Please to make your acquaintance."

Wynna smiled at her, a large gap revealing itself between her two front teeth. "We don't get many outsiders in our camp. It's nice to have someone new to talk to."

Amaleah knew exactly what the elf meant. After being locked in a palace for years without visitors, save for her father, Amaleah knew what it felt like to be friend starved.

"Well, now you do," she said, smiling at Wynna in what she hoped was her most charming smile.

She handed a stray paper to the elf, but not before she had read the title of page.

"The Art of Battle."

She snatched the rest of the papers from Wynna's hands. She didn't care how rude it was or if she was being disrespectful to their hosts. She needed to know what the texts were about.

There were papers discussing the current social climate in not only Lunameed but also Dramadoon, Szarmi, and the Island Nations. There were scrolls, their parchment so brittle that Amaleah was certain she'd crush them just by the small amount she was touching them.

"Be careful!" Wynna sniffed as if she knew what Amaleah were thinking. Amaleah delicately held out the slips of paper and rolled-up scrolls. The elf took them from her in a swift, yet somehow graceful movement. Her brow creased as she peered at the old manuscripts.

"I think you've broken them," she said, her lips pursing.

"What?" Amaleah asked, panic roiling within her. "But, I

couldn't have. I was…"

Her voice trailed off as she saw the corners of Wynna's mouth tugging upwards. She thrust her hands on her hips and said, "Next time I'll be sure to wreak havoc on your precious manuscripts, then we'll see who'll be laughing."

Wynna abruptly stopped laughing and glared at Amaleah. "You wouldn't!" she exclaimed.

"I guess you'll just have to wait and see," Amaleah replied, raising an eyebrow at the elf.

"Where were you off to?" Wynna asked as she bundled the papers and scrolls together. She undid the bit of ribbon in her hair to tie them together.

"Oh," Amaleah said, biting her lip to stall. "I was just exploring." She rubbed at her face, certain that it would reveal the tear stains from earlier. Her head felt muddled and her nose was clogged with mucus. She absolutely hated crying, but could never seem to stop when her body had made up its mind to cry.

"Alone?" Wynna pried. Her voice was casual and she didn't look at Amaleah as she spoke, but Amaleah sensed that there was a deeper meaning behind her question.

"I wanted some time to myself," she said.

"And now?" the elf asked.

A flicker of annoyance kindled within Amaleah, but she forced it aside as she said, "I still want to be alone." It wasn't entirely the truth. She did want to process her thoughts about Colin. She knew she would need to at some point. But, there was another part of her—a bigger part—that yearned to make friends with someone who's sole purpose wasn't to protect her.

"Oh," Wynna said, her face crestfallen. She looked down at her feet as she continued to walk alongside Amaleah in silence.

"I could," she began and then stopped.

"You could what?" Amaleah asked as they rounded another turn. She was certain this one would lead them back to the town center.

"Well, I could just walk with you, if you wanted. You wouldn't have to, of course. I would understand…"

"I would love to have you walk with me," Amaleah said, a smile creeping across her face. "In silence, of course."

Wynna laughed softly. "Of course."

Amaleah fully expected Wynna to break the silence. But, she didn't. Instead, they continued for several paces before Amaleah finally asked, "Do you know who I'll be training with while I'm here?"

Wynna gave her a curious look before blushing deeply. "I thought you knew," she said.

"Knew what?"

"That I'd be your tutor in magical technique, history, language, and application."

"What!" Amaleah exclaimed. She glanced sidelong at the elf walking beside her. She seemed too young to be a master teacher. "How old are you?"

Belatedly, she realized that the question might have seemed rude. Elves, much like the fae, were immortal creatures who could live for centuries and never appear to age a day.

"I was born just after the Wars of Darkness commenced."

"But that would make you nearly four hundred years old," she mumbled the words, not sure she completely believed what she was saying. She knew there were elves older than Wynna and that she shouldn't be surprised by any of the elves' ages, but she just couldn't wrap her mind around it. *Then again*, she reminded herself, *Helena, Castinil, and Armos were all significantly older than Wynna. At least they looked the part.*

"I'm still an infant in most elves' opinions," she said, her voice more bitter than Amaleah would have expected. She shifted the stack of papers and scrolls so that they nestled under her arm. "I think most of them were as amazed as you seem to be that I've received Elaria's approval to be your main tutor. There were several, more qualified candidates."

She clapped her hand over her mouth as if realizing she'd misspoken. "I wasn't supposed to tell you that," she explained after Amaleah coaxed her arm down. "My nana told me not to tell you that other people had been in the mix. She knows the only reason Elaria chose me was because we're so close in age."

"Uh, Wynna," Amaleah began, "you do realize that I'm only seventeen right."

"Well of course I do! By the Light, Amaleah, I'm not a dunce. I know full well you're still a teenager in human years. So am I, in elf years, that is."

"Right," Amaleah said, drawing out the word and nodding her head in an attempt to stall the conversation. She rolled her eyes. There was no way her seventeen years even came close to comparing to Wynna's nearly four hundred.

"Look, Amaleah," Wynna said, crossing her arms over her chest, "Like it or not, Elaria chose me and I'm here to do the job."

"Which clan are you from?" Amaleah asked, her ears perking at the mention of only being here to help her.

"None," she responded before disappearing into a cloud of smoke and ash. Amaleah coughed as the noxious fumes filled her senses.

When the smoke cleared, Wynna was nowhere to be found. Only a small, golden flute remained. The metal shone in the faltering rays of sunshine traipsing through the trees. Daintily, Amaleah plucked the flute from the ground and began examining it. It hummed in her hand and she felt as if ice were creeping across her flesh. Its coldness gripped her in a way she had never known was possible before. She tried to release herself from it. It was love and power and darkness and light all rolled into one. It was music on a winter night with stars falling from the skies. It was music on the wings of mighty beasts headed to war. It was—

"Amaleah!" Thadius called, his voice like a weight pulling her back into herself. She could hear him. Hear his heavy breathing. Hear the clomping of his hooves on the hard, frozen ground as he galloped through the trees. Hear the edge in his voice as he shouted her name again.

"Amaleah!"

She tried to call back to him. Tried to tell him that she was alright. But her words stymied in her throat. She coughed, as if choking on her own words. Tears welled in the creases of her eyes as she fought against the draw of the flute's magic. She could feel herself fading away, dissolving into nothing more than the song of the wind.

He reached her. Too late, she thought. His warm arm stretched around her, his finger twining in her hair as he cradled her head and peered into her face. He was all shadow and vague lines. Nothing distinct. He pressed his other hand into the small of her back. She could hear him whispering her name over and over again as he stroked her.

She did not speak. She did not move. She couldn't. Not

while the flute was still clutched in her frozen hand.

Thadius pulled away from her and the loss of his warmth sent a shiver down her spine. More than a shiver. She shook until her teeth chattered and all around her was nothing but blurred colors and lines. She felt his hands roaming her body, searching for any sign of injury, for any explanation as to why she wasn't reacting to anything he did.

His fingers found her clenched hand. She felt him prying at her fingers. Heard the faint snap as one of her joints dislocated as he tried to dislodge the flute from her grasp. His breath smelled of nuts and pine as he cursed under his breath. She wanted to tell him it was alright, that she would find a way out of the mist clouding her mind. She opened her mouth to speak and only a puff of mist escaped her lips.

Thadius rolled up his sleeves, his muscled arms bulging as he held her back with one hand and then deftly yanked the flute from her hand with the other. Every single finger cracked as he drew the metal from her icy hand. She had a momentary sensation of warmth and freedom before the agony of her broken fingers exploded on her senses. And then, she screamed.

Chapter Nineteen

Thadius was cradling her when Amaleah woke again. She knew only a few seconds could have passed as a wave of agony washed over her once more. Her hand ached in a way she didn't know was possible.

"Hold on," Thadius murmured as he increased his pace.

Amaleah leaned into him, his pine and citrus scent filling her as she breathed in deeply. His body rocked to and fro and he ran through the trees. Amaleah had to close her eyes to keep herself from fainting again. She couldn't remember where they were or why her body ached as much as it did. She couldn't remember why she felt so cold.

"Just hold on," Thadius repeated. There were people chattering all around her. She could hear their frantic cries. She tried to listen, to understand what everyone was so worried about. Thadius moved too quickly for her to concentrate on a single voice, save for his.

He didn't stop until they were back at Nylyla's house. She groaned as he carried her through the doorway, her broken fingers scraping against the wooden frame. Thadius hissed at her whimper.

Of course, Amaleah thought. *I was weak before I knew about my powers and I'm still weak now.*

He set her on an overstuff couch before standing back so that he could look at her. He pawed at the floor as he looked at her. She looked back at him, her body aching and her mind still muddled from—

"What happened?" Nylyla said as she rushed to Amaleah's side. Her cheeks were flushed and her eyes narrow and calculating as she assessed Amaleah's condition.

"I'm not sure," was all Thadius said. He continued to paw at the ground.

"Thadius," Nylyla said, "go fetch me a bucket of water. And heat it on the stove. I'm going to have to clean some of these cuts."

Amaleah tried to lift her hand, but Nylyla's grip on her wrist was too strong.

"None of that," she said as she brushed Amaleah's hair out of her face.

Amaleah tried to stir her magic, to call upon it to heal her mangled hand. All she found were the icy tendrils of whatever the flute had done to her.

"The flute," she whispered, her voice hoarse.

Nylyla looked at her, her eyes wide. "What did you just say?" she asked. She gripped Amaleah's hand more tightly as she leaned in to hear Amaleah's whisper. The agony of that grip was almost enough to send her back into unconsciousness, but Amaleah forced herself to concentrate on what Nylyla was asking.

"Tell me about the flute," the elf commanded.

Thadius clomped back into the room before Amaleah had a chance to tell Nylyla about the strange elf who had given her the flute. Instead, she simply said, "Thadius has it," before drifting back off into a fitful sleep.

———————◆———————

A warm fire crackled in the fireplace when Amaleah opened her eyes again. She groaned at the whimsical white and pink decorations and the scent of baking gingerbread permeating the room. And, to boot, she couldn't remember where she was. Despite the warmth emanating from the fire, she shivered.

"Ah," a voice said from the other side of the room. "You're awake."

Groggily, Amaleah sat up and peered towards the other side of the room. She did not recognize the oversized woman washing her clothes in a small basin in front of the fire.

"Who are you?" she asked, her voice piqued.

"Name's Claire," the woman said, still scrubbing at her dirty clothes.

"Where am I? What am I doing here?" Then, as if just remembering, she said, "Where are Thadius and Yosef?"

The woman wiped her wet, grimy hands on her apron before turning to look at her. She had a broad, ruddy face and shimmering blue eyes. Her ears pointed daintily above her white cap. Tendrils of curly red escaped the confines of the hat, giving the woman a halo.

"You   sure   do   have   a   lot   of   questions," Claire grumbled."Please," Amaleah begged. "Please just tell me."

"Can't say as I'm surprised," Claire continued, either ignoring or simply not hearing Amaleah's words. "Humans always did ask the stupidest questions."

"Please," was all Amaleah said.

"Hush now, child," Claire said as she ambled over to her, a

wet cloth in her hand. "They'll be up shortly."

She used the cloth to wipe down Amaleah's body. Although the cloth was warm, it left her feeling chilled and she shivered. Claire made a clucking sound as she placed a hand on her forehead.

"Is she awake?"

She turned her head towards the door in time to see Thadius and Yosef walk into the room. Yosef's black cloak billowed, as usual, as he moved into the space. Thadius strode towards her, concern etched on his face. She felt the tears swell in her eyes again. She balled her hand into a fist, trying to force herself from crying. She hated crying. Hated the way it made her feel powerless to her own emotions. Thadius reached her, trailing a long, delicate finger down her face. It left a tingling sensation on her skin and she shifted, uncomfortable with the touch.

"Thadius," Yosef said, a warning.

Amaleah turned towards the reaper. He leaned, almost casually, against the wall. Yet, Amaleah saw the way his body tensed when he looked at her.

"I'm alright," she whispered, though she wasn't certain her words were true.

Thadius turned away from her, his expression dark.

"I'm sorry," he whispered as he made as if to leave the room.

"For what?" she asked. Although her mind still felt murky and she only vaguely remembered what had happened to her, she saw no reason for Thadius to feel any guilt over her injury.

"I should have been there to protect you," he stammered. "I should have ensured that nothing like this could have happened." He paced across the room. "I should have waited to remove the flute from your hand until a more qualified person was available."

"You saved me," Amaleah said simply. She did not look at her hand. She knew what she would see and she wasn't sure she could bear it. Not while everyone else was there, at least.

"I hurt you," he snarled. "Look at your hand, Amaleah. Look at it." Spittle sprayed from his mouth as he spoke and Amaleah could see the crazed look in his eye as he said, "You may never be able to use your hand again, and it's because of me."

Amaleah shuddered. How would she be able to fight in the impending battle if she couldn't use her hand? Biting her bottom lip, she peered down at her injured hand. It was wrapped in thick, white bandages. Well, if she were being completely honest with herself, the bandages weren't completely white. Yellow stains covered the inside creases and Amaleah knew they were from puss seeping from her torn and battered flesh.

"Undo the bandages," she commanded, looking at Claire.

The woman stared down at her, eyebrows arched. "I'm not supposed to," she began, stumbling over her words. "I'm just supposed to change the dressing."

"Then change it," Amaleah said, her patience waning. Claire did as she was told. She drew and boiled a small bucket of water. She pulled clean bandages out of a small cupboard beside Amaleah's bed. Then, when everything was ready, she slipped a slender pair of silver scissors from her dress pocket and began snipping the bandages off her hand.

When the last of the bandages had slipped to the floor, Amaleah steeled herself before taking a look at her hand. It was worse than she had imagined. Green and yellow pus seeped from her broken skin. Her fingers splayed at odd angles. She tried flexing her hand, but stopped as intense agony overcame her.

"I don't understand," she said, still staring at her hand.

"How… how did this happen?"

Claire wiped Amaleah's wounds clean with hot water before spreading a thick, foul-smelling ointment on Amaleah's hand. it felt oily to the touch and she was instantly repulsed by it, but it made the agony subside, if only slightly. She deftly wrapped the hand again with clean bandages before bobbing her head at Thadius and Yosef and rushing from the room.

Amaleah peered down at her thickly bandaged hand. With the ointment and the bandages on, it didn't ache nearly as much as it had before, but she knew the truth. Unless someone used magic to heal her, she would never be able to use her hand again.

"Tell me," Amaleah commanded when she, at last, felt comfortable enough to look up at her companions.

To her surprise, it was not Thadius who responded, but Yosef. "Amaleah, how much do you know about the Creators?"

She chewed on her bottom lip. "Only what I've read in the histories of Mitier. And in the fae tales."

He nodded at her, the burned out black holes where his eyes should have been fixing upon her. She waited. He said nothing. Thadius drummed his fingers on his abdomen and began whistling softly. Amaleah glanced at the centaur askance, her face a mixture of bemusement and annoyance.

When neither of them explained why she needed to know about the Creators, she asked, "How do they fit into all of this? Who was the elf who gave me the flute in the first place?"

She thought of the unsightly elf who had been so pleasant at first. *She betrayed me*, Amaleah thought, her head pounding.

"In the beginning, there was only Light and Dark. The one needed the other. There was no ending, no beginning, no death without rebirth." Yosef's gravelly voice sent chills down her spine.

"A perfect balance," Amaleah said snidely. Her head felt as if she were under water. She could barely think through the fog. "I know this. It's in all the history books."

"Shh," Thadius chided her as he held a single finger to his lips.

"Together, they created our world. Everything we touch, everything we know, is because of them. And, when the Darkness blessed the whole of Mitier with rot, decay, and death, the Light forged the Creators to bring balance."

Amaleah leaned her head back against the pillows of her bed. Her vision was blurry and she was finding it increasingly difficult to concentrate on Yosef's words.

"The Creators performed wondrous acts. They created new life, gifted powers beyond our imagination to their chosen people, and provided hope to the masses. They were hope. They were life. They were Light. Throughout time, they became known for their actions. They were given the names of Mother, Warrior, Hunter, Wanderer, Blacksmith, Executioner, Gatekeeper, and Lover."

Amaleah mouthed Yosef's words as he said them. Thadius smacked—not hard enough to harm—her on the leg and raised an eyebrow at her. Yosef didn't seem to notice as he continued.

"In their time they created eight items, one for each of them, that they could use to store, channel, and siphon their abilities. The Mother was given a pitcher of water, so that she would always be in direct contact with the Light."

Amaleah bolted up. She had never read, never heard this part of the tale before. Everything, every history book, every fae tale, every story she'd been told, ended with the names of the Creators.

"The Warrior was given an ax, so that they would be able to

defend the Light at all costs. The Hunter, a bow, to stealthily take down both foe and prey. The Wanderer, whom many forget, was given the scrolls of knowledge so that they would always have the wisdom to make the correct choices. The Blacksmith was given a hammer to forge new life upon the world. The Executioner was gifted a sword, to keep justice at all costs. The Gatekeeper was given a key, to unlock the mysteries of the world. And, the Lover was given a flute, to remind others of the love and compassion the Light provides."

Amaleah's blood turned to ice as she listened to Yosef finish his explanation. *It couldn't be possible*, she told herself. *There was no way*. Her mind replayed her conversation with Wynna. The elf had given nothing away, at least not that Amaleah could detect.

"So, you think the flute she gave me was what, some kind of mystical relic tied to the Lover?"

Thadius stopped tapping his fingers as he met her gaze. He did not flinch at the hardness in her eyes. He only continued to stare as he said, "We have no doubt that it is."

"How is that possible?" she asked, her mouth going dry. "The Creators haven't been seen in over three hundred years. Why come back now? Why send cryptic messages?"

A dull ache had settled over her body and she leaned back against her pillows once more. She was cold, colder even than when she'd been holding the flute in her hand. She pulled the thick quilt up and over her shoulders, her body quaking slightly.

"Are you unwell?" Thadius asked as he moved closer to her bed.

Her teeth chattered so much that she was barely able to utter the single, "Yes," before Thadius had raced from the room. Yosef remained, though he made no move to comfort her.

Silence filled the room. For this, Amaleah was grateful. Yosef reminded her too much of the miseries from her home. Of her father. Of Sylvia.

Sylvia. The name sluggishly moved through her mind like wading through deep mud that had nearly frozen solid. Her body shook as she pressed onward. She needed to see her face, to hear her voice. She called out to her nursemaid, her friend. There was no reply. Tears leaked from her eyes as she remembered that there would never be a reply again.

There was fire.

All around her. Fire.

The fumes suffocated her, burned her. She cried out, but no one was there to save her. Her name echoed through the trees, like a lover's lament on the wind. She twirled and the flames leapt at her, biting her skin and singeing her hair. The smell overwhelmed her, brought her to her knees. All around her was laughter. His laughter, she realized.

"No," she whispered, to no one in particular, for there was no one there to help her. "No," she said again.

A path through the flames cleared as a lone shadow emerged.

"You will never escape me."

The madness. The total and complete madness.

Sweat dribbled down her cheeks. It lined her upper lip and formed on her brow. The flames licked at her, making her scream into the night.

"You'll never escape me," he cried at her. The command, the plea, reverberated through her. "You are mine."

She crawled away from the shadow, the flames catching her in their grasp as she moved closer towards them. She couldn't cry anymore; the air was so hot and dry around her.

"Amaleah."

She thrashed, sending tendrils of her power before her. A loud grunt followed by a sickening thud. Her eyes fluttered open in time to see Thadius shaking on the ground. His hand clutched as his chest as blood seeped from a wound.

"No," she whispered. "No. No. No. NO!"

She flung herself from the bed, though her head still ached and her skin was coated in a sheen of sweat. She pressed her hands across his skin, begging her abilities to flair, to heal him. She prayed to the Light, her wet breath mixing with Thadius's. His breaths came out in wet, ragged sobs.

She pressed more firmly on his chest, willing herself to give him whatever strength she could. She envisioned it. She called it.

Nothing happened.

His head lolled to the side. All she could see were the whites of his eyes as he stared up at her.

"Do something!" she hissed. She didn't care who heard or who responded. She just needed someone to save him. Blood coated her hands, her clothes.

"Please!" she said as Yosef knelt beside her. She was trembling now. Her head continued to pound and her thoughts became as muddled as murky water. The reaper wrapped his cold, dry hand around her shoulder, tucking her tight against him. She shuddered at his touch. Tears streamed down her cheeks as she grasped Thadius's hand in her own.

"Please," she whispered one last time.

It had been her. She knew it had it been her. If Thadius died, it would be her fault.

She was vaguely aware that Nylyla had joined them beside Thadius's body. She pummeled putrid smelling herbs into a fine powder. Amaleah watched the elf added a brilliant green liquid to the powder and began stirring until the mixture transformed into a thick paste. Nylyla dabbed the paste onto the centaur's wound. The bleeding slowly subsided and Amaleah heart sank. He was gone.

Yosef led her to the bed. Her body was numb. Her mind was numb. Everything within her felt numb.

"I'm sorry," she whispered. It was if she were a mocking bird, constantly repeating the same phrase over and over again.

"Hush now," Nylyla said, pressing a cool hand to her forehead. She held a glass to Amaleah's lips and forced her to tip her head back and drink the vile liquid within. It tasted worse than it smelled and it smelled like a horse's stall that hadn't been cleaned for three weeks. She nearly vomited as the thick liquid settled in her stomach.

"Rest," Nylyla whispered.

She fought to keep her eyes open. She needed to know. She couldn't sleep without knowing.

"Thadius," she whispered, her lips barely moving. She could feel her body relaxing, sinking into the sleep paralysis she'd only ever read about in books. "Is he…" her words trailed off as her body finally succumbed to the potion.

Chapter Twenty

The Lunameedian Countryside

Starla's boots sank nearly three inches into the muddy bank of the Estrell. She cursed as she tried yanking her boot out. It didn't budge. She heaved with both hands on her leg, trying to loosen the mud's hold on her boot. To no avail.

"Why don't you just take off the boot, miss?"

She snarled as she looked around the woods. As far as she could tell, she was completely alone.

"I'm serious," the voice called. "You'll never be able to get out of that mud if you wait too much longer. Your other boot is already sinking into its depths."

She glanced down and, sure enough, her other foot was sinking. Mud bubbles popped as her foot slid and splatted the hem of her dress. Her eyes immediately darted to the trees around her. She listened. She waited. She knew whoever was following her would make a mistake sometime. Then, she'd be ready.

She slipped a dagger from the knife holster stretched across her chest.

"I wouldn't do that if I were you," the voice called.

She turned in its direction, but saw nothing. Not even birds fled to the skies. She gripped the knife tightly in her hand, contemplating all the ways she could kill whoever lingered in the trees. She hissed as an arrow grazed her cheek. The cut stung as air hit it and she hissed again, clutching her hand to her cheek.

"Next time, I won't miss," the voice said. It seemed further away now, almost impossible to detect.

"Next time?" She yelled as she wiggled her foot around in the mud. It squelched, but her boot did not come free. "Next time I'll have your balls caught in my snare."

His laughter wafted through the trees like music during a party. Starla knew she needed to stall, to buy herself time as she dug her boots out of the mudhole. She flicked the drizzle of blood streaming from her neck and peered into the foliage above her.

"What's your name?" she asked.

He didn't respond for several moments. She clawed at the mud, now around her ankles. It filled her nails, leaving her feeling even more grimy than she had before. She pretended like she was fully involved in her pursuit of freedom, but she kept both ears open. She listened for any sound of movement above her. Birds cawed. Insects crawled over her hands and buzzed in her ears. A twig snapped.

She ducked just as another flew by her other ear. She knew by its path that it wouldn't have struck her. *A warning then*, she thought.

"Who are you?" she screeched as she covered her head with her arms. She crouched, low to the ground. In the flurry of her movements, she pulled another blade from its sheath.

"I told you not to do that."

She cringed, knowing that if he wanted, he could strike her now and no one would know the difference. She doubted even Viola would mourn her. Namadus certainly wouldn't. He had sent her on this fool's mission. She'd been searching for weeks, and still she had found so sign of the princess. Nothing. No one had seen her. No one had offered her aid.

She flinched as an arrow dug itself into the mud in front of her. A slip of paper was tied to its shaft. She looked at the foliage between her fingers, but saw nothing to indicate where her assailant was.

With a trembling hand, she wrenched the arrow free from the mud and slid the paper from it. Unfurling it, she read the message, first quietly, then out loud.

"Are you kidding me?" she asked. "Light's Wrath! Are you kidding me?" She crumpled the paper and dropped into the deepest puddle within reach of where she was stuck in the mud.

"It's your choice," he said.

Her eyes darted to the place where she thought she heard his voice. If she narrowed her eyes, if she concentrated, she thought she could see the shadowy outline of a person perched on a high branch.

"Women don't have a choice," she said.

The shadow moved. She saw it. Saw him. He swung from vine to vine until it was directly above her. Gritting her teeth, Starla readied herself to launch the first knife into his gut. She envisioned where she would need to strike. She saw his body jolt. She felt droplets of his blood fall on her like rain.

She took a steadying breath, her eyes locked on the shadow hovering in the trees above her. She knew she could do this. It's what she had been training for her entire life. She exhaled slowly, feeling her lungs collapse as she pushed out her remaining air. Then, in a swift, practiced motion, she threw the dagger home.

She heard the blade thud as it embedded itself in his flesh.

"You shouldn't have done that," he said, casually. There was no hint of an injury in his voice.

I heard it strike him, she thought. *I heard it*. She frantically pulled at her boots. Neither of them budged. She wiped sweat from her brow smearing mud on her skin as she did so. Her mind was a hum of frenzied thoughts as she wiped her hands on her leggings. An arrow clipped her left heel, leaving a trail of blood in its wake. With one final tug, Starla felt the will of the mud break and her foot come free.

Leaving her boots, she ran. Her lungs strained as she heaved in great gulps of air. Her side caught, sending a wave of pain through her. She tried concentrating on her breathing. She tried focusing on putting one step in front of the other. She wove through the trees, never staying on the same track long enough for whoever he was to take aim. She knew she was trailing blood behind her. Knew that, eventually, she would become too weak to run any further. He would be able to track her.

She stumbled over a thick branch blocking her path and went flying through the air. She slammed into rough limbs and rocks, the wind knocked out of her. Dazed, she rolled over and scanned the trees above her. She tried to hear, but her mind hummed and her ears rang.

Cursing, she pulled herself into a sitting position and examined her wounds. Her leg was scraped and bleeding where she'd tripped over the branch. Her hands were coated in mud. She could tell from the way they stung that they, too, were scraped and bleeding. The world swam as she turned her head at the sound of crunching twigs.

She scooted backwards, trying to cover herself with dead leaves and branches as she did so. It was a poor excuse of camouflage, but it was the best she could do. Gripping two more knives in her hands, she breathed in. Breathed out. Breathed in.

"I know what you intend to do," he said. His voice was close now, so very close. Still, she couldn't see him.

Breathed out. She flexed her wrist, ready to strike as soon as she knew his position. Breathed in.

"It won't work," he said.

He came into view and Starla breathed out at the same moment she lunged at him.

She put all her weight behind it. A snarl escaped her as she held the twin knives out. She saw his face, younger than she had been expecting. She heard his sharp intake of breath as she arched over him.

She slammed into the ground again, her head popping backwards on impact. She grunted as all the strength in her muscles slackened. She dropped her knives.

"I told you it would end poorly for you," he said as he knelt beside her. He held one of the arrows out for her to see. And, for the first time, she noticed the greenish tinge the tip had.

"Poison," she hissed through swollen lips.

"Poison."

Her eyelids fluttered. She tried to see his face, but he was clouded in shadow. "Who are you?" she asked again, though she had no hope that he would actually answer her.

She faded into darkness at the sound of his silence.

Sunlight streamed through the weeping willow's branches. The air was warm, but not muggy. Starla twirled in a frilly, pink dress as her sister, Viola, painted her from a distance. The air smelled of roses and jasmine and orchids. She glanced at the house behind her and saw the gardens. They were the most beautiful gardens she had ever seen, and probably ever would. She laughed as a butterfly landed on her outstretched hand, tickling her.

Not real.

Her sister's flowing white dress billowed behind her as she walked towards her and extended a glass of lemonade. She smiled at Starla as she linked arms with her and began walking towards the house. The tall, double doors were open, curtains fluttering outward. Viola squeezed Starla's arm as she whispered, "I can smell the lemon cake from here."

And she could, too. The buttery, citrusy scent of baking cake greeted them as they danced through the door. Viola laughed, her face flushed with merriment. She led Starla to the kitchen. A fire crackled in the hearth. Viola smiled at her as she sat at the kitchen table, her hair escaping its pins to fall in curls around her face.

Not real. Not real. Not real.

A broad, ruddy-cheeked woman turned to face them. Her orange hair was a frizzly mess under her stark white cap. She wasn't pretty, but she wasn't exactly ugly either. She was somewhere in between that instantly gave Starla the sensation that she was safe.

"Spot of tea, dears?" the woman asked, her voice warm.

Viola looked up at Starla then. Her eyes crinkled and her lips pulled into a wide, toothy grin. She nodded to the cook, who poured steaming cups of tea and set them before Viola at the table. Starla still stood. Something felt wrong. Something wasn't right. She looked around the kitchen, searching for answers. Herbs hung from ceiling beams and pots from nails at an oven.

Light streamed in through the large windows and fresh air filled the space. It was everything she had ever wanted.

Not real.

The cook brought over a plate, laden with fresh lemon cake, and handed it to Starla. The gap between her two front teeth when she smiled made Starla want to hug her. Instead, she returned the smile. The cook turned her back on Starla, her shoulders tensing. Starla watched her, analyzing her every move as she clutched the steaming teapot in her hands. The cook shook as she swung the pot towards Starla, boiling tea leaking from its open top. She didn't have time to move, to defend herself as the hot liquid washed over her.

Starla screamed and jolted upright. Ice water soaked her flimsy nightdress. She clutched at the dress, confusion sweeping over her. She tried to remember the last thing she'd done, but all she could recall was the faint scent of lemon cake and her sister's smile. She lifted her hands to wipe away the tear that had sprang in her eye.

She couldn't lift her hands. She writhed against the manacles holding her down; the thick iron links bit into her skin. There was nothing she hated more than being held in chains. She screamed again, her voice raw.

"Have you made your choice yet?" a male voice asked. Her head swam as she tried to remember how that voice was familiar to her.

"Who are you?" she managed to bark. "Where am I?"

A single candle provided light to the room. It was not enough to see the corners, but it was enough to see the iron bars and the stone floor. Water puddled in various places, shimmering slightly in the soft glow of the candle. The smell of excrement was overwhelming; Starla nearly vomited as a particularly foul stench reached her.

Footsteps echoed on the stone floors and she sensed a presence just out of reach of the light.

"You are in my home," the man said, his voice a juxtaposition of breeziness compared to the cell she was in.

She spat. "I don't want to be here."

He chuckled at her. "So much anger."

She snarled at him but said nothing. She had never considered herself an angry person before. She had been trained to fight, to spy, to kill. She was who her uncle had made her to be. She couldn't be anyone else but her.

"What do you want?" she asked, her voice flat. She twisted her wrists against the iron shackles. Pain seared her flesh as she realized that her skin had been rubbed raw.

"I thought I made myself clear in the note," he responded, his voice still breezy.

"And I told you, women don't have that choice."

"Tsk, tsk, Starla. I thought you were better than this. Smarter than this."

He stepped into the light. His face was shrouded in a dark cloak, though curls of golden brown hair fell onto his chest. Silver embroidery, depicting famous battles throughout Lunameedian history had been stitched around the hems. Starla raked her eyes over the embroidery; she had never seen such fine work before. He was tall, taller than she would have expected, considering how quickly he had moved during their skirmish in the woods. And, she admitted, though she didn't want to, he smelled of dark amber and timber. It was a spicy, manly scent that left her feeling slightly lightheaded as she regarded him.

"You'll have to forgive me," he said, tapping his foot on the floor. "I was rather nervous that you'd try to kill me again."

"You shot at me first," she hissed at him, her voice low. She struggled against her bindings.

She couldn't tell for sure, but she could have sworn he shrugged his shoulders before saying, "An unfortunate necessity."

"Necessity," she repeated. "Are you kidding me again? There is no Light forsaken way that hitting me with your arrows was a necessity."

"Well, actually, it was," he said. His voice a touch more petulant than it had been before.

Good, she thought, *let him sulk in his own mistakes.* Out loud, she said, "We all have choices."

"Touché."

They remained in silence for a breath of a second.

"You can call me Drez."

"Drez?"

"Yeah, Drez. It's what everyone here calls me."

"And where, exactly, is here?"

"Do you promise not to scream?"

"What?"

"Just what I said. Do you promise not to scream?"

"I don't know how I can promise that when I don't know what you're going to do. Are you going to hurt me? Inflict torture upon me to get the secrets you so desperately want? Tell me, Drez," she emphasized his name as she spoke, "What do you intend to do to me?"

"Nothing."

She didn't believe him, not for one second.

"There's no way that can be true," she said.

"It is," he interjected.

She considered his words. If he had wanted to, she reasoned, he could have simply killed her when she'd passed out. Instead, he'd brought her here, wherever here was.

"Fine," she snipped. "I promise I won't scream."

He drew the hood of his cape back, revealing the most scarred face she had ever seen. It was more like a massive ball of scar tissue than an actual face. His eyebrows were completely missing. His nose was a mere stump. His skin looked as if it had been melted and then reshaped into something resembling a face, but not quite achieving it.

She wanted to scream. She wanted to look away. But she didn't. Instead she just said, "Now will you tell me where we are?"

He smiled at her then and his face turned into something a little more hideous than it had been before. Still, she did not look away.

"We're on the outskirts of Encartia."

"You forged the river with me while I was unconscious?"

"Of course," he replied. "How else was I supposed to bring you here?"

She looked at him, dumbfounded. He wasn't following any of the rules she'd been taught by her multiple tutors. He didn't appear to be lying, but he wasn't telling the whole truth either.

"How did you get so good at shooting?"

"Practice."

She smirked at that. "And how did you learn how to mix nightshade like that?"

"It wasn't actually nightshade."

"Oh?" she asked, intrigued.

"No, it was a potion I concocted myself."

She raised one eyebrow at him. "I'm not sure I believe you," she said.

"Well," he said, a tad defensively, "it's true. I make all sorts of things."

She pulled on the chains a bit, wincing at the pain the metal on her raw skin caused. She held her hands out to him, a silent beg in her eyes.

He looked her over. "You won't try to run?" he asked at last.

She thought about it briefly, before saying, "No."

Shrugging his shoulders, Drez pulled a heavy-looking ring of keys from his pocket. Selecting one, he first undid the manacles around her wrists followed by the ones around her ankles.

"Better?" he asked, as he stepped away from her.

"Much," she said.

He gazed at her, unabashedly. Starla felt her cheeks heat and looked down at her hands. She decided that she didn't like how he was making her feel. She pinched herself in the soft spot between her thumb and index finger to stop herself from wondering what he saw when he looked at her.

"So," she said, "why ask me to betray my uncle?"

"Right to the point," he said. "I like that."

She rolled her eyes at him before standing. "If we're going to discuss your, er, proposition, then I'm going to need real clothes," she said, looking down at the sheer nightgown she was currently wearing. "And," she continued, "I'm going to need my belt and knives holster back."

Her stomach grumbled and she realized just how hungry she actually was. She couldn't remember the last time she'd eaten a proper meal. While she'd been traveling, she'd only eaten the food she'd packed and whatever she could catch while hunting. It hadn't been a lot.

"Come on," he said, motioning for her to follow him up a long flight of stairs. "I'll give you a change of clothes and your weapons back, but first let's get you something to eat."

He led her through a series of stone tunnels. She tried to count the number of steps they climbed and the direction of the turns they took. After she reached seven-hundred and seven, she stopped counting. Still, she tracked the turns they took and was fairly certain she could find her way back to the dungeon on her own if needed. The air grew less and less putrid the higher they climbed. She breathed in deeply when they stepped into a lavishly decorated room at the top of the stairs.

"What is this place?" she asked, breathily. She examined the various knickknacks placed carefully around the room. There were dolls for each of the kingdoms on the main island along with some from the adjacent, smaller ones. They each held tiny flags or other objects to represent their people.

"Have you been to all of these places?" she asked, trailing her fingertips over the dolls' porcelain faces.

"Of course not," he said. "But they make for great conversation starters."

"Sure," she said.

She sat in silence as he Drez prepared a meal of eggs and toast. The eggs were a bit runny for her taste, but she didn't say anything as she devoured the entirety of the plate he'd prepared for her.

When she'd finished the meal, Drez led her to another room. No fire blazed here and it was cold as she sank onto a straight-backed chair. She shivered, her head still aching slightly. She cradled her head in her hands as she waited for Drez to say something to her.

He stood behind an ornately carved desk at the far end of the room. Shelves of books lined the walls behind him. Starla watched as he fiddled with an iron door inset into one part of the shelving unit. It popped open following a soft click. His back filled the space, making it impossible for her to see past his shoulders.

"What are you doing?" she rasped.

He said nothing, but she heard three faint clicks before he stepped back, revealing a second door. He pulled her leathers, belt, and holster from the safe. The room was too dark for her to tell if her blades were still in the holster, but, nonetheless, she sighed in relief.

He lit a candle before coming towards her. His face was once again shrouded by his cloak. She wondered how often he had hid his face throughout the years, how many times he'd been scorned because of his features.

"Here," he said, dropping her gear into her lap. She gave him a wry smile before trailing her fingers over the well-worn leather of her knife holster. Each of her remaining blades was there. Without waiting for permission, she slipped her leather on over the nightgown and pulled the holster on over her top. The weight of her weaponry instantly made her feel more like herself again.

"So," she said, "What next?"

"Next we talk about that note."

She sighed heavily. "You already know my answer Drez. Why waste both of our time arguing over it?

"You're wrong," he said simply.

When he did not continue, Starla rolled her eyes and said, "What am I wrong about?" Her voice was the perfect imitation of boredom. She was anything but.

"You have a chance to be someone important," Drez said. "You could be the turning point…"

"I said no," she said, cutting him off.

"But," he paused, "but why? It doesn't make any sense."

"Maybe to you," she said.

He let out an exasperated sigh. "Your presence in our group could bring a lot of hope to the rest of us."

"No one knows who I am," she said, though a little less certainly.

"That's a pack of lies and you know it. You're the High Councilor's niece. You have everything to gain from the fall of the Bluefischer dynasty."

"I'm going to stop you right there," Starla said, her voice flat and her nostrils flaring. "My uncle stands to gain from the fall of the king. Not me. Not my sister."

"What a naïve notion."

She ground her teeth as she regarded him. "You have a hideous soul to match your hideous face," she hissed. She knew it was cruel. She didn't care.

"You could join us," he repeated. "Join us and we will ensure that you will never fall into obscurity."

"Join a rebellion that is most likely going to fail and you promise to make me legend?" she mused over his proposal. It was insanity.

"You have until midnight tonight to make your decision."

She opened her mouth to ask him more questions, but he had already opened the door and disappeared through it. The cold sank into her and her teeth chattered. When she was sure he wasn't coming back, she crept over to the fireplace and using the bit of flint she always kept in her tunic's pocket, she lit a fire. She stretched her hands out towards the fire, rubbing them together.

She contemplated his offer. She was not to bring the princess back to the palace. But, neither was she meant to kill her. No, this man—this Blackflame—wanted her to work with the princess. They wanted Starla to mould the princess into a killer. Her stomach squirmed at the thought. To do this would be to turn against her uncle. She knew Namadus' endgame. He wanted control. He wanted the throne.

Starla never had.

But then, there was the matter of her sister. If her uncle discovered her betrayal, he would be sure to marry Viola off to someone nastier than she could ever imagine. She couldn't do that to Viola. She couldn't.

The king was mad. This, she knew for certain. He had wanted to marry his own daughter. He had killed dozens of innocents in his pursuit to do so. She had seen the slaughter. She knew what would happen if he continued to rule. The entirety of Lunameed would fall. It would fare little better in the hands of his daughter. She was a weak, timid little thing that would never be able to control the kingdom.

I have much to consider, she thought as she leaned back and stared into the crackling fire.

Chapter Twenty-One
Miliom, Szarmi

Queen Vista wrung her hands as she paced across her bed chamber. The train of her dressing gown caught around her feet, making her stumble as she turned to face her door. She held her breath as she listened. *Surely,* she thought, *that was a knock I heard.* She paused a moment longer before returning to her pacing. Her heart pounded in her chest as she imagined the reunion she was to have with Coraleen. She hadn't seen nor heard from her during the four months she'd been at Ford Pelid. Even the guards she'd hand-selected to accompany Coraleen hadn't sent word to her.

A swift rap on the door stole her attention away from her thoughts. Queen Vista rushed the door, her trail fluttering behind her like a dark storm cloud on the horizon. She flung the door open, only to reveal one of her ladies in waiting. A scowl stretched across her face as she tried to recall the girl's name.

"What is it?" she snarled.

The girl bowed so low to the ground that Vista thought she might be sitting on the floor. Her chestnut curls bobbed at the movement, making her look like one of Coraleen's dolls of old.

"Pardon my intrusion, your Highness," the girl's voice shook as she spoke and she stumbled over her words.

Vista rolled her eyes at the girl. "Spit it out."

The girl bowed even lower, if that was possible. "It's just that," she mumbled the words, "Princess Coraleen."

"What about the Princess?" Vista asked, her annoyance rising.

"She's returned, your Highness."

A fleeting sensation of joy passed through Vista and then confusion. And then anger. "Then why hasn't she come herself?" she hissed.

"I'm sorry, your Highness," the girl paused and Vista realized that a tear had leaked from the girl's eye.

"Tell me."

"Princess Coraleen commanded me to tell you that she would not be joining the party tonight."

"What!" the queen yelled, her voice echoing down the hall.

The girl backed away, though Vista had not given her permission to do so. She snatched the girl's wrist in a tight grasp and demanded, "Tell me everything you know."

The girl began crying in earnest. She blubbered over her words such that Vista couldn't understand a single thing the girl was saying. Huffing, Vista dragged the girl into her room. She didn't struggle against her as she raked her fingers through the girl's hair.

"Hush now, dear one, I just want to know how my daughter is doing."

The girl continued crying, though her shoulder shook less and she breathed a little easier.

Vista poured the girl a glass of wine from her personal carafe. The girl's hands shook so violently as she took the glass that drops of red liquid sloshed onto the snow-white rug on the floor.

"I'm sorry," the girl repeated over and over again as she

dabbed at the stain with the hem of her gown. "I'm so sorry."

Vista exhaled slowly. She clenched her fists so hard, she felt the length of her nails dig deep into her flesh. *The servants really are vexing*, she thought as she slapped the girl on the cheek. The girl's head snapped back with a loud popping sound. When she straightened again, her eyes were glazed and she had difficulty concentrating on any one thing in the room.

Vista clutched the girl's arm firmly in her grasp. The girl squirmed against the tight pressure. Vista didn't care if she left bruises all along the girl's wrist. She had answers that Vista wanted.

"Tell me, how did the princess look?" she asked.

"She was tan, Your Highness. Her skin glistened in the sun like a thousand amber jewels." The girls stopped speaking, her head lulling forward. Vista pinched her jawline and the girl released a small scream before peering up into the queen's eyes. Though confusion lay in them, Vista could also detect the beginnings of hatred as well.

She smirked at the girl. "How did she sound?"

"Sound?" the girl asked, her eyes listless.

"Did she sound happy?" Vista clarified, her nails biting into the girl's flesh.

"I'm not sure," the girl said. Her breathing slowed. "I'm not sure," she said again.

"Useless girl," Vista snarled as she shoved the girl back into the chair. She thought about snapping the girl's neck. She could already envision the snap she'd hear as the neck broke. There wouldn't be any blood that way; no mess for the other servants to clean.

"Annaliese," she whispered. This girl was Annaliese Jeckpard. Vista sighed as she once again stroked the girl's hair. It was a pity, really, that her parents were so well connected among the Szarmian and Borgandian nobility.

"Leave," she commanded.

Annaliese stumbled from the room. She crashed into nearly every piece of furniture along her way. Vista watched her go, her eyes narrowing as she thought about what the girl had said. *Of course, Coraleen will join the party*, Vista reasoned, *it is in her honor, after all.*

———————◆———————

Instrumental music wafted through the air as Vista made her way down the marble staircase. The twinkling lights her husband had commissioned illuminated the gardens as she walked onto the veranda. Everything was as she had planned. Trays laden with carefully selected foods covered each of the tables scattered throughout the garden. Pink roses and orchids were in bloom. The fountains bubbled and hummed merrily at passersby. Women wore gowns that sparkled in the lamplight. Men wore black suites with stark white ties. Despite the heat, many of partygoers wore jackets and furs.

Vista had chosen a silver gown that dropped in a low V down her front and back. She knew all the eligible men of the court—and some that were taken—would ogle her from afar. *Let them,* she thought as she turned to stare at herself in a mirror. She was fairer skinned than most of Szarmi's subjects. Coming from her homeland of Borganda, her skin was kissed by gold and her long, curly hair held hints of red in it when the sun stroked it. Her hazel eyes were intelligent, cunning. When King Henry had been alive, no one had noticed how cunning her eyes had been.

It was a shame, really, she thought as she pouted her lips, *that no one ever noticed how lonely I was here. Not even Henry.*

His name gave her pause as she considered her reflection.

Her breasts were still plump, but they sagged just a little. Crinkles covered her skin around her eyes and lips. Her skin was less luminous than it had been when she'd first come here. She had never returned home. Her family had sent envoys and presents every year, but they had never deigned to come visit her. She had decided long ago that she would never return to her island homeland.

"Your Highness?" a voice called from the shadows.

She whirled around, the gems sewn to her dress catching the light in a myriad of color.

"Yes?"

"The, uh, Princess Coraleen has asked to speak with you."

Her heart lightened at the news. The time was drawing nearer for Coraleen to take her place on the throne. Vista needed to be sure that her daughter was ready for the challenge of ruling the Light forsaken land.

"Tell my guests that we will be down shortly," she said as she passed by him. He stepped out of her way without hesitation.

The walk to Coraleen's rooms was excruciating. With each step she took, Vista imagined her daughter rejecting her at her door. She saw the anger, the distrust in her daughter's eyes. In her gut, Vista knew that Coraleen would one day come to hate her. She just hadn't imagined that it would be so soon.

She rapped on Coraleen's door. At first, there was no answer. She knocked again, this time calling through the door. She could hear rummaging on the other side. She pressed her ear to the door, the blue diamonds in her ears smashing into the side of her head. She winced in pain as one of the backs nearly punctured her skin.

The door cracked a tad, Coraleen's gold-flecked eye peered out.

"Coraleen," Vista gasped, pushing on the door to open it

more. Her daughter held her ground.

"Mother," she said.

Her voice didn't sound right, didn't sound like the lovely, happy girl she'd sent to Fort Pelid.

"What happened to you?" she asked, her lips quivering. "What did the Captain do to you?"

Coraleen gave her mother a raspy, harsh laugh. "The Captain, as you call him, did nothing to me, Mother."

"Then," she paused as she considered her words. "Coraleen, tell me what happened."

She pushed on the door again. If she could only get in, only see her daughter, then maybe they could rectify whatever had happened. Coraleen shoved the door until it as a mere inch away from slamming shut.

"You're the one who chose my guards," she said, her voice bitter and cold.

"Yes," Vista said, her heart beating wildly in her chest. "But," she began.

Coraleen cut her off. "Then you're to blame."

"To blame?" she asked.

"Do you know what they let happen to me our first night out?"

Vista's blood turned to ice at her daughter's words.

No, she thought. *No, no, no.* She pressed against the door, yearning to see her daughter's face, to hold her while they spoke.

"What happened?" she whispered.

"What do you think?" Coraleen asked.

"I'll kill him," Vista snarled, pounding her first against the door. "Tell me who it was and I'll…"

"It's already done," Coraleen whispered.

Vista could hear the catch in her daughter's words and understood that she was mere seconds away from bursting into tears. Her throat bobbed as she stared at the door separating her from her daughter. She was the most precious thing in the world to her.

"Let me in," she said, her voice as soft and kind as she could make it. After years of perfecting her queen tenor, it was a difficult task to achieve.

"No," Coraleen said through the crack in the door. "I only came back because Captain Conrad made me. He said that he had signed an agreement with you that needed to be upheld." She scoffed as she spoke and Vista felt a piece of her heart shatter. All her plans. All her scheming. They meant nothing if Coraleen were not ready to rule.

"Open this door, Coraleen."

"No."

"You may be the princess heir to the Szarmian throne, Coraleen, but you are not queen yet. I demand that you open this door at once."

A pause. Vista breathed out heavily, her words reverberating through her bones. She had never, in all her years of commanding her daughter, used that tone on her before.

"No."

The single word hung in the air. Coraleen had never disobeyed her like this before. Even when she'd commanded her to kill her own brother, Coraleen had acquiesced without so much as an argument. She'd played her role well when she'd sentenced Colin to his death all those months ago. She'd gone to Fort Pelid without dissent. The word hung in the air. And, it shattered Vista's heart.

"Coraleen," the queen said, "please let me in. I promise you, talking with me will make it better."

Another pause. Hope kindled in the darkest places of Vista's heart as she leaned towards that crack, waiting for Coraleen to respond.

The door opened just the tiniest bit wider.

"You may come in," Coraleen said through that crack, "but, if I ask you to leave you have to promise that you'll do so without argument."

"Of course," Vista responded.

A moment's hesitation and then the door flung open to reveal Coraleen huddled by the fire. Even in the relative darkness of the room, Vista could see the dark circles under Coraleen's eyes. Her face was abnormally pale and Vista could see a smattering of freckles stretching across her daughter's cheeks, chin, and forehead. Her hair, once luscious and soft, hung in puffy braids that clearly hadn't been brushed or washed in days—possibly weeks.

"What have you done to yourself?" Vista asked, her voice shrill.

Coraleen glanced at her, her eyes hard before turning away from her.

"You can go, if you're going to scold me, Mother," she said.

Vista scoffed. "I have a right to know what's going on with my own daughter," she hissed through clenched teeth. Never before had her daughter been as insolent as she was tonight. It almost reminded her of Colin.

"You have a right to nothing," Coraleen responded, her back still turned towards the queen.

Vista crept up behind her daughter. Coraleen's shoulders shook and she knew that, if she were to look her daughter in the face, she would see the tears spilling down her cheeks.

"Tell me," she commanded, her tone harsher than intended.

"Tell you what, Mother?" Coraleen sniffled and she rubbed the sleeve of her traveling dress across her face. It came back shining. It took all of Vista's reserve to not shy away as her daughter turned to face her.

"Tell you that your chosen guards couldn't protect me? Tell you that I feel ruined? Tell you that I can't stand to be here with you!"

Vista stilled. *No*, she thought, *it can't be. It can't.* In her gut, she knew it was true. Still, she needed to hear Coraleen confirm it. Needed to know beyond a doubt what had befallen her daughter.

"I hate you," Coraleen whispered before Vista had a chance to ask her questions. "I hate your scheming, your betrayals. I hate the way you've manipulated all of us. Manipulated me," she chewed on her nails as she spoke. "I hate what you've done to our kingdom. To Colin," she added, almost as an afterthought.

"Coraleen," Vista said, her voice soft. She lifted a hand to stroke the back of Coraleen's head, but she jerked away from her.

"I hate you," she repeated.

Vista stared at her beautiful, golden daughter. She had been stronger than Colin. And smarter. She had been more adept at fighting. She was a true Szarmian. A true leader. Her bottom lip began to tremble as she considered Coraleen's words. She couldn't let her reject her title, her rule. Not when she was a true Szarmian princess.

"Coraleen, listen to me," Vista said, her nails clacking on the wooden armrests of the chair. "There is," she paused. If she took this step, if she told her daughter the truth about herself, there was no going back. "There is much for us to discuss," she finally finished.

"I don't want to talk to you," Coraleen sniffed, pulling farther away from her.

"Fine," Vista mumbled as she gathered her skirts and prepared to rise. A thought occurred to her as she stared down at her daughter. Her lips curled into a thin smile as she glared down at her. "But," she said, clutching her hands before her, "don't you think I deserve an explanation. I mean, I authorized you to go to Fort Pelid, I let Captain Conrad train you—even though you and I both know you were well-trained before, and I created the scenario in which you could rule. After your father…"

"Don't say it," Coraleen pled. "Please, Mother."

Vista rolled her eyes. "After your father chose your weakling of a brother as his heir, there was little else I could do. You were always meant to rule Szarmi, Coraleen. Not your brother."

Vista knew it was what Coraleen had always wanted. Her daughter was just as cruel, vicious, and power-hungry as she was. She had betrayed her only brother to take the crown. She had attempted to assassinate him.

"I don't want it," Coraleen whispered. "Not anymore."

"I don't believe you," Vista said, shrugging her shoulders.

"You should."

Vista sucked in a breath, her heart pounding in her chest.

"Tell me what happened to you," she demanded again. "I can't help you unless I know."

"Fine!" Coraleen shouted. "You want to know what happened to me? Your hand-picked guards couldn't stop a pack of vagabonds from killing them and then raping me."

Silence.

Vista couldn't breathe. She had known. Of course, she had known. How could she not? Still, the confirmation of it, the knowledge of it, sent a shard of remorse so deep within her that she doubted she would ever be able to remove it. Her blood pounded in her ears. Her head swam.

"No," she whispered. "Tell me it's not true."

"You asked, Mother, dear," Coraleen said, her voice impassive.

Vista gripped Coraleen's hand in her own.

"Tell me exactly what happened," she ordered.

A tear welled in the corner of Coraleen's eye. But, she began to tell her story.

Vista was reminded of the phrase her mother once said to her, all those years ago—before she was exiled to Szarmi. Vista had been a young woman then. Younger, even than Coraleen was now. And beautiful. A tragic beauty, her father had said the last time they'd spoken.

'There is nothing more tragic than having one's story locked away inside.'

She didn't know if the phrase was something her mother had coined or if she had found it somewhere, in another book or time. Or, more likely, if she had heard one of the servants talking and stolen the phrase from her.

Coraleen's lips trembled as she opened and shut them. In some ways, she looked like a fish gulping for air, but failing to find it. She brushed a stray strand of hair from her eyes as she peered up at Vista. Those beautiful, brown eyes, flecked with gold.

"They posted guards outside my tent when we were a mere day from Fort Pelid," Coraleen began. "They promised to keep me safe as I slept. I believed them. I believed they could protect me. They didn't. I woke to the sounds of their screams. Three men entered my tent and, before I could reach for my weapons, they gagged me."

Her voice was monotone as she spoke. She did not look Vista in the eyes. She only stared down at her hands, her cheeks pale, her eyes brimming with tears.

"I tried, Mother. I tried to fight them. But it was three on one and I couldn't reach my dagger."

She clenched one hand with the other. Vista saw her

daughter's hand pale where her nails bit into her own skin.

"They took me one at a time. They took turns as they held me down."

Tears leaked from her eyes. Her shoulder shook. Blood seeped from a wound on her hand where her nails had broken her skin.

"They told me that if I told anyone what had happened, I'd be ruined. You know how our laws work, Mother. You know I can never rule now. I'm soiled."

"You are not soiled," Vista snarled. Her daughter shrugged her shoulders but said nothing. Vista gripped Coraleen's shoulders firmly in her hands and said, "Listen to me, Coraleen. This changes nothing. You are still the rightful ruler of this kingdom. You deserve to reign. And we won't let any of those swine stop you."

"It's too late for them."

She released her grip on Coraleen's shoulders. "What do you mean? Did you tell Captain Conrad? Does he know…"

"I gutted them and made them watch as I used their own innards to cut off blood circulation to their cocks. They begged me for mercy, begged for a quick death when they realized that there was no hope for their survival."

She turned to stare straight into Vista's eyes. "I was covered in their blood, you see. I couldn't hide what I'd done. Captain Conrad helped me clean myself. He helped me dispose of the bodies." She quivered as she said, "He kept my secrets safe."

"Stop," Vista commanded. She clutched at her daughter's hands. Coraleen's skin was clammy and cold. Vista stifled the urge to let go of her daughter's hands. She always had despised clammy things. Yet, when she peered into Coraleen's hazel, listless eyes, she couldn't betray her trust like that. Instead, she gripped Coraleen's hands tighter.

"I'm sorry, Mother," Coraleen whispered. "I'm so very sorry." Tears streamed from her eyes, turning her skin blotchy and the whites of her eyes red.

Vista did not wave away Coraleen's apology the way her own parents had. She did not blame her daughter. And, she had no intention of letting the actions of those pigs destroy her daughter's rule.

"Listen to me, Coraleen," she drew her daughter's face closer to her own. "What happened to you, what those boys did to you, is not your fault."

Her daughter's lip trembled. Vista's resolve trembled with it. "You are stronger than you know and you will get through this."

"I don't know how."

The words were so lifeless; they made Vista cringe. She never cringed over other people's sorrows. Never. She stroked tiny circles across Coraleen's hand as she said, "I can teach you how."

Chapter Twenty-Two

Port Verenis, Lunameed, 333 Years Before

Kilian stashed the young girl under an apple tree several paces from the main road leading into Port Verenis. Her breathing was regular, yet shallow; he knew she would wake soon. So, he gagged her. And, he bound her feet and hands before tying her to the tree. She slumped against it, her face slack. A bit of drool dribbled from her lower lip. He hoped She would be pleased with his new find. New initiates were so difficult to find these days. The war had nearly destroyed all of them before their coming-of-age. Kilian prayed to the Light that this one would survive long enough to be of use to their goals.

Without delaying any longer, Kilian turned his back to the girl and began whistling as he strolled into Port Verenis once more. No one paid attention to him as he walked the street of the port city. No one stopped him. No one questioned who he was.

"Kilian," a young female voice said as he turned a corner.

He sucked in a breath as his gaze met that of the woman standing behind him. She was tall and willowy. Her silver-blue hair was a mass of curls that were pulled back into a thick bun at the nape of her neck. Even the pins he saw jutting out from her hair did nothing to contain the cowlicks that covered her head. Her skin, though still pale, was a sun-kissed peach color that spoke of endless days lounging on the beach.

"Cordelia," he whispered.

"I'm so glad to see you again," she said, her lips trembled as she spoke. "I could not see how our futures would intertwine in the future. I was so worried that we would not meet again."

She gazed past his head, her eyes glazing over. Kilian could have sworn that he saw her eyes roam aimlessly as she stared into the beyond. But then, as if nothing had happened at all, she looked back into his eyes.

"Our paths were always meant to cross."

Kilian smiled lopsidedly at her, his hand easing from the hilt of his ax, Wraith Killer.

"I hope that our paths continue to cross in the future," he said, smiling jauntily at her.

Her eyes took on an expression of deep sadness as she said, "The future is such a haze where you are concerned, Kilian. I cannot see through the mist."

Her words made his stomach clench, but he only said, "I need to speak with Bluebeard."

Wordlessly, she grasped his hand and led him through the streets. Kilian trailed after her, his thoughts jumbled as he reconciled the image of the little girl he'd met in Ula Una with the woman leading him through the streets now. So much had changed since his time in the court of mermaids.

"Uncle has been so worried about you," she said in that sing-song voice of hers.

"Has he now?" Kilian asked. He couldn't imagine Bluebeard ever being worried about him.

"Of course," she breathed.

They turned down a street Kilian had not taken note of earlier. It was windy and dark. Beggars crowded the streets. They stretched out their hands to him as he passed. Kilian dropped a few silver coins into the palm of a young woman nursing a babe. Her face was so dirty that he could barely see her expression of delight as she pocketed the money.

Cordelia turned down a street so narrow Kilian could only consider it an alley way. His shoulders grazed both sides of the buildings as they pushed their way to the end of the street.

"This way," Cordelia crooned as she tugged him through a narrow door on their right. The doorway was so short that Kilian had to duck to avoid smacking his head into the top of the frame.

Guards crowded the entryway room. Their knives were all angled directly at Kilian's throat as he stepped into the room. Cordelia squeezed his hand before dropping her hands to her side.

"I've brought him," she murmured to the guard closest to the door. "Notify my uncle that I have returned."

A young merman scuttled from the room. Kilian smirked at the remaining seven soldiers. If he swung his right shoulder upwards, he would be able to break the guard's jaw. And, with the guard out of the way, Kilian would be able to draw Wraith Killer from the belt at his waist. *All I would have to do is...*

"Kilian, me boy, it's been much too long," a gruff voice said from the doorway on the other side of the room. Cordelia slipped from Kilian's side to join the man.

Kilian unclenched his fist that he hadn't realized was now gripped around his axe's hilt. Shrugging his shoulders to ease the tension that had built there, he scrutinized the guards surrounding him. They wobbled from foot to foot, their unease palatable in the small room. Kilian bared his teeth at the youngest looking of them all. The poor lad jumped so high that he lost his footing and fell clear on his rump. The rest of the guards lowered their knives as Bluebeard laughed at the reaction of the young guard.

"There's no reason for ya to be wastin' time over there," Bluebeard said, his voice full of mirth. "There's much for us to catch up on." He motioned for Kilian to follow him.

Kilian gave the guard, still rubbing his ass from where he'd fallen, a lopsided smile before trailing after Bluebeard and Cordelia down the stone passageway.

"You've lost weight," Kilian said when they entered another room at the back of the hall. The guards had not followed them. After a quick glance around the room, Kilian determined that there were no guards stationed here either.

"Aye," Bluebeard said. He twisted one of the beaded strands of his hair as he considered Kilian from across the room. "What are you doin' here, son?"

Kilian barely glanced at Cordelia or Bluebeard as he flopped on one of the easy-chairs, his legs thrown over the armrest. He dangled Wraith Killer before him and breathed in heavily.

"I'm here on official business from the Creators still loyal to the Light," he said smoothly.

"I see," Bluebeard said. "And what does this official business entail?" he questioned.

Kilian stared into Bluebeard's eyes for a hard moment before replying, "They know what you've been up to, Bluebeard."

Kilian twirled Wraith Killer in his hands. The weight of his weapon was like a comforting blanket to a sick child. "You know why I'm here."

Kilian sat up straight in his chair and launched Wraith Killer straight at Bluebeard's head. He didn't wait to hear if his weapon had struck home before he wrenched free two of his daggers. He crouched behind another chair, breathing hard. A loud thwacking sound followed by the clang of metal on metal met Kilian's ears. His back stiffened as he heard the creak of wood beneath boots.

He breathed in slowly through his mouth, waiting for his

moment to strike. Bluebeard would overturn the chair, as he drove his sword home. Kilian could already picture the events that were about to unfold.

So, he counted; breathed in; exhaled.

"This isn't the right path for you, son," Bluebeard said. His breathing sounded wheezy and wet.

Kilian concentrated on the feel of the daggers in his hands. The pounding of his own heartbeat subsided as he breathed in once more.

"Can't ya see that, son?" Bluebeard asked.

Kilian heard his mentor's footsteps on the wooden floor creep ever closer to his position.

"Kilian?" Bluebeard said.

A floorboard creaked on the other side of the chair Kilian was hiding behind. *Time's up*, Kilian thought.

He shoved the chair back. It skidded into Bluebeard's chest just as Kilian launched himself over the chair. A yell escaped his lips as he drove the twin daggers home. The blades slid into cotton stuffing as they plunged into the chair. Kilian cursed as he spun around in time to see Bluebeard raise his sword.

My sword, Kilian thought as he saw its purple glow. *I'm the one who managed to wrench that sword from Malmadi's hide. I'm the one blessed by Clara.*

He used the bracer on his left arm to absorb Bluebeard's attack. Sparks flew as metal met metal. Kilian felt the impact as it traveled up his arm and into his shoulder. Grunting, he sidestepped Bluebeard's next attack.

"Just talk to me, son," Bluebeard said, breathily. Despite his lean body and muscled arms, the old pirate had lost quite a bit of his stamina over the years. He held the sword between them, preventing Kilian from striking him with his short blades.

Bluebeard jabbed his sword to Kilian's right so swiftly that

Kilian almost didn't move quickly enough to block the blow. He felt the bracer on his left arm crack as Bluebeard's sword smacked against it. The pirate twirled the blade around in his hand before once again holding it between the two of them.

Kilian took a step backwards. He could feel the heat of his ax calling to him, feel its power.

"Kilian," Cordelia whimpered. He glanced in her direction. She was huddled in a corner, her knees drawn to her chest, her swirling eyes streaming tears.

He hesitated.

He reached a hand out towards her.

Bluebeard whacked his sword against Kilian's bracer again. This time, the metal clanged to the ground, cracked into three pieces. A welt swelled on Kilian's forearm. Pain burned through him as he turned his attention back to Bluebeard.

"We are loyal to Lunameed, Kilian. I swear to ya. The merpeople's only allegiance is to the Light, to this kingdom, and to the city of Ula Una."

Kilian lunged for his ax. Bluebeard stabbed him in the foot. Kilian felt the cracking of bones as the sword bit into his flesh. Blood spurted from the wound. He stumbled, his foot utterly useless and fell to the ground with a loud crash. He scrambled for Wraith Killers. It was mere feet from him. Frantically, he reached for his weapon.

Bluebeard stomped on Kilian's mangled foot.

Kilian screamed in agony. He turned over so that he could face his advisory. Bluebeard rolled his shoulders, a grim expression covering his face.

"It didn't have to be like this, Kilian," he said. His beard glowed blue as a shield of hard air formed between Kilian and his ax. The sword, Frost, began to glow purple. Kilian knew all too well what that meant.

He pushed against the wall of hard air separating him from Wraith Killer. He beat his fists against the barrier.

Bluebeard raised Frost high above his head, his nostrils flaring. Kilian knew Bluebeard expected him to beg, expected him to play on their long-standing relationship as a reason to spare him. He knew his words would fall on deaf ears.

"I'm sorry, son," Bluebeard whispered as he brought the sword down.

"No!" Cordelia shouted. Her scream was but a faint buzz in Kilian's mind as he kicked both feet upwards and straight into the sensitive spot between Bluebeard's legs. The pirate grunted, stumbled, and let the shield of hard air drop as he fell to the ground.

A spike of dull pain shot through Kilian's foot at the attack, but he didn't feel any breaks as he leapt to his feet. His leg felt numb, the way it did when he laid on it for too long. Pinpricks of sensation swept through his leg and foot. He grimaced as he stooped to retrieve his ax.

Heat flooded through him the moment his fingers grazed Wraith Killer's haft. He felt powerful, as if he could squash anything in his way. He strode towards Bluebeard's prone body, his ax clutched at his side.

"Kilian!" Cordelia called. Her voice trembled as she spoke. His throat bobbed as he stood over the pirate turned merking.

"Rise," he said, his voice little more than a hiss.

Bluebeard stared up at him, his face wan. Wrinkles covered his skin and a dark spot aligned itself on his lower left cheek. Still, the older man held Frost between them.

"I said rise," Kilian repeated. His words sounded harsh and commanding, even to his own ears. He slapped the sword from Bluebeard's grasp with a single smack of his ax.

"Kilian."

Kilian rested the sharp blade of his ax beneath Bluebeard's chin. The metal gleamed red. Power seeped into Kilian's very veins as he stared down at the man who was once his mentor.

"You are pathetic," he said, as he spat on Bluebeard's face. The man didn't even flick off the glob of mucus as it trailed down his cheek. Instead, he continued to stare resolutely into Kilian's eyes. "To think that I ever wanted to be like you."

"Your father was."

"My father gave up on me," Kilian yelled. "He let himself die. He let them murder him!"

"Who, Kilian? Who?" Bluebeard asked.

"The Szarmians!"

Bluebeard shook his head, sweat rolling down his forehead and into his eyes. "I don't think they had anything to do with it."

"Liar," Kilian snarled as he brought the ax up and slammed it into Bluebeard's shoulder. Blood spurted from the wound, spraying Kilian in the face.

"I'm not lying, Kilian," Bluebeard managed to gasp. His arm hung loosely to his side. Dark red stains covered his once pristine linen shirt. Blood bubbled from his lips as he continued, "You have to believe me."

Kilian lifted his ax. Bluebeard closed his eyes just as Kilian brought the ax down again. It cleaved Bluebeard's skull in two.

Bone, brain matter, and muscle squelched as Kilian ripped Wraith Killer free from Bluebeard's skull. His hands trembled as he wiped the blood coating his ax on the hem of Bluebeard's pant leg. Grey matter slid from the blade and dripped onto the floor.

"He barely put up a fight," Kilian whispered, more to himself than anyone else. "He just let it happen."

Kilian ground his teeth as he stared down at the dead king. His green hair was matted and coated in blood. His eyes were still open, still staring at him. Bending down, Kilian silently closed them. She had warned him that he would try to beg, try to convince him that they were not the enemy. Kilian knew the truth. They followed Clara's path. They had been led into Darkness.

A loud trumpet sounded. Kilian spun around to find that Cordelia—and the sword—were no longer in the room with him. Heaving a sigh somewhere between annoyance and relief, Kilian raised his ax up and charged out of the room.

Soldiers, their iron and steel weapons held at the ready, pressed into him from all sides. Kilian ignored the pain of blades twisting in his flesh and tendons being sliced clean through. All he could see was red. All he could feel was the grip of his ax in his hand as he plowed into the soldiers as if they were nothing more than blades of grass.

His ax cut through knees and abdomens. It cleaved heads. Muck covered his entire body as he waded through the sea of corpses. The young guard from before sputtered on his own blood. His throat was a mangled mess of flesh and muscle. Kilian stared into the man's eyes as he brought down Wraith Killer and ended the boy's misery.

He released a guttural cry as he lifted his ax high. Already the wounds to his own body were healing. Already he could feel himself strengthening. He pounded Wraith Killer on his chest, taunting anyone left in the townhome to challenge him.

No one did.

He prowled through the house, searching every room for any trace of Cordelia. He found what must have been her bedroom. It was all shimmering cloth and whimsical paintings. It smelled of the sea and chocolate and flowers on a summer day. Clutching one of her gowns in his hand, Kilian stalked from the room. He kept to the shadows as he listened for any movement. He knew the bowmen on the rooftops would have heard of the attack on Bluebeard by now. He rolled his shoulders, cracking his neck in the process. It was a fool's task. No one could stop him.

He strode into a room occupied by a long, narrow table. Maps of Mitier covered its top. Wooden figurines depicting the sigils of the various kingdoms at play splayed across one of the maps. Kilian grasped the trident of Ula Una. It weighed heavily in his hand as he considered the map before him.

Borgandian ships laid anchor just miles from the port cities of Verenis and Recardi. If their ships could make port, the river access to the heart of Lunameed would be the death of the kingdom. Kilian trailed his fingers over the line Szarmi had drawn. They had already pushed the Lunameedian and Dramadoonian forces back. They already controlled the land between the Moorica River and the River Borad.

Kilian still had not heard from the envoys he'd sent to Smiel. If they were willing to defect from Szarmi and join forces with Dramadoon, they still had a chance to regain their footing in the Beoscuret Mountains. She had told him it would be a gamble. The Smielians weren't known for their bravery. Still, he had heard the rumblings of rebellion and seized upon the idea that he could convince the kingdom's people to aid in their fight to save the magical realm.

He clenched the trident in his hand until he felt the metal pierce his skin and blood began to ooz down his wrist. Bluebeard and his ilk had put the entire war at risk. They had jeopardized the future of the magical realm. They had chosen the path of Darkness.

His blood dribbled onto the map. It coated the ocean, turning the water into a sea of blood. Dropping the trident onto the table, Kilian strode from the room. Wraith Killer sung to him as he marched out the front gate of the building. Arrows rained down on him. Some met their mark. Others sank deep into the mud. Still others bounced off the cobblestone pathways. Kilian ripped each one that struck him from his flesh, blood and gore spraying the townspeople too slow enough to move out of his way.

Still the arrows kept on coming.

It was no matter to him. Let them fly their arrows. Let them believe that they could win. They would know soon enough. They would see the errors of their ways when their beloved ocean became coated with blood.

He began jogging, the pounding of his feet on the cobblestone streets distracted him from the pain he felt each time an arrow pierced him. He concentrated on his breathing, on putting one foot in front of the other. He was the Light's Hero, responsible for maintaining all that was magic in the world. He'd be damned if he let a traitorous Creator and a band of merpeople stop the Light from prevailing.

Chapter Twenty-Three

Amadoon Lake, Mitier, 333 years later

The boat creaked and freezing water crashed over its side. Colin clutched his cloak tighter to his chest as he sat at the bow of the ship. No light, save for the stars, guided their way. A wavering mist floated over the water's surface. Although it made navigating difficult, Rikyah had been insistent that traveling on a misty night was much safer than on a clear one. Colin hoped she was right.

There were three boats in total. Only five of their most trusted men had been allowed to accompany them across the lake. Intellectually, Colin knew that having the extra fifty men they'd left behind wouldn't be of much help in a fight against the Szarmian army. Still, he felt much less secure in his journey than he had since they'd embarked.

Colin's stomach felt queasy as the ship rocked. He hadn't vomited yet, which was a blessing, but he never had been able to stomach sea-travel. The one time he'd traveled to Borganda with his mother and father as a child, he'd been sick the entire way there. They hadn't returned to his mother's homeland since.

He contemplated how different his mother's homecoming had been compared to the one he expected now. Everyone he had ever cared about was either dead, believed him to be dead, or was responsible for lies. Despite Redbeard's optimism that he would be able to reclaim his throne, Colin wasn't as sure. He wasn't the fighter his sister was. He wasn't as cunning as his mother. He wasn't as loyal as Jameston had been. The thought of his friend sent a chill down his spine. By all accounts, the mad king had executed his friends. They had died trying to rescue him. It was time that he no longer had to be rescued.

"How far until we reach land?" Colin whispered.

"Shh," was the only response he received.

He stared off into the mist. He replayed the plan in his mind. First, they would make port on the beach right outside of Amadora. Then, Rikyah would lead them through the countryside—and the Dramadoonian mountains—until they reached the outskirts of Miliom. After that, they were on their own.

A hazy light in the distance caught Colin's attention. Despite the fog, the night sky was a brilliant labyrinth of stars. But, as Colin watched the light dip and bob, a terrible realization sank in.

"We've been discovered," he said hoarsely. When no one responded, he gripped one of Rikyah's people by the arm—Zeph—and said, "Someone's discovered us."

The silver-haired elf glanced in the direction Colin was staring. His already pale face paled even further as he watched the light bob, as if on waves. He wasted no time as he drew a silver dagger from his belt and slipped soundlessly into the water. The fog was too thick now for Colin to see if he resurfaced.

He inched forward in the boat. It rocked precariously, sloshing water into the base of the boat. Colin's stomach rolled with the waves, his skin turning clammy. Gripping the ledge of the ship's side, Colin eased himself into the still-warm seat that

Zeph had just vacated.

One of the men Redbeard had recruited leaned towards him and whispered, "What's happening here?"

Colin gulped down his fear. He knew there wasn't time to waste thinking about whether they'd make a mistake. If a Szarmian soldier had seen them, they needed to act quickly before a messenger could be sent to Miliom.

"Someone's seen us," he whispered, pointing towards the bobbing light. During the short time between when Zeph had jumped into the water and now, the light had made great progress in their direction.

"Oy!" the man shouted, spittle flying from his lips. "Look over there!"

Their company in the other two boats began clamoring noisily. Colin slapped his hand on his forehead. "So much for the element of surprise," he whispered as he sought out Redbeard in the dark. The mist was too thick for him to make the barkeep, even if he was a giant among men. Sighing, Colin drew his sword and watched at the boat approached.

It floated to their position. Colin squinted his eyes as the boat clipped their bow. The impact sent a shock through Colin's legs as he stood to address whoever manned the other vessel. He had just opened his mouth to speak with Zeph popped his head over the side of the ship.

"Well, I guess we have another boat now," he said.

Redbeard chuckled. Colin would have known that laugh anywhere by now.

"You're sure they were alone?" Rikyah asked from the boat adjacent to Colin's. Her voice held an edge to it that made Colin shiver.

"Yes," Zeph replied as he hoisted himself back into the Colin's ship.

"Who were they?" she asked. "What sigils did they bear?"

"Szarmians," he paused, "three of them. All armed."

"Alright then," Rikyah said. She lit a lantern. Its light illuminated the area around her boat and cast shadows on the rest. "We need three volunteers to take command of the Szarmian boat."

No one spoke.

"Well?" she snarled. "Who will it be?"

Still, no one volunteered.

"Listen here, men, fail to take a spot on that boat and I'll be sure to send ya overboard."

"Oh, that's no way to talk to them, Rikyah," Redbeard laughed. "You have to make them feel understood. Appreciated, even."

Although Colin couldn't see the glare, he could feel the cold tension in the air. His shoulders tensed as he waited for Rikyah to respond.

"You could be the first to go, Redbeard."

It happened so quickly that Colin barely registered the man sitting next to him draw his sword before all six of the soldiers were standing with their weapons pointed in Rikyah's direction.

"Honestly, Redbeard, I would have thought you'd train your men better than this," Rikyah scoffed.

Colin rested his hand on the hilt of his own sword. He glanced between Zeph, the soldier standing next to him, and the shadow he knew to be Rikyah. No one moved. For all Colin could tell, no one breathed.

The hair on Colin's arms prickled just as an arrow whistled past his ear. He jolted, rocking the boat and toppling the soldier standing behind him into the water just as another arrow dug into the wood where the soldier had just been standing.

Torches flickered to life around them, revealing a fleet of

twelve boats. Each one carried eight men. Colin scanned the boats for any sign of who they belonged to. They bore no banners, no sigils, to identify them. Their opponents' faces were masked with black cloth. Their clothes were a mixture of styles representing cultures from the Island Nations as well as Dramadoon, Lunameed, and Szarmi.

Colin glanced in Rikyah's direction. With the added torchlight, he could clearly see her face. He wasn't exactly sure what he had been expecting, but it certainly wasn't the wide, toothy grin she bore now. His jaw dropped as she lowered her bow and deftly dived into the water.

She resurfaced moments later in front of the boat closest to Colin's. Her muscled arms bulged as pulled herself out of the water and onto the enemy boat. She walked right up to one of the men and slapped him on the cheek. Colin sucked in a sharp breath as he waited for the armed men to attack.

Nothing happened.

Colin gripped his sword tighter as he took a step towards the stern of his boat. He stumbled as the boat shook and nearly fell overboard. He heard the soldier standing behind him snigger. Cursing beneath his breath, Colin sank to knees in attempt to save what dignity he had left.

"You should have sent word that you'd be passing through here," a distinctly feminine voice said.

Colin lifted his head just in time to see the person Rikyah slapped remove her mask and hood. Long, curly blonde hair cascaded over her shoulder as she shook her hair free. Her hair was so thick that it reminded Colin of a lion's mane. Her eyes were a stunning shade of jade green set in a face of pure bronze.

"I didn't know until two days ago," Rikyah responded. Though her stance was one of ease, Colin sensed the tension in her words.

"What? And the first thing you do to show me greeting is to slap me?" the girl feigned offense, but Colin could hear the underlying amusement in her words.

"You left me alone in that inn, stole my purse—and my horse, I might add—and you expect me to what, kiss your ass the first time I see you again?"

The woman belted out a hearty laugh as she clapped Rikyah on the shoulder.

"You wouldn't have me any other way," she said as she batted her eyes at Rikyah.

The masked men lowered their weapons as the woman raised her fist high in the sky. One by one, the boats extinguished their torches and slipped into the shadows as silently as they had come. Colin clung to his sword like a lifeline he wasn't ready to give up. He narrowed his eyes at the one remaining enemy boat.

"Do you attack all the ships crossing Amadoon Lake these days, Andra?" Rikyah asked, one hand on her hip.

"Best looting in the whole of Mitier."

Rikyah pursed her lips at that. "The people crossing these waters are either trying to escape persecution or have nothing left to live for. Stealing from them is akin to stealing from a blind beggar on the streets."

"A profitable beggar on the streets then," Andra retorted. "Don't get all high and mighty on me, Rikyah. You're no better than the rest of us, despite what you might think."

A cold wind whipped across the boats, sending a shudder down Colin's spine.

Rikyah let out an exasperated sigh before saying, "There's no need to get defensive, Andra. I just wanted to make sure you understood who you were stealing from."

"And why are you here, on these waters, then?" the woman countered. "Why are you in the dead of night?"

"What else?" Rikyah said. "Smuggling." She shrugged her shoulders, her gaze fixated on Andra.

Andra cast a glance over the small entourage of boats still bobbing in their general vicinity. "What do you have?" she smacked her lips as she spoke. Colin had the impression that he was watching a snake prepare its venomous attack.

"The usual fair," Rikyah replied dismissively.

Despite the cold, sweat dripped down Colin's brow. He shuddered as the wind picked up, rocking the boat. His stomach roiled as he tried to calm his rampaging heart.

"How much?"

"One hundred and fifty gold doubloons."

Andra whistled at the sum. "Who'd you find to pay you that?"

"You know a smuggler can never reveal their sponsors," Rikyah said as she flipped one of her jeweled daggers in her hand. The movement was practiced, calm even. Colin followed the blade as it slid through the air and then swan dived, hilt first, back into Rikyah's hand.

"I tell you what," Andra said as she continued to look over the remaining boats. "I'll strike a deal with you. Give me, oh let's say, twenty-five percent of the cut and I'll let the rest of your team live."

Rikyah snorted at the offer. "You're not going to hurt my team," she said as she continued to flip the blade into the air.

"I'm not?" Andra asked, disbelief dripping from her words like honey.

"No," Rikyah replied, "you're not."

Colin blinked.

He didn't see it happen, didn't know how it had happened. But there she was, holding her jeweled dagger to Andra's throat, her scarred eye pulsing in the flickering light of the torch. The blade was so close to her throat that Colin could see a thin line of blood pooling on Andra's neck.

Her guards—all two of them—stood with bows drawn. Instead of pointing them at Rikyah, one was aimed right at the waifish girl, Kaila. The other one had his arrow notched and pointed straight at Colin. He gulped, the hand on his sword shaking.

"It would be a shame to mar such a beautiful face," Rikyah crooned as she slid the dagger upwards. Andra did not fight against her. In fact, Colin got the sense that the woman rather enjoyed being toyed with by Rikyah. A sensual smile slipped over her face as she pressed more firmly into her captor. Rikyah's voice turned cold as she commanded, "Tell your men to lower their weapons."

Andra said nothing.

Rikyah dug her dagger into Andra's flesh. A gush of blood seeped from the wound. Andra barely flinched. Her eyes were wild as she leaned her head back and licked at Rikyah's face.

Rikyah snarled and pulled away from Andra slightly. Unfortunately, it was enough space for Andra to step onto Rikyah's foot before ducking out her grasp. She slammed her elbow into Rikyah's nose in one, swift motion. Her nose bleeding, Rikyah thrust herself at Andra with a vicious cry. Their entwined bodies shot over the side of the boat and splashed into the water.

Colin saw the look pass between the two guards before he saw the man loose his arrow. Without pausing to think, he held his sword in front of his face like a shield. Luckily for him, the arrow ricocheted off the sword and into the water. Unluckily, he didn't have to time to consider his luck as another arrow flew past him towards the man still standing behind him. He was not so lucky.

Colin launched himself into the water. It was so cold his entire body felt numb on impact. But, he knew he couldn't linger too long. Pushing himself through the water, Colin reached the bowmen's boat. *For Szarmi,* he thought as he heaved himself out of the water.

He flopped onto the boat's floor, water dripping into his eyes only to come nose-to-nose with the first of the bowmen. His eyes were open and staring blankly at him. Colin gasped and scooted away. A circular indent covered the man's temple. Bruising spread out from the indent. Colin's eyes roamed over the dead bowman until they landed on a fist-sized rock on the deck beside the man.

Grasping the rock, Colin read the inscription he knew would be written on it. 'Better luck next time, pig.'

"'Bout time you got here," Zeph said, pulling Colin's attention away from the rock. He swung his sword at the second bowman's feet, narrowly missing his mark. "Care to give me a hand?"

"Right," Colin mumbled as he stood. Still shaking, Colin swung his sword at the bowman. He could smell vanilla. Hear the flute playing in the background. See her dead, blue eyes staring up at him. And, he nearly gagged on his own vomit as he leaned over the side of the boat and spilled his guts.

"Tarnation!" Zeph bellowed. Colin barely heard the man over the pounding of his own heart in his ears.

He had killed her.

He vomited again. Well, it was a dry heave, as his stomach muscles contracted but only the tiniest amount of bile spewed from his lips. He wiped at his face with the back of his hand. Tears stung his eyes. *You're weak. You'll always be weak.* The words repeated in his thoughts. His mother's words.

"Colin?" Rikyah asked. A firm hand gripped his shoulder.

"Are you alright?"

Her face was a mixture of concern and anger as she peered into his eyes. Her damp hair clung to her skin and her scar seemed to glow in the dim light as she leaned closer to him. She was so close, in fact, that Colin could smell the garlic and onions on her breath from her lunch.

"Can you hear me?"

Colin squeezed his eyes shut. Her face still lingered there. His throat bobbed as he whispered, "I'm sorry."

A sigh. Cracking one eye open he saw Rikyah searching his face. "I'm sorry," he said again.

"For what?" she asked, her hand still grasping his shoulder.

"I should've helped. I could've..." he trailed off when he saw her expression.

"Tell me what you saw," she whispered to him.

"Nothing," he lied.

She raised an eyebrow at him, the movement elongating the sunburst of scars stretching over her skin. Colin broke eye contact with her. He knew his cheeks were flushing, knew he was being weak.

"I'm sorry," he repeated.

"Colin, I need you to tell me what you saw," her voice was compassionate, yet unyielding.

"I saw her," he whispered. "I saw her mangled body. Her eyes. I saw her beautiful, lively eyes empty of everything.""Hush," Rikyah said, her voice soothing. She wrapped her arm around his shoulder. "We cannot change the things we've done in the past, Colin. We can only choose to do things differently in the future."

His shoulders sagged.

"If you are to be king, and I believe you will, you will need to learn how to get past this barrier." She cradled him in her arms. "I promise you this, Colin. We will help you. I will help you."

He nodded into the crook of her arm. She patted him on the back as she silently held him. No one, not even Redbeard, interrupted them.

They reached the Szarmian beaches just as the first rays of sunlight crept over the horizon. The mist dissipated in the morning light, creating a clear path to the rocky beach. Colin shielded his eyes with his hand as he peered out over the short expanse of water. He scanned the beach and bordering tree line for any sign of the Szarmian guards he knew would be stationed there.

Nothing. Not even a curl of smoke from a night fire showed signs of life. Colin glanced at Redbeard's boat. The old barkeep was looking back at him, his expression grim. Katalina, the pigtailed member of Rikyah's crew, placed a heavy looking rock in her slingshot. Catching his eye, she winked at him. Colin blushed as he turned to face the beach once more.

Birds cawed overhead. A few fish leapt from the water as they glided through its depths. Already, he could smell the scent of fruit hanging from the nearby trees. And, if he really concentrated, he thought he could hear the whir of machines in the nearby village of Amadora. A sense of ease washed over him. He was home.

Their boats crunched into the underwater embankment. Colin jerked forward at the impact. Rubbing the back of his neck, Colin looked around the beach. He had never been to this corner of his kingdom before. His father had never deemed this bit of land all that essential. Although they were still closer to the north than they were to the south, the land was lush here. Plants of every size, shape, and color filled in the gaps between the trees. Mountains crested lofty clouds in the distance. Colin knew, from his memorization of maps, that this stretch of land still belonging to Szarmi was surrounded on two sides by mountains owned and occupied by the Dramadoonians.

He looked to the mountains now, his thoughts wandering to that night, all those months ago, when the Mad King of Lunameed had slaughtered his own people. The Dramadoonian royals had offered him a deal. Send Amaleah to them and they would side with Szarmi in the coming wars. He wondered what they would make of his situation now.

"This way," Rikyah said, motioning them to follow her across the rocks to the western-most point of the beach. The rocks were slippery and difficult to cross, but Colin managed. Redbeard huffed beside him, his irregular breathing a welcome relief to the sound of Colin's own thoughts.

"How does it feel, lad?"

Colin glanced at Redbeard. The barkeep's face was flushed and sweat ran in streams down his cheeks. But, there was an intensity in the man's blue eyes that made Colin consider the older man's words.

He shrugged. He knew it was a noncommittal answer, but he couldn't think of anything to say. He'd left Szarmi with his best friend, a troop of men, and the hope of a better world. He was returning with the loss of Jameston, the memory of his men being slaughtered by Szarmian soldiers, and a lost crown.

Redbeard clasped Colin's shoulder in his meaty hand. Even through his layers of clothing, Colin could feel the man's heat.

"If you want to take back your kingdom, you'll have to do better than that," the barkeep said. "You're part of a rebellion now, Colin. Best not forget that."

Colin was about to respond when Rikyah held up a fist and the small amount of chatter coursing through the band of men silenced. She pointed ahead of them, her ears twitching slightly.

Katalina drew her slingshot, her muscled arms bulging as she looked past Rikyah into the trees beyond. She crouched low to the ground. Her red hair, pulled back in customary pigtails, bounced as she dug into her rock pouch. Colin watched as Katalina discerned which rock she wanted with only her fingertips to guide her. She selected a round stone that was larger than her fist.

Her pointed ears perked and she leveled the slingshot towards the woods. Zeph, his tall, slender frame clouding Colin's periphery vision, muttered beneath his breath. Colin squinted his eyes, hoping to see what the others did. All he saw were the tall trees waving in the breeze.

Colin crouched lower to the ground. His foot slipped on the wet stones, sending him crashing to the ground. He yelped in pain as his ankle scraped against the coarse rock. Rikyah looked back at him, her eyes dark. A shadow shot across the morning sky. Colin watched in horror as it arched downwards and straight into the eye of one of the men guarding him. Blood gushed from the wound as the man slowly sank to his knees. His lips moved up and down as he fell forward and did not rise again.

Katalina released a screeching battle cry as she sent her shot hurdling towards the trees.

"Colin!" Redbeard grumbled as he shielded Colin's body with his own. "We have to take shelter. Can ya walk?"

Gingerly, Colin tapped at his aching ankle. Searing pain crept up his foot at his touch. When he brought his hand back up, it was coated in a thin sheen of blood.

"I'm not sure," he whispered. "My ankle."

More arrows rained down around them. Rikyah had her bow

out and was firing arrows in rapid succession. Her movements were fluid, almost elegant. She fired more quickly even than the automatic crossbow that had been used during the second assassination attempt against him. He wondered if they would ever be able to develop technology that fired arrows as quickly as Rikyah did naturally.

"Come on, son," Redbeard said, half-pulling, half-supporting Colin as they stumbled toward the mountain range to their left.

Screams echoed across the beach. Colin knew he needed to help their small band of rebels against the soldiers hidden within the trees. He knew the tactics the soldiers would use. And, he knew how to combat them. He just needed to reach Rikyah.

Redbeard poured whiskey from his flask on the wound, sending a shiver up Colin's spine. Colin ripped a strip of cloth from his shirt and made quick work of binding his ankle. Then, he tried to stand. He wobbled slightly and the pain was nearly unbearable, but there wasn't time to waste. Grinding his teeth, Colin forced himself to dash towards where Rikyah stood.

Her rapid-fire did not falter. She did not look at him as he took a place beside her. Fewer arrows sailed towards them now. Colin knew that could only mean one of two things. Either Katalina and Rikyah had reduced their number significantly, or—more likely—the soldiers had abandoned their post to circle around them.

Colin glanced at the rocky mountain to their left. Crevices several feet above them would provide the perfect cover for the Szarmian soldiers to attack from. They knew this land. They knew the paths to take. He squinted at the tree line again. It was too far for him to see much of anything but there, at the edge closest to the mountain, he saw darker shadows weaving through trees.

"Run!" He shouted.

"What?" Katalina asked, her freckled face flushed as she rushed to stand beside him.

"We need to get into the trees. Now!" he yelled.

"Colin!" Rikyah screamed.

He ignored her as he made a mad dash for the trees. He wielded his sword before him and prayed to the Light that whatever force had protected him thus far wouldn't fail him now.

Zeph and Katalina were on either side of him before he had made it more than a few feet. With his mangled ankle, he was more hobbling along than anything else.

"What are you doing?" Katalina asked, accusation in her voice. "We were wearing them down!"

"No, you weren't," he said. His voice came out in puffs.

"What do ya mean, 'no we weren't?'" she asked. "We were takin' them down."

He swept his free arm across the mountain on their left. "They abandoned their position in the trees."

Zeph turned his attention to the mountain. He maintained his pace with them, his feet remaining steady on the rocky terrain. Colin only wished he could be so graceful. He clenched his jaw as his foot caught on an upturned rock. He stumbled, but Zeph shot an arm out, catching Colin before he fell.

"Thanks," Colin mumbled as he righted himself and began running again.

"There," Zeph said, pointing to a specific location. "I can hear them taking position."

"Told you," Colin replied.

Zeph's lips pulled upward at the retort, but he said nothing as he raised one hand and made a gesture back to Rikyah.

"I think we had best get you out of the open," he said before plucking Colin from the ground and slinging him over his back.

Colin fought against him, but he was no match against the elf's strength.

Katalina went ahead of them. Her slingshot out. She released a whir of pellets as she reached the edge of the trees. Releasing another battle cry, Katalina dropped her slingshot into her belt pouch and drew a dagger. She was nothing but a blur as she weaved between the trees. Men fell in her wake.

By the time Zeph reached the trees with Colin on his back, all but one of the soldiers were dead. Their blank eyes stared up at Colin. *These were my men*, he reminded himself. *There is no other way*, he thought. He had to keep thinking that. He needed to believe that his father had chosen him to rule for a reason. If nothing else, he would prove to his people that their rightful king still lived.

Thomas and Kaila arrived moments later. Thomas placed a knife in Kaila's hands before urging her to stay hidden as he bolted towards the mountain path abutting the trees.

"Wait," Colin called after him, but it was too late. He was already gone.

The entire skirmish was over within a matter of moments. In the end, none of the Szarmian soldiers who had attacked them were left alive.

"Was that really necessary?" Colin asked when Rikyah finally strode through the trees. Thomas, Zeph, and Katalina were covered in Szarmian blood. They had been the only ones to engage the soldiers in hand-to-hand combat.

Rikyah shrugged. "These men were going to kill you. You would not have been able to convince them of your sovereignty, Colin. You need to let go of that notion. I doubt any of these met you or knew you personally. To them, you would have only been a Lunameedian impersonating their dead king."

"But there could have been a chance," Colin began.

"Listen to me, Colin Stormbearer. You may, one day, be a great hero to your people. You may be a great king, a great warrior. But today, you are a young, untested boy. If you want to reclaim your throne, these are the prices that have to be paid."

Colin knew she was right. Knew that, if the soldiers had been allowed to live they would have fought against him the entire time. It was what they had been trained to do. What he had been trained to do. Still, the killing of his soldiers left a hole in his heart that he wasn't sure he would ever be able to fill again.

Rikyah turned to walk away from him, but Colin caught her hand. "Will I ever be able to forgive myself for killing my people? Will they forgive me?"

Rikyah gave him a sad smile. Colin swallowed hard as he waited for her response.

She squeezed his hand as she said, "Welcome home, Colin."

Chapter Twenty-Four
Szarmi, Mitier

Rikyah led what remained of their group through the backroads of Szarmi. They kept the Beoscuret Mountains to their left. Rikyah claimed the wall of stone was good protection against surprise raids by the Szarmian armies. They had been traveling on foot for eight days now and still they had not reached the eastern bank of the Borad. From there, it would take another three days to reach Miliom.

Colin's feet ached. Despite his thick socks, his boots chafed against his heels. At times, he felt the hot liquid pop of his blisters when the pressure of his boot against them grew too much. He didn't complain. There was no good to be had in stating the obvious. They were a ragged group of rebels seeking an almost assuredly lost cause. His lost cause. So, every night before going to bed, Colin poured alcohol over the deepest and bloodiest of the wounds. The spirits stung like a thousand bees stinging him all at once, but Colin forced himself to bite onto a branch. If there was anything he had learned from his time at Fort Pelid, it was that a true leader demonstrated grit, especially in the direst of times. It was time for him to stop being the weakling his mother thought he was and be the ruler he had been born to be. Only Redbeard witnessed Colin peeling his soiled socks from his feet and binding the blisters each night. The old barkeep never seemed to even notice Colin's discomfort. Each night, he would strike a match and light a small amount of Mureechi before falling into his blankets for a bit of 'quick shuteye.'

Although his ankle had stopped bleeding on the second day, it was tender to the touch. Even if Colin barely grazed it, pain would shoot through his entire foot. Kaila had examined it. Her waifish fingers scrolled over page after page in her books as she sought a solution for his pain. All she found were vague references to cracked bones that simply needed to mend on their own. It didn't help that his nights were plagued with nightmares he couldn't explain to the others. Each morning, he'd awoken with dry, red eyes, a pounding headache, and vague memories filled with dark shadows.

To this, Kaila had offered him hot water mixed with valerian root and lemon. He'd gagged on the first sip he'd taken, but downed the rest of the mixture in one long gulp. That night—last night—was the first time he'd slept without a single nightmare. Still, he rubbed at his eyes with the back of his hand as he peered down the narrow path Rikyah had created.

His mind hummed with a flurry of thoughts. *What if Captain Conrad doesn't believe it's me?* he thought. His lips turned into a scowl as he considered what his next move would be. The captain was his last hope. His only hope.

"Let's make camp here tonight," Rikyah said.

Surprised, Colin halted. The sun was still above the line of trees. They could safely travel another hour before breaking camp in the twilight hour. Sweat dribbled down his face as he assessed their surroundings. Absentmindedly, he wiped it from his face with his sleeve. He'd almost forgotten how stifling the heat was in Szarmi, even during the traditionally colder months.

He'd been so consumed by his thoughts that he hadn't heard the faint chortle of the River Borad in the distance. He knew the closer they approached that the chortle would transform into a roar. He could almost imagine it now. The spray of the white; the muddy, putrid smell of dozens of fish swimming upstream; the miniscule bugs swarming around his face: these were the things Colin associated with the Borad. But, beyond the river, Colin knew his city was waiting for him.

"Tomorrow, we'll begin following the river until it forks. It's a six-day journey on foot from here. Once we arrive at the fork, you'll be on your own," Rikyah said as she approached him.

Colin nodded in response. The idea of Rikyah and her band of thieves leaving them scared him beyond what he was willing to admit. Awkwardly, Colin stared down at his feet, unsure how to respond.

"Listen, Colin," she continued. He glanced up at her, still unable to formulate the words brewing in his mind. "If this whole ruling a blood-thirsty kingdom thing doesn't work out for you, you'll always have a spot in my crew."

"You can't be serious," Colin finally said.

"'Course not," Rikyah laughed. "You're too scrawny to be on my squad."

Colin raised an eyebrow at this.

She punched him on the arm and said, "Naw, I need to take that statement back. I'd smuggle you across the border again, but then dump you in the ocean first chance I got."

"Rikyah," Redbeard boomed.

"Redbeard," she responded, shrugging her shoulders.

"Don't be tryin' to recruit me protégé. I've spent too much time cultivating this one for you to steal him away and turn into one of yer kind."

"One of my kind?" Rikyah repeated, pressing her hand to her

chest. "Why, Redbeard, I would never. Us scoundrels never recruit anyone. No need to. You know the recruits come to us."

Redbeard's only response was to puff on his pipe.

Colin huddled in his blanket as he stared into the fire. The flames danced, sending glowing embers into the night sky in a swirl of vibrancy before disappearing into the abyss. In a way it was comforting. It reminded Colin that, no matter how brightly one shines, we all end in the same darkness. And then the wind shifted and a cloud of pungent smelling smoke enveloped him. He coughed, his eyes watering.

"Smoke always did follow beauty," Rikyah remarked.

Colin couldn't see anything through the haze of smoke, but he could hear the humor in her voice.

"So that's why it never blows in your direction," Redbeard chortled.

The wind changed direction yet again and Colin was given a moment of reprieve. His eyes still stung and he knew he would smell of the pungent odor until he was able to bathe again. *Gears*, he thought, *no wonder they mock me*.

"Aren't Szarmian monarchs supposed to be all burly and macho and stuff?" Thomas asked as he whittled away at a twisted and knotted branch. Despite the growing pile of wood chips growing at Thomas's feet, it was too early to tell what he was shaping the branch into.

"Yeah," Katalina said as she bit into an apple. Juice sprayed from the fruit and dribbled down her chin. She smacked her lips loudly and ran her tongue across her cheeks and chin—as far as it would reach—to gobble up the juice. Colin was, at once, appalled at her lack of decorum and highly impressed with the agility of her tongue. "Szarmi is known for its military prowess." She wiped her lips with the back of her hand. "As far as I can tell you're just a pretty boy who looks good in a uniform."

Colin felt the heat rise in his cheeks. He had never, in all his years at Fort Pelid, under the tutelage of the best dualist in the kingdom, or within the grasp of his mother's temper felt as targeted as he did now. He wanted to throttle them all. He wanted to prove himself worthy of the throne he was determined to fight for—determined to claim as his own. It was his birthright, but, more than that, it was his duty to protect the people of his kingdom. He balled his hands into tight fists, his nails biting into the soft spots of his flesh. *How dare they*, he seethed.

"Eh, now, don't be treatin' the new king of Szarmi so poorly there, friends."

All eyes turned towards Redbeard as he popped his pipe back in his mouth. He blew rings of smoke into the night sky as he, presumably, considered the sister moons and stars. Colin gaped at the man. None of the others spoke. Their silence was louder than a thousand voices in the chilly night air. Despite the fire, Colin shivered beneath his blanket. He still couldn't fathom why Redbeard was so devoted to helping him reclaim his throne. After all, his ancestors had terrorized the Lunameedian people for centuries, even before the Wars of Darkness. He peered over the members of Rikyah's troupe. Their support didn't make any sense.

"How did you come by your scar?" he asked abruptly.

Rikyah shot a glance at him that seemed to say, 'bugger off,' but Colin stared her down. Her lip curled into a sneer as she said, "That is not a tale for a bedtime story."

Colin shrugged his shoulders. "I see no children here who are terrified of the dark."

She rolled her shoulders and absently flipped one of her jeweled daggers in her hand. It always landed hilt first in her palm. Colin gulped as he waited for her respond. It was one thing to think of a witty comeback, he decided; however, it is quite another thing to deliver the quip well.

"I'm a smuggler, yer Lordship," she emphasized the 'lordship' as if it were a slur. "Injuries are merely part of the job."

"But it's so distinctive," Colin pressed.

Zeph and Katalina collectively sucked in a breath. Colin noticed their response to his retort and felt ice form in his veins. He needed Rikyah more than she needed—or even wanted—him. He chided himself for being such a dolt and opened his mouth to apologize when she raised her fist in the air, instantly quieting him.

"This scar," she said as she trailed a finger down the coiled flesh bursting from her eyepatch, "was caused by one of the cruelest men I've ever met." Her fingers traced the edges of the eyepatch and Colin swallowed hard. He could only imagine the emptiness that lay behind the patch. "I earned it during a dual to the death. Clearly, I was the victor."

Colin found himself nodding. Her tale was a short one and left much to be desired, but he found himself engrossed in it.

"That's it?" he asked when it was clear that she was not going to provide any more details about the dual.

"That's it," she replied before standing up and lumbering towards her pack. "I think it's best for us to try and get some shut eye before departing in the morning. Zeph, you take first watch. I'll take next."

She didn't look to make sure the rest of the group followed her orders. They all did, even Redbeard. Colin watched them all—except Zeph, who drew his bow and settled down before the fire—clamor for their packs and pull out their extra blankets. No one spoke. Eventually, Colin did the same.

Chapter Twenty-Five

The Silver Moon Camp, Encartia

"She's dangerous."

"She's not. She just doesn't know how to control her powers."

"How can you say that? Did you see what she did to the centaur? Imagine if that had been…"

"Enough."

Amaleah's eyes fluttered open at the sound of voices in the room. Her limbs felt numb, as if she hadn't consumed enough water that day. Her head swam as she sat up to see Nylyla, Elaria, and Yosef conversing with heads bowed in the corner. She squinted at them, her vision hazy. Nausea swept over her and she clamped her hands over her cramping abdomen. The coppery scent of blood and singed flesh filled her. There had been so much blood. She hadn't meant to.

"Where is he?" she croaked, her parched lips splitting along cracks. She sucked on her bottom lip to clear the blood before pleading, "Please, tell me he's alright."

Nylyla pulled herself away from the others and knelt beside Amaleah's bed. Her brows knit as she peered into Amaleah's eyes. There were tears in those eyes. Amaleah swallowed the lump that formed in her throat as she waited for Nylyla to tell her what she feared she already knew.

"Just tell me," she said, shutting her eyes tightly.

The waifish elf ran her chilled, slender fingers over Amaleah's forehead. She smelled of mint leaves and dew on a summer night.

"It is too early to tell if he will live or not," the elf whispered.

Amaleah heard the creak of floorboards as someone else approached her bed.

"What happened?" Elaria demanded. Her voice was tight with thinly veiled distain coating each word.

Amaleah stared straight into the matriarch's eyes. "I don't know what happened."

Elaria sniffed. "Of course not." She glared down at Amaleah. "You are nothing more than an untrained child.""Of no fault of her own," Nylyla chided. She did not flinch as the older woman turned her icy gaze upon her.

"You will remember your place here, Nylyla."
"Stop," Amaleah whispered. She pushed her hands down to lift herself from the bed. It was then that she noticed her hand, which had been so mangled before, was now completely healed.

"What?" she asked as she examined her flesh.

"The only thing we can conclude is that your flare of magic healed your wounds," Elaria said. Her voice was like an ice pick slowly chipping away at what remained of Amaleah's resolve.

"I don't understand," Amaleah whispered.

Elaria sighed loudly and rolled her eyes at the younger woman. "Honestly, Amaleah, you will need to be much quicker at learning if you are to be the Harbinger of the Light so many of our brethren have talked about for all these centuries."

Amaleah mouthed a small 'oh' before shaking her head and saying, "I want to learn."

"The first lesson: your magic has the ability to heal your own wounds and do wondrous things. But, until you gain control of your abilities, you will continue harming others, just like you did today."

Amaleah looked down at her hands. She hadn't meant to harm him. She didn't know where the visions of her father emanated from and, in some ways, it didn't matter. She was at fault. She had lost control of her powers and she had hurt her friend.

"The flute," she murmured softly as she replayed the day's events in her mind.

"The flute is none of your concern now, child," Elaria said as she dusted her tunic off and began walking towards the doors.

"But," Amaleah began, a retort rushing to her lips.

Elaria turned a hard-eyed gaze upon her and Amaleah promptly closed her mouth. She left the room without another word. Ice filled Amaleah's veins as the matriarch disappeared into the hallway. Now that she had slipped through her father's grasp, she was determined to never allow another person to rule her. She would claim her own destiny.

"If you're feeling up to it, I think it was time that we began teaching you how to control your powers," Nylyla said. Her voice was smooth and flowed like a gentle stream over Amaleah's ears. She immediately felt at peace.

"Let's begin" Amaleah responded.

Nylyla led Amaleah to a sparring ring on the outskirts of the encampment. Yosef trailed behind them. His shadow shielded Amaleah from onlookers as they slipped through the crowd. She was thankful for his presence.

Trees lined the circle of stones separating the ring from the forest. Amaleah stopped dead in her tracks as they entered the ring. The most beautiful man she had ever seen grappled with a woman. His ebony hair was tied back with a ribbon the color of the ocean. His bare chest bore a strange scar on his left side. It nearly consumed the entirety of the skin over his heart, though he was moving too quickly for her to distinguish what the scar was. Her eyes trailed over his toned body. She quickly looked away, knowing that her cheeks would bear the evidence of her thoughts.

"Are you unwell?" Nylyla asked, stretching out a hand to stroke Amaleah's forehead.

"No, I'm fine," Amaleah replied quickly. "Just a little winded from the walk." She fanned herself with her hands as if to demonstrate the veracity of the lie. Nylyla raised an eyebrow at her, but shrugged her shoulders before turning her attention back to the sparring match.

The woman brought her elbow up in a quick jab to the man's jaw. He spat blood before rushing at her and tackling her to the ground. The woman struggled against him, slamming her fists into the soft spots around his collar bone, abdomen, and groin. He grunted in pain, but continued to pin her to the ground. A few seconds later, she conceded the match.

The man slumped back, his chest heaving upwards with each breathe he took. The woman clapped as she sat up.

"Well done, Nikailus," she said. "You are learning quickly."

"I learn from the best," he replied, smiling.

He turned his attention towards Amaleah and Nylyla. Amaleah's cheeks still burned from the elf's line of questioning, but she found she couldn't look away from his gaze. His eyes met hers and her stomach fluttered in a way she had only ever read about. Her lips formed a small 'oh' before she quickly looked down.

Now wasn't the time for this line of thinking. She chided herself for her wondering thoughts as her eyes noticed a series of faint scars stretching over his toned abdomen.

"Are you sure you're alright?" Nylyla whispered from the corner of her mouth. "You really are quite red, Amaleah. If you need to rest, we can come back to the ring later."

"No," Amaleah said quickly, her eyes darting up to Nikailus's face. He searched her face and the concentration with which he looked at her left her feeling bare. "I'm fine," she reaffirmed.

"Alright," Nylyla responded, though her tone indicated her reticence. "As long as you're sure…"

"I am."

"Amaleah Bluefischer," the elf in the ring said. Her voice was hard and her face was, if possible, even harder. Amaleah gasped as she noticed the jagged scars bulging from the elf's cheeks.

The elf raised an eyebrow at her as she flipped a dagger in the air. She had several belts strapped across her chest and hips. Metal glinted in sunlight, casting strips of white light across the arena. "It is rude to stare, Princess."

Amaleah gasped again, this time from her humiliation. She clutched a hand to lips and stammered an apology.

"Is this how everyone reacts when they first meet you, Anno?" the man asked. His voice was like smooth velvet on a cold winter night.

"Pretty much," the elf responded as she caught a twirling dagger, hilt-first, from midair. She proffered the blade to Amaleah.

Gulping, Amaleah accepted the blade and stepped into the arena.

"Nikailus, meet Princess Amaleah Bluefischer of Lunameed. Amaleah, meet Nikailus Sindarthian of no title."

"Yet," Nikailus added. He winked at Amaleah as she

glanced up at him in surprise. She knew her cheeks must have been several shades darker, but she couldn't control her reaction to the sound of his voice.

Stop acting like a foolhardy youth, she scolded herself. She chewed on her bottom lip before holding out her hand to shake his. His fingers were cold as they trailed across her skin. Every fiber of her tingled at his touch. He stepped closer, close enough for her to smell the fresh scent of citrus and sandalwood.

"Pleasure," he said as his lips grazed her knuckles.

Amaleah nearly swooned. In fact, she might have, if it hadn't been for the two elves and Yosef standing there, watching them. Instead, Amaleah ripped her hand out of his and forced her attention onto Anno.

"Drink this," the elf said as she pressed a vial into Amaleah's hand. The milky-white liquid swirled inside the glass bottle.

"What is it?" Amaleah asked.

Anno sighed loudly. "Just do as I say, girl."

"I am no girl," Amaleah retorted, crossing her arms over her chest defiantly.

"Until you learn to control your temper, I will always consider you to be a 'girl,' girl."

Amaleah's jaw slackened at the elf's tone. Although she greatly desired to, she refrained from replying to the other woman's tone.

"You've got spunk, girl. That's a good thing, if there ever were one."

Amaleah beamed at the elf's words. She had not been anticipating praise. Despite her skill with the bow, she was certainly lacking in her staff and blade work.

"I'll return for her in two hours," Nylyla said as she began to stroll back down the path they'd come down. Amaleah watched her go, her shoulders sagging.

"Drink up," the elf said, her tone commanding.

Amaleah sniffed at the liquid and inhaled a whiff of what smelled like rotten eggs and fungi that had been sitting in the sun for too long. She coughed, her eyes watering slightly.

"There's no way in darkness that I am going to drink that," she said. She stoppered the vial and held it out to the woman.

"It's not so bad," the man said. His voice was deep and husky. It reminded Amaleah of the sound of a summer storm before it goes into total chaos. As a child, she had always enjoyed rushing outside to listen to the storm roll in and watch as the dark clouds billowed over the land. She stole a quick glance at him. He met her eyes and smiled at her.

"It smells disgusting," she said, wrinkling her nose in distaste.

"It tastes even worse," he replied, his tone neutral.

She looked between him and vial. "What does it do?" she asked.

"Dims your powers," the elf answered. "Now, drink up so that we can begin."

"But I thought the point of me being here was so that I could learn how to control my abilities," Amaleah protested. "Doesn't this defeat that purpose?"

The elf sighed heavily and rolled her eyes. "This is the first part of your training, Amaleah, but it is possibly the most crucial. You must learn to control your emotions or your powers will control you. All magic is born from the Light bound within us. You've probably heard it referred to as your soulfire."

Amaleah shrugged but said nothing.

The elf sighed again, her frustration evident in her exasperated breath. "Have you ever noticed that your magic is strongest when you are having an intense emotion?"

An image of the wildfire circling her. The smoke filling her eyes, and nose, and mouth. She couldn't breathe. She couldn't escape. Her father barreling down at her. *You'll always be fine.* A shiver ran down Amaleah's spine as the words reverberated through her. It was as if she were there again. She looked up at the elf, silver lining her eyes.

"Then you do know," the elf said. Her expression softened as she searched Amaleah's face. Still, she shoved the vial back into Amaleah's hand. "Now drink," she said.

Amaleah complied.

Ice coursed through her veins. She thought she screamed, but she couldn't be sure. All she could hear was the rushing of her own blood as the poison was pumped through her body. Her fingers went numb from the pain. Her teeth chattered. Her toes curled as the putrid liquid sloshed around her stomach.

A warm hand grasped her shoulder, steadying her as she nearly tottered over. She clamped one clammy hand down upon her supporter and felt the bile rise up the back of her throat. It burned. She coughed some more.

"Steady now," Nikailus whispered. His breath tickled her neck and momentarily made her forget the terrible pain in her gut and the ice in her veins. "It'll be alright," he said.

She clung to him like a babe. Tears slid down her cheeks and she moaned softly as he placed a cool cloth upon her brow. She wasn't sure where he'd gotten the cloth, but she was grateful.

Within seconds the poison passed through her system. She gulped in fresh air and let the calming sensation of staring up at the trees ease her rapidly beating heart into the steady tenor of a bass drum. Her mind cleared. The burning sensation ceased.

Hesitantly, Amaleah reached for the wild, uncontrollable side of her that she hid deep within. It was but a mere flicker compared to the burning star she normally found. She frowned at the realization that she had been made entirely normal.

"How long does the poison last?" she asked.

"The dosage we gave you will wear off within a matter of hours," the elf responded.

"Some take days," Nikailus offered. There was a tone to his voice that warned Amaleah not to cross the elves.

"Yes," Anno said, drawing a silver dagger from the bandolier that stretched across her chest. She flipped it in the air before catching it hilt first in her palm and instantly throwing it at a target several paces away. It dug into the heart of the bullseye.

"You're good at this," Amaleah said before instantly realizing how dumb that made her sound.

"And you will become even better," the elf replied, not even phased by Amaleah's naïve comment of amazement. "You may call me Anno, girl."

Anno tossed Amaleah and Nikailus staves. "Since you are both beginners, you will start with the beginning weapon."

Amaleah eyed her rod. It was long, but not so long that she couldn't hold it properly. Etchings had been carved into the wood and then sanded over until the entire length was smooth. Despite the carvings, it was smoother than any other staff she had ever used.

"This first test will just be to measure your skills. On my mark, I want you to fight until one of you is pushed out of the inner circle."

Amaleah looked down to find that a violet circle had been painted on the floor of the arena. It didn't look big enough for them to maneuver in, much less fight.

"You can't be serious," she said.

Instead of answering, Anno simply motioned for Nikailus to take his position within the smaller ring. Amaleah clutched the staff in two hands, her knuckles turning white from how tightly she held it.

She bit her bottom lip, considering. She didn't have time to be a coward, but, even after all the time she'd spent with Yosef and Thadius training, she was still so unsure of her abilities, especially after watching Nikailus strike Anno only moments before.

She looked up at her opponent. A lazy smirk covered his face and, when he caught her looking at him, he winked.

Amaleah pretended to gag before falling into the familiar stance Thadius had taught her. She swung her staff out in a wide, low strike. He jumped to avoid being struck in his ankles. She anticipated his rebuttal in time to bring her staff up and stop his staff from slamming into the top of her head.

Sweat beaded on her brow and rolled in her eyes. She blinked away the sting but did not allow herself to loosen her grip on her weapon. He tossed his staff from one hand to the other, his smile growing wider as Amaleah breathed in deeply. She watched the staff jump through the air. Saw his fingers wrap around the sturdy wood. Heard his heavy breathing. Felt the gentle breeze caress her bare shoulders. She lifted her chin to the breeze, welcoming its cooling effect.

He jabbed his staff at her abdomen in one, swift motion. She didn't have time to jump out of the way. The force of the impact on her gut sent her reeling. She doubled-over, dry heaving. His shadow flitted across her as he brought his staff up for the finishing blow.

Before he landed on her, Amaleah dropped her staff and propelled herself at him, feet first. His violet eyes widened in surprise as her feet connected with him and he fell to the ground. She heard the loud thunk of his head hitting the ground and smiled in satisfaction. Without pausing, she grabbed him by the hands and heaved him towards the purple line in the sand. He was heavier than she'd anticipated and she barely moved him an inch before his eyes fluttered open.

Amaleah gasped in surprise as Nikailus gripped her wrist in his hand while simultaneously kicking his feet up towards her already aching middle. The force of his kick sent her air born. For a single moment, she was suspended in air above him. He smirked at her again, the insufferable man, before she landed in a heap on the outside of the purple ring.

"Well done, Nikailus," Anno said, her voice imperious.

Nikailus stuck out a hand for Amaleah to take. Her eyes trailed up his arm, lingered on his scarred chest, and then finally met his gaze. There was no malice in his brilliant, violet eyes. Just warmth. She couldn't understand it. She wasn't sure she wanted to understand it. All she knew was that he made her feel at peace. Smiling, she took his hand.

Chapter Twenty-Six
Szarmian Countryside

They reached the river's fork exactly at the time Rikyah had predicted. There were only three days left in their journey to Miliom. Colin still wasn't sure what he would face upon his arrival, or if he would be able to win the trust of his captains. He had little hope that General Nabine would follow him. The general had been an admirer of his mother for quite some time now. Still, if he could even convince five or six of the army's twelve captains to join him, he would be able to reclaim his throne. He was sure of it.

The night was crisp as they crowded around the lone torch Rikyah had allowed them to light. Hidden in the shadows of a few straggling trees, they whispered their goodbyes in hushed voices. Rikyah and Redbeard feared, perhaps justifiably so, that with Fort Azoma being a day's ride from the river fork they needed to exhibit even more caution than usual. Redbeard had surprised them all when, two days earlier, he'd left camp in the wee hours of the morning only to rejoin them the next day when they broke for the midday meal. He explained that he'd ridden ahead to meet with one his spies.

"You have spies?" Colin asked, his innards cringing at the thought of revolutionary spies infiltrating his kingdom. Of course, he knew—and expected—Dramadoon, Lunameed, and even Borganda to send spies to the kingdom. He'd had little inclination that there were other stakeholders investing in intel.

"And be thankful that I do," Redbeard replied. He stroked his beard absently as he spoke. "You'll want to be hearin' what I discovered," he continued.

Colin folded his arms over his chest and waited for the old barkeep to reveal what he knew.

"Yer mother has convened a special session with the captains and generals of the realm."

"And?" Colin replied snidely.

"And," Redbeard said, raising an eyebrow at Colin's impudence, "they are rumored to all be stayin' in the palace."

This wasn't exactly news to Colin. His sister had sentenced him to die when she'd denounced him as a Lunameedian imposter on that bridge. She'd committed treason. Against him. Her own brother. Even if she believed he was dead, the most strategic move she could make upon her return to Miliom would be to call a council meeting of the army's commanders. It's exactly what their father would've done.

"You know I already had my suspicions…"

"Yes, yes," Redbeard said dismissively. "But now they're confirmed." He emphasized the confirmed part. Colin nodded, not fulling grasping what Redbeard was implying.

Redbeard sighed heavily when Colin offered no retort. "Fine," he fumed, "I think it's time that we discussed an alternative plan."

"The quickest way to gain an audience with my mother's council members—with the commanding officers—is to enter the throne room and declare my mother and sister liars," Colin growled. "We've been through this, Redbeard. It's the only choice I have."

"And what if I told you there could be another choice?" Redbeard queried. He tugged on his beard as he spoke. Colin had come to realize that this was Redbeard's tell. He'd seen him use multiple times, especially when he had a yearning to smoke on his mureechi pipe.

"I'm listening."

"I seem to recall you mentioning having a relationship of import with one, Captain Conrad."

"Yes, and," Colin interrupted.

"And he's here, boy."

Colin clenched his fists. He should have known Captain Conrad would be in attendance. He was the commanding officer in the army's training facility, after all. He would be needed to help prepare the men and women drafted when the time came for war. Even so, it would be nice to see a familiar face in the room.

"It'd be a great time to discuss changing some things in our plan, Colin," Redbeard said gruffly.

"I want to stick to the plan," Colin replied without the slightest hint of hesitation. "We made this plan together. It's a good plan."

"It's a terrible plan and you know it," Redbeard retorted. "Don't try to fool yourself into thinking we've developed something that will actually work, Colin. No one in this city is going to let you walk into your mother's throne room and let you denounce her. You'll be thrown into the dungeons quicker than you can spit." Redbeard, of course, spat into a copper cup when he finished his speech. Colin assumed it was for good measure.

"And what do you propose we do?" he quipped.

"I suggest that we take in as few of men as possible and seek out your Captain Conrad for support. He was your mentor, was he not?"

"Yes, but…"

"Then it's settled," Redbeard proclaimed before Colin had a chance to finish his thought. "We'll sneak in, find your captain, convince him of who ya are, and use him to persuade th'others to our cause."

"You make it sound so easy."

Redbeard shrugged. "If it were too easy there'd be more rebellions."

Colin hadn't been able to argue with that. Now, as he stood beneath the tranquil moons and listened to the gurgling of the Miliom River, he wondered if he were making the right choice. It was possible his sister would make a fine ruler. She was young, and terribly naïve, but she loved their kingdom almost as much as he did. But, it was too late to turn back.

Kaila, the waifish little elf, hugged Colin tightly. She wiped at her eyes as she turned her back on him. Colin pressed two fingers to his lips and held his hand out to hers in return. Thomas nodded at Colin before wandering off in the same direction as his daughter. Colin could hear the man grunt loudly as he wrapped his arms around Kaila's slender shoulders. "Promise me we'll see each other again," Kaila said into the night sky. Her voice carried on the wind. Colin nodded in her direction.

"Well, it was nice knowin' ya, kid," Katalina said as she wrapped one arm around Colin's neck. He didn't struggle against her as she rubbed her knuckles over his scalp and continued, "I won't be missin' ya too much, though. You snore something awful and I don't have time to be savin' yer sorry…"

"Oh, lay off him, Kat," Redbeard rumbled. He stroked his coppery beard as he spoke.

"Ain't said nothin' that wasn't true," Katalina retorted. She glanced sideways at the old barkeep.

"Thank you for that," Colin murmured. He wriggled out of

her grasp and stood back to survey her.

"Whatcha lookin' at?" Katalina spat. She raised an eyebrow at him and smirked.

"I was just thinking that you'll have to teach me how to use a slingshot as well as you, if we ever meet again."

She chuckled and clapped him on the shoulder. "I don't know about that. Might be too dangerous with that terrible aim of yers."

Colin shrugged. "Still, I'd like to learn."

A shadow lengthened over Colin's shoulder. He turned to see Zeph and Rikyah standing behind him. Zeph said nothing as he nodded at Colin and then joined Kaila and Thomas as they finished packing their gear.

"Thank you," Colin said, extending his hand towards Rikyah. "For everything."

"It might not seem like it, Colin Stormbearer, but I have thoroughly enjoyed learning more about you over these past weeks. You might not be the best fighter," she gave him a sympathetic half-smile at that, "but, I believe you have the making of a great king."

Colin was thankful his face was shrouded in shadow and that, despite the sister moons and stars, the night sky was dark.

"I hope that one day you won't have to smuggle people across our borders."

Rikyah casually flipped a dagger in hand. The jeweled hilt landed, hilt-first, in her palm. "What fun would there be in that?" she chided.

Though she exuded a sense of cocky nonchalance, Colin heard the edge in her tone. Too many innocents had been killed for simply having magic in Szarmi. It was time for that to change.

He was about to promise political reform if he won the

crown back when Redbeard boomed, "Time to go," and gripped the back of Colin's neck with a meaty hand.

"Farewell, Colin Stormbearer. May the wind propel you onward and the Light guide you," Rikyah said.

"Yeah," Katalina chimed in, "what she said." Her short pigtails bounced as she looped her arm through Rikyah's and pulled the smuggler away.

"I sincerely hope we meet again," Colin called after them.

"That would be something, wouldn't it?" Katalina retorted. She shoved Rikyah towards the river. Colin had no idea why they had decided to travel further south, but he wasn't in a position to question their motives.

Redbeard guided him towards the road that followed the Milo River straight into Miliom. Only two of the guards the old revolutionary had recruited for their mission back to Szarmi accompanied them. As Redbeard had explained, now that they knew they had a potential ally in the palace, their plan would work on secrecy over outright claim. Although Colin still wasn't convinced this was the best strategy, he was at the mercy of Redbeard and his group. Without them, he most likely would've been dead already.

"Three days from now and we'll be in Miliom," Redbeard commented after they'd traveled for several moments in silence.

"I know," Colin replied.

"No matter what happens, or what condition we find your home in, Colin, promise me that you'll keep pushing forward."

Colin glanced at Redbeard. It was difficult to tell in the darkness, but he though he detected a hint of worry in the man's rough face.

"My father wanted me to rule, Redbeard."

"Yer not yer father."

"No, I'm not, but it wasn't just him who wanted this. I do

to," Colin snapped. "It's not just about having power for me." He paused. The roar of the Milo River deafened his thoughts and left him feeling at peace with what he knew to be true. "I want to bring peace back to this place. People always say that the Wars of Darkness ended all those years ago, but I think they're wrong. We're still fighting. We'll always be fighting until every race in the whole of Mitier is recognized. Maybe, just maybe, something I do as king will put a dent in the terror we've spent the last three hundred years creating for ourselves."

Colin breathed heavily at the end of his speech. His heart hammered in his chest and his hands twitched as he considered the implication of what he had just said. He couldn't tiptoe around his beliefs anymore. Szarmi deserved better than to waste away in squalor. That's what hate does to people. He had seen it in the way his kingdom had denounced the beauty of the magical world. He had known it as he'd thought about the advances his engineers could make with a little magic to go with their technologies. He had believed it when he'd met her. Amaleah believed the same things he did. He knew it. Together, he had no doubt that they could break down the barriers between their two nations. They could become a united whole. It was the stuff of which his dreams were made.

"You have the making of a revolutionary yet," Redbeard commented, pulling Colin out of his thoughts.

Colin beamed, "Do you really think so?'

"I wouldn't be here if I didn't."

Chapter Twenty-Seven

Colin barely recognized his city. It appeared more like a city of ash and bones than it did the wonderous place he'd dreamed about since leaving. Ash swirled around his boots as he passed buildings burned to cinders. The air smelled of burnt flesh and decay. People, their faces gaunt, roamed the streets. Children, their noses dripping and their eyes listless, begged for coin, their lower lips quivering. Guards, their weapons held firmly in their hands, patrolled. The glass orbs he and his father, King Henry, had worked so hard to install had been smashed into shards and dust. What remained of the lamps speckled the cobblestone pathways in a glittering rainbow as Colin wandered the streets of his home.

Colin had never seen such despair in Miliom before. Even when his father had prepared war campaigns and taxed the people to feed his armies, he had always calculated a fair amount so that the people wouldn't starve.

His gaze met that of a small child. She couldn't have been more than four or five years old. Her brilliant blue eyes, so rare within Szarmi, were dull as she met his gaze. Snot slid from her nose and her hair hung in matted clumps about her narrow face. Fire burned within his stomach. This was why his father had chosen him to rule instead of Coraleen. This was why he had returned to reclaim his throne. His people deserved mercy, justice, and compassion, not this miserable life his mother and sister had carved out for them.

Reaching into his jacket pocket, Colin grasped for a bit of coin he'd hidden away. The little girl watched him, without curiosity. Even that had been taken from her during these hard times.

"Easy there, son," Redbeard mumbled as he gripped Colin's arm tightly. "There's no reason fer ya to be bringin' attention to yerself jus' yet."

Colin slid his gaze over the crowd. Several of them peered at him, interest covering their features. Without looking at Redbeard, Colin released his grip on the coin and withdrew his hand from his pocket.

"Let's go," he said, drawing the scarlet scarf Rikyah had given him more tightly across his face. Only his eyes were visible above the thin material. When his father had been alive, the city had been filled with shops and little places to eat. The city had thrived on military pensions, trade, and scientific endeavors. It had teemed with the latest fashions, including brilliantly embroidered scarves. Now, as he searched the crowd, all he saw were guant faces and dirty slips of cloth hanging from loose clothing.

Colin counted the number of children he saw wandering aimlessly about the streets as he led Redbeard and two guards through the city streets. They reached a seedier part of the city— located on the outskirts of the mercantile district—just as the sun was setting on the horizon.

The streets were clogged with sludge and foul odors. Colin didn't want to think about what he trudged through as his boots sloshed in small holes where the cobblestone had crumbled. Boys, no older than ten, threw knives at targets drawn onto building walls. Colin shivered with each thump he heard as the blades found their home in the clay bricks of the buildings. Each time he imagined that the boys had decided he and his men looked like more promising targets.

Women, their tunics cut low across their bosoms and wearing curly wigs dyed blonde strolled the streets in pairs. Their overly sweet perfume reminded Colin of rotting figs on a summer day. He coughed as one leaned in and placed a wet kiss on his cheek before giggling and walking away.

"Perhaps we should rest for the night," one of his men suggested.

Colin felt inclined to agree. With the sun setting and the gas lamps shattered, the city would be encased in darkness. Already, he felt the eyes of the boys trailing their small party. Several of them ran past Colin, their hands grasping at his scarf, his tunic, and his belt as they went. He clutched the walking staff Rikyah had given him more tightly and pretended to hobble a bit as he walked. It wasn't difficult to do. His feet ached and his legs were exhausted from their long journey. Still, he wasn't sure his gait was as convincing as he'd hoped it would be.

He ducked down an alleyway and his men followed. He heard more footsteps behind them, but did not hurry his pace as he led the other three through an intricate web of Miliom's city streets. Still, whoever was following them, continued to keep pace. The hair on the back of Colin's neck stood on end as he rounded a corner only to find a group of older boys—though still younger than him—standing in a group in the middle of the street. They carried torches and wore small blades tied to their waists.

Colin turned an immediate about face and took a different path heading in the same direction. He'd gone no further than a single block when he came upon another group of boys playing dice and twirling daggers in the air. The smoke from their torches made Colin cough as he caught a whiff of it at exactly the wrong moment.

The boys jerked their heads up and turned in Colin's direction. Colin stepped to go back the direction he'd came, but, past his men, he could see the first set of boys boxing them in.

"What's the meaning of this?" Redbeard asked. His voice sounded calm, but Colin could sense the tension coating each word.

"Give us ya money and we'll let ya go," one of the boys said.

"Yeah," another continued, "or we'll stick you with the pointy end of our blades."

One of the boys, Colin estimated the leader based on his broad shoulders and rakish grin, stepped forward. He sneered at the scarlet scarf covering Colin's face before ripping it off and throwing the material to the ground.

"Real men don't cover their faces," the boy said gruffly while the rest of the boys gasped.

Colin dropped his head and covered his face with his hands. He peered up at the boy who'd stripped him of his one disguise. The boy's eyes narrowed and bore straight into Colin's.

"Traitor," the boy whispered. His lips quivered in the shadows cast by the boys' torches. He pointed a long, bony finger in Colin's direction. "Look boys, it's the missing son returned to us."

Members of the gang whooped and hollered at their leader's quip. Colin scoffed.

"If I am the missing prince, then that makes me your king," Colin said in the most imperious voice he could muster.

The boy before him considered. He scraped one his bony fingers across Colin's face. He smelled of manure, sweat, and urine. Colin jerked away from the boy's dirt encrusted nail scraped against his skin. The boy smirked, his yellow teeth flashing in the setting sun.

"We have no king now," he said, his voice mocking. He jabbed his bony finger into Colin's chest. "A king never brought us nothin.' A king never put food in our bellies or took care of our mammas on their deathbeds. A king…"

"Uh hem," Redbeard cleared his throat.

Internally, Colin groaned. Despite the barkeep's intimidating stature, there was no way that he would be able intimidate or bribe this group of ruffians. He was Lunameedian, after all.

"It seems ta me that you lot would be much better off treatin' yer sovereign with the respect he's owed."

The leading boy spat on the ground between himself and Colin. He looked Redbeard up and down before wiping his nose with the back of his hand and saying, "That's all the respect he deserves."

Redbeard shrugged his shoulders. "That's too bad."

Before Colin had a moment to register what had happened, Redbeard had pulled his ax from his belt and used the handle to knock one of the boys out. Colin wasn't sure how a man of his size was capable of moving as quickly as he did. He swung his body around in a surprisingly graceful arch, and slammed the blade into the gut of another of the boys. Wasting no time, Redbeard quickly wrenched the ax free with a squishing sound and flung it into the head of a third boy.

He then knocked a fourth boy against the stone wall of the building closest to them, his forearm choking off the boy's air. He pressed against the boy's throat until his eyes bulged and he stopped struggling. As the boy dropped to the ground, Redbeard stared down at his hands. His cheeks were ruddy and he breathed heavily as he looked over his shoulder at Colin. The prince couldn't be sure, but he was certain he saw silver lining the barkeep's eyes.

The two guards, evidently bolstered by Redbeard's quick display of power, drew their swords. Colin brandished his staff, the metal tip out, as he surveyed what remained of the gang. In the shuffle, several of them had vanished into the shadows of the city. There were only four left. He turned to face the leader once more.

"You were saying?"

The boy laughed. It was really more of a wheeze. He shook his head as he said, "More's a'comin.' If I were you, I'd go back to where you come from."

"That's what I'm trying to do," Colin said, exasperated.

"Life weren't never good under yer father. Don't expect life would've been good under you, neither. Least now we have a pretty face to look at when yer mam and sis ride through the city."

Anger boiled in Colin's veins. Despite his estrangement with his family, he still cared for them. Nothing would ever change that. He whacked the boy in the face with the metal tip of his staff. The boy's head snapped back and he slumped to the ground, cradling a bloody mouth. He spat and shards of broken teeth came with the blood. The sight made Colin queasy.

Colin stood over the wounded ruffian. "If you were in charge," he said, his voice low, "what would you do differently?"

It wasn't the question he'd intended to ask. In fact, Colin wasn't sure he had intended to ask a question at all. But, as he stared into the boy's defiant eyes, even as he bled onto the cobblestone streets, he found himself curious. He and his father had spent years building a better city for their people. Although King Henry had been ruthless in war, he'd also been kind to his people. Colin would be damned if he let a lowly cutpurse defile his father's name.

"I'd dip my wick in yer sister. And maybe that mam of yer's as well."

Colin felt a mixture of rage and disgust as he lifted his staff to smash into the face of the leering cutpurse. His muscles tensed as he brought the staff down.

His arm jolted as something caught the staff in midswing. He traced the deeply muscled arm that held his staff aloft until he met Redbeard's gaze.

"Don't do it, son," Redbeard whispered.

The gang member sniggered from the ground and spat more blood. "No, yer highness, don't do it." His tone was all mockery.

"Let go of my staff, Redbeard," Colin demanded. He glared at the barkeep. He seethed as he tried to rip the staff from Redbeard's grasp. Unfortunately for Colin, the pounds of muscle lining Redbeard's arms overpowered his weaker stature.

"No," Redbeard said. "I can't do that, son."

"Stop calling me son," Colin muttered as he struggled to regain control of his staff. "I'm not your son."

Redbeard tugged on the staff and Colin nearly stumbled forward. The bigger man placed a meaty hand on Colin's shoulder and said, "Look at him."

Colin stared down at the still-bleeding ruffian crouching on the cobblestone street. His clothes were tattered and he cradled in his mouth in his hands. It was hard to judge, but Colin doubted the boy was no more than thirteen or fourteen years of age. Dirt smeared his face in streaks from the obvious tears he'd shed. Something in the back of Colin's mind tugged at him.

"I see nothing more than a vagabond," Colin sneered, though his tone did not match his words.

"People can't help what they were born to," Redbeard said.

His voice was gruff and Colin could hear the underlying pain beneath the barkeep's words. He glanced up at the older man to find him staring intently down at the injured boy. "Those born into power never have ta know the worry of never kn'win' where their next meal will come from nor if they're good enough for this life. You sit on your thrones and you think you do well enough by the people, meanwhile, the poorest among you are deprived of the things they need most."

"That's not true!" Colin shouted. He didn't know who Redbeard thought he was. His father had dedicated his entire life to ensuring the prosperity of the Szarmian people. He'd done good deeds. He'd invested in technologies to make life easier for his people. Colin had always wanted to be like him.

Redbeard squeezed Colin's shoulder. "Think 'bout it, son. You sat in your palace, were given the best of an education, the best of a chance to live well. What did the people get?"

"You think I haven't struggled?" Colin asked. "You think I haven't faced hardships? Let me tell you…"

"It's not the same. You know it's not."

The wind left Colin's words as he stared at Redbeard, who continued to stare down at the bleeding boy.

"Maybe he deserves what's been given to him in life," Colin said defensively.

"Maybe," Redbeard replied, "But when you start on the bottom rung of life sometimes you can't help but stay there. Too many of the poor young ones in our kingdoms have been left to either waste away in squalor or do what this one's done, try to make a life for himself in the only way he knows how."

"Through stealing?" Colin sniffed.

"Through surviving."

"I'd hardly call this surviving," Colin retorted, waving a hand across the remaining gang members.

"If it's the only world you've ever known it is. You were raised to be the king, Colin. Yer father declared you his heir, even when he didn't have to. From yer youngest memories, all you've known is power and privilege. But, what if you had been born in the slums of your city the way this poor soul was. You might not have turned out so different."

Redbeard squeezed Colin's shoulder again and released his hold on the staff. Colin jolted slightly as the full weight of the staff caught him off-guard.

"More often than not, men follow the paths they were born to. If yer going ta be the ruler I think ya will be, you need to understand the experience of yer people, son."

Colin let the tip of his staff fall to the ground. He didn't know if he agreed with Redbeard or not. Never, in all his years of training, had anyone ever offered him this perspective. He'd been raised to believe, as had all Szarmian people, that the person makes their destiny, not the other way around.

Torchlight cast shadows on the alley walls before them.

"Well, then," the bleeding boy said as he clumsily rose to his feet. "Thanks for wastin' all that time with yer jabberin.' Looks like me men have finally come back fer me."

"I think that's our cue to go," one of Colin's guards said as he turned about face and began running in the opposite direction of the torchlight. Colin and Redbeard shared a short look before shrugging at the same time and doing the same.

Chapter Twenty-Eight

Colin wheezed slightly as he rounded a corner and was pulled through a tent flap by rough hands. He struggled as whoever his captor was clamped a hand over his mouth.

"Shh," his captor whispered.

It was so dark in the tent that Colin couldn't even see his hand in front of his face. Over the stench of the man, the scent of hundreds of spices filled the air. He'd been in markets like this as a boy. His mother, Queen Vista, had always said they reminded her of her youth in Borganda. Of course, she'd also said that the spices used in her island nation were some of the only fond memories she had of her time there.

Voices muttered beyond the flap he'd been pulled through and several footsteps padded down the cobblestone street. The hand holding Colin captive tightened its grip. For a moment, Colin couldn't breathe, but then the torchlight filtering through the hung tapestries faded, as did the voices.

"That was a close one," a voice murmured in the dark.Colin heard the faint ping of stone striking against rock and a small yellow blaze illuminated the room. His captor, who turned out to be one of his guards relaxed his hold. Colin sighed in relief when Redbeard emerged from behind a sturdy-looking wooden table laden with jugs of alcohol.

"I think it best we stay here tonight, m'boy," he said as he laid the jugs on the dirt floor. He pulled a wedge of hard cheese from his pack and added it to the jugs.

"I blame you, you know," Colin grumbled as he plucked a rug from one of the displays and spread it on the ground. "If you would've just let me finish him off none of this would've happened."

Redbeard sighed heavily before uncorking one of the jugs with his teeth. He spat the cork clear across the room and into a clay bowl in the corner. He drank deeply from the jug, the amber liquid spilling down his chin the longer he held the clay to his lips. When he had finished slaking his thirst, he drug his arm across his mouth and smiled at Colin above the lip of the jug.

"If you're even half the ruler I think ya could be, you'll think about what I said t'night. I wouldn't be here if I didn't think it were true."

He passed the open jug to Colin. Colin's first instinct was to shove the jug away. He was not some child to be scolded by an irreverent barkeep from the savage nation to the north. He was the heir to the Szarmian throne. He almost said as much but then the image of the younger boy slumped on the ground, shards of his teeth scattered over the stone bubbled to the forefront of his mind.

Colin had done that.

In all his time practicing combat with Captain Conrad, even his time spent in Lunameed fighting for his life, he had never faced off against a weaker opponent. Sure, the ruffian had bated him with his cocky remarks about his family and his flippant disregard for the royal family. But he had been younger and clearly starving. Colin shivered as he remembered the way the boy's slender shoulders had shaken as he'd laughed at Colin. He tried to reason with himself, tried to tell himself that the boy's misfortunes were a result of his own faults. Somehow all of his justifications fell short.

He snatched the jug from Redbeard and sipped at the alcohol. It carried hints of vanilla and coconut in it, which surprised Colin. He'd only tasted alcohol like this in the palace. It was specially imported from Borganda for his mother. As far as he knew, there was only one merchant who traded for the beverage in the whole of Miliom.

"I know where we are," he said, his voice shaky. He peered around the tented shop more closely. It was then that he saw what he hadn't before: the wall tapestries depicting Borgandian myths, the statue of the Hunter on the shop table, the dried flowers hanging from the tent's wooden frame. These were symbols of his mother's homeland. A sinking feeling filled his belly. If they were where he thought they were, then they needed to leave the shop, and quickly. Just to be sure, Colin stalked to the table and peered beneath it. Despite the dimness in the room, he saw what he was searching for. There, hung on a golden nail, was a talisman of the sea foaming over the world.

"We can't stay here," Colin stammered.

"What's all this 'bout?" Redbeard asked through a mouthful of cheese. "Don't be daft, son. We can't leave while that gang is still out there."

"We can't stay here," Colin repeated as he ran his fingers over the talisman. He remembered the day his mother had given it to the shopkeep. They were friends.

"You're talkin' nonsense, Colin."

"No, I'm not. My mother knows this shopkeep. They're friends, Redbeard. She used to bring me here as a boy."

Crumbles of the cheese fell from Redbeard's mouth. He didn't seem to notice as he jumped to feet and strolled towards Colin.

"Surely, he won't check on his shop at night," the old barkeep said.

"Ahem," a high-pitched chirp came from behind the table.

Colin spun around in time to see the tent flaps drop as a short, slender figure ambled into the room. His blood turned to ice in his veins. It was too late.

"Who are you and what is your business here?" the woman said as she entered the sphere of light cast by the lamps. Colin caught Redbeard raising his eyebrows in surprise at the firmness of the woman's voice. Her papery skin was pulled tight over her bony flesh. White curls adorned her heart shaped face in a halo. Like many Borgandians, silvery tattoos covered her caramel skin.

"Vecepia," Colin whispered.

She carried a thin dagger in her hand, its jeweled hilt more fashionable than functional. Still, her presence in the shop was undeniably powerful.

"Colin Stormbearer," she replied. When she finally looked at Colin, he could see that her once chocolate eyes had turned milky blue. Colin was even more surprised to find her defending her shop alone following this revelation.

"I'm surprised that you still recognize my voice," he said.

She chuckled at him. "I'm surprised you still know your way around the city."

"I didn't, really," he said, shrugging before he remembered

that she couldn't see his actions.

"How long has it been?" she asked, tucking the dagger into her belt. "You two over there," she motioned towards the guards, "make yourselves useful and find the prince a stool to sit upon."

They shuffled across the shop, shooting glances at Redbeard all the while.

"There has been much discussion in the city about you," she said.

"Oh?" Colin asked. It wasn't unexpected. Still, he was curious to hear what the people had been saying about him.

She reached out a hand and Colin came to stand close enough to her that she could touch him. At her request, he guided her hand to his face. Her fingers were like ice on his skin as she explored his features. Muttering to herself, Vecepia plucked a hair from Colin's head and rubbed it between her fingers.

"You always did resemble your mother," she said. It was the only distinguishable phrase she'd said for five minutes.

"I know," was all Colin could think to say.

Vecepia sighed. She sank down onto a small wooden stool behind the table. She looked frail as she cradled her head in her hands and continued muttering to herself.

After a moment, Colin asked, "Are you going to turn us in?"

She belted a hearty laugh at that. "Boy, if I were going to turn you in, I would've called the guard before I entered my shop."

Colin took in their surroundings. It would be easy for the city guard to surround them. If that happened, Colin knew his life would be forfeit. The queen mother couldn't risk Coraleen being dethroned by the rightful heir. They'd attempted to assassinate him before and, when that didn't work, they'd concocted the ruse that he'd been killed by the Lunameedians. He was a dead man walking.

Slowly, he dragged his eyes back to the shopkeep. For all he knew, she could be stalling for more time.

"Did you?" Colin asked, clasping her hand in his sweaty one.

She cocked an eyebrow at him. "No," she said wryly.

He wasn't sure he should trust her, but he found that he did.

"If you're not going to turn me in, then why are you here?" he asked, still clutching her hand in his own.

"Do you remember coming here as a child, Your Highness?" she asked. There was no mockery in her voice as she offered him the title and a spark of hope kindled in Colin's stomach.

"I do," he said.

"You were always a curious little boy," she squeezed his hand as she spoke. "Always looking about the shop, asking me questions. I didn't mind it, but your mother, oh well, she didn't like how you stole attention away from your sister."

Colin shrugged. It had always been that way for him.

"I'm not sure how this explains why you're helping me."

"Patience," she said as she slipped her hand from his. Her stooped body creaked as she bent to retrieve a tea kettle from one of the lower shelves of the desk. Colin didn't know the extent of the woman's relationship with his mother or why she would risk her stature within the Szarmian court, but he was thankful she was.

"I used to tell you stories about the Motherland, do you remember?" she asked. She lit a small gas burner as she spoke and poured water from a clay urn by the back door she'd entered through. "You used to sit," she pointed at a spot near where'd they entered, "and stare up at me with such eagerness it was hard to tell you no."

The wisp of a smile passed over her lips as she turned her milky eyes back to him. "Do you remember any of those tales?"

"Only one," Colin said. He wished that he could remember more.

"Would you tell it to me?" she asked. The kettle she'd set on the small burner whistled. Colin couldn't fathom how she knew where to reach or where to pour, but Vecepia managed to fill five glasses full of the steaming liquid. She thumbed small bags full of tea leaves into the water and swirled them around as she handed them to each of Colin's companions in kind. When she reached him, she whispered, "I would dearly love to hear how you butcher the tale."

He jerked back, expecting abhorrence on her face, but found only a half smile.

He sighed, loudly, before beginning the tale, "There once was a king named Jamad who dreamed of nothing more than giving up his throne and living as the commoners did. Some say he was the greatest emperor to rule in Borganda. None could match his strength or speed. None could best him."

Vecepia braided her thin fingers together. Knobs from the age stiffness bulged from her knuckles. Colin found himself wondering how much pain she lived with every day. He hoped it was minimal.

"One day, he encountered an old man wandering through the woods who, after Jamad helped him across a raging river, offered him a wish in return. The foolish king asked for relief from his duties as king. The old man simply smiled at Jamad before disappearing into a cloud of smoke. Jamad, fearful that he had angered the Creators, crept back to his palace only to discover that another man sat on the throne. Despite his attempts to convince his people that he was the king, no one believed him. Branded as a mad man, Jamad wrestled in street duels to earn his bread. He saved for years as his bones cracked and his body slowly deteriorated. Eventually, he was able to save enough for passage to the ancient lands that later became known as Szarmi. Using his brutal force, Jamad fought his way to a place of power once more. He became the first king of Szarmi."

Vecepia sipped her tea and sighed as Colin came to the end of the story. The lamps flickered as a gust of wind and dust swept through the shop. Shadows danced across Vecepia's face, her milky eyes flashing like lighting in the sky.

"It is strange that the one Borgandian story you remember from your childhood so closely mirrors your own," she mused. She traced the lip of her cup with her finger as she spoke.

Colin weighed her words. "I'm not sure I agree. I don't think I'm anything like the old king. I want to rule," he replied petulantly.

She chuckled. "All men are fools when it comes to power."

Colin raised an eyebrow at Redbeard as if to ask if the older man understood Vecepia's quixotic ponderings. The old barkeep just shrugged his shoulders and slipped a pinch of mureechi into his pipe. He had just lit the herbs and puffed once when Vecepia set her cup upon the table. Colin was no closer to understanding Vecepia's strange requests. He sighed loudly.

"I will help you enter the palace, Colin." Her voice came like a gentle caress on the wind. It slid across Colin, leaving him shivering in its wake.

He waited for the demand he was certain would follow her

declaration. None came.

"I don't understand why you're helping me."

She set her milky gaze upon him. Colin's entire body went rigid and he felt like that little boy from all those years ago who'd gotten in trouble for breaking one of her special clay pots. With sweaty palms and a racing heart he forced himself to stammer, "Please tell me."

"There is no reason," she responded.

"But…" Colin began. He did not believe her in the slightest.

"But nothing, Your Highness. Please, either accept my help or leave my shop and take your chances with the city's vagabonds."

Colin swallowed the lump that had risen in his throat. This old woman was willing to risk her life to help him. He wasn't even sure he was up to the challenge and here this old, blind woman was: willing to help. All Colin could feel in that moment was humility.

"We accept," he said.

"Then we have no time to lose," she whispered.

Chapter Twenty-Nine

When Colin accepted Vecepia's help in entering Miliom's palace, he had not anticipated her leading them through the sewage. He swore the murky water and the squelch of his boots plunking into refuse was worse than the stench. Though, he wasn't sure how that could be possible when the smell of excrement made him want to vomit each time he sucked in a breath. How the blind Vecepia knew her way through the tunnel system was a mystery about which Colin didn't dare ask. He made the mental note to assume she had spent hours wandering through these tunnels until she found the one leading to the palace. Whether this was the truth or not didn't matter as long as she came through on her promise to lead them to the palace's underground gates.

"We're almost there," the older woman wheezed. Her shoulders shook in the flickering torchlight.

"You best be right 'bout that," Redbeard mumbled as he passed Colin to take the lead. With his overbearing stature and thick, Lunameedian accept, Colin expected the old woman to shy away from Redbeard. To the contrary, Vecepia seemingly ignored the man as she licked her fingers and held them up to the air.

"This way," she said, motioning towards an off-shoot of the

tunnel in which they were walking. They rounded a sharp bend in the tunnel before coming to a halt before a set of iron bars. Rust covered the long poles that had been drilled into the top and bottom of the tunnel. The sludge here was shallower and the fumes much less repugnant.

"This is where I leave you," Vecepia murmured. She clutched at Colin's hands and drew him close to her. She stood on tiptoes and wrapped one of her arms around Colin's neck. Her breath was moist and hot and smelled of tea as she whispered into his ear, "Never forget that everyone suffers, faces challenges, and—at times—feels alone. The mark of a true leader is that, in these difficult moments, they rise up. They never give up. They do not cower in the corner while their people despair." She pulled away from him, her face clouded in a shadow as she declared, "Do not miss your chance to rise up, Colin Stormbearer."

She did not give Colin a chance to respond to her statements. As smoke curled around her body, she disappeared into the darkness behind them.

"Well," Redbeard mumbled as he rubbed the back of his neck. "She was a peculiar one, wasn't she?"

Redbeard's words pulled Colin from his thoughts. Ignoring the barkeep, he turned to face the iron bars. Redbeard held his torch closer to the bars, revealing a gate on the left-hand side of the barrier. Although the gate showed the same deterioration as the bars, a shiny new chain and been wrapped around the gate and a robust lock sealed it shut.

"Now what?" one of the guards groaned. "I don't remember the way back to the shop," he continued in a whining voice. "She shouldn't have left us here until we were through the gate!"

Colin rolled his eyes at the man before reaching up to examine the mortar around the bars. With a small amount of force, the sealant crumbled into little more than dust and crumbs. Drawing his sword, Colin pounded its hilt into the mortar. Chunks of the sealant plopped into the sludge all around them, splashing them with the murky water. Colin didn't care. All he could think about was crossing this barrier—of being home again.

Sparks flew as his sword met iron.

"Easy now," Redbeard shouted, clamping a firm hand on Colin's shoulder. He held his ear up to the bars and listened to the darkness beyond. "Can't ya see that this used to be an easy entrance into the palace? Someone clearly wanted this place to be under higher security."

Colin shrugged. Dropping his sword into the water, he gripped the pole he'd left bare at the top. Heaving in a massive breath, he flung his shoulder against the bar. A loud scraping sound and a cloud of dust followed.

"Stop it," one of his guards hissed. "Our greatest asset right now is stealth and surprise, Colin."

Ignoring the pleas of his men, Colin slammed his shoulder into the bar again. More dust fell. He gripped the bar in his hand, the cold metal sent a shock up his arm as he began to jiggle the bar. It wiggled from the top. Colin smiled as he reached as high as he could and pulled down. For a moment, he dangled in the air as he hung from the bar, then with a loud crunching noise, the bar pulled away from the remaining mortar in the ceiling and fell downwards.

Colin grinned as the bar cascaded into the water. Stooping to retrieve his sword, he wiped the grime off on his pants.

"That wasn't so hard," he proclaimed as he side-stepped through the hole.

Redbeard chuckled before squeezing through the bars. Several of his buttons caught on the metal and popped off when

Colin gripped the barkeep's arm and tugged. The release of tension of Redbeard's body sent him propelling forward. He flailed his arms before knocking into Colin and sending them both into the grimy water.

Colin spluttered as his head became immersed in the fowl smelling sludge. Futilely, he tried rubbing the refuse from his face with his own dirty shirt. All he achieved was smearing the grime across his cheeks in brown streaks. One of the guards removed his coat and wiped Colin's face off as best he could, but Colin knew he must smell and look atrocious.

"Thanks," he mumbled as he stripped his shirt off and threw on the coat. Never, in all his time imagining what it would be like to return to Miliom, had he ever envisioned returning home covered in dung. Still, he was that much closer to seeing the marble halls of the palace once more.

"Let's go," he commanded. Neither of the guards nor Redbeard grumbled as Colin led the way. It is a strange thing to come home when one has been disavowed from the place. Yet, Colin found himself eager to see the marble halls, smell the mustiness of his father's libraries, and hear the patter of the servants. With each step he took forward, the faster his heart hammered. He was almost there.

The tunnel on the other side of the bars inclined upwards at a gradual pace. The farther they traveled upwards, the less repugnant the air became. Colin was just about to comment on the gentle breeze that grazed his face when he saw long shadows cast on the sides of the tunnel ahead of them. Throwing his arm up, he halted Redbeard and the two guards. He pointed at the guards and motioned for them to drop their torches in the water. The torches sizzled as their fire was extinguished and a plume of smoke rose. They pressed their backs against the tunnel wall and waited in silence and darkness.

Gruff voices echoed down the tunnel. Although he hadn't seen the telltale uniform, Colin assumed they were palace guards. Gripping the hilt of his sword, Colin prepared himself for the skirmish he knew would ensue. He never had been good at fighting. *Maybe this time*, he thought as he silently counted to three and then spun around the corner.

Redbeard beat him to the attack. Using his elbow, he knocked the helmet off the closest guard before twisting around and cleaving the man's skull with his ax. Colin felt his stomach squirm at the sight of the crimson blood spraying across the wall behind the man. Redbeard threw one of his daggers at the next guard. It lodged itself in the man's eye. He collapsed to the ground, his torch extinguishing as it hit the water. It had been the only light left in the dark tunnel.

Colin blinked into the sudden darkness. If he had counted appropriately, that left two more guards to dispatch. Afraid to swing his blade around in the tight quarters, Colin scooted back until his back touched the wall. From there, he fiddled with his flint and striker as he attempted to relight one of the torches. Grunting sounds echoed all around him. His hands trembled and he nearly dropped his flint into the murky water below.

A man moaned. Water splashed. A scream pierced the tunnel air. Colin struck his flint again and a small flame blossomed into life. He lit one of the torches his men had carried. At first, Colin didn't register the destruction all around him. Five bodies were strewn across the tunnel floor. Their crimson blood pooled around their wounds. Colin shook as he approached the bodies, fearful of what he would find.

Two palace guards and both of Redbeard's men were dead. Their lifeless eyes stared aimlessly upwards, as if calling to the Creators for salvation. Colin closed their eyes, careful to only touch the bodies for as long as necessary.

Splashing water drew his attention away from the deceased. Colin spun around in time to see Redbeard fall to his knees in the shallow water.

"What have I done?" he asked, his voice hoarse. He laid his hands on his knees and bowed his head. "What have I done?" he repeated.

Colin stood motionless, looking between the bodies and Redbeard. Both men they'd traveled with bore wounds congruent with an ax. He bowed his head as realization dawned upon him. Redbeard had been the who'd killed them all. He'd turned on his own men. He had known that Redbeard was a vicious fighter, capable of fighting against the odds. But this, he looked at the mangled men before him, didn't make sense. He shivered as another breeze from the passageway ahead grazed his cheeks.

"You saved us," Colin cooed as he took a step towards the man. Redbeard brandished his ax. Blood dripped from the blade. Colin stood still as Redbeard peered up at him from knitted brows.

"You're a liar, Colin Stormbearer," Redbeard growled, "A bloody, filthy liar."

Redbeard's words stung. It wasn't so much the words themselves as much as the wrath each syllable carried with it.

"I'm sorry," Colin whispered.

Redbeard barked a cold, harsh laugh. "I should never have pledged myself to your cause, Colin."

Taking his chances, Colin stepped towards his companion. "I'm glad you did," he said.

"You won't be."

The words hung in the air between them. Even with the bursts of anger he'd seen in the old barkeep, Colin trusted the older man without limit. He'd gotten him this far, Colin had no reason to doubt that Redbeard would fail him in the future. *Sometimes*, he reasoned with himself, *people just need time to process the things they've been through*. There was no doubt in Colin's mind that Redbeard had faced a great number of hardships. The faint scars on his skin and his nonchalant demeanor told him that. The way Redbeard fought told him the rest. He dropped to his knees before his companion, his friend.

"Whatever you've faced in the past, Redbeard, whatever you do in the future, I am glad that you're my friend."

Redbeard stared down at his meaty hands. He breathed heavily for several moments, his breath coming out in hot gusts that tickled the back of Colin's neck. The prince supposed that he should be afraid of the man. He'd certainly demonstrated enough bloodlust in front of Colin that there was little room for interpretation. Redbeard was a killer, regardless of the reforms he'd attempted to make in his life.

"There's not too many in this world that call me friend," Redbeard mumbled.

At first, Colin thought that he had imagined Redbeard talking to him. The older man's voice was soft and gruff and almost too jumbled to understand. But, when Redbeard looked into Colin's eyes and said, "I will try to stop the fury that rises within me, Colin. It is difficult for me to know who is a friend or foe in this world."

Colin clamped a hand over Redbeard's shoulder and squeezed. "You never have to worry about where you stand with me, Redbeard. We are friends."

Redbeard nodded but did not respond.

Colin took Redbeard's silence to mean that he agreed with him. He squeezed the older man's shoulder again and Redbeard met his eyes. There was no madness in them, only a sorrowfulness that made Colin's chest ache. *What has this man seen?* Colin asked himself.

"We need to keep moving," he said, glancing at the empty passageway before them.

"I think you should go on without me," Redbeard huffed.

"What?" Colin asked, "No!"

Redbeard held up his hand, stalling further exclamations from Colin. "Listen to me, boy, you know the palace better than I do. Without the additional guards, I'll only slow you down rather than aide you in your quest."

"But," Colin began.

"No," Redbeard repeated, "No arguments on this one, Your Highness."

Redbeard so rarely used Colin's title that its use left him feeling jarred.

"I need you to help me in this," Colin pled.

"Yer more capable than you recognize," Redbeard contended. "Please, Colin, just go."

Colin stood. The idea of returning to the palace alone made his insides squirm. But, the image of the burned buildings and swollen stomachs of the children in the streets propelled him to act. His father had chosen him as his heir ahead of Coraleen for a reason. It was time that he made his mother and sister see his strengths rather than his weaknesses. He was fighting for so much more than his right to the throne. He was fighting for his people. He vowed that he would let nothing stand in his way of providing aide to them.

"Will you be here when I return?" he asked, his voice emotionless.

"I will be," Redbeard replied, without looking up from his spot on the ground. "I promise ya this, Colin: I started down this path with you and I will finish this task with ya. I just," he paused as his voice broke, "I just need some time," he managed to finish.

Colin nodded and turned to head down the tunnel leading to the palace.

"Wait," Redbeard commanded, gripping Colin's wrist. He pulled several daggers from beneath his clothes and handed them to Colin. "Take these," he said, "they might come in handy."

Colin stared at the blades. They were all different shapes and sizes, but they had the same design engraved into their blades. Rising from the hilt, each blade depicted a merperson raising a weapon. Intricate nautical knots framed the merpeople from hilt to tip. Colin had seen designs like these only once before, in an old book about Mitierian lore.

"The lost daggers of Ula Una," he breathed. His eyes widened in awe as he studied the design more closely. Miniature seahorses and fish had been etched into the designs so delicately that, if one were to simply glance at the blades, they would miss these details. A different precious jewel was pressed into the hilt of each dagger. He trailed the tip of his fingers over the engraved blades and bejeweled hilts. "They're beautiful," he whispered, more to himself than to Redbeard.

"Aye," Redbeard grunted.

"But how?" Colin asked in astonishment.

Redbeard shrugged. "Found 'em in a pile o'junk I was cleanin' one day."

Colin didn't entirely believe the older man's explanation, but he decided it didn't matter how Redbeard had gotten them. Rumor had it that the blades were blessed and would return to their owner, no matter how far he or she traveled or how much time had passed. And now, Redbeard was bequeathing the daggers to him. Flush with gratitude, Colin accepted the blades without another word and strapped them to his belt and beneath his clothes. The blades were surprisingly heavily, but their weight was a comfort as Colin began the trek through the tunnel alone. Redbeard had not lit his own torch as the last flickers of Colin's flame disappeared around a bend. Colin prayed to the Creators that the older man would be fine until his return.

As his boots continued to slosh through the mud and grime, Colin remembered those who had accompanied him the day he'd left Miliom all those months ago. His heart sputtered as he thought of his dearest friend, Jameston, and all that the large, jolly man had missed. *He'll never meet his child*, Colin realized with a sinking sensation. He vowed that he would visit his friend's widow and offer aid, once the fighting had ceased. For now, he could only hope that he would leave the palace with more men and more hope than he currently had.

Chapter Thirty

Silver Moon Camp, Lunameed

Amaleah crouched beside Thadius. His breathing was shallow and his skin pale. She trailed her fingers over his brow.

"I'm so sorry," she whispered, bending down to kiss him on the cheek.

His eyelids fluttered but did not open. It had been a week now and he still had not opened his eyes. Nylyla said that can happen sometimes, especially when magic was involved. She told Amaleah there was no way of knowing whether Thadius would ever regain consciousness.

A tear slid down Amaleah's cheek and plopped on Thadius's arm. "You were only trying to help me," she murmured, "and I hurt you for it."

She clutched at Thadius's hand. She had visited him every day that Nylyla and Elaria allowed her to. Most of her time was spent in the training ring with Nikailus and Anno. Each day, she was expected to drink the milky white potion to stop her powers from manifesting. So far, she hadn't had another uncontrollable outburst, but she feared stifling her magic would make it even stronger the next time she used it. None of the elves had taken the time to discuss magical control with her.

A light knock drew her attention away from Thadius and her

own thoughts. Nylyla stood in the doorway, a tray laden with tea and cookies in her hand.

"I thought you could use some company," the waifish elf said. She motioned for Amaleah to follow her.

Amaleah squeezed Thadius's hand. "I'll be back," she promised as she kissed his brow once more and laid his hand across his chest. She wished she could go back to the moment when her magic exploded from her and stop herself from harming him. *But,* she reminded herself, *wishing for things that can never come true is futile.* She laid another blanket over his shoulders and tucked it in tight.

Nylyla led her to the back patio of her home. It was really more of a small, flat surface with cushions on the ground instead of chairs, but it provided a peaceful atmosphere. Trees stood like rows of soldiers before her. Golden light filtered through the foliage and tiny dust particles sparkled as they wafted through the air.

Amaleah breathed in heavily. She knew her time in Encartia was limited. Once she was trained to an acceptable level, she would be expected to perform whatever tasks the others believed would fulfill the first prophecy. No one had told her what that meant; she hated being kept in the dark. She hated that she had escaped from one set shackles only to be bound by another.

"Anno tells me your training is going well," Nylylala said. Her birdlike voice drew Amaleah's attention back to the present moment.

"Did she?" Amaleah asked. "I'm surprised. Nikailus has bested me in every match so far."

Nylyla shrugged. "The point of your lessons isn't to win as much as it is to learn to control your body and emotions."

"My entire body aches from the practices," Amaleah complained. "I can barely walk some days."

"The stronger you become, the more the pain will fade."

"Hasn't gotten any easier yet."

"It's only been a week, Amaleah," Nylyla chided, "you must have patience."

Amaleah sipped at her tea to stop herself from saying something she would later regret.

"How have you and Nikailus been getting along?"

Amaleah shrugged. "He's very strong. And arrogant." She wanted to confide in the elf that she had been dreaming about her mysterious sparring partner but she didn't know how to describe what she was thinking. He had the unnerving ability to make her feel empowered and helpless all at the same time. To make matters even more complicated, she found that each time she touched him, an image of the Szarmian prince would spring into her mind. It was all so frustrating.

Nylyla bit into a cookie and waggled her eyebrows at Amaleah. "Go on," she said through a full mouth. "Tell me more."

Amaleah sighed. She wasn't convinced there was much to tell. "Have you ever had the feeling that you were meant to find someone?"

"Sure," the elf responded. She smiled knowingly at Amaleah. "When I first met Rikyah I knew she would always be my first love, if not my eternal one."

Amaleah bit her bottom lip. That wasn't exactly what she was trying to say. "I'm not sure it's like that," she admitted. "I mean, he is very handsome," she fumbled over her words, "but it's as if something is drawing me to him. I want to be around him. I want to learn more about his past. I want to see what we can do together."

"Sounds to me like it's 'like that.'" Nylyla leaned forward, cupping her hands around her tea cup. "Why don't you think it is?"

Amaleah shrugged. She wanted to explore her conflicted feelings on her own time without anyone else influencing her.

"Well," the elf said, leaning back again, "I suppose the best thing you can do is just continue what you're doing."

"Am I interrupting?" Nikailus asked as he stepped out of the doorway and onto the patio.

Amaleah felt her cheeks flush and jumped out of her seat. *How long has he been standing there?* she wondered. Her tea spilled down the front of her tunic. She caught his amused smile as she hastily blotted at the stain with a cloth.

"If I knew I could scare you this much by simply talking to you, I'd goad you more during practices," he said.

Amaleah glared at him. He really was an arrogant, insufferable man. She gave a pointed look to Nylyla as if to say, 'see, this is what I have to deal with,' before brushing past Nikailus to go change her outfit.

"Anno is expecting us," he called after her. "She sent me here to collect you."

Amaleah didn't respond as she stormed up the stairs to her bedroom. She pulled open the closet door with a loud bang and began rifling through her belongings. The fur coat and the three dresses were hung in the furthermost back corner of the closet. She didn't know why she'd kept them. She never intended to wear them again, not after what she'd been through. But she couldn't bring herself to discard them either.

Huffing, she yanked down a forest green tunic and tugged it on. She made the mistake of glancing in the mirror. Her cheeks were still flushed and her hair was disheveled. She didn't give herself time to fix it. Instead, she pulled it back into a tight ponytail and rushed from her room. Maybe sparring would help calm her nerves.

Nikailus didn't say anything as they made their way to the ring. Amaleah glanced at him several times during their short walk together. This was the first time they'd been alone since meeting the week before. His expression was stony and he kept his gaze locked ahead of them. Amaleah had to bite the inside of her cheek to stop herself from saying something to him. She was determined not to be the one to break the ice.

"Finally," Anno called as they climbed into the ring. "I was expecting you thirty minutes ago."

Amaleah glared at Nikailus, who only passively nodded at Anno.

"Why didn't you collect me sooner?" she demanded.

"I was having such a fun time listening to your conversation," he goaded.

She knew it. Amaleah's blood boiled as she stared at him. "You had no right," she said.

"And you shouldn't have been talking out in the open."

"I wasn't!" she shouted. "We were on the back patio."

Nikailus smirked at her and gave a lazy yawn.

Amaleah's arms shook as she accepted the milky vial from Anno. "When I'm finally allowed to use my powers, I'll wipe that smirk off your face," she remarked snidely as she gulped down the potion. The smell and taste didn't bother her as much as it had before.

"I look forward to it, Princess," Nikailus replied. He assumed a defensive stance and waited for Amaleah to do the same.

When Anno gave the sign to begin, Amaleah swung out with her staff in a wide arch. Anticipating that he would try to jump over the staff, she abruptly flipped the staff upward, catching him between the legs. He flopped to the ground, groaning. Not wanting to give him an edge, Amaleah walloped him over the stomach with her staff. He groaned again.

She approached him warily. He had done this to her before. He let her think she had the upper-hand before launching himself into a quick, tight, offensive attack that left her defenseless. She vowed she wouldn't let him take control like that today.

She prodded him with her staff and he twitched. Knowing the tell-tale signs of him faking injury, she drew her staff to her and then jabbed him in the side. She rushed towards him, staff pointed down.

He swung out with his staff and leapt to his feet. She soared into the air and used her staff to spring over him. Bending her knees as she landed to reduce the impact, Amaleah used her momentum to swing around and smack her staff right in Nikailus's jaw. A bruise spread out from the point of impact.

His eyes widened in surprise as Amaleah jerked the bottom half of the staff up and hit him again between the legs. She smiled as he dropped to the ground. She was close enough now to level her staff at his throat.

"Move and I'll shatter your windpipe," she hissed at him.

"There's no reason for that," Anno called.

"Do you concede?" Amaleah asked, staring down into Nikailus's eyes.

He smirked at her, blood bubbling from his lips at the movement.

"Do you concede?" Amaleah asked again, pressing the staff a little more into his throat.

He nodded.

"This exercise was not about destroying your opponent, Amaleah. It was about strategically maneuvering him out of the ring."

Amaleah spun on Anno. "But I beat him," she said. "This is the first time I've ever gotten him to concede. You should be proud of me."

"You beat him because you let your anger get the best of you," Anno replied as she stepped into the ring and offered Nikailus a hand. He accepted the war elf's aid. "If you can't learn to control your emotions, Amaleah, how can you expect to control the magic inside of you?"

"Maybe if you gave me a chance to learn!"

"This is your chance."

They stared at each other. It wasn't that Amaleah didn't appreciate the lessons the elves were trying to teach her—she did—but she couldn't waste any more time waiting for them to determine if she was worthy of the prophecy or not.

She stormed away from the ring.

"Where are you going, girl?" Anno called after her. "We still have several more hours of lessons for the day."

"I'm done," Amaleah yelled. "Find someone else."

She didn't know where she was going. All she knew was that she couldn't be there anymore. *Who does he think he is, listening to my private conversations with a friend?* she fumed as she started running. In most situations, Amaleah detested running. But now, as she put foot in front of the other and felt the wind whipping through her hair, all she felt was free.

Chapter Thirty-One

It was several minutes later that Amaleah stopped running. She panted as she doubled over. Her side cramped. *And this is why I hate running*, she told herself. She felt lightheaded when she stood up again. She couldn't believe that she had just run away from the training ring. She knew she needed to be better equipped to fight. The damage she had done to Thadius was enough to convince her of that. But, after seventeen years of being kept in the dark and controlled by her father, she was determined to not let anyone else determine her fate.

She punched one of the trees. And instantly regretted it as her knuckles popped and her skin was scraped off. Whining a little, she clutched her hand to her chest.

"You should apologize to Anno," Nikailus said as he stepped from behind a tree to her left.

"Great," she mumbled, still clutching her hand. "How long have you been watching me this time?"

His eyes narrowed on her injury. "What did you do to yourself?" he demanded as he stepped forward and gripped her arm.

"Nothing," she began. Blood seeped from the wound when she tried to flex her fingers.

"Yeah," Nikailus retorted, "that really looks like nothing." He trailed a finger over the scrape. His touch sent a shiver down her spine. Tiny bruises were already beginning to blossom over her knuckles and fingers. "I think you broke your hand."

"I think you're right," she said coldly and tried to rip her hand away from him.

"Why are you so angry with me?" he asked. He turned away from her as he spoke. His voice was soft and carried with it none of the snide arrogance it normally did.

"Why did you listen to my private conversation?" she retorted.

"I," he paused. His back stiffened and Amaleah wondered what lie he was trying to work out in his mind. "I heard my name and I wanted to know what you and the elf were saying about me," he confessed.

"And that gives you a right to eavesdrop on me?" she asked.

"No," he responded quickly. "But…"

"Listen, Nikailus," she cut him off, "I don't really care why you listened to my conversation. There's no excuse for it."

He spun on her and gripped her shoulders between his hands. The nearness of him made Amaleah's stomach squirm. His citrus and sandalwood aroma was intoxicating. "I feel drawn to you, too," he whispered as he bent down and kissed her lightly on the lips.

Amaleah froze. She didn't respond to his kiss but she didn't push him away either. He must've taken this as an invitation because he pulled her closer to his chest and deepened the kiss. He was warm and that pull she always felt when she was around him exploded within her. Dropping her injured arm to the side, she wrapped her other one around his neck. She coiled her fingers in his hair.

He moaned softly as he pulled back just far enough to peer into her eyes. "I've been searching for you for so long," he whispered as he leaned in to kiss her again.

She returned the kiss. And the one after that. And the one after that. When he finally drew back, she barely remembered why she had been mad at him in the first place.

"We should head back," he whispered, his voice husky.

"Not yet," she murmured as she reached for him again.

He kissed her on the forehead. "I don't know all the reasons why you're here, Amaleah, but I've heard enough of the rumors to know that you need to complete as much training as possible if you're going to take the throne away from your father."

She stepped away from him, "Where did you hear that?" she demanded.

"What?"

"Where did you hear that I wanted to seize the throne from my father?"

"Nowhere," he said quickly. "I just assumed..."

"You assumed what? That because my father tried to force me into a marriage with him that I would want to face him again?"

"I'd heard he'd gone mad," Nikailus tried to explain.

The vision of her father standing before her, shrouded in smoke and flame filled her. *You're mine. You'll always be mine.*

She shoved away from Nikailus. "What I want for my kingdom and its people is none of your concern," she snipped. She hated that all he had to was mention her father for the memories to bubble up inside her. "I'll make my own way back."

With that, Amaleah began walking down the path that led to

the training ring. Nikailus didn't say another word, but she heard the steady patter of his feet behind her. She ignored him even as the lingering warmth from his kiss remained on her lips. *What have I gotten myself into*, she thought as she entered the clearing where the ring was located.

"What did you do your hand?"

It was the first thing Anno asked when Amaleah couldn't grip her staff properly

"Punched a tree," she replied, sheepishly.

Anno raised an eyebrow as her clucked her tongue. She lifted Amaleah's hand close to her face so that she could examine the damage. "Broken," she sighed. "We'll have to wait for the potion to wear off so that you can heal yourself before doing any more training."

"Is there anything I can do in the meantime?" Amaleah asked. She didn't want to waste any more time.

"Elaria wanted to meet with you after training today," Anno responded. "I suppose you could just go now."

Amaleah groaned. The Silver Moon matriarch was kind—most of the time—but also stern. Amaleah never knew how the older woman was going to react to her.

"I'll go with you," Nikailus offered.

Amaleah glared at him. "No," she said. "I don't need your help."

His expression fell at the tone in her words. Anno's eyes flicked between them, but Amaleah did not care if the weapon's master saw her fight with Nikailus.

"Fine," he replied with nonchalance. He picked up his staff and motioned for Anno to join him in the ring. "Good luck with the matriarch," he called as he began going through the various stances Anno had taught them.

———————◆———————

Amaleah waited in Elaria's main sitting room. It smelled of cinnamon and old books. A tapestry hung on the wall with each of the twelve elvish clans listed. Their sigils blazoned in gold. Although Nylyla had been attempting to teach Amaleah to read the written language of the elves, she still only knew the basics. The only words she recognized on the tapestry were "Silver Moon."

Footsteps thudded in the hallway beyond and a small girl wandered into the room. "Elaria sent me to fetch you," the girl chirped. Amaleah had to do a double-take of the girl. She had antlers growing out the top of her head, yet she had the body of a human. She had never seen anything like it.

"Come on," the girl said. She ran a hand over her antlers and patted her hair down, as if trying to hide them from Amaleah.

The princess followed the strange girl in silence. She felt remorse for how she had treated the girl. If she was ever going to lead her people into peace, then she needed to be able to set aside her own biases.

"I don't want to sound rude," Amaleah said, though she immediately realized that starting off her question like that made it rude, "but what type of magical creature are you?"

The girl stiffened, but responded to Amaleah's question, "A Tief, Your Highness. My ma was the daughter of a farmer not too far from these parts. My pa was a wood nymph."

"Do they live here with you?"

"No," the girl replied, but did not elaborate further.

They arrived at the end of the hall and the girl knocked briskly on the wood.

"Send her in," Elaria's voice came from the other side. The girl bobbed a curtsy at Amaleah as she opened the door wide and the scuttled away. Amaleah realized that she hadn't even asked for the girl's name.

"Amaleah," Elaria greeted her coldly, "have a seat." She motioned toward a green, padded chair opposite her own. "There is much we need to discuss."

Amaleah sank into the oversized chair. It was so big it nearly engulfed her.

"I have heard reports that your father is gathering an army to find you and bring you home. There have even been rumors that he knows you're here."

Amaleah's jaw dropped at the revelation. She had thought— well, she wasn't sure what she had thought.

"Anno tells me that you've made quite a bit of progress in your use of the staff, though she worries about your control over your emotions."

The princess nodded but continued to say nothing.

Elaria continued, "Although I have serious reservations about your ability to serve as the Harbinger, we cannot wait any longer for you to begin learning the basics of magical control. Your powers are unlike any I have seen since I was a child."

Elaria sipped from a glass of water. "I do not agree with the Creators' choice, but I accept that you are the Harbinger."

Amaleah had had enough talk of the prophecy for one day. "Tell me of my father's plans," she demanded.

"What do you want me to tell you? That his forces will far outnumber our own? That he will also have magic wielders in his forces? That his soldiers are superior to ours?"

Amaleah dug her nails into the arms of her chair. "I know what kind of man my father is," she said coolly. "How much time do we have before his army arrives?"

"A timeline has not been provided. Our spies have confirmed that he has been drafting boys as young as twelve into the army. They have also reported that he's been spending more and more time locked away in his war room with his councilors. That is all we know."

Amaleah's pulse drummed in her ears. She could barely hear Elaria over its rhythm. He was taking children. To find her. To have her returned to him. How many people would die because she had chosen to flee from him?

"Amaleah?" Elaria asked. She was leaning forward in her chair, her eyes uncharacteristically full of concern.

"It's all my fault," she whispered. "I should never have left the palace. I should have faced him on my own. He wouldn't be doing this if I had just kept my promise to him." She knew she was rambling, but she didn't care. The thought of hundreds, if not thousands, more of her people dying simply to save her from her fate made her skin crawl. She would not be the reason for their despair.

Elaria backhanded Amaleah across the cheek. Amaleah's head whipped to the side and she saw twinkles of sparkling light before everything came back into focus. "What was that for?" she asked, placing a hand over her swelling cheek.

"This is no time to play the 'oh woe is me' card, Amaleah."

"I'm not…"

"You were," Elaria reprimanded firmly. "Only the Creators know why they chose you to be the savior of this land, but there's nothing we can do about it now. Either stand tall and face your fate for what it is or cower and die and drag the rest of us into darkness with you."

The passion with which Elaria spoke sent a shiver down Amaleah's back. "I'm sorry, Elaria," she murmured. She sat up straighter and looked Elaria in the eye, "What do we do now?"

"Our forces cannot defend you without help," she said. She stood and gathered an armful of papers from her desk. "I know the Keepers have promised to help you, that they sent you here to be trained. They always did like to let other people fight their battles," she sniffed. "Perhaps you will be able to convince them to aid us when the time comes."

"So, you are not going to abandon me?" Amaleah asked. She was surprised, given how much she felt the older woman's wrath since she'd let her magic explode from her with catastrophic effect.

"No, child," Elaria responded, her voice softening, "the Silver Moon clan will not abandon you. My hope is that the other eleven tribes will also aid us, for if they don't our entire way of life could be destroyed."

Amaleah nodded. She now understood the risk Elaria had taken in allowing her to take refuge in Encartia. "The Dramadoonian royals offered me aid once," she recalled. "Perhaps they would offer it again."

"Perhaps," Elaria said thoughtfully as she laid out a map over the table between the two chairs. It showed, in detail, the Lunameedian countryside. Amaleah traced her finger over the space between Estrellala and Encartia.

"How many days will it take my father to move his forces this far south?" she asked.

"With the numbers that have been reported to us, it could take up to six weeks."

"Six weeks," she repeated softly. It seemed like such a long time to her, but she knew the weeks would pass quickly.

"That includes the remaining prep time we've calculated he'll need to train his new recruits," she said. "I hear that he's been in contact with one of the dark sorcerers to the north."

"But my father hates sorcerers," Amaleah objected. "He's always had a great distrust of them. He told me once that they were too independent to count on. I don't believe he would change his mind now."

Elaria shook her head. "He may distrust them, child, but he will use their gifts like he does the rest of the magical creatures in the realm."

Amaleah has always been taught to fear sorcerers. By far, they were the magical beings her father despised the most. She'd heard the Baron Blodruth and his daughter talking once about how King Magnus had sought out the help of the sorcerers when her mother had been dying. None of them had heeded his call. The memory sparked an idea.

"Do you know where the Baron Blodruth and his daughter went after they were exiled from court?"

"I've heard rumors…"

"Let me write to them," Amaleah squeaked. "There was a time when Nicolette Blodruth was like a mother to me. If there's a chance, no matter how small, that she and her father would aid me now, I have to take it."

Elaria slowly folded her hands in her lap. "I'm not sure that is the wisest choice for an ally, Amaleah," she said.

"Why not?" she responded. "They were always so kind to

me…"

"Do you remember why they abandoned the palace?" Elaria asked.

"Yes," Amaleah stammered. The vision of her father barricading the Blodruth's servants inside of their corridor and burning them alive bloomed into life. She could smell the putrid smoke and feel the heat rising in the palace. "My father used it as a lesson on loyalty. He told me that to break a promise was unforgivable." She shivered as she remembered how cold it had been on the balcony as they watched the baron and his daughter flee from the palace.

"I never met the Blodruth's, Amaleah. I cannot tell you how they would react to you reaching out to them for help."

Amaleah pulled her knees up to her chin and hugged herself as she said, "If I am to lead my people, then I have to learn how to build trust even with those who may despise my family."

Elaria lips twitched at her response.

"What?" Amaleah asked, still hugging her legs.

"Sometimes I catch glimpses of your mother in you," she replied. "And," she continued, "I see the ruler you could become."

Amaleah beamed. She was thankful that the matriarch didn't entirely despise her. She clapped her hands and said, "I think it's time that we began drafting a letter to everyone who may come to my aid."

Chapter Thirty-Two
Solmani Palace, Miliom, Szarmi

Colin marched down the marble hallway of Solmani Palace. It was exactly as he remembered it. The pillars were dusted in a thin coat of gold powder. Gas lights twinkled in uniform intervals. Their light poured in from the open windows. Colin could hear the distant sound of music wafting upon the wind. Unlike the songs from his memories, the tune of this song brought sorrow with it. Gone was the jubilee he was used to. Colin paused a moment to glance out one of the windows with a view of Miliom.

This is my city, he thought. *It will always be my city.* From his vantage point, Colin could see the destruction that had riddled the capital. Entire burrows were little more than black scorch marks. The once pristine white and red stone the city had been constructed of was dull and dirty. Colin clutched the windowsill so tightly that his knuckles turned white and his fingers ached. Of course, he had known, after wandering through the streets and being attacked by the ruffians, that his city had been beset with turmoil. But seeing how far reaching the destruction was left Colin feeling interminably furious. There was no excuse his mother, or his sister, could give that would convince him to forgive them for what they done to their capital or to their people.

A cool breeze whipped through the empty corridor, trailing winter in its wake. *So soon*, he realized. He had been gone for so long that he hadn't realized how close to the months of darkness they were. Based on his observations of the city, he had little reason to believe that his mother and Coraleen had prepped the larders for the vast amounts of food that would be needed to survive a bitter winter. With the impending war, their people would suffer even more, especially since he knew his mother would draft boys as young as twelve and girls as young as fifteen to fight in the war. Farms would be left to waste away come spring, only furthering the hunger felt by the people. Colin had read about such things during his studies at Fort Pelid. Captain Conrad had always spoken about planning for the dark months as being of the utmost importance. Colin knew that, even if he could regain control of his throne before the cold months set in, he wouldn't have enough time to store up food to last everyone through the winter. He ground his teeth as he considered the state of his kingdom.

"And so, the prodigal son has returned," a smooth voice hissed from the shadows.

Colin clenched his jaw. Sweat beaded on his brow as he slowly turned towards the sound of his mother's voice.

"No help to you," he responded in kind. His eyes trailed across her attire. He had never seen his mother wear anything other than the finest of dresses. Yet, here she was, clad in the blackest tunic he had ever seen. Her hair was pulled into a loose braid that hung behind her back. Colin raised his eyebrows as he noticed how much silver was woven into her ebony hair. During the months he'd been away, she'd aged.

She held a slender sword in her hand. It reflected blue light pouring in from the open window. He had never seen his mother fight before. He doubted she knew how to wield the sword she carried and he almost laughed at the thought of her attempting to stop him from reaching Captain Conrad's rooms. The laugh caught in his throat as he saw the hatred in her eyes.

"Why?" he whispered. The single word hung between them. Colin clenched and unclenched his fist so many times he lost count as he waited for his mother to respond. She blinked at him, her expression cold and blank. He took a step towards her. "Tell me why," he commanded.

His sister stepped from the shadows in a motion so swift, Colin barely had time to maneuver away from her blade. Her sword was identical to the one their mother carried and Colin could see intricate engravings sprawled across the metal. He recognized a few of the symbols. They were the symbols of the Stormbearer house. They were the symbols of a ruler. A fire roiled within him as he stared at those symbols that should have been his. He positioned himself so that his back was to the smooth wall on the other side of the corridor. He couldn't risk any of his mother's guards slipping from the shadows and surprising him the way his sister had. The coldness of the stone provided some measure of comfort. He knew these walls, these corridors, this kingdom. He was the rightful heir.

He locked eyes with his sister and said, "Do you intend to murder me, Sister?" His voice was bitter and it took all his reserve to keep himself from lunging at her. She was the reason his people believed him dead. She was the reason he had lost everything.

Her eyes were wary as she spoke, "No, Brother. I do not intend to kill you." Her lips trembled as she continued, "At least not yet."

At that, Colin released a low growl. Growing up Coraleen may have been the better fighter, but now that Colin had faced the trials of the past few months, he knew he was scrappier than his sister. He had no intention of ever letting her best him again. This was his only chance to find Captain Conrad and convince him the rumors about his death were lies. He had to believe that Captain Conrad would believe him. There was no other option. Even if he and the captain could only convince a few of the other royal councilors that he was, in fact, the rightful king of Szarmi, it could tip the scale in his favor.

His eyes darted to his mother's face. She bared her teeth at him, her pearly white incisors gleaming in the blue light. Releasing a long breath, Colin asked, "Why do you hate me, Mother?" He needed time to think, to plan, to escape.

She barked a harsh laugh at him as she brandished her sword in his direction. The tip of her blade cut a loose button from Colin's tunic. He heard it bounce across the marble floor as he sidestepped closer to the small passageway to his left that would lead him to the rooms reserved for military officers. He remembered which one Captain Conrad reserved for his personal quarters. Without taking his eyes from his mother's, Colin batted the blade away from his chest with the back of his hand. She glared at him, and poised the blade against his chest once more. A smirk spread across his face at her games. Had he been the child of his youth, her actions would have plagued him. Now, they only made him recognize how petty and insecure his mother truly was. He could use this to his advantage.

"Hate you, Colin?" Vista cooed. She batted her eyes at him. "Why would I ever hate you?" she purred as she slid the blade down his chest, slicing off more buttons as she went.

Colin ducked just as the tip of her blade skimmed across his bare chest. Blood seeped from the wound in a crisp, red line. He barely noticed the pain as he continued to lock his eyes with her.

"Mother," Coraleen reprimanded, a warning. Her voice was

cold and passionless, yet her eyes bore into their mother's back like a predator about to attack. "We discussed this." She looked at Colin as she spoke. For an instant, he thought he saw a flicker of doubt there. And something else. Something that he couldn't quite describe, but it gave him hope.

"Everyone believes he's dead. As long as he accepts the truth, there's no reason to kill him," Coraleen continued. Colin stared at his sister. Her lips were set in a hard line as she stared at their mother. "Please, Mother, at least give him this one chance."

Colin inched away from his mother as she and Coraleen glared at each other. He knew they were communicating without words about what to do with him. He was determined to take his fate out of their hands.

"What truth?" Colin asked. He forced his voice to quiver slightly. He knew his mother, at least, would fall into his trap. She had always viewed him as weak; why not let her now?

Coraleen tapped her foot against the marble floor. The sound echoed down the hallway. "It's time that he knows," she said. She pouted slightly, the way she always did when she was about to demand something go her way. It had always worked on their father, but rarely on their mother.

"Fine," Vista spat. Her caramel skin had turned a faint shade of puce that made Coin's skin crawl.

She rounded on Colin. Her face was twisted into a disgusting display of anger, hate, and disbelief. Colin gulped, a whisper of fear shivering down his spine. She advanced upon him, pointing her slender sword towards his heart before abruptly stopping just as the point of the sword pierced his linen shirt. In the blue light, Colin almost would have mistaken her for one of the magical creatures of Lunameed. That is, if it hadn't been for her twisted features. Her scowl deepened as Colin continued to stand his ground.

"You always were a sniveling little mongrel," she hissed. "You were always the weakest runt." She spat on his shoes and Colin resisted the urge to wipe it off on the side of his pants.

"You've always hated me," he said, shrugging. "There's no reason for me to expect anything different now."

He deftly slipped his hand into his tunic and pulled out one of the seven daggers Redbeard had given him. Although his palms were sweaty, the weight of blade was reassuring. He proffered the blade, hilt first, towards Vista. "I'm tired of fighting you, Mother," he bowed as he spoke. He knew it was a little theatrical, but didn't care. If now was the time for grand gestures, he would comply. "Just tell me what you have to say and let us move forward."

Coraleen and their mother shared a look. Colin fought the urge the flip the dagger and strike out at their mother. He could only imagine the lies she had fed Coraleen throughout the years. He could see the internal struggle in his sister's face. Whatever their mother had done to his sister, Colin vowed he would make her pay.

Vista sighed loudly and Colin stole a quick glance at her. Her nostrils flared when she caught his gaze. "You really want to know, don't you?" she asked. Her eyes roamed over his face and Colin thought—at least for an instance—that he caught a glimpse of remorse in her expression. It quickly faded as she nodded and Coraleen advanced upon him with such speed that Colin barely had time to react as she slid her own dagger from her belt and pinned him from behind. She pressed the blade into his throat.

"Whatever you think, promise me that you'll accept her words as truth," Coraleen hissed softly. Her breath was warm and wet against his ear. Although the dagger was cold against the exposed skin of his neck, Colin felt how gently his sister held him. He nodded in an almost imperceptible manner and felt her body sag as if all the tension she'd been carrying had suddenly been released.

"Please, Mother," she said. Her voice was softer now, more like the child he remembered. Her breath tickled his skin as it swept over him. He could smell the hint of chocolate and wine on her breath as she continued, "Maybe we were never meant to kill him. Maybe…" Coraleen paused and Colin felt the shuddering breath before he heard it. "Maybe we should give him a chance to fade into obscurity. Everyone thinks he's dead so there's really no reason to…"

"When I was a girl, your father was the bravest man I knew," Vista said, cutting Coraleen off. Her hands shook as she sheathed her sword. Her golden skin was a dull, tan color and her brow was furrowed. Colin couldn't remember a single time in his life that his mother's brow had furrowed the way it was now.

She dug her cold hand beneath his chin and lifted his face until he had no choice but to stare into her cold eyes. They gleamed as her nails cut into the soft spot beneath his chin. Still, Colin refused to flinch against her touch.

She sighed before saying, "I admired your father, Colin." She tapped her fingernail against his cheek as she spoke. "I thought I loved him. He was the young, rising star of the military and I thought he only had eyes for me. Of course, at that age, I only had eyes for him." A sad smile played across her lips as she spoke and Colin thought he saw the glint of a tear in her eye. Her nail was still tapping against his cheek.

"How could you love a man you had only met once before your wedding day, Mother?" Colin asked, a smirk spreading across his face. He knew he'd catch her in this lie. She hadn't known his father long enough to form an opinion about him before their marriage. She couldn't have loved him. Colin didn't believe in love at first sight and, since he knew they'd only met the once before their marriage, he couldn't imagine a scenario in which they had fallen in love. By all accounts, his parents hadn't even spoken to one another during King Henry's visit to solidify the marriage pact between Szarmi and Borganda.

Vista narrowed her chocolate brown eyes at him, her nostrils flaring. Her knuckles turned white and her arms shook slightly as she wrapped them around herself. For once, she did not resemble the polished, controlled woman to which Colin was accustomed. He found that seeing his mother rattled this way brought him no joy. Despite everything she had done to him, he still loved her. He would probably always love her.

"Before the wars broke out among the islands, my people had been a mighty breed. We were fierce and loyal. We were rich, not just in gold and jewels, but also blessed by the Creators. All the island nations admired us. This is why King Henry agreed to my father's terms of marriage. He wanted the social capital I would bring to Szarmi."

Colin fidgeted as his mother spoke. He knew the histories of the Island Nations. Borganda had been a mercantile leader for years before dozens of civil rebellions and the eventual decline of their aristocracy. In the wake of the political turmoil, the islands had joined together to form the United Islands. But, that had happened after his mother had sailed across the ocean to join his father in Szarmi.

"I don't understand what this has to do with me," Colin said flatly.

His mother patted his cheek as she stared past him. Her eyes took on the glazed look of someone seeing beyond the present.

"It was the harvest festival and I had been given a new dress to celebrate my betrothal to King Henry. Every man in court was envious of the foreign king that would sweep me away. I flirted with them as the bonfires burned bright and the lute players dazzled us with their skills. I danced so much that I could barely breathe."

Colin didn't know when, but his mother had stopped tapping her nail against his skin as she spoke.

"I don't remember who heard the beating drums first. I do not know who blew the war horn as the armies approached. At first..." she shivered, but continued, "At first, we thought it was just a demonstration. We thought it was part of the festivities. But then they broke down the gate. My ladies swarmed around me, their blades drawn. My father had ensured that each of them was a member of the Nightshades. They trained me against my mother's will, but my father encouraged my education."

She glanced at Coraleen. "I passed my knowledge onto your sister," a smile danced across her lips. "She has surpassed even the greatest among those included in my retinue."

Coraleen's blade dug into Colin's skin at the compliment. He felt the warm trickle of blood slide down his throat before she relaxed her grip. He had heard tales of the Order of the Nightshade in his youth. They were lady warriors—assassins, really—who were trained in the art of poison, seduction, and stealthy death. The Szarmian soldiers had boasted about how they would make a conquest of the women beyond the Paralosa Sea, though Colin knew none who had met one of the deadly assassins.

"Screams filled the castle. The guards posted at the doors to the great hall were the first to turn against us as we fought to reach the hidden tunnels behind the throne. Nahaila, my truest friend, was the first to fall." There was no tremble in her voice as she spoke. There was no glimmer in his mother's eye as she continued, "It happened so swiftly, there was no time for her to react. One of my father's guards turned against us. I can still see the agony on her face as the guard twisted his fist within her hair and yanked her head back. There was so much blood."

He felt Coraleen stiffen beside him and wondered how much of this tale his mother had told her before. He would have thought that his mother had prepared his sister for this lie. His mother shook her head before staring directly into his eyes. "He reached for me next, but my second stepped between us. She told me to go, to run as fast as I could to the safe room further in the palace. And so, I did. I wouldn't know what befell her until the following morning."

Throughout his childhood, Queen Vista had only spoken about her childhood in Borganda in terms of the things she either desperately missed or hated beyond reason. Most of the stories he heard about the other half of his birthright came from Vecepia or from the Island Nations' ambassador during his short visits to Miliom over the years. Although his mother imported tea from her home nation and, occasionally, made food with Borgandian spices, Colin could count on one hand how often she had discussed her childhood experiences.

"In my panic, I didn't escape through the secret passage that led to the safe room. My father always had been paranoid about slave rebellions since the events in the Jade Islands that he'd had a powerful sorcerer add enchantments to a room close to my mother's quarters. Only those of his bloodline or name could enter." Queen Vista paused for a moment. Her eyes stared past Colin and took on a listless expression. For once in his life, Colin began to wonder what his mother had experienced in Borganda before coming to Szarmi. He had always assumed she'd lived a life of leisure and comfort. Now, he wasn't so sure.

"Instead, I rushed to my bedroom and bolted the door shut. I could hear the screams of my maids as they tried to stop the soldiers—the traitors—from reaching me. They gave everything to protect me." She began tapping her nail against his cheek again.

"The sounds of fighting had ceased, yet I was still terrified. I had heard my ladies—my friends—as they gave their lives. When the pounding on my door started, I hid beneath my bed, too frightened to open it. But then, as if in answer to my pleas for safety, your father's voice called through the door."

Vista looked straight into Colin's eyes as she spoke, her expression all hard lines and sadness. "I thought I was saved. He was there to protect me. I knew it. He had always been so kind to me."

"Father never spoke of this," Colin said.

"Haven't you figured it out yet, Colin?" Vista goaded. "Or do I need to explain, in detail, what befell me the moment I opened that door?"

Colin's insides squirmed and, despite his best efforts to still them, memories of what he'd read about military coups and war poured into his mind. Men could do terrible things when they were set on destruction.

"Your father strode into my rooms covered in grime and gore and blood. His face was flecked with it. I asked him where my father was. He told me he'd taken refuge in the safe room with my mother and siblings. I was the only member of the royal family not in the safe room. I remember my skin turning to ice at the thought. I had been so stupid."

"You're anything but stupid, Mother," Coraleen whispered. Colin had a moment of reprieve from the knife cutting into his neck as she loosened her grip.

Vista shifted her gaze towards Coraleen, "Thank you, dear one, but I am who I am now because of what happened to me on that day. And trust me, I was stupid." She turned her gaze back to Colin. She waved her hand at Coraleen and the princess dropped the knife held to Colin's throat. Before Colin had time to react, Queen Vista gripped a handful of his tunic and pulled him into an embrace.

Colin stiffened as his mother hissed in his ear, "Your father was a rising star in the military until the day he took everything away from me."

Her voice was so bitter that Colin accidently jerked his head in surprise. Coraleen's blade was back at his neck in an instant, leaving a small red stain on his skin as it cut a thin line across his throat.

"I don't understand," Colin said, his voice tight. He feared he understood too much.

"King Henry was not your father, Colin. How could he be when you were already in my belly by the time my father put me on a ship to sail to Szarmi?"

"That's not true," Colin proclaimed. "You're lying." He turned his expression to Coraleen, despite the fact that her blade continued to slice at his neck. "Coraleen," he pled, "don't tell me you believe this? She's trying to pit us against each other, can't you see that?"

Vista cackled coldly. "You really are as stupid as my spies have reported," she said.

Colin sought out his sister's face. Tears glistened on her cheeks and her lower lip quivered. He turned his attention back to Vista. "Why should I believe you? You've usurped my power; you've placed Coraleen on the throne; you've done everything you could to destroy my life. Tell me, Mother," he scoffed at her name, "why should I believe anything you say?"

"Because it's the truth," Vista replied. She did not look away from him when she spoke. She stood with her back straight and her chin held high. Although she wasn't wearing her usually elegant garb and her hair was tied back in a braid, Colin thought he had never seen her look so regal.

There was so much defiance and anguish in her expression, Colin found it difficult to maintain eye contact. It was like looking into a mirror and seeing his own feelings reflected back at him. His hands shook and he gripped the dagger tighter to hide his emotions.

"If you're telling me the truth, why didn't you say something sooner? Why didn't Father ever tell me?"

"He didn't know."

Colin's mouth formed a small 'oh' at her response. What she and Coraleen had just revealed to him finally clicked into place. If his mother was telling the truth, he wasn't the true heir. His father—King Henry—hadn't known. Sweat formed on his brow. *It's not possible,* he told himself. *It can't be.*

"I'm sure you have lots of questions," Vista said softly. For once, her voice was kind as it passed over Colin.

He shook his head. "No," he said.

"Colin," Coraleen chimed in, her voice as delicate as a

budding flower on an early spring day. She lowered her blade and placed her hand on his arm. Her warmth made him jolt as if he had been struck instead of caressed. She pulled her arm back, her expression that of a wounded animal as he turned on her.

"This is why you let them shoot me from the bridge?" he asked. He knew her answer even before she whispered 'yes.' He didn't respond. He didn't look at her or at Vista as he stormed down the hallway towards Captain Conrad's quarters.

"Let him go," he heard Vista say as he rounded a bend in the hallway. "We'll deal with him later."

Colin stood just out of sight of his mother and sister; his entire body quivered. Szarmi was his home. Not Borganda. King Henry was his father. Not some unknown soldier in a distant land. He was the rightful ruler of Szarmi. Not Coraleen. Colin ground his teeth as he considered. As he hesitated outside of Captain Conrad's quarters, a quiet voice inside of him whispered that his mother's words were true.

Chapter Thirty-Three

Colin sipped at the steaming cup of hot tea he clutched in his hands. The liquid scalded his lips as it crested the top of the cup. Still, the warmth emanating from the porcelain calmed him. Captain Conrad sat in a straight-backed chair across from him. He twiddled his thumbs and looked everywhere except at Colin.

The captain cleared his throat and finally looked into Colin's eyes. "I know you've been through a lot, son." His voice was hollow. Even from across the room, Colin could tell that the Captain's eyes were rimmed in red. He scanned the small sitting room. Papers were strewn about the room in disorderly fashion. Dirty dishes laden the floor closest to the captain's desk. The captain's quarters held little of the order and cleanliness they had at Fort Pelid. Colin scrutinized the captain.

"Tell me what's happened since I left for Lunameed," he demanded, cutting the captain off.

Captain Conrad flushed a dark shade of purple, sputtered a moment, and then said, "It's no use, Colin. Everyone believes you're dead. We had a burial for you."

"I don't care," Colin replied, impetuously.

"Colin," the captain said with a little more of his usual commanding tone, "there's something I need to tell you, something your mother..."

343

"If it's the allegation that I'm not the legitimate heir, then I already know."

Colin was surprised to see relief wash over Captain Conrad's features. He wondered how many others his mother had spread her lies to. He wondered how many of them had believed her. He set the still-steaming cup of tea on the small table between them.

"King Henry, whatever my relationship with him was, chose me as his heir. I am the rightful king."

Captain Conrad paled at Colin's statements. This was not going the way he had imagined. Throughout his journey home, he had always envisioned Captain Conrad supporting him from the moment he laid eyes on him. He had always been Colin's mentor, his champion, his friend. He couldn't understand why he hesitated now, when Colin needed him the most.

"Ethan," Colin said, using the captain's given name, "please…"

"You will not, under any circumstances, address me so informally, cadet," Conrad commanded. He scowled at Colin, his eyes turning dark.

Colin shuddered at the captain's expression. If he couldn't convince the military leader who knew him best to follow him, then how could he expect any of the others to follow suite?

"Captain, I need your help."

The captain sighed loudly. "I know that, Colin."

Colin didn't know how to respond. It seemed as if everything he said was an affront to the captain. But, he was the rightful heir. No matter what his mother said, King Henry had chosen him to rule. That thought reverberated through Colin and gave him strength.

"Even if I wanted to help you, Colin, my vow was to the crown, not to an individual."

Colin's mouth slid open as he regarded the captain. His heart beat faster in his chest as the realization of what was about to come next settled on him.

"I'm sorry, but no matter what you say, I cannot break that vow."

The captain's jaw clenched and Colin could see the vein throbbing in the captain's neck.

"Your vow was to defend the crown. I am the crown."

Captain Conrad laughed at that. "No one person is the crown, son."

"But I am the rightful heir."

"No matter how much I wish that were true, it's not."

The finality of Captain Conrad's words slammed into Colin like a bolt from one of their army's automatic crossbows.

"Queen Vista told me her story, Colin. And, Creators save me, I believe her." He rose from his chair and strode towards Colin. Silver lined the captain's eyes as he placed a hand on Colin's shoulder and whispered, "You are good, kind and incredibly intelligent." He squeezed Colin's shoulder. "You are a great leader, son."

A single tear slid down the captain's cheek as he spoke. "I'm sorry that it's come to this."

"That's it?" Colin shouted as he shrugged off Captain Conrad's touch and stood. His head ached as he turned to face the older man. "You give me condolences and you tell me what a great leader I am, but you can't admit that I should be the ruler?" He strode towards the captain's doors. "I risked everything to come back to Szarmi, Ethan." He spat the captain's first name as if it were poison. "Have you even been in the city streets since my mother took control of the kingdom? Have you seen the destruction? Have you seen the hunger?"

Everything that had been building within him seemed to boil to the surface as he continued to glare at the captain who had trained him. "You sit here, in this palace, with all its finery. You serve a tyrant, Ethan, did you know that? Was it you who ordered your soldiers to smash the gas orbs that provided light to the city? Was it you who set Miliom ablaze?"

Captain Conrad threw Colin's still-full mug of tea against the wall. The porcelain cup shattered into hundreds of shards and tea exploded across the room. Colin stilled as he stared at the man before him. Conrad's shoulders heaved up and down as he breathed heavily.

"I would never," the captain said, enunciating each word, "turn my men against the people of this city."

"Then who did?" Colin asked defiantly.

Conrad glowered at him but said nothing. Colin knew it had been a low blow. He knew how much the people—how much Szarmi—meant to the captain.

"I'm sorry," Colin finally said.

The older man shrugged before stomping across the room and retrieving a broom and dust pan. He turned his back on Colin as he swept up the remnants of the mug.

"I just want what's best for my people," Colin continued. He didn't care if his words fell on deaf ears. "All this time, I've been worried about whether or not I'd make a good king. It took losing my throne to learn what it means to truly be a great one."

Conrad turned to face Colin at those words. His face had turned ruddy and there was still an edge to his expression as he regarded Colin, but he asked, "What makes a great ruler?"

Colin considered his words carefully before responding. He wasn't sure how Captain Conrad would react or what he would say, but Colin knew this was his one chance to gain the captain's help. He was not going to waste it.

"You weren't there when the Lunameedians turned on us. We waited for as long as we could for Jameston and the others to return. They never did." Colin's voice cracked as he spoke. He had so rarely spoken about Jameston that, now that he was, he found it difficult to control his emotions. "We had nothing as we traveled across the Lunameedian wilderness. And then, when we finally made it to the border, my own sister denounced me and sentenced me to death."

Colin paused as the memory stung him. "Through this, I learned that leaders can never take their power or the people who support them for granted. I learned what it was like to be hungry, and cold, and miserable for days on end."

"Plenty of people know these things, son," Conrad said softly. "That doesn't mean they make great leaders."

Colin's lips lifted at that. "That's true," he said, "but I also learned what it means to have compassion for others. Princess Amaleah taught me that."

Conrad perked up at the mention of the princess. "You spent time with her?" he asked. "But how? It was reported that she disappeared into the wilds of Lunameed without a trace."

"Let's just say I ran into her while I was making my way home."

Colin didn't feel like sharing his experiences in Encartia with the older man. With the reactions the captain had been having since opening his door to Colin, the prince wasn't sure he could trust him.

"Honestly, Captain, I think leading a kingdom is more about compassion, confidence, and trust than it is anything else. King Magnus butchered his own people. I saw their dead bodies strung up on poles as we proceeded to the Palace of Veri. His own daughter fled from the palace to escape him. My mother and sister are letting our people starve and resort to thievery to survive. My father—he will always be my father, Captain— taught me to be tough and strong. But, he also encouraged me to seek out knowledge and truth."

Colin felt like he was rambling, but he didn't care. Captain Conrad would either side with him or he wouldn't. At this point, Colin had nothing to lose. "I am ready for this, Captain. I know I am."

Captain Conrad shook his head. "I'm sorry, Colin."

The prince bowed his head, crestfallen. He had pinned everything on Captain Conrad's acceptance of him. Without it, he didn't know what to do next.

"It's not because I don't believe you," the captain said. "I do," he continued quickly. "But I am a man of my word and I cannot abide myself breaking my vow to the throne."

Colin sighed loudly. "That's it then," he proclaimed, his shoulders sagging. He turned to leave the captain's rooms.

"It doesn't have to be," Conrad replied softly.

He turned back, hope spurring in his chest, and raised an eyebrow.

"Think about it, Colin," the captain prodded. "You already know what you need to do."

"I don't," Colin began.

"How close did you become with the lost princess?"

Colin wavered. He knew how he felt about Amaleah. Despite their separation, thoughts of her had pervaded his thoughts since their time traveling together. He doubted she felt the same way. Besides, they were both refugees in their own countries.

"As close as you can become in a limited amount of time," Colin responded judiciously.

"Ah," the captain said, "I see." He quieted as he regarded Colin with a knowing stare. "Perhaps your path to the throne will not be a straight one but a strategic one."

Colin would be lying if he said the thought hadn't crossed

his mind. He had nothing to offer her. His position in Szarmi was, if it were possible, even more precarious than her own in Lunameed. If they formed an alliance and they failed, he was certain King Magnus would execute him. If they succeeded in taking back the Lunameedian throne, there would be no assurances that they could beat the superior Szarmian armies. There were too many possibilities, too many questions left unanswered. Besides, Colin reasoned, he knew that he found her intriguing, beautiful, brave, and incredibly intelligent. But, he was unsure she saw him in the same way. He had always wanted to marry for love, not country.

"What if she declines?" he pondered.

"Then she says no," Conrad replied, a smile playing across his lips. "The surest way to never know the answer to that question is simply not ask it."

"I have nothing to offer her."

"You have yourself."

"Ha," Colin laughed. "I'm not sure that's worth much when it comes to reclaiming one's throne. Look at me, I can't even convince my own captain to side with me."

He meant it as a joke, but the sadness in Captain Conrad's eyes pierced Colin to his core. "I'm sorry," he said quickly. "I didn't mean…"

"You meant it," Conrad cut him off. He sighed. "I'm sorry, Colin, but I can't keep apologizing or defending my position. Please, just accept my stance for what it is."

Colin didn't like it. He didn't agree with the captain. And, he certainly did not understand it. "Fine," he managed to grind out.

"But," Conrad mused and he stroked his chin, "perhaps there is a way to help you without breaking my vow."

Colin cocked an eyebrow at him, "Which would be?" he inquired.

"Just because I'm not willing to break my vow to the throne doesn't mean that others won't."

"You do realize you're speaking of treason," Colin pointed out.

The captain nodded once, his expression grim.

"And you're still willing to do that?"

Conrad nodded again.

"Why?"

"Because I believe in you."

It didn't fully make sense to Colin. He couldn't fathom why Captain Conrad would be willing to help him recruit soldiers to his cause without joining him as well. Still, he wasn't about to reject what aid the captain was willing to supply. They cleared the captain's desk and set about drafting their plan.

⸻

Hours later, after Colin's fingers were covered in ink and Captain Conrad had finished an entire bottle of amber-colored alcohol, they leaned back in their respective chairs with smiles on their faces. The plan was set; now, all they needed to do was set it in motion.

They had decided that the less amount of time Colin spent in the city the better. Captain Conrad was concerned about the queen's reasons for letting Colin escape her as easily as she had. He was certain Vista had a plot up her sleeve to do something vile to Colin—something that would require him being freed from the dungeon. And so, they had agreed that Colin would vacate Miliom within twenty-four hours.

In that time, Captain Conrad would call a meeting of his soldiers along with any recruits who had spent considerable amounts of time with Colin at Fort Pelid during their training days. At first, Colin had been resistant to including those who had trained with him. He never had been a strong fighter, much to the chagrin of his father and mother. But, he had been well respected by his peers. And, he reminded himself, they all knew that he had only ever lost one training exercise in which he was the commander. Conrad believed this would be enough to sway many of the younger men to Colin's side.

Conrad clanked his tankard of ale against Colin's glass of water. Clear liquid sloshed over the sides of the glass and puddled around its base. The water soaked through the edges of notes Colin had scattered across the table.

"Was that really necessary?" Colin asked. His head ached and his fingers felt slightly numb. He wasn't sure if it was because of drinking too little water or if he was just that anxious about the next step in their plan.

"Maybe," Conrad replied, his speech slightly slurred. Colin wasn't sure he had ever seen the captain drunk during all his time at Fort Pelid. He was about to chide the older man when a knock pounded on the door.

"What's that?" Conrad asked. His eyes had taken on a glassy sheen as he clumsily stood from his chair.

"Captain Conrad," a voice bellowed from the other side of the door. "You're needed in the queen's chamber."

"Am I now?" Conrad responded in kind. Colin rested his head in his hands. If he was pulled away into some long meeting, there was no chance of their plan succeeding.

"Captain?" the voice asked. "Is everything alright?"

Conrad ambled across the room. He swayed with each step and Colin was fearful the man would fall completely over. He didn't, thankfully, but he did slam into the door. "Everything's just fine," he yelled. He flung the door open, a broad smile spread across his face.

Colin dove behind the desk. His knees crackled as he squatted. Even after walking the countless miles between Estrellala and Miliom, his legs quivered at supporting himself in a crouching position.

"Are you alone, Captain?"

Captain Conrad glanced behind him. Colin peeked around the edge of the desk. He hoped that the corner he was hiding behind was shrouded in enough shadow to conceal him, though he was not entirely convinced. It was then that he saw the tankard of ale and the glass of water still sitting on the low tea table.

"Well, now that you mention it," Conrad spluttered, "I may or may not have a little company over." His speech drawled and a bit of drool slid down his chin as he spoke. "But, a lady never kisses and tells so I won't be sharing her name with you."

The soldier blushed a deep crimson red and stumbled over his words.

"It's alright, son," Conrad boomed, clapping the soldier on the shoulder. "She'll leave once we've gone."

The guard nodded slowly, though Colin caught him peering around the room. He slid further behind the desk and prayed the shadows continued to conceal him. He didn't peep out again until he'd heard the soft click of the door latching shut.

The room felt empty without the imposing body of Captain Conrad to fill it. He hoped the next time they met it wouldn't be on the battlefield, but he knew that was too much to ask. Conrad had made his choice. Colin needed to respect that.

Colin did a quick sweep of the room, collecting the notes he and Conrad had taken and maps of the Lunameedian-Szarmian border. He was determined not to leave anything incriminating behind. It would be bad enough for the captain if any of the soldiers chose to leave with Colin on the morrow. If they didn't, the plan Colin and Conrad had concocted would be of little use. He needed troops to offer to Amaleah in order to set their accord. No matter how much she liked him, he knew she would never agree to bind herself to a Szarmian and pit herself against entire swaths of her people just because of how she feels about him.

Checking the room one last time for any remnants of his being there, Colin cracked the door open and peered into the empty hallway beyond. *It's now or never*, he told himself as he dashed from the room and made his way back to the tunnel.

Chapter Thirty-Four

Thank the Creators for hooded tunics, Colin thought as he rounded a corner and nearly slammed into a maid carrying a tray laden with pastries. Instinctively, he pulled his hood lower over his eyes. If his mother had kept the same servants, there was a chance this one would recognize him; Colin couldn't take that chance. He bobbed his head and sidestepped around her without a sound. The butter and honey scents of the pastries washed over Colin, making his stomach growl. He realized that he hadn't eaten since the night before when they'd taken refuge in Vecepia's shop. He and Conrad had been so focused on figuring out a plan that they hadn't taken time to eat a meal.

He encountered other servants carrying platters filled to the brim with food, wine chalices from his father's private collection, and gold and jewels from the treasury. None of the servants stopped to talk to him, most of them averted their gazes and kept moving forward. Their behaviors troubled him. When his father had still been alive, he'd ruled with iron in his fist but also mercy in his heart. Clearly his sister, under the tutelage of their mother, had gone down the path of might over compassion.

Without realizing he had done it, Colin found himself in front of his father's study. It had been the one place his father threw down the mantle of 'king' and had always simply been 'father.' The gilded doors had been commissioned from an Island Nation's artist. Swirls and waves of ocean revealed miniature fish and merpeople and sea monsters roaming the seas. Despite their capital being deep within their borders, Szarmi had a love of the ocean that had prevailed since the dawning of its foundation. Colin often wondered if the stories about King Jamad were true. If he truly had been the first king of Szarmi and had traveled here from Borganda, it would make sense that he would continue to pay homage to the sea.

Colin trailed his fingers over the door handle. No dust collected there. He wondered if Coraleen or his mother had been spending time in the study or if the servants had been diligent in their dusting. Secretly, he hoped the latter. This had been their special place. For years, King Henry had taken Colin to his study to discuss new technologies and advancements in medicine. Coraleen had never shown any interest in these topics so she had never been invited. No, they had spent their time sparring or riding together. His sister had been tough—certainly tougher than Colin could ever imagine being. But she had lacked Colin's desire to learn.

Before he could second-guess his decision, Colin pulled the latch and slipped into his father's study. No fire had been lit and the curtains were drawn tight. Darkness enveloped him. During his younger years, Colin would have been able to walk through the room blind, now he bumped into tables and chairs as he made his way across the room to the hearth. His father had had it custom built for him. Natural gas, similar to what had been used in the glass orbs in the city, had been fed into the study's fireplace. Colin lifted the level that released the gas and struck a match he found on the mantel—just as it had always been.

Fire blazed in the hearth, sending uncomfortable warmth to meet Colin. Mirrors had been strategically aligned throughout the room such that the firelight filled the entirety of the study. Colin smiled as he remembered when King Henry had the mirrors installed. He had told Colin that enlightenment was about taking steps forward and constantly seeking truth as well as beauty. His father's study was a testament to how much he had believed those words. Gilded books were organized in neat rows along the bookshelves lining the walls. Masterful paintings hung above the fireplace and his desk. Floor-to-ceiling windows—when open—revealed Miliom and the countryside beyond. His father's desk was laden with papers and drawings of new technologies his scientists had been working on.

As he sat down in his father's leather chair, he noticed just how much dust had settled upon the desk. He couldn't blame his sister. If he was being honest with himself, he would have to admit that he'd only visited his father's study once after his death. He glanced to the side and saw the shards of glass still on the floor from where he'd shattered a vase against the wall. Not even the servants had been here to clean. The more closely he looked about the room and at the items on the desk, the more he realized how dilapidated the space was becoming. It was more than just dust. Dead bugs covered the window sills. A bit of food had sprouted mold that was slowly spreading across one of the tables closest to the hearth. He chided himself for never having asked the servants to clean the room. It was if this place had been made into a shrine that was gradually rotting away.

Colin shook his head. He couldn't let himself think like that. He was his father's legacy. Gingerly, he slid his finger under the table until it caught on the key he knew would still be there. Sure enough, his finger met the cold touch of metal and Colin quickly yanked the key from its holster. He breathed in deeply before slipping the key into the one drawer his father had never let him see. The only reason he knew how to open it now was because of the letter his father's advisors had given him before that last trip to Ducal House and his eventual, ill-fated, journey to Lunameed. He wondered what secrets his father had kept from him.

Did he know I wasn't his true son? The thought crept through Colin's mind like a reaper did its prey. His hand stilled on the drawer's handle. He still wasn't convinced he could trust his mother's account of his heritage. If his real father had been violent with her—if he forced her—then Colin was little more than a bastard, born of a victim and a rapist. His hands shook. And, if King Henry had known, if he had believed his mother's account, then he had betrayed Szarmi in choosing him as the heir.

"She could also be lying," he whispered. Even as he said the words, even as he recognized her story was the perfect way to supplant him, there was a part of him that knew she wasn't.

He wrenched the drawer open. His hands shook as he lifted the contents. There was only a thick, leather bound book inside. He knew because he ran his fingers all over the interior of the drawer searching for anything else his father meant to give him. But it was just the book.

It had no adornments. The pages were not gilded. The leather was rough in places, as if his father had opened and closed the book so many times that it cracked. A cord wrapped around the book, sealing it shut. Colin tugged on the cord, slowly unraveling it. He hesitated before opening to the first page. He had no doubt of what this book was. His father had told him once that every ruler should keep an account of his life. The first date was the year of his coronation.

Loud footsteps from the other side of the study doors drew his attention away from the book. It was the sound of marching and that could only mean one thing: his mother and sister had finally organized a search party for him.

Colin wound the cord around the journal once more and slipped the book into his chest pocket. He hoped he would have time to read it in the future. He made quick work of relocking the drawer, slipping the key into its hiding place, and extinguishing the fire. In darkness once more, Colin ambled across the study and pressed his ear against the door.

"He can't be dead," he heard someone say from the other side. "I just saw him…"

"The Princess-Heir found him. There is no doubt in her words. She claimed to have seen the Lunameedian shapeshifter posing as her brother wandering the city."

Colin's heart sank at the words. At least now he knew why his mother and sister had let him go so easily. They were using him as a political scapegoat to dispose of a rival. He ground his teeth as he waited to hear more.

"Have you found the imposter?"

"Not yet. If you see anyone suspicious wandering the halls, report them immediately. Remember those murderers to the north can fool us into believing they're someone else entirely."

Colin wondered who his mother and sister had assassinated. Who he was being blamed for murdering. *This is why he chose me over Coraleen*, he thought as he waited for the voices to fade. He had to believe that his father knew he wasn't his son. He had to believe that King Henry had chosen him anyways. It was the only way he could continue fighting for his throne without feeling like a usurper. His mother hadn't provided proof and she had every reason to lie, yet, for whatever reason, Colin couldn't dispel the feeling that she wasn't. He shook his head again. He didn't have time to consider all the possibilities. He had to choose between accepting his sister's rule and the apparent destruction of his homeland or he could choose to fight, knowing that he might be a fraud.

"I choose to fight," he whispered, although there was no one there to hear him.

He listened for sounds on the other side of the door but heard nothing. Deftly, he slid the door open and slipped into the hallway beyond. He had nearly made it to the tunnel entrance when a shout rang from behind him.

"You there, halt."

Colin didn't look behind him or hesitate. He sprinted towards the room leading to the tunnel entrance.

"Stop right there!" the guard called again. A dagger flew past his head and imbedded itself in the wall ahead of him.

"Next time I won't miss."

Colin dove, sliding across the tiled floor until he collided with the door at the end of the hall. He yanked the dagger free and flung it, without aiming, behind him. He heard it skitter across the floor. Wasting no time, he pulled the door open. He had just moved to enter when two more daggers clipped the wall where he had just been standing.

"I don't want to kill you," the guard yelled.

"Then don't," Colin replied before pulling the door shut. Thinking quickly, he heaved on the tall, wooden shelf standing beside the door. It fell with a bang, barricading the entrance. He knew it wouldn't last long. The guard was already pounding against the other side of the door. Colin flipped back the rug and pulled open the trap door that dropped into the tunnel below. The odiferous fumes from below wafted upwards and Colin gagged. Still, better to be alive and in sewage than captured. He dropped through the hole and into the muck below.

Chapter Thirty-Five

Redbeard was exactly where Colin had left him. The bodies were not. His heart hammered in his chest and his lungs burned. He hadn't stopped running since his feet first hit the ground. He knew the barricaded door wouldn't hold for long. They needed to leave. Now.

"How did it go?" Redbeard murmured in the near darkness of the tunnel. His voice was sober and his face looked as if he had been clawing at his own flesh.

"Captain Conrad isn't willing to join me," Colin said, hurriedly. "We can't…"

"Then what comes next?" Redbeard asked, cutting Colin off.

Colin frowned at Redbeard and said, "We have to go. Now!"

"Wha' do ya mean?"

"I mean," Colin replied, his voice icy, "that I've been found out. There's no time to explain, Redbeard. A guard saw me. There'll be more. Please, we need to go," he pled.

Redbeard pulled his pipe out as if he was going to smoke a bit of his mureechi, peered at Colin's face for several moments, frowned, and then replaced the pipe into his tunic pocket. "Ya best be explainin' what happened," he growled. "But let's go."

He began barreling his way down the tunnel. Colin had a momentary feeling of remorse at leaving his home once more, but squashed it when he remembered that guards would soon be upon them. He followed the older man.

"Where to next, son?" Redbeard breathed heavily.

"The Beoscuret Mountains, as close to Fort Pelid as possible."

"What!" Redbeard shouted. "Ya can't be serious, Colin. We can't go there. It's a trap!"

"We have to. It's our only hope."

"I take it ya didn't meet with yer Captain Conrad, then." Redbeard's tone wasn't malicious. Colin could tell that. It just felt sly, as if Redbeard were expecting Colin to break down at any moment. He supposed it wasn't without due reason. He had been acting like a complaining coward for much their journey together.

"I did, actually," he responded. "Captain Conrad is going to organize a summit for me to meet with several squadrons and a few of the other commanders."

"That doesn't sound like much. 'Sides didn't ya say the captain won't be joinin' ya? Why would he help ya recruit men if he ain't going ta help ya get outta yer situation?" Redbeard probed, his eyes narrowing on Colin.

"Because," Colin responded, "he believes in me."

Redbeard laughed. His voice echoed down the tunnel and reverberated back, distorting the laughter into peals of sorrow. He clapped Colin on the shoulder and said, "Do you honestly believe him?"

"I do," Colin replied automatically. If he was being truthful, Captain Conrad was the only person in the whole of Mitier that he trusted implicitly.

"Then let's hope he ain't settin' ya up fer a trap."

"He won't," Colin said. He glanced at Redbeard, "If you want to go back to Lunameed, you can. You owe me no allegiance."

"Actually, I do," the man said.

Colin fell into silence at that. He could think of nothing he had done that would merit a debt from the old barkeep. If anything, Colin owed him a great debt for keeping him alive this long and for helping him cross the border back into Szarmi.

They continued onward. Only the squishing sound of their boots in the murky grime below interrupted the silence. They crossed the gate, still without speaking. Colin wanted to know what to do next. He had lost everything: his throne, his kingdom, his family, and now, even his own identity. He didn't know if he would be successful. He didn't know if he could overcome the depth of the rumors his mother and sister had spread about him.

All he could do was continue to hope.

"I know where we can get horses," Colin said, breaking the silence. "It'll make traveling to the mountain range quicker."

"And leave a trail," Redbeard muttered.

"We can travel by night, try to keep to the country passes instead of the main roads. Once there, we can send the horses on ahead of us. Hopefully the guards I know will be sent after us will think we've crossed into Dramadoon."

Redbeard raised an eyebrow at him and his lips pulled upwards into a cockeyed smile. "Yer beginnin' to think like a leader," he said.

"Maybe," Colin replied. "But I still have a lot to learn."

"It's good that ya recognize that, son," Redbeard said.

Colin shrugged. For once, he was at a loss for words.

"Do ya have any ideas about how we can get out of the city?" Redbeard whispered.

"One, but you're not going to like it," Colin replied.

Chapter Thirty-Six

Colin borrowed clothes from Vecepia and disguised himself as a woman. A long scarf covered his hair and he wore the traditional robes of a widow in mourning. Vecepia had chosen them, knowing that the color and shape of the cloth would stop nearly everyone from harassing him. For Redbeard, who was too large and broad and hairy to readily pass as a woman, she trimmed his beard and provided a fresh cloak. It was decided that he could pass as Colin's guard.

They weaved through the streets of Miliom with barely a word passing between them until they reached the back wall surrounding the city. It was higher than Colin remembered. He placed a hand upon its cool stone.

"What's the plan, Colin?" Redbeard asked. His voice pitched and Colin stole a quick glance at the older man. He would not have anticipated Redbeard being nervous about breaking out of the city.

"Don't chide me when I tell you," Colin hissed. A pair of guards passed behind them. Their swords were drawn and they glared at each person they passed.

Redbeard waited until he was sure they were out of earshot. "Just tell me yer plan, son."

"Fine," Colin replied. "Tonight, when fewer people are out

363

and about, we should climb the wall."

Redbeard stared at him without speaking. His face grew ever redder the longer they remained silent.

"Yer kidding, right?" the older man asked. "Ya can't possibly expect both of us to be able ta scale this wall without getting' caught? It won't happen."

"We can't go through the main gate, Redbeard, they've been checking everyone's face as they pass. Someone is bound to recognize me. What other choice do we have?"

Redbeard stroked his chin, tugging delicately on the ends of his beard. "I may still have a contact who could get us out."

"What?" Colin roared.

Redbeard shushed him and pointed at another pair of guards strolling through the streets.

"What?" Colin whispered, his voice clipped and angry.

"I have connections here."

"Uh, care to elaborate?"

"Not really."

"Fine," Colin fumed. "But you better be able to deliver on this, Redbeard. The longer we stay in the city the more likely it is that we'll get caught."

"Follow me," Redbeard commanded, starting down a side street. Begrudgingly, Colin followed.

Redbeard led Colin down a winding web of streets. Colin tried to keep track of the route in case they ran into trouble, but they took too many turns and side streets Colin had never traveled to remember. The old barkeep finally stopped in front of a rickety looking tavern. The teal paint was peeling from its store front and the iron sign out front was completely rusted.

"Broken Ax?" Colin read as they passed through the door.

"Friend of mine runs the place," Redbeard whispered.

"Then why didn't you bring us here in the first place?" Colin chided.

"Didn't want ya to know all my secrets," Redbeard responded.

Mureechi smoke engulfed them as they entered the dimly lit room. A piano player at the back of the room played a dreary tune Colin had never heard. Redbeard led Colin to the bar and placed a thick, silver coin on the water-stained wood. A pair of crossed axes was stamped on the front of the coin. Colin had never seen that kind of money before. He was about to ask where it was from when the bartender palmed the coin and jerked her head towards the back room.

Her dark hair was braided and coiled atop her head and, even in the dimly lit room, Colin could see the vibrant purple color her hair was dyed. She wore all black except for a ruby pendant clasped around her neck. A black dagger hung at her slender waist and she laid a hand on the hilt as she motioned for them to pass her into the next room. She said nothing as she pulled the door closed behind them.

"Jorah," a woman's voice called from the shadows.

"Myrah," Redbeard responded with a smile.

"I thought you were out of this business."

"And I still think you're the loveliest woman I've ever met."

A tinkling laugh filled the room as a tall, plump woman emerged from behind a silk curtain. Her dark hair was curled and framed her heart-shaped face. Her emerald eyes were ringed in amber. They were the type of eyes that you never wanted to look away from. Colin gaped as the woman stood before them, hands on hips, smile stretching wide across her face.

"How long has it been?" she asked as she poured a brilliant green liquid into three glasses.

"Twelve years, if I reckon correctly."

"Twelve years?" she gasped, placing a hand over her heart. "Why, I was only a love-struck teenager the last time I saw you." Her words were kind, yet Colin caught the edge to her tone and the way she glared at Redbeard beneath her eyelashes.

"You were the best, even then," Redbeard said, clearly missing the nuanced way the woman addressed him.

"I still am," she said, throwing back her head and gulping down the green liquid in one go. Colin sniffed at the liquid. It smelled like green apples on a summer day. Shrugging, he sipped at his drink. He immediately regretted it. It took all of his willpower to suck down the bitter, burning toxin.

Redbeard drank his own glass down in a single gulp as well. He wiped his lips with the back of his hand and said, "It's been too long, Myrah."

She sniffed. "What are you doing here, Jorah? When you left, you promised that you wouldn't return until you'd found a ruler suitable to end this Creator forsaken feud between Szarmi and Lunameed." Her gaze narrowed as she met his eyes.

"By the hammer!" she hissed, stepping back. "What have you done, Jorah?"

"He's the one," Redbeard whispered.

"No," Myrah said, inching backwards, "I don't think so." She pointed a shaking finger at Jorah, "You've brought the missing heir here. I would recognize his eyes anywhere." She made a loud cawing sound and the bartender burst into the room. Myrah drew a crossbow from behind the curtain and pointed it straight at Colin's heart. He gulped.

"Give me three good reasons why I shouldn't kill him now and be done with it," Myrah said to Redbeard. The bartender pressed her dagger to Redbeard's back. The older man stiffened, but gave no other sign of distress.

"He wants to form an alliance with Lunameed," Redbeard said, holding up a single finger. "Two," he continued, flipping another finger up, "he wants to end the destruction his mother and sister have brought upon the kingdom." He paused as he returned Colin's gaze. "And three," he continued, holding up a third finger, "I trust him to be the right leader for the cause."

Myrah glared at them both. "Things aren't like they used to be, Jorah. When we lost that last rebellion…"

"We lost that battle because I made a stupid mistake," Redbeard cut in. "It was my fault she died. If I had been more careful…"

"If you hadn't come when you did, all would have been lost."

Redbeard shook his head. "This could be a second chance."

Myrah lowered her crossbow ever-so-slightly. Her expression softened as she peered at Redbeard. "I miss her," she whispered, her voice catching.

"I do, too."

Colin wanted to chime in and ask what in the bloody world they were talking about, but the dagger pricking at Redbeard's back gave him room for pause. They clearly had a history together of which Colin had no place. It wouldn't serve them well to interrupt their moment.

"It's too late," Myrah whispered. "I gave that life up."

"But you accepted my calling card," Redbeard said.

Myrah shrugged. "I wanted to see who of our old gang had finally come out of hiding. You know I haven't heard from any of the others since that night either. Everyone disappeared into the wind. Except me. I stayed here and built a place for myself. Despite what it might look like, this is one of the most popular tavern's in Miliom."

"I believe it," Redbeard responded. "You always did have a mind for business. It's why we chose ya for the job."

"The job?" she barked. "The job?" her voice came as a sarcastic snap. "You picked me up off the streets when I was barely eleven and trained me to spy for you. Sure, you made sure I never wanted for anything and you were always kind to me. But you made me into what I am."

"And look at you now," Redbeard snapped, his patience clearly waning. "Look, girl," he growled, "I only came here because I need help. Yer either in or yer not, but I need ta know yer answer."

Myrah jerked her head and the bartender gripped Colin around the neck. Her dagger pressed against his skin like a sliver of ice. Colin shivered but kept his stance as stoic as possible.

"Let the kid go," Redbeard growled out.

"His mother offered quite a nice price for his head," Myrah responded, sliding her finger over the point of her bolt.

"If you want me to say I'm sorry for leaving you here, then I will. I'm sorry," Redbeard proclaimed. To Colin's surprise, he heard a hint of panic in the older man's voice.

Myrah laughed at him. "You think that an apology is going to make up for you abandoning me?" she hissed. "You made me believe you loved me. I certainly loved you." She aimed her crossbow at Redbeard as she spoke. "I've waited all this time for you to show up again. To think that I would be your friend after everything you did to me. Do you know what I had to do to survive once you'd left me?"

Her lower lip trembled as she spoke.

"You don't want to do this," Colin said.

"Quiet, boy," Redbeard warned.

Colin ignored him and instead spoke louder, "I can see that our mutual friend here has hurt you." The blade at his neck tightened across his flesh. Colin already had one wound from the day, he figured another one wouldn't be any different. "But I don't think you actually want to hurt him, do you?"

She fired the crossbow. Colin's jaw dropped as he watched. As if in slow motion, the bolt found its home in the floor directly in front of Redbeard's left foot.

"Tell me what I want again and I'll be sure to drive the bolt home next time," she hissed at Colin. She turned her attention back to Redbeard.

"Convince me," she said.

Redbeard yanked the bolt from the ground and snapped its shaft in half. He threw the broken wood to the ground before striding across the room and wrapping his arms around Myrah's shoulders. "I've missed ya," he said, lowering his head to kiss her.

Colin closed his eyes. He had no interest in watching the two of them make up. Which was the exact reason why he missed watching Myrah slap Redbeard across the cheek so hard that blood flew from his lip as his head whipped to the side. All Colin saw was the aftermath.

"What was that for?" Redbeard asked, cradling his lip in his hand.

"That," Myrah retorted as she stepped away from him, "was for being the biggest fool I think I've ever met."

The bartender dropped her dagger from Colin's neck when

Myra motioned for her to do so.

"Does this mean you'll help us?" Redbeard pled, his gaze turned boyish as he peered down at Myrah.

"I suppose," she responded, "but only on one condition."

"What's that?" Colin asked.

Myrah shot a glare in his direction but returned her attention back to Redbeard, "You have to promise you'll never come to the city of Miliom again."

"And here I thought you'd want me to take ya with me."

"Maybe once," Myrah responded, running a hand along Redbeard's ruddy cheek. "But not now." Her expression softened. "Now, I just want to make good on my life without the drama associated with your dreams, Jorah."

For a moment, Colin thought the older man would decline her bargain. "I truly am sorry," he whispered to her.

"It doesn't matter anymore," she said, dropping her hand from his cheek. "Do we have a deal or not?"

Redbeard glanced at Colin. "It's a deal."

To Colin's surprise, they didn't have to go far to reach their escape route. Myrah flipped back an ornate rug from the floor to reveal a trap door.

"Great," he said, "More tunnels."

Myrah raised an eyebrow at him, but motioned for him to descend the wooden ladder pressed against the tunnel wall. "This one isn't connected to the sewage tunnels beneath the city," she explained. "I've worked on this escape route for the better part of five years." She shrugged when Colin gave her a startled look. "I think you'd be surprised, Your Highness, to discover that there are several secret passageways beneath this city."

Colin made a vow to himself to spend more time learning

about the ins and outs of his city if he ever reclaimed the throne. Knowing about one's people would certainly make ruling them easier.

"Thank you," Redbeard said, saluting Myrah before he descended the ladder.

"Don't thank me yet," Myrah responded. "If I know the queen, she'll be sending out search parties beyond the city wall in search of that boy." The way she referred to Colin made his insides squirm. "She's been trying to convince everyone that he's dead and replaced by a Lunameedian shapeshifter. If I were you, I wouldn't trust anyone."

"Including you?" Redbeard asked.

"Yes, including me," Myrah responded before ushering them down the ladder and closing the door atop them. Colin heard the distinctive click of a lock being snapped into place.

"Umm, Redbeard," he asked, "are you sure we can trust her?"

"Who knows," was all the older man would say.

Chapter Thirty-Seven

Colin didn't know how long they'd walked in darkness, but it must have been for at least a day, maybe two before they finally ran into a dead end. Colin felt around until his hands grazed the rough wood of a ladder. Hastily, he clamored up the steps. His head banged into the door at the top.. He shoved, but the door wouldn't budge. He shoved again, this time harder, and clumps of dirt fell on his head.

"Careful," Redbeard warned, only a few steps below Colin.

"I can't get the door to open," Colin called down.

"I can see that, son," Redbeard responded. Amusement coated his words, but Colin found the sound of Redbeard's voice grating. "Climb down and let me try."

Colin slammed his shoulder into the door once more to no avail. "Fine," he mumbled as he began his descent.

Redbeard immediately began climbing the ladder the moment Colin's feet were on the ground. Colin heard the older man grunt, felt clumps of dirt fall on his head, and then smelled the sweet, fresh scent of clean air.

His stomach growled from lack of food as he lifted himself from the other end of the trap door. He emerged from the tunnel just as the sun was at its peak in the sky. Colin blinked, momentarily blinded by the sun's brilliance. He fell to his knees, clutching at the grass all around them.

"We haven't got time for all that," Redbeard chided. He inspected their surroundings, his face tight with worry. Colin did the same. As far as he could tell, they were utterly alone.

Redbeard sniffed at the air. "Do you smell that?" he asked, pointing his nose to the mountain range behind them.

Smoke. Colin lowered his body even further to the ground as Redbeard dropped to a crouching position. They listened for any sounds coming from the mountains, but heard nothing other than the sounds of animals scurrying about the trees and over rocks.

"Come on," Redbeard commanded, walking in the opposite direction of the smell of smoke.

Colin looked to the sky. "Wait," he called after Redbeard. "You're heading north."

"So?" Redbeard asked.

"That's the wrong way."

Redbeard turned on Colin, his face a glowering mess of rage, sweat, and ruddy cheeks. "We need to be getting back to Lunameed," he bellowed. "Or have you changed yer mind?"

"Not yet," Colin said. "Not until I rendezvous with Captain Conrad. Please, Redbeard, I at least have to try."

Redbeard stomped his foot. "Can't you see that the captain is most likely setting ya up, Colin? Why else would he send ya on yer merry way only to discover yer being framed for murdering someone?"

"I don't know," Colin responded.

"It's a trap."

Colin shook his head. "Conrad is one of the oldest friends I have. He's the only friend I have left from Szarmi. I can't…" he paused, "I can't give up on that right now."

Redbeard sighed heavily. "Fine," he said, "but if you end up dead because of this, don't blame me."

He undid the strap holding his ax in place and carefully pulled the weapon from his belt. Colin drew his sword, mimicking Redbeard's actions.

"Lead the way," Redbeard commanded.

Chapter Thirty-Eight

Colin crouched behind a large stone formation overlooking Fort Pelid. Despite having crossed the border into Dramadoon and back to Szarmi on multiple occasions, he and Redbeard had not crossed paths with soldiers from either kingdom. In fact, they hadn't seen any sign of other people except for the camp fire on their first day out of the tunnel. Now, as he peered down at the fort, Colin couldn't help but feel his anxiety creeping up within him. He was putting all his hopes in the hands of the man who'd mentored him since he was a boy. He thought he knew the man. And, Captain Conrad had given him every reason to believe in him. Yet, as Colin watched the rows upon rows of soldiers set up camp around his old training ground, he became increasingly aware that the older captain could be setting him up for betrayal.

"It's now or never," Redbeard prodded. He loomed over Colin as he stared down at the mass of soldiers. "They certainly look like a young lot, don't they?"

"They are," Colin replied.

"Doesn't yer precious captain have connections with anyone a little more experienced?" Redbeard inquired. He tugged on his beard as he spoke.

"We thought it best that I focus my attention on winning

over the soldiers who trained with me at one point or another," Colin replied, sheepishly. "With all the rumors abounding that I'm an imposter, I need some way to prove that I'm the real Colin."

Redbeard pulled out his pipe and stuffed it full of mureechi. The small flicker of flame followed by the pungent odor of the herb gave Colin a sense of unease. He wasn't ready for the army to spot him.

"Don't do anything that's going to get us noticed," Colin reprimanded.

Redbeard shrugged and puffed on his pipe. "Seems ta me that it's better ta get this done now than ta wait. They'll either turn ya in or they won't."

Colin knew the old barkeep was right. The soldiers would either believe him or they wouldn't.

"Captain Conrad said he'd send me a sign when it was time," Colin said. It was true. They had discussed a signal. Although, Colin couldn't quite remember what they had agreed upon.

"Look, son, the longer we toil here, the more likely it is that these soldiers—or worse, ones that have no interest in making nice with ya—will find us."

Colin sighed, his exasperation growing. "I hear you, Redbeard, I think we just need to give it one more…"

He abruptly cut off his retort when a giant plume of smoke rose from the fort below. Embers cascaded into the sky and then fluttered down as ash all around them. Colin coughed and bent down low to monitor what was happening in camp.

"I think that might've been yer sign," Redbeard said as he knelt beside Colin. He reeked of mureechi and Colin had a difficult time breathing between the stench of the other man and the ash.

"I think you might be right," he replied, noticing that the captain was marching among the soldiers camped outside of Fort Pelid. He wondered what the captain had told the men to convince them to join him at the fort.

Redbeard patted Colin on the back. "No more excuses, Colin. Let's go."

Colin nodded in response and, without further ado, began climbing down the mountain pass towards the fort. It was a steep incline. Even following the man-created path, keeping his balance as they trotted down the mountain was tedious, hard work. He was covered in sweat by the time they'd made it half-way down the slope.

Panting, Colin said, "Let's rest a moment."

Redbeard, still apparently out of shape, agreed.

They settled on the ground, breathing heavily. Colin passed Redbeard his water canteen and the older man drank heavily from its contents. Colin patted his breast pocket, ensuring that his father's journal was still there. He hadn't read any of it yet. Although he had had time while they'd been waiting for the army to arrive, he hadn't been able to bring himself to pry into his father's innermost thoughts. Maybe it was because he was afraid of what he would find there. The idea that his father had known about his true birthright and had chosen him to be his legacy gave him hope while at the same time marring his image of King Henry as a traitor to their kingdom. He still hadn't decided how he could rectify those two opposing images in his thoughts. He was still struggling with his own demons.

A branch snapped somewhere nearby. Colin sat at attention. He strained to hear any other sounds that indicated someone was approaching. Redbeard cradled his head in his hands, but Colin could tell from his posture that he too was listening for the sounds of intruders. A moment passed and Colin heard nothing else.

"Let's keep moving," he whispered as he rose from his perch on the ground.

Redbeard nodded in agreement. He drew his ax and motioned for Colin to draw his sword. Colin hoped they wouldn't have to fight anyone, but he readied himself for the possibility all the same.

"State your name and your business here," a voice called from above them.

Colin whirled around but saw no one. "I could ask you to do the same," he said.

Silence.

The silence was unnerving. If their intruder was moving, he should be able to hear them. But, there was only the sound of the wind rushing between the mountain peaks.

"It'd be better for everyone if you state your name and your purpose," the voice said again, this time closer.

"Tell me this and I'll answer your questions: are you from Dramadoon or from Szarmi?" They were so close to the border that Colin wanted to make sure he knew who they were dealing with first.

"Dramadoon," the voice replied. "Now, tell me your answers."

Before Colin had a chance to say anything, Redbeard had whipped around and flung his ax straight at where the voice came from. There was a sickening crunch and Colin knew the older man's weapon had struck true.

"Why did you do that?" Colin screeched. "You know Prince Freddy and Princess Saphria wanted to ally with me! You are too quick to fight rather than talk," Colin lamented.

"And yer too eager to die," Redbeard snapped as he bent down and picked up the man's bow. "It was drawn and aimed straight at ya, Colin. My job is to protect you. Don't be forgetin' that."

He tossed the bow aside and strode past Colin. "Let's keep moving," he grumbled as he moved ahead of Colin.

Colin looked between the dead body and Redbeard. He knew the older man was just trying to protect him, but he also feared the bloodlust he sometimes saw in him. He wondered what the older man had experienced that had turned him into such a killer. Although he would never admit it, Redbeard's ferocity scared him.

They made it to the last plateau of the mountain pass before reaching the base of the mountain. Colin crawled on his hands and knees towards the plateau's edge. The sun was just disappearing behind the horizon and fires had started to spark into life among the tents below. Curls of smoke rose into the sky, bringing with it the smell of roasting meat. Colin's stomach grumbled again. He hadn't had a decent meal for more than a week now.

"Do you want to stop for the night or keep going?" Redbeard asked.

"It's late," Colin replied. "We should wait until morning."

They decided not to start a fire. The mountain air was chilled and Colin, covered in sweat, was cold. He groaned as he nestled in between two large rock formations. His father's book pressed against his sternum. Its weight was a reminder that, regardless of anything else that happened, he had chosen Colin to be the next leader of Szarmi.

Morning came early. A soldier wearing Szarmian garb jabbed the blunt end of his staff into Colin's chest. Colin opened his eyes to find that Redbeard's hands were tied behind his back. A nasty looking bruise covered one side of his face. Two more guards flanked the older man. Colin wondered how he'd slept through the ruckus Redbeard must've caused but didn't fight against the Szarmian soldier as he bound his hands together. They looped a rope around his neck and connected him to Redbeard. Surprisingly, the older man didn't fight back.

"Come on," the soldier said as he shoved Colin in the back. Colin stumbled slightly but was able to stay on his feet as the guards led them down the final mountain slope.

"I hope you know what you're doing," Redbeard hissed.

Colin glanced at the soldiers. They gave no indication that they had heard Redbeard's words.

"I hope so too," Colin whispered.

The soldiers led them to the heart of the camp. Captain Conrad was drilling the men as they approached. The familiarity with which Colin watched the younger soldiers performing routines set his nerves a little more at ease. He recognized a few of their faces. They must have recognized him, too, because several of them stopped engaging in the drill and instead began to point at him.

"Murderer," he heard someone from the crowd shout.

"Imposter," said another.

A rock flew through the sky and smacked Colin in the head. His vision went white and nausea overcame him. Colin emptied what little contents he had in his stomach on the ground in front of him. Blood ran down his face and fell to the ground in tiny crimson droplets. The sight of it nearly had Colin retching again.

"Sorry," he squeaked at Redbeard as some of the chunks hit the man's boots.

Redbeard didn't respond to Colin, but he jeered at the crowd of soldiers.

Captain Conrad stepped forward, his eyes full of concern. He ripped a strip of cloth from his own shirt and wrapped it around Colin's wound. The captain peered around the camp. His features contorted into the hard, angry lines of a commanding officer. "You should be ashamed of yourselves," he snarled at the soldiers. "Do you have any idea who this is?"

"Yeah!" one of the soldiers shouted. There were too many of them for Colin to pinpoint exactly who had spoken. "It's one of them Lunameedian shapeshifters. My pa told me he read about them in the papers."

"Colin Stormbearer is dead, Captain," another soldier said. "Queen Vista performed a burial service for him, or have you forgotten?"

"How many of you trained with Colin at some point or another?" Conrad asked, his voice as loud as a crack of thunder during a storm. "How many of you served on teams with the prince-heir? How many of you grew to know the man behind the royal title?"

Many of the soldiers rose their hands. Colin leaned down and spat out a mouthful of bile. He coughed but forced himself to stand up straight.

"I know there has been much confusion over the past several months. We have all experienced a great amount of loss."

Colin met the gaze of several of the soldiers as Captain Conrad spoke. Even when they sneered at him, he did not cower. There was no reason to. If the soldiers killed him here, at least he could die knowing that he tried.

"I believe this man is the real Colin Stormbearer," Conrad said, gesturing towards Colin. "Now, I can't tell you lot what to do, not when it comes to this, but what I can tell you is that if he is the Prince-Heir, then we must do everything in our power to maintain the throne."

"What you're saying is treason, sir," one of the men called.

Colin cleared his throat. "I remember when we were boys together, Xander."

The soldier who called treason turned bright pink as Colin turned towards him. "We used to play with wooden swords in the palace's courtyard. Do you remember?"

He turned to another soldier, "And you, Chip, do you remember running along the Milo River trying to catch flying fish as they sprang from the water?"

He locked eyes with yet another soldier, "Christopher, you were the first person to dual me in the training ring. You beat me soundly and then were so afraid that I would punish you that you begged for forgiveness."

He lifted his chin higher. "We are the soldiers of Szarmi, keepers of the land and watchers of the people," he paused as the words to the oath every Szarmian soldier has learned since the Wars of Darkness filled his mind. He could recite this pledge in his sleep if he had to. They all could. When he began again, several of his comrades joined him. "We will fight for home and country. We will protect our sovereign and the royal line with our dying breaths."

"To this, we pledge our lives and our bodies," Captain Conrad joined in the last line.

"I am not your enemy," Colin said. His voice took on the tenor he remembered his father using when addressing the people. His words were slow and definitive. He measured his breaths. He infused each word with conviction. "I have seen the destruction my mother and sister have laid upon the city and the farmers across the land. I know the danger King Magnus poses to the north."

His hands were sweaty and his mind still fuzzy from the blow to the head. Still, this was his moment and he was not going to waste it. "My father, King Henry—may the Creators keep him and bless his name, chose me as his heir. You know the law. If he had desired Coraleen to be the heir, he would have proclaimed it thus. My mother has coerced Coraleen into usurping me. She sent me to Lunameed as a ruse. She always intended to either assassinate me or to supplant me through lies."

"But I am here now. I have faced many hardships and dangers over the past several months. But I have also come to realize what it means to choose country over self. I was born to be your future king. If you rise up and help me now, I can promise you, that when the time comes, I will not forget who my true friends were."

Several of the men cheered at the conclusion of his speech. Conrad shushed them by raising his fist in the air. Each soldier bowed his head and raised his fist in salute to the Captain until the entire encampment was silent.

"You all have your own squadrons. You all have been trained as officers in our nation's army. But you also have a choice. Choose the crown as you see fit. I will not force any of you to serve at the leisure of the prince-heir. But if you do, I promise that I will not press charges against any of you."

His words sobered the crowd. Colin could see it in their faces.

"If you do choose to go with his Royal Highness, I implore

you to offer your men the same choice I am offering you now."

Colin stepped forward. "I cannot promise that following me will be easy. I cannot promise that I will be triumphant in the end. All I can tell you is that I love this country. I love its people."

"You're asking us to fight against our brothers in arms," one of the men said.

"I am," Colin replied. There was no use in denying it. He was asking these men to join him in civil war. "But, I don't think we'll be alone," he continued. "My goal is to help the Princess Amaleah crush her father's power and take back the throne. I intend to sign a marriage pact with her. With your help, I know that we can defeat the Lunameedian army. We are the best soldiers in the known world. Together, we will be unstoppable. My hope is that once she has control of her kingdom that she will aid me in reclaiming the Szarmian throne."

Murmurs passed through the crowd of soldiers. Colin hoped revealing his full plan would spur them to action. Whether they chose to support him or not, he wanted them to know they wouldn't be jumping into civil war immediately.

"So you want us to die on foreign soil to help the witch who burned down her father's throne?"

One of the soldiers stepped forward. Colin recognized him. He was the fourth or fifth son of a minor duke in the kingdom. Colin remembered him as a snake who was only out for self-gain.

"Marius," he said, calling the soldier by name, "our kingdom is at a precipice. We will either fall over the edge to our destruction or survive by letting go of our past hatred." Here came the part where he feared losing the men. "I spent time with the Princess Amaleah during my journey home. I have every belief that our goals are aligned. Each of us wants what's best for our nations. I believe that we will be stronger together."

"Count me out," Marius shouted.

None of the other soldiers said a word as Colin shook his head and said, "Do as you please, Marius. I will not force you to follow me. I won't force any of you to follow my lead. All I ask is that you consider this: King Henry was a great king. He served our nation well. And he chose me to be his legacy. In the few short months my mother has been in power as regent to my sister, how many of you can say she's done a good job for our people? If you believe that I can do better, follow me. If not, I will meet you on the battle field."

Captain Conrad spoke once more, "This is not a decision to make lightly. Take the rest of the day to consider. You will each announce your decisions at the evening meal."

The captain undid the binding around Colin and Redbeard's wrists. He cut the rope linking them together. Colin gingerly rubbed at his raw skin as he followed the captain to his quarters within the fort's walls. It was just as he remembered it. Organized, cool, and, most of all, fresh-smelling.

"You did well, Your Highness," he said, using Colin's formal title.

"Thank you," Colin replied. "I hope it was enough."

"We will know soon enough."

"That we will."

Redbeard puffed on his mureechi pipe, his eyes roaming over the captain's quarters.

"So, you're the great and heroic Captain Conrad." He pierced the captain with a penetrating gaze. "The boy is always talking about you as if you were some kind of Creator."

"I am," Conrad said, eyeing Colin.

"Well," Redbeard said as he blew out a giant ring of smoke, "I suppose I should be thankin' you for helping our young friend here find his path."

"And I suppose I should be thanking you for bringing him home."

The two men sized each other up. Colin felt the tension rise in the room.

"That's enough, you two," he said. "We don't have time for your pissing contest."

The two men turned their attention back to Colin. "No matter what happens tonight, Redbeard and I will be leaving in the morning."

"Why?" the captain asked.

"Because," Colin replied. "The longer I stay in Szarmi the more likely it is that my mother will successfully assassinate me. And, more than that, I need to return to Lunameed as quickly as possible. If I am going to have any hope for success with the princess, I need to be at the forefront of the marriage proposal line."

"Then let us hope enough of the officers choose to serve you and that enough of their respective men choose to as well."

"All I have is hope," Colin replied.

Chapter Thirty-Nine
Silver Moon Camp, Lunameed

Amaleah concentrated on the candle wick. Sweat beaded on her brow and she could smell the odiferous stench of her armpits when she lifted her hands and tried to create fire. Nothing happened. She released an exasperated howl and tried again.

"Be careful," Nikailus said as he twirled a dagger in his hand. "You might just lose your voice with all the yelling you've been doing."

Amaleah stuck her tongue out at him. It had been three weeks since she and Elaria had drafted and sent letters across the whole of Mitier. So far, no one had responded to her pleas. With only three weeks left until the anticipated assault on Encartia, Amaleah was beginning to believe that she would have no other choice but to surrender to her father.

Angerly, she shoved her hands forward again and tried to command the wick to burst into flame.

"Let me help you," Nikailus said. He wrapped his arms around her from behind and guided her hands forward. His touch, like it always did, sent a shiver down her spine. She breathed in his scent. They hadn't kissed since that first time all those weeks ago, but they had continued to train together.

"Close your eyes," he commanded.

His breath tickled her ear and she leaned back into him, ever so slightly.

"Good," he said, "now, imagine the feel of fire. The smell of it. The taste of smoke on the air. Call to it. Coax it into life."

Amaleah tried to do as he said. In her mind's eye she could see the candle burst into flames. She could see the embers dancing on the air as they floated about the room. She could smell the smoke.

Her eyes flew open and she disentangled her body from Nikailus.

"I'm sorry," she heaved. "I just...I can't do this." She wrapped her arms around her torso and went to stand by a large oak tree. With her back to him, she let herself face her father. She told him to go away. She commanded him to. It was something she and Elaria had been working on for the past three weeks.

When she'd first told the matriarch of her nightmares and the visions she sometimes had of being trapped by her father—how it had been that vision that had forced her to expel her power on Thadius—the elf had folded her into her arms and cradled her as Amaleah wept. She'd told Amaleah about a disease called 'warrior's shock,' that they had been studying for some time now. Although Elaria knew of no cure for the infliction, she began meeting with Amaleah to work through her fears and anxieties associated with her father.

Amaleah breathed in deeply; counted to six as she held her breath; and then released her air in a steady stream. Her heartbeat slowed and the image of her father slowly receded. She had been dreading working on calling flame to life for days. She'd already 'mastered' the art of pushing and pulling items at will and creating massive blasts of energy. They also had her practicing weaving light and air. Elaria told her that was an extremely rare gift and the fact that she had it meant that she should train with it even more. So far, she had not found any of the tasks they put before as challenging: except for calling fire to life.

"Don't do that," Nikailus said, coming up behind her. "Don't shut me out." He wrapped his arms around her again and pulled her against his body. She didn't struggle against him as he nestled his head in the crook of her neck. "No matter what it is you're facing, Amaleah, I will always be there for you."

Amaleah nodded against his cheek but said nothing. She wasn't sure she could offer what he desired.

"You are so powerful, Amaleah," he whispered in her ear. "You don't even recognize how amazing you are."

Amaleah shook her head. "Please don't," she pled.

"Why not?" he asked, turning her around to face him. "I've seen how much you've grown over the past three weeks, Princess." He stroked a rogue strand of her hair from her brow. "You have more potential in your little finger than half of all the magical creatures combined."

"Don't say that," she said, shaking her head. She didn't want to be. She knew that with her abilities came greater responsibility for the people she served. As the Princess of Lunameed, she was charged with caring for her people. As the Harbinger, well, she wasn't quite sure yet what that meant for her, but she knew that she had a responsibility to serve and protect those who could not do it for themselves. Her power was not meant to be used for personal gain.

"I know you don't believe this, Princess, but I have no doubt that if you had been given more time to master your magic, you would be able to take back your kingdom on your own."

"But I don't have more time," she said, chewing on her bottom lip.

"What if there was a way to find the Creators?" he asked, his voice became more emphatic. "What if we could release them?" He rubbed her cheek with the back of his hand, "We could save the world."

"No one's seen the Creators in over three hundred years, Nikailus."

"No, but what if there was a way to find them?" he pressed. "We are the two most powerful magical beings to roam this world in hundreds—if not thousands—of years. What if we could do it?"

"You're crazy," she said, playfully pushing him away from her.

"Maybe," he conceded. "But I'm not going to give up. I know they're out there somewhere, Amaleah. I can feel it in my bones. What if we were meant to find each other? What if this is what we're meant to do?"

"I don't know," she admitted.

"At least promise me that you'll consider it."

She peered into his violet eyes. She had never noticed before but they contained a core of silver that seemed to shimmer as his expressions changed.

"Please, Amaleah," he whispered, leaning in closer to her face. She swore she could feel his lips graze hers, but knew they were too far apart.

"Ahem."

They sprang apart. Amaleah felt her cheeks burn as she met

Nylyla's gaze. "Someone has been asking for you," she said, smiling.

Amaleah cocked an eyebrow. "Really?" she asked, "Who?"

"Thadius."

Amaleah rushed towards Nylyla and wrapped her arms around the waifish elf. "You're telling me the truth?" she gushed. "You promise?" She lifted the elf off her feet and twirled her around in the air. "He's really awake?"

"Yes," Nylyla laughed. "Now put me down so that you can go and see him."

Amaleah didn't even glance at Nikailus as Nylyla led the way back to her house.

Chapter Forty

Arcadi Forest, Lunameed

Starla panted. Her head felt light and her side cramped as she continued running through the trees. Branches whipped at her face, scratching her otherwise porcelain skin. It had been almost five days since she'd been released by Drax. He'd been true to his word. He hadn't forced her to do anything she didn't want to. He hadn't forced her to tell him about the inner workings of the Lunameed throne. He'd just sat with her. He'd listened to her, even if she had nothing to say.

His final words reverberated through her. *Kill the king.* It's what she wanted. More than anything, she wanted to dispatch the king and his insipid daughter. She wanted the monarchy to descend into chaos and for a new ruler to rise. She would be damned if that ruler were her uncle. There was no place for him on the throne.

She clutched at her side. Her muscles burned as her breathing sputtered. She slowed her pace. Birds cooed in trees high above her head. Dried, dead leaves rustled on the ground. Several of them lifted into the air and danced before riding a lightwave into the beyond. In the shadowy places beneath rocks and giant trees, snow still clung to the earth. She doubted it ever fully melted, even during the summer months.

As children, she and Viola had chased each other through the autumn leaves. She had loved how the brightly colored leaves crunched beneath her feet and the smell of the wind turning chill. She knew the plants were dying. She knew the colors of the leaves were their death pallors. She knew the world would turn into a flurry of snow and ice within just a few weeks. None of that had mattered. All there was in the world was her sister's smiling face, the multicolored leaves, and the undeniable tenor of change.

The dying world held no comfort for her now.

Icy tears stung her cheeks as the weight of her decision settled upon her. The Light help them all—if there even was a Light to pray to. She wasn't so sure about that one anymore either.

Her skin prickled and the hair on her arms stood on end. She tilted her ears to the wind and sniffed at its scent. An odd stench clung to the air. It was like rotting wood and sandalwood mixed with leather. Deftly, she slid a knife from her belt and ducked beneath a low hanging branch.

The sound of her own heartbeat drowned out all other sounds. Breathing in deeply, Starla concentrated on the forest. Birds sang. Animals scrambled between trees. A twig snapped.

She jerked her head in the direction of the sound.

"Who are you?" a male tenor asked. The voice reverberated through the trees. It was nearly impossible to discern from where the sound originated. She crouched even lower. Her back ached and her heart beat more rapidly. She didn't even know how that was possible.

"I'm seeking refuge in Encartia," she said. She managed to keep her voice from quaking too much.

"Step forward," the man commanded. There was no room for negotiation in his tone.

Despite the cold, sweat beaded on her forehead. She refused to miss her chance at finding the princess. Maybe then she could make a decision about what to do next.

She held up her hands and dropped the blade into a small pile of leaves. It barely made a sound as it sank into the soggy ground. "Please," she said. "I have been traveling for days on my own." She stumbled a little as she came forward and sank to one knee. She panted loudly. "I just needed to find my way here." She stole a glance around the forest. Even from her current vantage point, she saw nothing out of place within the forest.

"Who are you?" the man asked again.

"Starla," she replied, keeping her eyes low. She did not give her family name.

"From where do you hail, Starla?" The voice sounded as if it came from all directions. Cold wind whipped all around her, sending shivers down her arms.

"From the capital," she responded. "I came in search of the princess."

Silence.

There was so much silence that Starla began to believe that the mysterious man in the woods had either been a figment of her imagination or that he had slipped away without her realizing it.

"I know the princess," she said. "I served her in the palace. It is my unyielding desire to be of service to her once more."

Still silence.

She huffed loudly, examining her nails. Dirt was caked beneath them. She hadn't bathed in days. Her stomach growled at the worst possible moment. She knew her breath probably matched the acrid taste in her mouth. If only her uncle could see her now, he'd be appalled.

"I know I don't look like much," she said, "but I'm here to help her." *Even if I end up killing her in the end.*

"Why do you believe that the princess is here?" the man asked.

"It makes the most logical sense," Starla said firmly. "The elves have always been amicable with the Bluefischer line. There is no reason to believe that serving the princess would be any different."

"You should return to the palace."

"I can't."

It wasn't a lie. If she returned, empty-handed, to her uncle, she knew he would stop at nothing to ruin her sister's life. Until women were seen as more than property for the pleasure of men, her sister would always be at risk.

An arrow flew past her ear, grazing her skin. She slid her finger over her wound and it came back coated in blood. She clenched her fist, anger filling her.

"It is cowardice to hide within the forest and take shots at me. You must be scared to lose to a woman." She forced herself to sound cockier than she felt.

"You have a fire within your heart."

This time, the voice was louder and sounded as if it were

right behind her. Starla seized another blade, this one hidden in the lining of her vest, and slashed outward with it.

Sniggering filled the air.

"You can't hurt me, Starla."

She spun in a circle, searching the forest for any sign of who her assailant was.

"You won't find me."

Cursing beneath her breath, Starla gathered her meager strength and leapt onto the path from her hiding spot.

It was at that moment that Starla realized three things. She was surrounded. There was no chance for escape. And, she had discovered the entrance to Encartia.

Chapter Forty-One
Silver Moon Camp, Lunameed

Amaleah crouched beside Thadius's side. His body was covered in sweat and his skin was gaunt and yellow, but he was awake. After weeks of being nonresponsive, he was finally awake. She wrapped her arms around him and pulled him into a tight embrace.

"Careful," Nylyla chided. "He is still quite ill."

Amaleah released the centaur and sat back enough to examine his face again. "I'm so sorry, Thadius. I'm so terribly sorry."

His chapped lips cracked into an open smile. "You have nothing to be sorry for," he replied. There was a glimmer of his roguish self in there, Amaleah was sure of it. "It was arrogant of me to think that I could break whatever power the flute had over you."

"No," she cooed at him, "it was my fault for rushing out like I did. I shouldn't have ever put myself in that position." She paused as she dabbed a cool, wet cloth across his brow. "I should never have put you in that position."

"We all make mistakes, Your Highness."

"Yes, but most people's mistakes don't send their friends into unconsciousness for five weeks."

397

Thadius laughed at that. "No, I don't suppose they do," he responded, grinning up at her. "But then again, not all people are meant to be the Harbinger."

Despite Amaleah's happiness that Thadius was awake and finally recovering, the mention of her prophecy sent ice coursing through her veins. She was tired of everyone and everything around her trying to control her.

"Hey now," Thadius said, "what's that look about?"

Amaleah shrugged. "It's nothing," she said, kissing him on his brow. "I promise."

"I could hear you, you know."

"What do you mean?" she asked.

"All those times you came to visit me," he explained, "I might not have been able to respond to you, but I could hear you."

Amaleah's breath caught in her chest. She was glad that he had heard her words—her apologies. She was thankful her explosion hadn't caused too much damage. "A lot has changed since you've been injured," she said, her voice small and plaintive.

"What do you mean?" Thadius asked. He coughed slightly and nodded his head towards the jug of water sitting on his bedside table. She held the glass to his lips as he drank some water.

"I've been training with Anno and Nikailus, and Elaria."

"That's good," he responded. "That's why we came here."

"I know," she said. "But there have been other things, too."

He narrowed his eyes at her. Amaleah sighed. She had been dreading telling him about the impending battle that was expected any day now. She knew he would want to fight. But, in his condition, that would be out of the question.

"We've received word that my father has been gathering his

forces to march on Encartia. Elaria has been trying to convince Kileigh to ally the elves with me. So far, only a handful of the clans have said that they will fight with me when the time comes."

"Amaleah," Nylyla scolded. "He needs his rest."

"Wait," Thadius said, closing his eyes for a moment. "Tell me the rest. I need to know."

Nylyla raised her eyebrows at Amaleah as if to say, 'I thought you knew better,' and then walked out of the room. Nikailus stood in the doorway and Yosef stood in the corner on the other side of the room. Amaleah was glad they were both there.

Amaleah recounted everything that had happened while he'd been unconscious. He didn't ask any questions or comment on the things she told him. He just listened. Occasionally, he nodded. When she had finished, he turned his gaze to Nikailus.

"And you're the one who's been helping her control her magical abilities?" he asked.

Nikailus nodded once in response.

"I see," Thadius said. His lips formed into a small scowl.

Amaleah glanced between the two men. She had so hoped that they would get along. She would need them both in the coming days.

"Yosef, my dear friend," Thadius said, stretching out a hand towards the reaper. "I'm so glad you didn't decide to cut my life short."

Yosef, his ever-present billowing cloak fluttering behind him, glided over to Thadius and peered down into his face. Well, as much as a creature of death with no eyes would peer at anything.

"You don't say?" Thadius chortled. "I would never have guessed you'd vouch for me in the darkness beyond," he croaked.

Yosef made a strange sound, as if he were trying to laugh but not quite succeeding. Amaleah couldn't remember a single time she'd heard the reaper make a sound like that.

"Really?" she said, "You're joking about our friend almost dying?" she glowered at the reaper who simply floated back to his corner.

"Don't be too hard on him, Amaleah," Thadius scolded. "He is a reaper, after all."

"How can you be so casual about all of this," she asked, her voice pitching. "I almost killed you."

"Yeah, but you didn't."

She opened her mouth to respond when a shadow loomed over her. Elaria was there, her lips pressed into a thin, hard line.

"Your presence is needed. Now," she hissed the last word and yanked her from the room. Yosef and Nikailus crowded the doorway as Elaria pulled her down the hall.

"What's going on?" Amaleah asked.

"One of Kileigh's guards caught an intruder in the forest. She claims to have been one of your servants."

"What!" Amaleah pulled her arm free from Elaria's grasp and hurried her steps. "Who was it? Did you get a name?"

"No," Elaria responded. "She claimed that she had an important message for you about something happening in Estrellala, but that's all she would say.

Elaria rushed ahead of Amaleah to lead her into the town center. Crowds of people filled the streets and Amaleah saw the gold dust on the ground that she now associated with Kileigh, the matriarch of the twelve elvish clans. The petite, golden toned elf stood at the head of a long procession. A figure, bound in rope with a black bag over their head lay in the fetal position on the ground before the matriarch.

Fearlessly, Amaleah strode forward and bowed her head before the matriarch. "I am glad that we finally get to meet," she said. She managed to keep her voice steady, despite the quivering she felt inside.

"Yes," Kileigh said. "I had hoped that you'd come to me once you were done trifling with our dear Elaria's help, but you never did."

"I'm sorry," Amaleah stammered. "I wanted to complete my training here."

"You wanted," the matriarch began before devolving into a low laugh. "You thought that the mighty Anno and the experience of Elaria could help you win the fight against your father." She giggled girlishly at that and Amaleah began to wonder just how old the elf before her really was. "Oh, my dear little princess, how little you know."

Amaleah wasn't sure how to respond to the golden matriarch's verbal spar against Anno and Elaria. She decided to ignore it for now and press the elf for information about the servant who had arrived from Estrellala.

"I hear you apprehended one of my servants. I would like to speak with her."

The matriarch's face darkened as she regarded Amaleah. "She was trespassing on elvish land without permission. Need I remind you that the elves are not under the jurisdiction of the Lunameedian royalty? We are a free people," she spread her arms wide and her crowd of elves cheered her.

"I'm sorry if I have given offense," Amaleah stumbled over her words. "But I would like to see to her. I need to know what word there is from the palace."

Kileigh stepped towards Amaleah. Her golden eyes gleamed as sunlight struck them. She was the most regal, beautiful creature Amaleah had ever seen, even ahead of Cordelia, but the coldness she felt from her made her shiver.

"You know my father plans to march on Encartia."

Kileigh's smile slithered into a sly smirk, "I do."

"I intend to defy him."

"I know what you are, Harbinger," the elf stated. She stood directly behind the hooded figure now.

"Please don't hurt her," Amaleah found herself pleading. She didn't know where the flash of urgency came from but it was there, pulsing within her. Her finger began to tingle as she took a step towards the matriarch.

"Uh-uh," Kileigh whispered as she wagged a finger at Amaleah. "Don't get too close or I may have to order my guards to kill her." She flicked her wrist towards a group of soldiers stationed near the entrance. They were taller than any of the other elves Amaleah had seen in Encartia and she was pretty sure their arm muscles were as thick as she was. Amaleah audibly gulped.

"What do you want?" she asked the golden elf.

Kileigh's ears twitched at that and she peered over at Amaleah with a conciliatory smile. "I thought you'd never ask."

Something screamed at the back of Amaleah's mind that there was danger, but she forced it aside. She didn't know who this servant was or why she had made the journey to Encartia, but she was determined to find out.

"Let us strike an accord," Amaleah offered. "Tell me what you want and we can negotiate terms."

Kileigh stepped around the hooded figure and came to stand directly in front of Amaleah. She gripped her chin, her golden nails bit in the spot spots of Amaleah's flesh as she examined her face. "You really do look like Orianna, don't you?" she asked rhetorically. "Except for those eyes." She patted Amaleah on the cheek.

"If the entirety of the elves helps you push back your father, I will need some assurances that, should you become queen, you will give us back what is ours."

"I don't know what you're talking about," Amaleah admitted. "What do I have that's yours?"

"It's not what you have, per se, but what the kingdom of Lunameed has stolen from us."

Amaleah wracked her brain for any memory she had of reading about her royal bloodline stealing from the elves. She couldn't remember a single story.

"Whatever it is, I'm sure we can find a way to negotiate," she said carefully, fearful of any traps the matriarch may have laid for her. She searched the crowd for Elaria, but couldn't find her. She longed for the older elf to aid her in this political battle.

"A long time ago, the entirety of the Arcadi Forest was our home," Kileigh explained. "My people want it back."

"But what about all the people who dwell there now?" Amaleah asked, surprise coating each of her words. "would you send them away?"

"They are not our problem," Kileigh hissed. "Those lands belonged to my people's forefathers and we long to have them returned to us."

Amaleah paused. Giving that much land away would be devastating to her kingdom. She hung her head. She couldn't make that agreement.

"Kileigh," Elaria's voice rang out over the crowd. "You know our forefathers willingly gave that land to the Bluefischer line when they defended us against the Szarmians."

"They stole that land from us!" Kileigh shrieked. "They waited until we were vulnerable and then struck us with a blow that has forever diminished our power."

Elaria sighed as she stepped up beside Amaleah. "Then you

are no better than the men of old," she hissed.

Amaleah's eyes widened at the strength the older woman demonstrated. She defied her matriarch. She stood her ground. She did not back down even as Kileigh focused her golden eyes upon her.

"You always were a human sympathizer," Kileigh hissed.

"And you always carried a chip on your shoulder," Elaria countered. "Even as a little girl, you felt the world owed you something. I was disappointed when your father named you his heir. You've always been a spoiled, self-indulgent…"

"You dare call me names in front of representatives from each tribe?" Kileigh cried out. "You dare defy your leader?"

Elaria's mouth snapped shut. She peered around the precession. Amaleah watched as the older woman's knees began to quake.

"Make a fair trade, Kileigh. That's all I'm asking for."

Kileigh snaked her eyes over to Amaleah. The elf's gaze made Amaleah's skin prickle with gooseflesh as she waited for the matriarch to say something. When it appeared that Kileigh was through with talking, Amaleah lifted her chin high and said, "I am willing to give you half of what you ask for."

Elaria shot her a glare, but Amaleah ignored it. "I can't promise to give you all of the Arcadi Forest, but I can give you the entirety of the eastern woods. What stretches from the Seppiet River along Amadoon Lake and the Cervantu River is yours—given that you release my servant back to me and help me defeat my father."

Kileigh raked her eyes over Amaleah's face. "We already occupy half of that," she said.

"I know. But this is all I can offer you today."

Kileigh turned her back on Amaleah and strode towards a group of elves closest to her guards. They whispered among themselves for several tense moments. Amaleah thought about stepping forward and unmasking her captive servant, but decided against it when she saw the angry gleam in Elaria's eye.

Eventually, Kileigh faced Amaleah once more. "We will have the accord drawn up," she said. She shoved the servant towards Amaleah. "Until then, consider this a sign of our good faith."

The servant stumbled and Amaleah caught her in her arms. She weighed barely anything and Amaleah easily helped her servant gain her footing once more."

"Thank you," Amaleah said as Kileigh and her entourage of elves prepared to leave.

"It is I who should be thanking you, Amaleah. We have attempted to negotiate for our lands to be returned to us for centuries. You are the first to begin making amends for the horrors of the past."

Amaleah wasn't sure she had done the right thing. Elaria's glare certainly gave her pause. But, she had to trust her instincts. And, her instincts were telling her that this was the first step to building a stronger Lunameed.

Using one of her daggers, Amaleah made quick work of cutting her servant's hands and feet free. She sighed, readying herself for whatever damage the elves had done to her servant, before pulling the hood off the woman's head.

She blinked as recognition hit her. "You!" she shouted.

"Me," the blonde-headed wisp of a girl replied.

Amaleah didn't hesitate a moment longer before punching Starla in the face.

Chapter Forty-Two

Starla scrambled away from Amaleah. Blood flowed from her nose. She pinched her bridge and held her head forward, trying to get the bleeding to stop.

"What are you doing here?" the princess screeched at her.

Starla released her hold on her nose and flipped on her hands. She kicked the princess backwards. She stepped forward too tackle her when a pair of strong arms gripped her around the middle. Starla struggled against the hold on her. Lifting her legs, she used her own body weight to force herself backwards. Her captor wobbled for a moment, but kept his feet under him.

Cursing, Starla tried a different approach. She jabbed the man in his stomach multiple times with her elbow. His hold on her loosened for a moment. It was all she needed. She twisted in his arms and brought her knee up and between his legs. He yelped and let go of her altogether.

"Did my father send you here to kill me?" Amaleah asked. She was back on her feet, an arrow notched in a bow. "Did he?" Her lips were pressed into a hard line and she looked as if she could release her arrow with little to no justification.

"No," Starla responded.

"I don't believe you," Amaleah shouted.

"You should."

Amaleah trained the arrow on Starla's heart. *She's certainly got more fire in her than she did before*, she thought as she held up her hands and said again, "I promise you. Your father didn't send me here."

"Namadus then," the princess said her uncle's name like it was a curse.

"I came on my own."

"How did you know I was here?" Amaleah asked.

Starla thought about lying. It would have been so easy to beguile the naïve little princess. But there was something about the glint in Amaleah's eye that stopped her. "There are still those in this kingdom that want to help you," she said.

"And you expect me to believe you're one of them?"

Starla chuckled at that. She made her voice sound as nonchalant as possible, "Believe me or don't, it doesn't matter. I'm here to help you."

The man she'd kneed in the groin groaned loudly. Amaleah made the mistake of glancing down at him, a frown spreading across her face. Starla took her chance and dashed towards the princess. With one hand she gripped the bow and with the other, she flipped Amaleah around so that her back was pressed against Starla.

"Listen to me," Starla hissed in Amaleah's ear. "If I wanted to kill you, I could do it right now." She squeezed on Amaleah's neck for good measure. "But I don't," she continued. "I'm here because, whether I like it or not, you're a much better candidate for ruler than your father or my uncle."

Amaleah squirmed in her grasp so she tightened her grip again. "Stop fighting me," she whispered. When Amaleah didn't, Starla wrenched the bow from her grasp and flung it into the crowd of onlooking elves. She quickly pinned Amaleah's arm to her side and gripped her by the middle. "Stop. Fighting. Me."

Amaleah stomped on her feet. The force of it stung and made Starla's eyes water, but she maintained her hold.

"Let the princess go," a voice commanded from behind Starla. She slowly pivoted, Amaleah still in her grasp, until she came face-to-face with the stoutest, most scarred elf she had ever seen.

"Well ain't you a beauty," Starla said, mockingly.

The giant elf threw a dagger that grazed Starla's ear. Blood flowed down Starla's neck from the wound and coated Amaleah's shoulder.

"I said, let her go," the elf said. "I won't miss again."

Starla assessed the situation. She was surrounded. Her weapons had been confiscated by the first set of elves who'd taken her prisoner. The princess had obviously learned the basics of fighting and was slowly working her way out of Starla's grip. There was really only one solution.

She pushed Amaleah into the warrior elf and bolted in the opposite direction. She thought she'd cleared the crowd when a dark shadow darted from the trees and tackled her. She fell, face-first, into a pile of rabbit dung.

"Was that really necessary?" she asked as she spat grass and pellets from her mouth.

Her assailant didn't respond. He simply hoisted her up and flung her on his shoulders. He smelled like rotting carrion and really bad eggs. A bit of bile rose up Starla's throat but she choked it down as the man carried her back to where Amaleah stood waiting.

The princess bound her feet and hands again. And then, much to Starla's dismay, she tied her to a pole in the middle of the street.

"Tell me why you're here," the princess commanded.

Starla let her head loll as she searched her surroundings for anything that might be useful in her escape. The muscled warrior elf wore a series of bandoliers across her chest. Knives filled each loop. *Useful,* Starla thought as she scanned the rest of the area. There wasn't much, mainly just the weapons other people carried. *But,* she reasoned, *if I could just get my hands on one them, then I could set myself free.*

"I already told you, Your Highness," she used mocking tone for the princess's title, "I came here to help you."

Amaleah released an exasperated cry. Starla smirked at her ability to affect the princess so.

"You really do need to learn how to control your emotions," Starla said, shrugging.

Amaleah stomped her foot and a blast knocked Starla's head against the poll. *What was that?* she thought as she looked over at the princess, who was staring at her hands in dismay.

"Enough," a wizened elf said, laying a hand on Amaleah's shoulder. She cast her gaze on Starla with unreadable expression on her face. "You will dine with us tonight," she said.

Starla didn't fight as a pair of male elves untied her from the pole and half-carried, half-dragged her to a house at the end of the row.

Chapter Forty-Three

Nikailus slipped his hand into Amaleah's as they walked back to Nylyla and Rikyah's home. He traced circles over the back of her hand with his thumb. Her palm was clammy and sticky, but he maintained physical contact with her. Her emerald eyes searched his face and he was tempted to kiss her again.

"I'm sorry she hurt you," she whispered.

Nikailus shrugged. He was used to beatings. The Blackflame had ordered its pupils to be beaten daily for the first seven years he lived with them. The brand on his chest throbbed at the memory. They had given him the brand when he'd been initiated into their order. He could still smell his flesh melting and hear it sizzling as the brand left its mark.

"She did nothing to me that I can't handle," he replied, squeezing her hand. "You did well," he added.

"No, I didn't," she responded petulantly. "I used my powers to hurt her. I didn't even think about what I was doing. I just... reacted."

"Still, you didn't hurt anyone else and you disarmed her."

"She wasn't armed to begin with," Amaleah corrected him.

He rolled his eyes at her. "You know what I mean," he said. She shrugged.

"Amaleah, I don't know how else I can say this to you. You are the most amazing person I've ever met."

He noticed the smile that played across her lips at his words. He hungered to kiss her lips again. To taste her again. But he knew she would resist him. It was fine. He could be patient when he wanted to be.

"Thank you," she murmured as they reached the house. "You're not so bad yourself."

Chapter Forty-Four

Amaleah didn't like it. And, she certainly didn't agree with Elaria's decision to let Starla stay in her home with her. She tried to explain that the golden-haired girl was an assassin who had almost killed her during the night of her escape from Estrellala. She told Elaria what Starla had done to Prince Colin. But no, it didn't matter what Amaleah said. Elaria was set on letting the girl take refuge in the Silver Moon encampment and that was how it was going to stay.

She paced around her room as she fumed. She didn't have time to learn how to control her powers, fight better, and watch her back for blood thirsty assassins. A tap on her window drew her attention away from her pacing. She cracked open the glass and peered down. Nikailus stood there, his black shirt unbuttoned, revealing his muscled chest. Her heart beat faster in her own chest and she found it surprisingly difficult to breathe. He motioned for her to join him. She shook her head but he motioned again before sitting down on the ground with his head propped on his fist.

Smiling, she closed the window and rushed down the stairs. She didn't care if Nylyla or the others heard her leaving. None of them had taken her side when she'd tried to convince Elaria that letting the assassin stay with them would be a mistake. No, all they did was shrug their shoulders and say that everyone deserved a second chance.

But Nikailus had agreed with her. That thought brought a smile to her face as she approached him. He sprang to his feet the minute their eyes met and rushed towards her. He embraced her, his warm arms encircling her.

"I've been thinking about this all day," he whispered into her ear as he nuzzled her.

His words, although they made her smile, also made her stomach do flips. She didn't want to mislead him and she certainly didn't want him to think that she could, in any way, be his. At least not yet. She wasn't ready to tie herself to anyone. Besides, she was still having dreams about Colin. And she still had her throne to win from her father. And she had to fulfill the prophecy. She didn't have time for romance right now, especially when she was so confused about her feelings. She shook her head against his shoulder and pulled away from him.

He frowned down at her. "What's wrong?" he asked, still holding her shoulders in his hands.

"Nothing," she lied. "I just," she paused, trying to think of some way to change the subject. "I just wanted to go on a walk."

"Oh," he said. He slid his thumb over her bottom lip and leaned in as if he were going to kiss her again.

She turned away and began walking towards a path she enjoyed taking in the evening. She heard him sigh but didn't turn around to see if he was following her. She knew he would.

Within moments he had caught up with her.

"Have you given my proposition any more thought?" he asked.

"What proposition?"

He halted and gripped her wrist in his hand. It wasn't hard enough to bruise her, but she certainly didn't like him touching her like that. "Please don't play games with me," he said. "Not tonight."

His eyes held so much sadness that Amaleah almost kissed him right then and there. But she didn't.

"Remind me," she prodded.

"About finding the Creators," he said.

"It's a fool's errand, Nikailus," she said.

"What if it wasn't?" he pled. "What if all it required was someone as strong as you to break the spell that trapped them."

"I don't know," she said, annoyed. "I suppose we would have heard about others seeking them out. No one knows what happened to them, Nik. All we have are rumors and conflicting stories."

"What if I told you that I knew how to find them."

She searched his face. He seemed so sincere. She brushed a lock of his dark hair away from his eyes and peered up at him. He crinkled his nose at her and stuck out his tongue. She laughed and began walking again.

They walked in silence for several paces. A cool breeze swept through Amaleah's hair, making it flutter about her face. Even with all the tension and worry she felt, being out here, in the woods, with Nikailus set her mind at ease. She inhaled deeply and released her breath slowly. This was exactly what she needed.

"Think about all the good we could do together," Nikailus whispered in her ear.

"What?" she asked, startled. She hadn't heard or felt him get that close to her.

"I said, think about all the good we could do together. We're the most powerful magical beings Mitier…"

"I know. You said that earlier," she said.

"But it's true."

"Why are you so insistent that we search out the Creators, Nikailus? The way I see it, they either exist and have chosen to ignore us for the past three hundred years or they were always myths."

"That's blasphemy," Nikailus said coolly.

"Maybe it is, but it's how I feel," she replied.

He hung his head. "Finding them could be the turning point in the upcoming battle, Amaleah. If you can't see that then I don't know what else to do to help you."

He stormed away from her and Amaleah found herself alone in the woods. The chilly night air caused gooseflesh to prickle on her arms. She loved going on walks, but she hated doing them alone.

Rustling sounds surrounded her. She forced herself to believe that the sounds were just animals scouring for food. She hadn't brought a torch and the sister moons were but tiny slivers in the sky above. There was not enough light filtering down among the trees to guide her way.

The rustling grew louder. She could tell that whatever was moving in the shadows was too big to be a woodland animal. Flexing her hands, she tried to call her magic to her.

"Come on," she whispered, "please work."

Sparks danced on her fingertips, but flickered out the moment she moved her hand. She breathed in deeply again and thought about what Nikailus had told her to do. Imagine the flame. A twig snapped nearby and Amaleah jolted. Fire burst from the palm of her hand as she caught herself from the fall. Fed by the trees, the flames began to rapidly spread.

Men screamed and horses brayed.

"No," she thought, panic swirling within her. It was her father's army. It had to be. Who else would be there.

She envisioned blasting the army away. She could see the

men flying through the air, could hear their panic as they fought to maintain their footing.

She brought her hands up to launch the attack.

"Wait!" a voice called from the shadows. "We mean you no harm."

She recognized that voice. Her heart thrummed in her chest as she dropped her hands to the side. It wasn't possible, she thought. It couldn't be. She raced through the trees. Men in red uniforms formed tight rows. Some were on horseback. Many were on foot. Wagons laden with weapons and food barely squeezed through the trees.

"Colin?" she called. She had been so certain it had been him. She searched the faces of the men. None of them were Colin. There were so many of them. How had he mobilized so quickly? Why hadn't anyone told her that he'd reclaimed his throne.

"Colin!" she called again.

The soldiers cleared a path. In the distance, she saw the tall, slender outline of the prince as he approached her.

"I'm here," he said as he stepped into the flickering light of her fire.

Chapter Forty-Five

Kiela Rainforest, Smiel, The Second Darkness

Water dripped onto Rhaelend's forehead, stirring him from his slumber. The air was hot and muggy. Oppressive. Even with the heat, Rhaelend shivered. His parched lips cracked when he opened them to lap in the water rolling down his face. The water tasted stale, as if it had been sitting in a cistern for far too long.

Rhaelend opened his eyes.

Agony flowed through his bones. He was trapped in darkness. Neither the sister moons nor starlight filtered through the tiny cracks running up and down the walls. No torchlight cast aside the darkness.

"Guard," his voice barely came out in a husky whisper. "Guard!" he called again.

Gingerly, he trailed his fingers over his temple. He winced in pain. He remembered the shadow emerging from the forest. And the pain of something slamming into his head. He remembered what he had done.

The pungent scent of smoke filled his nose, but he could see no fire. Distantly, screams pierced the air. Rhaelend felt around him for any sign of where he was. His skin flared with fire. *How*

417

long have I been here? he thought. His mind worked sluggishly. *What had happened? Where was Kiwanai? And the ring? Were they safe?*

A dirt floor was beneath him and stone stood all around him. He crawled across the room. It was barely twice his length. Cautiously, Rhaelend felt for the door. There was nothing. Nothing. *It doesn't make sense. All of the dungeons in the palace have doors. Unless I'm not in the palace.* The thought sent a wave of nausea through him. If he had not been apprehended by the princess and returned to the palace, then he had no idea where he was.

"Hello?" he called. "Is anyone there?" he banged his fists against the wall as he spoke. Only dust and crumbling rock responded.

Cradling his head in his palms, Rhaelend sank against the wall. He really had made a mess of everything. He tried to identify the moment that had defined everything. The First Darkness had left Smiel relatively untouched. They'd heard rumors, of course. When the news of the young Szarmian prince's assassination had reached their remote kingdom, the war had already begun without them. Szarmi did not ask for aid until near the end. In that first war, his kingdom had declined, claiming that they wished to remain neutral in the dispute between Lunameed and Szarmi. In secret, Kiwanai's grandfather, Delinai, had set up a training regimen for his armies. Rhaelend had been selected to serve as Kiwanai's personal guard. They'd prepared for the worst: an invasion from the west. But none came.

In the end, Lunameed pushed the Szarmian forces from their

territories. They'd sent sorcerers to set the Barbery Woods ablaze. With forces to the north and wildfires spreading across their southern border, the Szarmian ranks broke. And, as King James of Szarmi sought to keep control of his armies, he negotiated a surrender.

A reluctant peace had followed. For a time, Smiel had thought that would be the end of the fighting. Delinai had relaxed the training regimen of the Smielian armies. Smiel continued its tradition of focusing on music, art, and beauty. That was the world Kiwanai was raised in. Even as a child, she'd been protected from the rumors of war. She'd been left in the dark about the horrors the other kingdoms of Mitier had faced. But Rhaelend had known.

His father, a trusted emissary to Delinai, had been sent to negotiate an accord between Lunameed and Szarmi. He had never returned. He could still remember the rumble of his mother's body as she clung to him when delivering the news. "Your father is dead."

Squiggling worms crawled over Rhaelend's skin as he sat in the mud. Grunting, he wiped them off his arms and legs. Water continued to drip from the ceiling, creating puddles all around him. His stomach rumbled and he wondered, again, how long he had been locked in this cell. The shouts from outside grew louder. He couldn't discern what the people were saying. He prayed to the Light that they were the result of the rising force of rebels. It was time for the Smielian people to be free.

The peace between Szarmi and Lunameed did not last long. Within fifteen years, the truce between them blazed into nothing more than ash. Kiwanai's father, Moordai, assumed the throne following a lapse in Delinai's memory. By that time, Rhaelend and Kiwanai had fallen in love. She'd meant everything to him. More than his position on the guard. Even more than the safety of their kingdom. Moordai had never approved of the match. Kiwanai was to wed someone of more stature. She'd begged her father to let them wed, but Moordai had refused.

Rhaelend ground his teeth at the sour memory. After her father's refusal, Kiwanai had stopped coming to see him. She'd stopped fighting for him. But, Rhaelend had never stopped fighting for her, even if she couldn't see that truth right now.

Everything changed when Moordai agreed to aid the Szarmians. He claimed it was in the best interest of Smiel. Rhaelend knew the truth. Moordai wanted to align himself with the military prowess of their western neighbor. Through marriage, they would be a great alliance. He wasn't surprised when he learned the news of Kiwanai's betrothal to the Szarmian heir. But, he was surprised when he was reassigned to another part of the palace. Still, she had not fought for him.

But he still fought for her.

He knew her secret, the fire she controlled when she thought no one was looking. She was a sorceress or fire goddess or simply blessed by the Light. To Rhaelend, it didn't matter. She was the sun in the darkest of nights. She made everything warmer, brighter, better. If there was one thing Rhaelend knew above all else it was this: the Szarmians would crush her. There was no other narrative. Kiwanai possessed the very thing they were waging war to destroy. Rhaelend knew that Kiwanai would go, that she would attempt to change the prince's mind about magical creatures. He also knew she would fail.

Bells clanged. Despite the pain in his head and back, Rhaelend jumped to his feet at the sound. He counted. *One, two, three, four.* He gasped. "No," he whispered. He sagged against the stone wall. "No."

Everyone in Smiel knew what the tolling of the bells meant. Each number signified something different. One-a new royal had been born. Two-the king was dead. Three-war. Four-the fall of the kingdom. The people were so accustomed to the first two tolls that they barely listened for the third and fourth. Before Moordai's rule, Smiel had been a place of peace and prosperity. Rhaelend had always believed that the king's greed would be Smiel's ruin. And now, it seemed, he had been proven correct.

Chapter Forty-Six

The Silver Moon Camp, Lunameed, 325 years later

Amaleah sat at the head of the long table that had been set up in the Silver Moon camp's town hall. Elaria sat at the other head, much to the chagrin of Kileigh, who sat at Amaleah's right-hand side. Thadius, still recovering from what Amaleah had done to him lay next to Elaria. Nylyla sat next to him. Amaleah smiled as she watched the young elf force feed the centaur berries with herbs and water. He was slowly regaining his strength, and for that, Amaleah was thankful.

Nikailus and Colin sat next to each other to Amaleah's left. She did not like how they glared at each other when they thought she wasn't looking. She wanted them to be friends, but it appeared that they had no interest in getting to know one another better. Redbeard, still as grizzly as ever, sat on Colin's other side. He puffed on his pipe and peered about the room. He seemed leaner to Amaleah and more muscular. Colin, too, appeared leaner and stronger. She wondered what the two of them had faced on their journey to Szarmi. She had gathered enough information to know that Colin had been unsuccessful in reclaiming his throne but had gained the trust of about a quarter of the Szarmian army.

Starla, her expression smug and a new bandolier strapped to

her chest sat to Elaria's left. Her blonde hair was pulled back into a tight bun at the back of her head and she wore soft black leather that seemed to move with her body perfectly. Amaleah had tried to convince Elaria to leave the assassin at home, but the matriarch had refused, stating that since the girl was Namadus' niece and had been in the palace only a few months ago that she would be crucial to understanding the mindset of the king.

Rounding out their meeting were Anno, Yosef, and one member each from the other ten elvish tribes.

Amaleah cleared her throat. "Thank you for coming," she said. Her voice shook slightly. She detested public speaking. She always had, especially since Namadus had forced her to do it so often during her time in Estrellala.

"As many of you know, I recently escaped the clutches of my father, King Magnus of Lunameed. It is my belief that insanity has taken his mind and he is no longer fit to rule our nation." She paused, letting her words sink in. "I have received reports that he plans to forcibly retrieve me and force me into wedlock with him." Her stomach churned and a single phrase passed through her mind. *You'll never escape me.*

"I have no intention of letting my father," *or any man,* she thought, "rule me against my will."

"I consider each of you to be an ally. I come to you now, not as the Harbinger, but as a woman seeking help. Help me defend myself against my father. Help me reclaim my throne. Help me do these things and I swear to you that I will do everything in my power to fulfil the prophecy spoken of in old."

Murmuring filled the room as the matriarchs of the clans all began speaking at once. Amaleah glanced at Nikailus, who smiled at her, and then to Colin, who frowned.

Elaria shushed the room and rose from her seat. Her bones audibly creaked as she stretched out a hand towards Amaleah. "I, for one, offer you the resources of the Silver Moon Clan. You are one of us, child, and we will not abandon you in this time of need."

Kileigh stood next. She smirked at Amaleah as she tossed a rolled scroll at her. "The accord we agreed upon," she said. Amaleah's fingers tensed around the parchment. Now that she knew who the prisoner was, she regretted bargaining away part of her kingdom in return for Kileigh's help.

Her hands trembled as she unrolled the scroll and scanned through its contents. It was written in the common tongue instead of elvish, for which Amaleah was grateful. she still had not mastered the language, despite her hours of practice. Everything appeared to be in order.

She laid the scroll down and then looked Kileigh straight in the eyes. "And you promise to help me win back my throne, no matter how long it takes," she prodded.

Kileigh rolled her eyes. "Didn't you see that clause in the agreement?" she asked. She smiled conspiratorially at Amaleah. "My councilors advised me against it, but I told them I was going to do what I pleased."

Amaleah reread the document, this time without skimming over the longer passages. Sure enough, the clause was there. She finished reading the document, just to be sure Kileigh hadn't tried to slip something else into, but found nothing amiss. She passed it over to Thadius to examine. He and Nylyla began reading the entirety of the document as Amaleah thanked Kileigh for the accord.

"I know not all of us have always been on amiable terms," her gaze shifted to Starla who was picking her nails with one of her daggers. She still didn't understand why Elaria thought it was a good idea to arm the assassin. The younger girl flicked the dirt she'd collected on the blade on the ground. She winked at

Amaleah when she noticed her staring at her.

"Umm," Amaleah paused. She'd forgotten what she was going to say next.

"Princess Amaleah," Colin stepped in. The room fell silent as he stood and approached her. "I know that I don't have much to offer. In truth, only four-thousand of my men joined me for this campaign. They know that leaving their post means civil war for Szarmi. They chose this path because I promised them I would do everything in my power to regain the throne."

"I know that," Amaleah replied. She glanced between Redbeard and Colin. The older man stared down at his hands and appeared intent on looking everywhere but at her. She looked back at Colin. His hazel eyes widened as he kneeled before her. *Oh no*, she thought, her heart hammered so rapidly in her chest that she thought it might explode. This could not be happening.

"We are both rulers without a kingdom," he said. "Perhaps together, we can change that."

Amaleah swept her gaze over the attendees. All of them stared at her and Colin with rapt attention. Nikailus scowled at them, his violet eyes narrowed on her face. Her skin prickled as she looked down into Colin's eyes once more.

"Perhaps we should discuss the terms of your proposal in private," she said. Her voice shook and she chided herself for being unable to just tell him that she had no desire to marry at the moment, perhaps ever.

"No," Kileigh said. "I think that any proposal the prince without a kingdom has for you should be heard by everyone."

Colin blushed. Amaleah wished she could give him the answer she knew he wanted.

"Yes," Elaria agreed, "I, too, think that would be best."

Amaleah groaned internally. "Fine," she acquiesced. She placed a hand on Colin's shoulder and squeezed it gently.

"Please go back to your seat," she whispered.

He searched her face. She could see the disappointment in his eyes as he stood and strode back to his chair. He leaned into Redbeard and whispered something Amaleah couldn't hear as he took his seat.

She took a sip of water and tried to slow her breathing. It was no use. "What did you have in mind, Your Highness?"

He didn't look at her as he responded. "It's a simple trade, really," he explained. "I will pledge my four thousand men to your cause and help you take control of the Lunameedian throne. In exchange, you will help me take back Szarmi once the fighting has ceased here."

Amaleah sighed in relief.

"It was suggested to me by my advisors that we seal the pact with a betrothal." He looked into her eyes as he finished telling her the pact arrangement. He had the kindest eyes she had ever seen.

She swallowed and sipped at her water again as she contemplated how she should respond to him. She needed his soldiers. Szarmian forces were known for their strength, fortitude, and group maneuvering. More than that, she wanted— she needed—Colin to be a part of her campaign. Although they had only spent a few short weeks together, she wanted their friendship to continue growing. In him, she saw a fellow ruler who wanted to leave Mitier a better place.

"I accept your offer," she said, her voice quivering slightly. "But I cannot accept the betrothal."

"Amaleah, be reasonable," Elaria chided, "this is the only way to ensure that both sides of the pact will be upheld. Prince Colin needs assurances."

Amaleah shook her head at Elaria's words. She did not want her frustration at the situation to mar what she said next. She looked straight into Colin's eyes as she said, "I will sign whatever contract you draw up, Colin." He flinched at her informal use of his name. Amaleah's gut wrenched at the sight of his suffering. She never intended to hurt him. He looked away from her, but she continued, "I have no intention of using myself as a bargaining tool. I want us to be friends as well as allies, Colin."

He gripped the arms of his chair so tightly that his knuckles turned white. For a moment, all Amaleah wanted to do was take back everything she had just said and accept his proposal. She cared for him. She thought she could even grow to love him. But he clearly saw marriage to her as a way to shore up his ability to take back Szarmi. She had had enough of people using her and controlling her life. She just wished he could see that and not take her refusal as a personal affront.

"I'll draw up the pact," Colin said, his voice was devoid of emotion and he barely glanced at her as he stood to take his leave.

"Thank you," she said. She wished they were able to speak in private, so that she could explain how she felt—why she had rejected him.

He bowed to the members of her council before striding to the door. As Amaleah watched him go, she silently begged him to turn around, to look at her, to give her an assurance that their friendship was intact. He didn't even pause as he opened the door and left the room.

"Well," Kileigh said, a smirk covering her face, "that was certainly entertaining." She clicked her nails on the table before asking, "Why didn't you tell me he wanted to marry you, Amaleah? I mean, I know he's a Szarmian, but the way he proposed." She fanned herself. "I don't think I could have turned him down the way you did."

"Right, well," Amaleah stammered over her words. "I think it best that we carry on, don't you?"

She wasn't in the mood to continue discussing strategy, but their time was running out. Elaria had predicted that her father's army would arrive within three days. There was no time but the present to make all the arrangements and determine a strategy.

She had just asked Redbeard to walk them through the strategies he'd used during his days as a rebel leader when a loud horn sounded from outside. Elaria rose from her seat and rushed to the window. Throwing it open, she revealed total chaos on the other side.

"It's too late for strategy," she said. The older woman's voice shook as she continued peering outside. "Your father's army has arrived."

Chapter Forty-Seven

Well, Amaleah thought, *he was going to come after me at some point*. She glanced around the room. Half of her councilors were staring at the elves preparing for an assault. The other half were looking at her. For the first time in her life, she was expected to have the answers. She didn't. She would never admit that to the members gathered around the table, many of whom were older, more experienced, and probably did have the answers.

"Um," she began. She met Elaria's gaze. The older elf nodded to Amaleah, a small smile playing across her lips. The encouragement was all Amaleah needed. "Redbeard, find Colin, let him know what's happening if he doesn't already. Tell him that I'll agree to anything he requests—except the betrothal. Tell him," she paused, "tell him I need him in this fight and that I look forward to returning the favor once I've claimed the Lunameedian throne." Redbeard nodded and rose from his chair. He shared whispered conversation with Anno and Elaria, but slipped from the room within moments.

Amaleah turned her gaze to Kileigh, "Our pact is signed. Ready your troops," she glanced at the other elvish matriarchs, "ready all of your troops. We must defend Encartia. If you cannot find it in yourselves to do it for me, then do it for your homeland."

Finally, she looked to Nikailus, "Walk with me." She left no room for discord as she hastily left the town hall. The rest of her councilors followed suit, each of them taking a different direction as they readied themselves for the impending battle.

Amaleah had barely gone six paces when Elaria gripped her arm, halting her.

"You did well in there," the matriarch said. Her wrinkled face tightened as she leaned forward and whispered in Amaleah's ear, "I pray that the Light gets you through this. When you see your father on the battlefield, remember what you have learned. Do not let your emotions rule you." She leaned back and cupped Amaleah's cheek in her hand, "You are who we've been waiting for, Amaleah."

Tears welled in Amaleah's eyes at Elaria's words. She didn't have the words to tell the matriarch what her confidence in her meant, so she flung her arms around her shoulders and hugged her. At first, Elaria was stiff and stood with her arms by her sides. As Amaleah squeezed her gently, the matriarch slowly wrapped her arms around the princess's shoulders and returned the hug.

The sound of another horn blast drew Elaria's attention. "You'll find armor in your rooms," she said. Her voice was tight as she scanned the woods. Smoke curled above the trees in the distance. "I had it custom made for you." She cupped Amaleah's cheek again. "May it serve you well."

With that, Elaria drew away from her and disappeared into the crowd. Amaleah sought out Nikailus, who was standing nearby. He gripped her hand as they made their way to Nylyla and Rikyah's home.

"Even with Colin's four thousand, we still only have around fifty-five hundred fighters. My father will have nearly double that number," she slipped her hand out of his as she spoke. She noticed when his hand clenched and unclenched.

"Yes," he said, "Colin may not be the hero he wants to be."

Amaleah gave Nikailus a sharp look and hissed, "He's my friend, Nik, and my ally. We need him."

"No, we don't."

"How can you say that? Do you not see the terror the elves feel?" she strode through the entrance to her home with the elves. "If the battle turns, I am going to surrender myself to my father. No matter what the outcome is, it is better than watching them all die."

She turned her back on Nikailus, her shoulder shaking slightly. Now that the time had come for war, she wasn't sure she was ready.

"Colin is a skilled strategist," she said. "His soldiers are some of the best trained men in the whole of Mitier. Even facing nearly double their forces, the Szarmians may turn the tide. Besides," she said as she began to climb the stairs to her room, "none of the others I sent letters to responded to my pleas."

Nikailus followed her up the stairs. She was glad to have his company. Though her feelings were still mixed and confusing to her, her need to have Nikailus in her life outweighed anything she was feeling.

"What if I told you that I'd discovered how to release the Creators," he whispered from behind her.

Not this again, she thought, whirling on him. "I would say what I have always said when you've brought this up, Nik. You're chasing a dream."

He gripped her hand and pulled her towards him. The warmth of his hand on hers made her worries begin to fade. All the tension she'd been feeling in her shoulders and back began to recede. Even the headache that had been growing in strength ever since she'd refused Colin's marriage proposal dissipated slightly.

"I'm not," he said emphatically. "I found a book in Elaria's archives that talked about the Wars of Darkness in great detail. The author described a world-ending battle during the Third Darkness. The Creators were there, Amaleah."

His eyes shone with excitement as he continued, "The Blackflame, for better or worse, carried a secret with them. They claimed that the Creators did not willingly abandon Mitier during the Wars of Darkness. Rather, they were imprisoned by those who were jealous of their power. The Order knew how to release the Creators and they taught me what was required."

He wrapped his arms around Amaleah's shoulders, "All we have to do is find them," he whispered in her ear.

His breath tickled her neck and set her senses on fire. It was an alluring fairy tale. But that was all it was.

"I cannot go chasing after a dream when there is a real battle about to begin," she replied.

Nikailus stepped away from her, his face stricken. "Is this because of him?" he asked. There was so much vehemence in his voice that, for a moment, Amaleah thought she was speaking to someone else entirely.

"No," she responded definitively, "this has nothing to do with him. The only reason my father's army is here is because of me. I have a duty to do everything in my power to help the elves, the few magical creatures who have joined us, and now Colin's army be victorious." She crossed the threshold into her room. "If the battle turns, if we begin to lose, I need to be here to surrender." She didn't wait for him to respond. There was nothing he could say that would change her mind.

The armor Elaria had commissioned for her hung from a headless dummy. Amaleah was surprised by the simplicity of the design. Thin strips of cloth had been quilted together to form a flexible yet sturdy tunic. Soft leather pants completed the under pieces of the armor. They both had been dyed in the Lunameedian colors of blue, green, and brown. Silver thread had been used to embroider designs representing the Creators into the cloth and leather. Silver mail, so delicate it looked more like a spider's web than metal, lay atop the tunic. Amaleah was afraid to touch the metal for fear that it would break apart in her hand. Finally, hard leather pads had been tied around the wrists, shoulders, knees, and abdomen of the entire ensemble. She trailed her fingers over the outfit. It was perfect.

"Are you going to help me put this on, or not?" she called through the open doorway.

Nikailus trudged into her room. He glowered at her, looked at the armor, and then sighed loudly.

"Although I would be delighted to see you without any clothes on," he purred, "You should probably put the tunic and pants on by yourself."

Amaleah's cheeks burned as she realized her mistake. "Yes, of course." She shoved him out of the room and closed the door in his smirking face. At least he wasn't holding her decision to stay for the battle against her.

Amaleah made quick work of changing into the new set of tunic and trousers. The material, despite its multiple layers of quilted cotton, was lightweight and breathable. The material seamlessly moved with her body. The mail slid over the tunic like water. It fell just below her hips and fit tight against her body. Despite how delicate it looked, the chain links appeared to have been forged from a single piece of metal. It sparkled like starlight and Amaleah found herself wondering how the mail had been crafted. It was certainly lighter than any metal she had seen or felt before. Despite the comfort she felt in wearing it, she hoped it wouldn't be needed during the battle against her father's army.

"You can come in now," she said as she opened her bedroom door.

Nikailus entered her room once more. "The mail is becoming on you," he said. "Everyone will know what a true warrior you've become."

He brushed back her hair as he tied the leathers around her abdomen. "Promise me you won't put yourself in too much danger once the fighting begins," he murmured in her ear. He let his fingers glide along her chest as he moved to adjust the shoulder straps.

She pressed her body against his. His warmth soaked into her and she let herself wonder what it would be like to accept him into her arms, to do more than just steal kisses from him. Her cheeks flushed at the thoughts.

"I already told you. If it comes to it, I will choose the lives of those who fight for me over myself. May the Light protect us," she responded. She stepped away from him to admire herself in the mirror. With her leaner, more toned muscles and armor she was a far cry from the princess she had been a year ago. Gone were the frilly dresses and jewels she'd been expected to wear in court. She smiled as she admired the way the chain mail sparkled beneath her leathers. Nikailus was right. She was more warrior than princess now.

"I've never noticed this before," Nikailus said, sweeping a hand over the silver chain of the conch shell necklace Cordelia had given her. Although she had always kept it hidden beneath her clothes, it now laid atop her tunic. She brushed her fingers over it, the pink and silver colors shimmered in the light pouring in from her window.

"It was a gift," she said simply.

"From whom?" he prodded.

Amaleah met his gaze in the mirror. There was something in his expression that gave her pause. "From a friend who wanted me to remember that I will never be alone."

"From the Szarmian scum then?"

She whirled on him, jabbing a finger in his chest. "You have no right to speak of Colin that way," she roared. His eyes widened as she shoved him backwards. "You have no right to demand answers from me. You are not my father nor my husband."

"You've certainly made that very clear," he shouted back at her.

She faltered. "But, you are my friend," she said, in as placating a voice as she could muster.

He shook his head. "And what if I want more than that?"

She stiffened and her voice came out colder than she intended, "No one and nothing can induce me into a betrothal at this time."

"Because you have feelings for a prince without land or fortune."

She scowled at him and shook her head. "No," she said softly, "not because of him, Nikailus. Can't you understand that I have been told what to do my entire life? My father controlled my every action, my every move. Even now, my 'friends' want things from me that I'm not sure I can give." She crossed her arms over her chest and continued, "I know being royalty comes with responsibility. I understand that. But I want to decide when

I marry and to whom."

"Say what you will, Princess," Nikailus seethed, "but I can tell how you feel about him."

"And can you tell how I feel about you?" she quipped.

Stricken, his features softened. "No," he declared, "I cannot."

"And therein lies the problem." She laid a hand on his arm and squeezed gently. "Let's just get through this battle and see what happens next."

A darkness settled over his face as he peered down at her. Without a word, he ripped his arm from her grasp and stormed from the room. Amaleah sank onto her bed. In less than a day she'd ostracized two of the people she cared about most. Cradling herself, she wept.

Chapter Forty-Eight

Amaleah didn't weep for long. The sound of a third horn trumpeting the approach of her father's army spurred her to action. She strapped a dagger to her hip and both of her thighs before selecting her favorite bow. She'd pick up at least one quiver of arrows from the armory. Ideally, none of these weapons would be necessary. She intended to use her magic to push back her father's army. Though, if she were being honest with herself, using her powers against others was also one of her greatest fears. Even with the newfound control she'd developed, she worried that she wouldn't be able to stop herself from exploding outward—from hurting everyone around her, even those she cared about.

She trailed her fingers along the conch necklace once more. Cordelia had told her it was a blessing from her people. But the merpeople were dead. The sirens had sung their last song. She didn't even know if Cordelia still lived. The conch shell turned as cold as ice in her hand. So many of the magical beings had 'blessed' her. The lone siren. The fae. Even the Tiefs. Where were they now? She stared at her reflection in the mirror for a moment longer. They had all abandoned her.

"You can do this," she told herself. Somehow, she believed

herself more than she did the voices telling her she wasn't ready.

She strode from the house, her back straight and her chin high. The Silver Moon encampment was a flurry of activity. Those too young, too old, or too frail to fight were being housed in safehouses. Spellcasters placed charms around the perimeter of the dwellings to keep the occupants safe. Amaleah prayed to the Light that the enchantments would hold if their armies were pushed back.

Thadius, his face still gaunt from the magical blast she'd attacked him with, trotted up beside her.

"I want to fight," he proclaimed.

"You can't," she said. "You're still too weak."

"I think that's a decision for me to make, Your Highness, not you."

She glanced sidelong at him. Here she was demanding that people respect her autonomy and she was attempting to strip him of the same privilege. "You're right," she sighed. "I shouldn't forbid you from fighting, but I will ask it of you. I don't want to see you get hurt."

"And I can't sit around twiddling my thumbs where there's a battle ahoof."

"And here I always thought you were just a foppish scoundrel," she teased.

"Who me?" he asked, pointing at himself. "Never, Your Highness."

She rolled her eyes at him. "I still remember the first time we met—before you shoved me into that well."

His cheeks turned pink and he shrugged his shoulders. "Had to be done, I'm afraid, Princess."

She ignored his retort. "You were late because you were

flirting with a fae."

He shrugged. "A centaur never kisses and tells."

She laughed. It was the first true laugh she'd had in days. It made her sides hurt and her breathing laborious. Still, she wouldn't have traded it for the world. "You really are a scoundrel, aren't you?" she asked.

"Only with the right conquest," he replied, wagging his eyebrows at her.

They continued bantering back and forth until they reached the backend of the troops. Elaria, Anno, and Kileigh had negotiated the exact location they would stage the battle. Her father's army was approaching from the north. Beyond the forest, there were only open hills and farmland. Anno had predicted—accurately—that King Magnus would send his forces down the shortest path. Word had been received that he'd sent ships down the River Estrell laden with soldiers. Several of Kileigh's scouts had discovered carts and rows of soldiers as far as the eye could see marching down the river bank. Based on these reports Anno had surmised that King Magnus had deployed a force of some fifteen thousand men.

It was more than what Amaleah had anticipated. Even with Colin's four thousand, they would be outnumbered three to one on the battlefield. If the rumors were true, her father had even extended a peace offering to a variety of sorcerers and magical creatures he had long since affronted by never including them in court celebrations or political deliberations. The idea that her father wanted her returned to him so much that he had resorted to allying himself with creatures he found repulsive made her insides quiver. She did not want to find out what he would do to her if he ever got his hands on her again.

She couldn't think of the odds. They would either win or she would turn herself over to her father to save the others. Those were the only outcomes she could accept. She hoped it would be the former.

Although many of Colin's forces remained in camp, he had ordered that teams of skirmishers be sent forward to harry the enemy, attempt to slow them, and cause disarray in their lines. The elves sent their rangers forward to protect the Szarmian forces and guide them through the forest trails. The small force of spellcasters born to the elves would be stationed with Amaleah and Nikailus near the frontlines. They needed to be able to see where they were sending their blasts of magic in order to wage an effective campaign.

Amaleah wasn't sure where Colin or Redbeard would be stationed during the battle. She searched for Colin in the confusion, but couldn't find him anywhere. She promised herself that she would ask Elaria where he was once she arrived at her designated position. She wished, more than anything, that she had had an opportunity to speak with him before the fighting began.

She and Thadius walked in silence as they passed rank after rank of Szarmian and elvish troops. *There are so many of them,* Amaleah thought as the trees finally began to thin. The sound of men shouting and horses neighing drowned out all other sounds as she approached the wood and steel dais Anno had insisted the spellcasters stay on. It, too, had been charmed for protection.

Amaleah stepped out from behind the last row of trees and surveyed the scene before her. Her heart skipped a beat at the immensity of the green and blue clad force. Two squadrons of three ships each filled the river channel in the distance. Her fingers itched to send a blast of power at them, to disable them even before the fighting began.

Thadius laid a hand on her shoulder. "Wait," he whispered.

Amaleah didn't question how he knew her thoughts, but she did as he requested. She scanned the troops. They stretched further than she had even imagined. There were cavalry and archers and infantry with long spears as well as swords. The stench of sweat, horses, and excrement filled the air. Amaleah stepped back into the shadow of the trees, but continued to survey the army before her.

A lone soldier, waving a white flag approached. Elaria and Kileigh emerged from the trees, each wearing garb similar to that of Amaleah's.

"We should shoot him," Kileigh said. She had painted elvish symbols on her brow and wore her long, golden hair in a braid down her back. Even in war attire, the elvish matriarch was beautiful.

"We should hear what he has to say," Elaria countered.

The younger matriarch glared at Elaria. "When this is over, Elaria, we will have to have a chat—you and I—about your respect for our order."

"Should we?" Elaria quipped. "I rather thought I showed all the respect that was due."

Kileigh glowered at the older elf. "You certainly have become more daring since the princess arrived."

"Call it finding my voice again," Elaria said. She stepped out from the protection of the trees and approached the messenger. Amaleah did not miss the movement of several archers aiming their arrows at the messenger as Elaria approached him. She would bet anything that her father's archers had done the same to the Silver Moon matriarch.

"His Majesty, King Magnus Bluefischer, Lord over the Lunameedian Waters, Ruler of the Magical Realm, and Father of the Light, sends his regards to you and the elvish people," the messenger called. Even from the distance separating them, Amaleah could hear his words. "My master bids you to relinquish his daughter to him. Deliver her now and all will be forgiven." He paused, apparently for dramatic effect because he waited for several moments before continuing. "Refuse to return her and he will rain upon you with fire and brimstone."

Amaleah watched in amazement as Elaria shrugged her shoulders at the messenger.

"You can tell your master," she replied, her voice booming across the open plain, "that if he wants his daughter, he should ask for her himself."

"Is that your final answer?" the soldier asked. Amaleah thought she heard a slight quiver to his voice, but she couldn't be sure.

"I don't speak for the Princess Amaleah," Elaria responded, "But I can tell you this, if she wanted to return to her father, she would have done so already. The elves will not force her to return to His Majesty. Not today. Not ever."

It was hard to tell what reaction the messenger had to Elaria's words. He seemed to sputter for a moment. But then he bowed to her and quickly retreated back to her father's line.

Amaleah narrowed her eyes at her father's army. He had to be in there somewhere. She doubted that he would send an army to retrieve her without also accompanying the forces.

"He'll stay at the back of the army," Elaria said as she rejoined Kileigh and Amaleah.

"What?" Amaleah asked.

"Your father," Elaria explained. "It is customary for the ruler to remain protected at the back of the army."

"I see," Amaleah replied. The idea that she, most likely, would not have to engage with him brought a small smile to her face.

"You're smiling at the onset of battle," Kileigh remarked. "You must be as mad as your father."

"No," Amaleah replied, shaking her head. "I'm just relieved that I won't have to see him."

Kileigh shrugged. "If he's as mad as they say, I wouldn't put it past him to join the front lines in search of you."

"Thanks for that," Amaleah retorted.

"What?" Kileigh asked. "It's true."

Amaleah turned her attention onto Elaria. "Do you know where the Prince of Szarmi will be during the battle," she asked. She tried to control her voice as much as possible.

"Didn't you just decline his marriage proposal," Kileigh remarked, "in front of everyone?"

Amaleah rounded on the young matriarch. "He's still my friend," she said, though doubt had already begun to set in.

"Is he?" Kileigh prodded, "He didn't seem too pleased with you when he stormed out of the council meeting." She picked a stray thread in her tunic. "Oh well, I guess he's on the market now."

Amaleah rolled her eyes at the elf. There was no sense in conversing with her if all she was going to do was goad her. She turned her attention back to Elaria. "Well?" she asked.

"I heard he had found a tree high enough to see the entirety of the battlefield," Elaria responded hesitantly. "He plans to climb to the highest point possible and direct the troops from there."

Amaleah stared up at the height of the massive trees all around her. These woods were thousands of years old. She couldn't even begin to fathom how high Colin would have to climb in order to reach the highest peak he could manage. "He'll be safer there than on the frontlines," Elaria assured her. "Besides, I lent him a mail shirt and had our spellcasters provide him with an amulet for protection."

Elaria's reassurances did nothing to quell the feeling that their argument earlier that day would be the last thing they ever said to one another. Once again, she found herself wishing she had insisted that they had talked alone so that she could explain her position.

"Don't look so worried," Elaria said again. "The prince will be fine."

Amaleah's attention was drawn to the sound of clanking metal from across the plain. She looked past Elaria to see that her father's army was pounding their weapons against their shields. They began cheering as a robust man adorned by gleaming golden armor drew to the front of the line. To Amaleah's amazement, her father withdrew his helmet and scanned the woods before him.

He was too far away to see his face, for which Amaleah was thankful. She practiced the breathing technique Elaria had taught her. It helped. Barely.

He strode forwards. A billowing green and blue cape fluttered behind him as he approached the woods.

"My messenger tells me my daughter won't return home until I personally request her to."

His voice boomed through the trees. Amaleah clutched at the conch necklace around her neck. It hummed slightly beneath her fingers.

"The choice is yours, daughter. Return to Estrellala with me now or watch your friends die."

Amaleah's skin turned clammy. All the doubts that had been building within her bubbled to the surface. She had brought this destruction to the elves—even to Colin. She took a small step forward.

A warm hand rested on her shoulder, stalling her. "Do it now," Thadius whispered in her ear.

She looked at him, her eyes full of terror. "I'm not sure I can."

"I believe in you. We all do."

Amaleah clenched her hand into a tight fist. She needed to remember why she fought, why she wanted to save her people. Her father might not have started out as a monster, but he had certainly turned into one.

She exhaled and punched her hands out. Power exploded from her like a barreling wind before a storm. She dug her feet into the ground as the force of her magic shoved her backwards. Grinding her teeth, she focused her blast on the first ship, then the second, and then the third before her energy gave out and she collapsed in a heap upon the forest floor.

Shouts filled the air, drowning out all other sound. Weakly, Amaleah lifted her head and peered beyond the tree line. The three ships she had struck listed in the water, massive holes torn through their hulls. Soldiers clad in green and blue abandoned the vessels as fires slowly blossomed into life. The lines of soldiers who had previously been standing at attention before the ships had scattered and broken the line. Amaleah smirked. *Perhaps we do have a chance*, she thought as her gaze drifted to her father.

He crouched on the ground, his face a blazing red. "Was that your response, my dearest?" he called. His voice sounded strangely calm. "If that is the best you can do, then this battle will end more quickly than I had anticipated."

His words chilled Amaleah to the bone. She shivered as Thadius helped her rise to her feet. She leaned against him, her energy completely drained.

"Get her to the dais," Elaria commanded as one of the elves hiding in the trees handed her a bow. "Protect her," she added as Thadius lifted Amaleah and swung her onto his back.

"You're still injured," Amaleah protested.

"Now," Elaria said, her voice tight.

Amaleah peered through the haziness in her head to see that her father's forces had regrouped. With a mighty cry they surged forward. The battle had begun.

Chapter Forty-Nine

Amaleah clung to Thadius as he rushed through the trees. Her head spun and sweat dripped down her brow, but she managed to remain conscious. She wanted to tell him to stop, to let her down, that she could walk, but she couldn't muster her voice to work.

The sounds of battle filled the air. Men screamed, their voices abruptly cut short by what Amaleah could only imagine as death. Horses neighed, their cries piercing the air like peals of thunder. Metal clanged, adding to the pounding in Amaleah's head. Although she couldn't see the bodies of fallen soldiers or the bursts of blood as men were cut down, she could imagine the destruction of her father's army clashing with the smaller one that supported her.

The tattoo on her ankle burned as an arrow grazed her arm. Its tip was deflected by the leather bracers on her wrists. Thadius jerked as another arrow pierced his shoulder. Amaleah flew from his back. She rolled, striking the trunks of trees as she went. She screamed as her back finally struck a taller, sturdier tree.

"Amaleah!" Thadius called weakly. Amaleah's heart thrummed in her chest. *No*, she thought as she rolled onto her side. Through the trees, she could see another arrow protruding from Thadius's side.

She clawed her way forward. Each movement was agony. She watched as another arrow lodged itself in Thadius's chest.

"NO!" She cried. Blood seeped from the wound. Thadius's eyes rolled to the back of his head. He slowly sank to the ground, his breathing laborious.

She pulled herself to a standing position. She swayed, her body still weak from using the full force of her magic.

"Run, Amaleah," he whispered. His voice sounded so wet.

She took a step towards him. *Maybe I can heal him*, she thought.

"Go," he pled. "Please."

A lone archer emerged from the shadows. Starla. It was Starla.

Amaleah released a ferocious cry as she ambled forward. "Why?" she demanded, her voice as cold as ice. She dropped to Thadius's side. There was so much blood. She didn't know where to apply pressure. She didn't know how to make it stop. She clutched at the centaur's hand. His pulse beat against her palm. It was so desperately slow.

Amaleah looked up at the girl to whom Elaria had offered refuge and kindness. A second chance. For a moment, Amaleah could have sworn she saw regret etched on the assassin's face, but her features quickly slackened into a black stare.

"Why?" Amaleah demanded again.

"Did you see your father's army?" Starla scoffed. "You have no chance at winning this campaign, Princess."

Amaleah shook her head. "So, you…" she paused, looking down at Thadius. His heartbeat was even fainter now. She tried to will power into her fingers. There was nothing.

"I had intended to take you alone," Starla replied. There was a tone in her voice that gave Amaleah pause. "But," she continued, "there are always casualties in war."

Starla strode forward, her blonde hair falling into her face. She gripped Amaleah's hair and pulled her head back until she could peer in the princess' eyes. Amaleah felt Thadius's pulse sputter and slow. She tried to turn her head, to look at him, but Starla yanked on her hair, keeping her in place. "Even with your magic and your training, Princess, you don't deserve to rule Lunameed."

Amaleah reached for one of Starla's daggers. The assassin swatted her hand away.

"Tsk, tsk, Amaleah," she hissed. "Someone should teach you some manners." She pulled one dagger from its holster and held it against Amaleah's throat. The cold metal made Amaleah shiver, but she kept her gaze locked on Starla.

"Go ahead," she whispered. "Do it."

The assassin's eyes widened.

"What?" Amaleah asked, "Can't force yourself to do it?"

Although she had conflicted feelings about the assassin, although the witch of a girl had mortally wounded Thadius, Amaleah still saw a glimmer of something lurking beneath her hard exterior. In that moment, she didn't see an adversary, she saw a broken girl—much like herself—who would stop at nothing to survive.

Amaleah heard the rasp of Thadius's voice as he sucked in a mouthful of air. There was a pause. An exhale. He did not breathe in again.

Starla must have heard it to. She glanced towards the centaur, her expression vacillating between horror and determination. Her grip on Amaleah's hair slackened just enough for her to peer down at her friend. His eyes unblinking met hers.

Uncontrollable tears flowed down her cheeks as she fixed her gaze on Starla. "You didn't have to do this," she said.

For a moment, Starla looked stricken. That moment quickly

faded as she pressed the dagger more closely to Amaleah's throat.

"I think it's time we returned you to your father," she hissed in Amaleah's ear.

Amaleah tried to step on Starla's feet. She slammed her head back, hoping to catch the assassin in the nose. She even jabbed her elbow into Starla's side. Her blows either missed their mark or, if they did connect with Starla, only served to make the assassin press her blade tighter against her neck. Amaleah already felt a trickle of blood sliding down her neck.

A loud popping noise sounded from behind them. She felt Starla stiffen and then fall to the ground. Spinning around, she came nose-to-nose with Nikailus.

"Where did you come from?" she asked, followed quickly with, "Thadius."

Nikailus considered the dead centaur. "There's nothing we can do for him now," he said calmly as he wrapped his arms around Amaleah's shoulders. She leaned into him, thankful for his warmth and his sturdy presence. She closed her eyes as she thought of the carnage of the battlefield. Even from the distance, she could hear the screams of dying men. Her eyes flashed open as she remembered that Nikailus had not been with her at the battlefront.

"Where have you been, Nik?" she wrapped her arms around his neck, tears still streaming from her eyes. Thadius's legs were visible as she looked over Nikailus's shoulders. She quickly shut them again.

He traced circles down her back and cradled the back of her head with his other hand. The sensation was calming, but Amaleah was in no mood to be calmed. She wanted answers.

"Tell me where you've been, Nikailus. How did you get here without us hearing you?" Her voice came out more as a whine that a command. She tried pushing away from him. She wanted to see his face when she spoke to him. He held her tightly against his body.

"One day," he said, "you'll forgive me."

She squirmed in his arms, but his grip on her was too tight. She felt a pulling sensation at her navel. Heard the same loud popping sound from before. And then, the world was darkness.

Chapter Fifty

Colin knew they were outmanned. But that did not mean that they had to be outmaneuvered. He held up the spyglass Kileigh had given him. She'd promised him all the support the elves could muster, but it still wasn't enough to compete with the numbers King Magnus had rallied. Five thousand troops against fifteen thousand. If they survived, the bards would be singing about them across the ages.

Elaria sent a peregrine to carry messages from Colin to his commanders on the ground. It surveyed the battlefield with unflinching yellow eyes.

"I hope you are as fearless as they," he whispered to the bird. He stroked its blue-grey back and the bird squawked at him with a preternatural cry. "I'll take that as a yes." The bird's only response was to turn its gaze back to the field.

From his vantage point, Colin could see just how far King Magnus's troops stretched across the plain. Six ships were anchored in the harbor. Hordes of troops shuffled from the gangplanks. With the spyglass, he could see that many of them wore little more than quilted tunics for armor. They carried long spears. Few had anything else. He wondered how much training the soldiers had received, or if their king had simply recruited them to die.

Colin trained the spyglass on the troops already in formation. He counted at least three battalions of heavy infantry stationed in front of what he assumed to be the king's pavilion. A banner barring the Lunameedian sigil—a bow and arrow encased by a laurel—flew high above the pavilion. He estimated the three battalions to hold at least three thousand soldiers, if not more.

Ahead of the heavy infantry, a company of heavy cavalry waited to be called to action. The sight of them made Colin's stomach recoil. He knew that if they couldn't take out the heavy cavalry as quickly as possible they could punch a hole in his line, leaving his forces scrambling to fight both from the front and the back. He could not let that happen.

Thousands of light infantry, clad in similar garb to the men still shuffling off the ships, stood in front of the heavy cavalry. All of them carried spears. Some of them sported wooden shields. None of them had a single piece of metal armor from what Colin could see through the spyglass. Light cavalry flanked the rest of King Magnus's forces. Even from the cursory glance Colin gave them, he could tell that their riders were more than double that of his own.

At least a thousand archers formed three rows ahead of the light infantry. Colin watched as their commanding officer raced in front of them, shouting orders. He was too far away to hear what they were, but his heart sank as the archers drew back on their bows and aimed at the tree line.

A lone soldier emerged from the Lunameedian ranks, waving a white flag. Colin trained his spyglass on the soldier. The man appeared to be unarmed. Captain Conrad had told him once that forces who try to negotiate before a battle are cowards. Colin had never believed that little tidbit of advice to be true. Rather, he preferred to believe that there were times when diplomacy was a much better weapon than the sword. He doubted this would be one of those times.

He was surprised to see Elaria join the soldier in the middle of the plain. The conversation did not appear to be going the way the soldier had hoped. Colin prepared to give his first command as the soldier retreated into enemy lines. Colin lost sight of the man in the sea of disorganized light infantry. By the time he trained the spyglass back to the spot where Elaria had just been standing, she was gone. Colin breathed a sigh of relief. Neither side had launched the first attack. He knew it wouldn't be long, that the fighting couldn't stall forever, but still he hoped to figure out some plan of action that would save them all.

He peered down at the tree line, where he knew his forces were waiting to rush out and defend the very people they had fought centuries to defeat. Colin had never been prouder of the Szarmian troops than he was in that moment. The ones who had chosen to follow him gave him hope that, if he was successful in his campaign to win back his throne, he would be able to create peace between his and Amaleah's nations.

Her rejection still stung. Even thinking of her now made it difficult for him to concentrate on the impending battle. He found himself searching for any glimpse of her he could find through the densely packed trees. To no avail. He knew she was supposed to be stationed at the dais that Elaria had commissioned to be built just behind the protection of the first line of trees. He let himself imagine her safe among the ranks of the other spellcasters before blocking all thoughts of her from his mind. There would be time enough for him to process her rejection following this battle—assuming they both survived.

Alone, a rotund figure stalked from the tent and made his way to the front of the archers. Even without the spyglass, Colin could tell the man was King Magnus. He wore golden armor with a crown melded into the helmet.

"Well, that's ballsy," Colin whispered to the peregrine, who, of course, did not respond. The king did not step as far out as the messenger before him had. Instead, he planted himself right in front of the archers, hands on hips in an imposing stance.

"My messenger tells me my daughter won't return home until I personally request her to."

His voice boomed through the trees. Colin knew there was no way for the king's voice to carry like that without magical enhancement. Using the spyglass, he scanned the enemy lines. Sure enough, figures cloaked in black and emerald robes stood close to the king's pavilion. One of them had their arms outstretched in the king's direction. Colin cursed beneath his breath. He had not anticipated sorcerers in this battle.

"The choice is yours, daughter. Return to Estrellala with me now or watch your friends die," the king continued.

Colin dropped his gaze to the tree line. "Don't do it, Amaleah," he pled as he scanned the trees for any sign of her giving into the king's demands. His heart pounded in his chest as he waited. He found himself counting the seconds as they passed. He had just reached thirty when a giant gush of wind rushed across the plain. He heard an earsplitting crash.

Scrambling to raise the spyglass, Colin saw the second blast strike the second ship just as the first began to lurch and then sink. What few men remained on deck abandoned ship just as a third blast punched a hole in the hull of a third ship. He had no doubt that he had Amaleah to thank for the listing, sinking ships. He smiled as he watched the light infantry at the head of the army break.

As King Magnus sank back into the safety of his forces, his archers began raining arrows upon Colin's troops as they emerged from the trees. Colin had orchestrated the combined forces of the Szarmian and elvish troops to enhance their strengths while at the same time mitigate their limited numbers. The central force was comprised of four battalions of heavy infantry, each with five hundred men. Colin had trained with many of these men at some point during his time at Fort Pelid. They were an organized, unified force that would not break, even under the most desperate of situations. He was forever grateful that so many of them had chosen to leave behind their families to join him on his quest to reclaim the Szarmian throne. He hoped their faith in him would not be unfounded.

Flanking Colin's men was a mixture of elvish light infantry and Szarmian crossbowmen. Though these forces were only comprised of eight hundred, Colin hoped the automatic crossbows and the speed of the elves would be enough to support the battalions of heavy infantry during the assault. The Szarmian forces were well equipped. Even the crossbowmen had been assigned a dagger, a light metal helmet, a hauberk, and a large shield—to protect themselves during the reloading period. Each bow was capable of firing seven shots in a row with enough force to pierce through armor at close range. Colin hoped that, when the Lunameedian heavy cavalry decided to charge their lines, his crossbowmen would be able to take down a number of the horses.

The elves had provided six hundred archers for the battle. Colin had read account after account of the devastation elvish archers could perform during battle. He had always hoped to see their skills in action, he just wished it wasn't under these circumstances. Though the Szarmian forces were not known for their archery and only two hundred heavy longbowmen had traveled with Colin to Lunameed, these warriors had trained with their weapon since the age of three.

Behind the archers, Colin had kept a battalion of heavy infantry and crossbowmen in reserve. His meager three companies of light cavalry were grouped to his extreme left flank, where he hoped to be able to exploit some opening in the Lunameedian ranks.

The Szarmian battalions of heavy infantry were equipped with metal shields, a spear, and a short sword. Colin ordered the four battalions on the front line—each containing five hundred men—to advance. They locked their shields over their heads. Arrows bounced harmlessly off the metal barrier.

Seeing that their archers were ineffective against the unity of the Szarmian forces, King Magnus's commanders called for their archers to retreat. With a little prodding, they sent the thousands of ragged light infantry charging across the field.

Anno, the bulky, scarred war-elf who had trained Amaleah during her time in Encartia, had told Colin before the fighting began about a tactic the elvish archers were highly skilled in. Colin prayed to the Light that the maneuver would be as effective as Anno had proclaimed.

The six hundred elvish bowmen formed three lines behind the Szarmian heavy infantry. The archers, almost as one, raised their bows at a high angle and released. While the arrows were still arching upwards in the sky, the archers drew and released again, and again, and again. Each time they lowered the angle of their bows. Within a matter of seconds, over two thousand arrows blotted out the sun from the sky. Colin watched in awe as the arrows dropped down upon King Magnus's underequipped light infantry at the exact same moment. Although not as impressive as the skill the elves demonstrated, Szarmian heavy archers launched their own volley of arrows. Hundreds of Lunameedian soldiers fell to the attack. The sound of men screaming filled the air.

Even with the Lunameedian army taking heavy losses, it still wasn't enough. King Magnus's archers returned the volley as the thousands of light infantry continued rushing across the field. Not even the speed of the elves could keep up with the onslaught of the masses.

Colin gave the order and all four battalions of heavy infantry moved their shields to the front of their formations. They formed a solid line across the length of the battlefield. Using their spears, the infantry began pushing back the Lunameedian light infantry. Without shields or armor, the Lunameedian front line began to falter. The poorly trained soldiers in the back ranks began to drop their spears and run. Lunameed used their light cavalry to cut off the soldiers' path of escape. More and more of the light infantry fell as they were herded forward like cattle to slaughter before the might of the Szarmian heavy infantry.

Lunameed released a torrent of arrows. Colin watched in dismay as they fell upon the first and second battalions. Already engaged with the light infantry, his forces didn't have time to raise their shields against the onslaught from above. Dozens of Colin's men fell. Colin ordered for his small reserve of crossbowmen to fill the gaps as his soldiers regrouped. Bolts zipped through the field, killing many soldiers on impact. The elvish archers proved their worth as they yet again blotted out the sky with thousands of arrows arching over the Szarmian forces and into the middle of the Lunameedian light infantry.

It wasn't enough.

Colin scanned the battlefield trying to determine what his force's next maneuver should be. Elaria's peregrine soared through the air, arching over the Lunameedian light cavalry on Colin's left flank. There was a gap. Using the spyglass to confirm, Colin saw how a number of the light infantry had managed to slip past the light cavalry on that side. The horsemen, obviously ill-trained compared to the Szarmian forces, floundered. He could exploit that blunder.

Colin sent the order and the two hundred crossbowmen on his left flank charged forward under cover of their massive shields. At the last moment, they thrust the shields into the ground, forming a metal divide between the Lunameedian cavalry and them. Without pausing, they discharged the full might of their crossbows into the Lunameedian forces. It was a terrifying display of sheer grit and might as they discharged and reloaded multiple times in a row. Each time, they took out more of the cavalry.

A blast of power from the elvish spellcasters knocked dozens of the horsemen back. A dark shadow moved across the Lunameedian calvary, leaving only withered corpses in its wake. Colin wasn't sure if he should be thankful for Yosef's killing powers or terrified by them. The Lunameedian light infantry, clearly noticing the gap between the ranks and the piles of the dead, rushed away from the left flank, abandoning their position in a disorganized mob. A small smile crept across Colin's face as he watched the Lunameedian commanders futilely attempt to retake control of their forces.

His smile slowly turned into a frown as a figure forced its way through the fray. Having seen the sorcerers stationed at the king's pavilion, Colin had no doubts about who and what the figure was.

"Stop him!" he shouted. The peregrine flew through the air at a torrential speed. It reached the company commander leading the crossbowmen just as a strike of lighting shot from the sky. All Colin could see was the flash of white light before the screams began. Through the spyglass, he could see the charred bodies of his men splayed across the ground. A second strike pierced Yosef through the chest. His black cloak momentary floated above ground before dropping in a heap. Colin's commander ordered the retreat of what little forces remained.

Colin cursed beneath his breath. If they'd just had a little more time, he was certain the tactic would have broken the Lunameedian line. As it was, the light infantry that had broken away from the Lunameedian forces raced back to their positions. The sorcerer strode back to the king's pavilion. Even as arrows from the elves rained down upon the light infantry once more, the enemy forces continued to advance.

Colin searched the skies for the peregrine, but could find him nowhere. A commotion to his right flank drew Colin's attention away from the destruction on the left. A hooded figure, clad all in black with a scarf covering his face slashed through the enemy lines. Even without the spyglass, Colin could see that the warrior's axe glowed a brilliant red color.

"It can't be," Colin whispered enraptured. Throughout history, there had only been one warrior who wielded an ax that glowed red. And his name had been Kilian Clearwater.

The figure decimated the furthermost right flanks of the Lunameedian light infantry, as if they were nothing more than ants. Colin watched the warrior's progress through his spyglass. Taking his chances, Colin relayed his command to the runners he'd requested as backup in case something happened to the peregrine. He had hoped he wouldn't need them, but now he was thankful for his foresight.

Within moments, his crossbowmen on the right flank had turned their bolts on the Lunameedian light cavalry. Colin shifted the spyglass to the king's pavilion, wary of the retaliation the sorcerers would take against the warrior or against his troops. To his surprise, King Magnus gave no command. The sounds of his light cavalry being slaughtered by the crossbowmen sent a shiver down Colin's spine. He gripped the branch he was perched on and stared out over the field.

A horn blasted and the Lunameedian forces abruptly fell

back. One last rain of arrows fell upon the retreating forces, leaving bodies in their wake. Colin raised his spyglass, searching the enemy lines. He could see no reason for the retreat. Despite their heavy casualties, King Magnus still had the advantage. He hadn't even deployed his heavy infantry or heavy cavalry.

Colin's stomach dropped as he realized what King Magnus had in mind. The Lunameedian troops stepped to the side, leaving a clear path right down the middle of their forces.

He called for his troops to fall back. But, without the peregrine, the message was conveyed too slowly. The ground began to rumble. Even from the treetop, Colin could feel the jolting of his bones as the heavy cavalry charged forward. It was a thunderous sound that drowned out even the cries of the men they trampled on their way to meet the Szarmian battalions. Heavy infantry followed in the wake of the riders.

Colin's men began to retreat to the relative safety of the trees. The hooded figure disappeared into the scurry of soldiers as if he had been a figment of Colin's imagination. Elvish archers released a volley of arrows at the heavy infantry, but they glanced off the metal armor without causing many casualties.

A squad of sorcerers leapt off the backs of the heavy cavalry as they abruptly changed direction. As one, they raised their hands and sent a stream of fire down the middle of Colin's forces. It happened so quickly that his men didn't even have time to scream as they were incinerated. Fire tore through the trees, cutting off the escape route for what remained of the elves and Szarmian soldiers.

Smoke billowed around Colin. He coughed and peered down through the branches. Flames were creeping up the trunk of his command post. He shook his head and turned his gaze back to the battlefield. The Lunameedian heavy cavalry had regrouped in the middle of the field. Behind them, King Magnus strode through the battlefield detritus.

The mad king's voice boomed across the field. Even above the deafening sound of hooves and cries.

"You will always be mine," he shouted towards the tree line. "You can never escape me, Amaleah. Never."

The king raised his fist in the air and the cheering from his army ceased.

"This is it," Colin whispered, coughing as his lungs filled with smoke. "I'm so sorry I couldn't save you, Amaleah."

Colin forced himself to watch as the mad king lowered his arm and the heavy cavalry rushed forward to crush what remained of his forces. He watched as the horses picked up speed and the heavily armored riders lowered their lances. Colin's infantry locked shields and leaned forward, as if bracing for a storm. Colin knew his men were brave, but the sight of them holding the line even with the crushing force of the Lunameedian heavy infantry upon them, made his heart swell. He was proud to have served with them, even if he couldn't save them now.

A loud popping sound filled the battlefield and a gust of cool wind ruffled Colin's hair. His jaw dropped as he saw thousands of glowing figures winnow into the field. The fae had arrived. And they had brought hundreds of centaurs with them.

Chapter Fifty-One

Amaleah lurched forward. Her stomach roiled and bile filled her mouth. Closing her eyes, Amaleah focused on her breathing. Her head pounded and felt as if someone was slowly sliding a dagger through her brain. She coughed and clung to the warm body holding her.

Nikailus.

She opened her eyes wide and stared up at him. They were no longer in the forest. Dilapidated stone surrounded her. She could smell it now. The musty scent. The decay. The rot.

She slapped him so hard that his head jerked away from her. "Where are we?" she demanded. Her voice shook. He had let Thadius die. He had forced her to abandon the battle.

He slowly rotated his face towards her. Rubbing the red spot on his cheek from the impact of her hand, he smiled down at her.

"I knew you would never agree," he began.

"What have you done, Nikailus?"

"This is the only," he continued. "It's the only way we can save the world we were meant to rule." He caught her hand and whispered, "Together."

Amaleah fought the urge to slap him again. "Tell me what you've done, Nikailus."

"I discovered the way to free the Creators," he replied

emphatically. "I tried to tell you. I tried to give you the choice, but you ignored me," he frowned at her. "This is the only way," he repeated.

"What are you talking about!" Amaleah nearly shouted. "I am needed at the battlefront, Nik. I can't be chasing down foolish dreams that might not even be true."

She twirled around the room. Sunlight filtered in through the overgrown ivy on a window to her left. She could see no doors, no stairs, no way for her to get out.

"Where are we?" she demanded again. "And please, no more riddles."

"I found a text in the elvish library that spoke about the Wars of Darkness. Their historians recorded that, during the final battle at the Tower of Alnora, the Creators just disappeared."

Amaleah released an exasperated sigh. "I know the histories, Nikailus. Do you not understand what you just said? The Creators are gone. They have been over three hundred years."

"Yes," he said, his voice smooth and cold.

Amaleah continued searching the walls for any sign of a door. The ivy was so dense that it was difficult to see the stone beneath it. Even if she did find a way out, she was too far away to reach the battle in time to provide help. The Ruins of Alnora were more than a week's journey on foot. Even if she could find a horse, it would still take her three days to get back to Encartia. She ground her teeth as she considered.

"But there was a secret text, one that the Order of the Blackflame kept these past three hundred years. One that tells of the imprisonment of the Creators," he strode towards Amaleah and clutched both of her hands in his. "I have found what the forefathers before me could not. They knew the secret of releasing them, but knew not where the Creators had been locked away." He slipped one of his hands into the folds of his jacket and pulled out a tattered, flaking book.

"We can do it, Amaleah."

Amaleah chewed on her bottom lip.

"Your heart is beating so quickly," Nikailus whispered, rubbing the back of her hand with his thumb. He bent closer to her face. "Please," he begged, "just trust me."

Everything in Amaleah wanted to revolt. To pull away. To desert him. He had betrayed her in a way that she feared was unforgivable. And he had known. Known that all she wanted was control over her own life. He had taken the choice to stay and fight away from her. He had forced her to abandon Colin to the mighty forces of her father.

And for what?

Some rumor in a book that probably wasn't even as old as the Wars of Darkness.

She peered into his violet and star eyes. There was so much hunger there. So much desire. For her or for the power of the Creators, Amaleah wasn't sure.

"If I help you, will you take me back?" she asked, her voice came out in a small chirp. "I cannot just abandon the fight."

"You mean you can't just abandon him," Nikailus glowered.

"No, I mean I can't abandon any of them!" Amaleah shouted her response. "The elves, the Szarmian soldiers, everyone who has joined the fight. They are risking everything for me, Nikailus. Everything."

He dropped her hand and turned away from her. "When we release the Creators, Amaleah, you have to promise me that you will rule with me. We could do such great and wondrous things for the magical creatures of Mitier. Just think of it."

He whirled around to face her once more. His eyes seemed to glow as he flipped the book open. Amaleah didn't know what to say to him. There was a part of her that saw his vision. That hungered to be the iron fist that united the whole of Mitier, not just her kingdom. She could envision their lives together. With their powers combined, they would be too formidable a force to stop.

A smile spread across her face.

"Tell me what to do."

He returned her smile before turning his attention to a large stone formation in the middle of the room. Waving his hand across the formation, the ivy slithered back, revealing carved figures in the stone. Amaleah stepped forward, trailing her fingers over the tops of the sculptures. Their features were so lifelike that Amaleah had a momentary sensation of touching a corpse.

"Do you feel it?" Nikailus whispered in her ear as he wrapped his arms around her from behind. He pressed the full length of himself against her and tugged her more tightly to him. "The power? It's them, Amaleah. And we can rescue them."

"How do you know they weren't locked away for a good reason?" she murmured, a sudden fear creeping into the back of her mind. The conch shell necklace hummed against her chest as Nikailus laid his chin atop her head. "The only reason someone would lock away the Creators is to destroy the magical world. Think about it, Amaleah. Magic has been in decline since the Creators disappeared. If we release them now..."

"Maybe we can bring it back," Amaleah finished.

"Exactly," he whispered into her ear. He kissed her lobe as he positioned his face so as to be able to see the page he'd turned to in the book.

"Once we've finished the incantation, we need to consecrate the statues with blood."

Amaleah's stomach squirmed. "How much blood?" she asked.

"Don't worry," he whispered. "All we'll do is slice our palms open and let our blood flow around the statues. With our combined power, we will release them."

Although the thought of cutting herself scared her, she felt as if she had no other choice. If his spell worked, then the Creators would be free and they could turn the tide of the battle. If it didn't, then she was sure she could convince him to take her back. Trying was the only way.

They read the incantation together, their voices melding into one. At the end of the inscription, Nikailus sliced her palm with a silver dagger and then did the same to his own. Amaleah forced herself not to flinch as the cold metal bit into her skin. They walked around the stone pillar where the statues and etchings had been carved. Her blood mixed with Nikailus', forming a complete circle around the pillar.

They stepped back and waited. For a moment, it seemed as if nothing was happening. But then, a tremor ran down the pillar. Dust floated into the air like tiny sparkling diamonds. Amaleah took a step back, her mouth going dry. Nikailus took her hand. They watched as the figures etched into the pillars slowly peeled away from the stone.

A blinding white light filled the room and then encapsulated them in utter darkness. Amaleah clung to Nikailus's side.

"You have come at last," a feminine voice whispered from before them. Slowly, a blue orb began to glow. And then a golden one, and a green one, and a violet one, and a red one, and a white one, and a pink one, and an orange one. The orbs illuminated the faces of eight beings. Amaleah opened her mouth and then quickly shut it.

The golden and violet orbs dissipated along with the faces. Amaleah blinked in confusion. There were eight Creators in total. Where had the two gone?

"Cowards," the feminine voice behind the blue orb hissed. She turned to her brethren. There were three men and three women. All of them of insurmountable beauty. The woman who had spoken stepped forward. Her dark, chestnut hair fell in curls about her face. She was petite, but Amaleah could see the toned muscles beneath her silvery dress. Through the glow of the blue orb, Amaleah could see that the woman's eyes were a mixture of ice and sky. They were haunting.

"Amaleah Bluefischer." Her voice caressed Amaleah's name as if it were a breakable thing. "The Harbinger."

Amaleah did the first thing she could think of. She curtsied.

The woman's lips quirked into a small smile. "We have waited for you since the dawn of creation," the woman continued. Her voice echoed in the room. "And now, you have set us free."

She glanced at the others. Each of them stepped forward in turn, bowing their heads to Amaleah. They did not acknowledge Nikailus.

The woman with the blue orb stepped closer to Amaleah. She smelled of coconut oil and vanilla.

She cupped Amaleah's cheek in her hand. The woman's skin was surprisingly cold to the touch and it took all of Amaleah's willpower not to jerk away from her.

"This is our gift to you," the woman said.

Chapter Fifty-Two

Starla woke to the smell of smoke and burning wood. She coughed, as the thick air filled her lungs. Shaking her head, she tried to remember what had happened. She remembered shooting Thadius. And capturing Amaleah. Afterwards, though, was a haze. Rubbing the back of her head, she felt the warmth of her own blood soak into her fingers. She grunted, realizing what must have happened.

She coughed again as the smoke continued to curl around her. Thadius's dead body lay not ten feet from her. Whether it was from the smoke or the sight of the centaur's prone body, Starla's eyes began to water. She cursed herself before forcing herself into a standing position. Flames licked all around her. She thought about racing back to the Silver Moon camp. She knew it was her best chance at surviving this Creator forsaken battle, but her curiosity overruled her need for safety.

Wrapping herself in her cloak, Starla dashed through the line of flames. Szarmian soldiers and elvish archers rushed towards the flaming trees. Behind them, Starla could see heavily armored soldiers on horseback preparing to charge. Her heart skipped a beat as she realized what she had feared from the very beginning: the elves and Szarmian forces were no match for the sheer numbers of the Lunameedian army. She cursed whoever had stopped her from taking the princess to the mad king. She knew she could have saved them all. Elaria. That wimp of a prince, Colin. Even the golden matriarch of the elves. Now, they were as good as dead—if they weren't already.

Over the shouts of men and the neighing of horses, Starla heard the mad king's cries.

"You will always be mine. You can never escape me, Amaleah. Never."

Starla crept along the tree line, ignoring the heat from the flames as they licked at her back. She climbed a tree that wasn't quite burning yet. And there, just beyond the mass of cavalry, was the king.

Starla nearly tumbled from the tree as King Magnus brought down his hand and his cavalry began to charge. Her teeth chattered and her ears popped. She swung down from the tree and raced as far away from the oncoming forces as she could. As she ran, she kept glancing back at the last place she'd seen the king.

Just as the cavalry was reaching the first lines of Szarmian soldiers, a loud popping noise filled the air and a gust of wind disrupted the battlefield. Starla whirled in her tracks, peering out at the field. Thousands of fae and centaurs materialized out of thin air. They glowed different shades of colors as their forms took shape. Each one of them wore golden armor and carried majestic swords. She watched in awe as the centaurs bore down on the flanks of the heavily armored Lunameedian cavalry. Blood sprayed their gleaming armor as they cut through the ranks.

Cheers rose from the Szarmian and elvish forces, who began to rally once more. The fae bomblasted the sorcerers surrounding King Magnus with glowing orbs of power. Starla smiled to herself as she watched one of the sorcerers crumple to the ground, black smoke billowing from his robes.

She searched the battlefield for her uncle, but couldn't find a trace of him in the fray. *This could be my chance,* she thought as she trained her eyes on the mad king. She calculated what it would take to reach him. With the fae, centaurs, elves, and remaining Szarmian forces pressing in upon them, she heard his advisors calling for retreat. He continued calling for his daughter.

Fool.

Deftly, she pulled one of her daggers from the bandolier across her chest and began stalking towards the king. She wove in and out of the fighting. More Lunameedian heavy infantry were rushing forward, providing reinforcements to the king's army. She cursed as a stray arrow grazed her cheek. Blood sprinkled the ground as she pressed a hand firmly against the wound.

She was a mere twenty feet from the king when the wind changed. Dark clouds, boasting purple lightning swept over the battlefield. Gusts of wind buffeted her from both sides. She crouched low to the ground, trying to keep her footing. Peals of thunder shook the sky. The fae, their faces stricken, peered up at the sky. Starla had seen her share of storms over the years and this one was anything but normal.

Clenching her teeth, she inched her way toward the king. Despite the heavy wind and bolts of lightning, she drew ever closer to his position. All of the fighting had ceased as the soldiers peered towards the skies. As Starla watched, their faces slackened and their eyes glazed over. The hair on her arms stood on end and a nagging voice at the back of her mind roared at her to run, to get out while she still could. But, she was too close to the king to turn back now. She crouched even lower to the ground as she maneuvered between the silent, still soldiers.

A loud clap of thunder ripped through the air. The clouds with their purple lightning disappeared as quickly as they had appeared. For a moment, the soldiers continued to stand, listlessly peering up at the sky. And then, as if being controlled by invisible strings, they began attacking one another.

Warm blood splattered across Starla's face as a Lunameedian soldier cut down one of his own. He turned his gaze on Starla. There was nothing in his eyes as he raised his sword to cut her down as well. She threw the dagger in her hand straight into his eye. He swayed for a moment, took another step forward, and then tumbled to the ground. Starla wiped the blood from her face with the back of her sleeve.

All around her, soldiers killed indiscriminately. Her heart beat wildly in her chest as she searched the fray for King Magnus. Despite the chaos all around her, she knew she needed to take this chance to rid her kingdom of its greatest foe: its own king.

A Szarmian soldier jabbed at her with his spear. Starla dodged the attack by jumping into the air. Gripping another dagger from her bandolier, she shoved the blade deep into the soldier's throat and twisted. Blood sprayed the air in a mist as she continued advancing on the king's position.

Members of the king's council—the ones whose faces were not slack—demanded a retreat. Starla watched as the remaining sorcerers disappeared in plumes of glittering smoke. The councilors' cries rang across the battlefield. King Magnus continued to shout for his daughter, either he ignored them or simply didn't hear them over the sound of his own voice.

The sound of ground being stripped from the earth tore her attention away from the king. She watched as two fae turned on each other, their golden armor crimson with the blood of their victims. They sent bursts of energy at each other. Each blast shuddered the entirety of the battlefield.

Starla forced herself to stop watching. The king was directly in front of her. She was surprised he was still standing. A faint blue glow emanated from his body. She raised an eyebrow at the sight. She wondered if that was the source of his protection. *It doesn't matter*, she told herself as she pulled another dagger from her bandolier. There was no doubt in her mind that this was what she needed to do.

She shoved herself from the ground. The king whirled on her as her shadow passed over him. There was a look of surprise in his eyes as she landed on his back and wrapped her legs around his middle. Using her free hand, Starla tore the golden helm from the king's head. His ruddy cheeks were coated in sweat.

"She'll always be mine," he whispered, his mouth frothing. "She'll never escape me."

"Not if I can help it," Starla hissed as she plunged her dagger into the king's throat and twisted. His eyes widened as she ripped her dagger free and then stabbed him again, this time right below his left ear. Crimson blood spurted from the wound, coating her face. The coppery taste filled her mouth as she wrenched her dagger free and slammed it into him a third time.

The king's body stilled beneath her. She leapt from his body as it tumbled to the ground.

The councilors locked gazes with Starla as she turned on them. Blood dripped from her body to the ground. They looked to each other and then back at Starla.

"The King is dead," they cried. "Retreat!"

Lighting filled the sky, nearly blocking out the councilors' words. Wind stung Starla's cheeks as it gusted through the plain. Its roar blocked out all other sound as she sank to her knees. Within seconds, the lightning and wind subsided, leaving behind the destruction of the battle.

All around her, soldiers blinked at the hazy sunlight filtering through what remained of the clouds. Soldiers who had been fighting only moments before dropped their weapons, their expressions dazed.

"Retreat!" a lone shout rang out over the plain.

That single word seemed to propel what remained of the Lunameedian soldiers into action. Commanding officers ushered their troops along the path leading back to Estrellala. Shouts of 'the king is dead," and "retreat," echoed among the soldiers.

Starla stumbled to her feet. She had made her choice. King Magnus was dead. She had no doubt that her uncle would seize control of Lunameed. It had been what he'd always wanted. Power. Starla sucked on her bottom lip as she considered. She could leave now, slip away in the chaos. She doubted anyone would be able to find her. Maybe, after enough time had passed, she could find a way to communicate that she was alright to her sister, Viola. She could set herself free from the tyranny of the Lunameedian court—of her uncle.

She glanced at the diminished lines of Szarmian and elvish forces. Even with the odds stacked against them, they had held their line. She knew their work was far from over. With King Magnus dead and the Lunameedian forces retreating, this was a decisive victory for Amaleah and Colin. But, Starla knew the war was far from over. Grinding her teeth, Starla ambled back towards the Silver Moon camp.

Chapter Fifty-Three

The Ruins of Alnora, Lunameed

The woman released Amaleah's cheek. Tears streamed from the princess's eyes as she peered up at the woman.

"What have you done?" she asked, her lips trembling. She had seen it all. The soldiers turning on one another. Her father's body, coated in blood. The fires. The destruction. The death.

"You mean, what have you done," the woman corrected.

"Me?" Amaleah asked.

The woman laughed, her voice like silver bells. "Oh, Amaleah, if it hadn't been for you, we would never have been able to come back to power."

"Who are you?" Amaleah hissed. She stole a glance at Nikailus. His face was shrouded in shadow.

"We are the Creators," the woman replied. "You may call me Tavia, if you wish."

Amaleah shook her head. It couldn't be. The Creators were good. They did as the Light commanded. They were everything that was beautiful in the world.

Tavia smirked at Amaleah. She raked her pointed nails across Amaleah's cheek before clutching the princess's chin in a vice-like grip. "Dearest Amaleah, the Harbinger of the Light," Tavia mocked. "We created this world. We molded each living

475

thing from dust and light. You owe your very existence to us."

Amaleah struggled against Tavia's grip, to no avail. The woman flashed a snake-like smile at her as she leaned in close and whispered in Amaleah's ear, "We will do great and terrible things together, you and I." She kissed Amaleah on the forehead. "When we're through with this world, not even embers shall remain of those who defy our power."

End of Book Two...

Epilogue
Silver Moon Camp, Lunameed

Colin paced around the councilroom. Plumes of mureechi smoke filled the room as Redbeard puffed on his pipe from the corner closest to the fire. Elaria, her arm in a sling, sat beside Kileigh at the head of the table. The golden elf scribbled notes on a scroll. Representatives from the fae and the centaurs waited just beyond the door. Colin was thankful for their aid, but unsure how they would react to his taking command now that Amaleah was missing.

Nylyla shuddered as Colin passed behind her. He placed a hand on her back and felt the waifish elf suck in a breath. He knew she had been crying. He couldn't blame her. They had found Thadius's body in the woods, but, so far, had discovered nothing to indicate what had happened to Amaleah. Part of him wanted to join her, but now was not the time. Their forces were diminished. Their princess was missing. The Lunameedian king was dead.

Colin glanced at Starla. She had come to him, drenched in blood, while the forces were retreating. The final storm had extinguished the flames trapping him in his command post. She'd stumbled into him, her eyes glassy, and confessed that she'd killed the king.

Colin couldn't say he was sorry for her actions. He just wished he knew what had become of Amaleah and Nikailus.

"We have to make a decision," Elaria said, her voice hoarse.

Colin nodded. He knew the matriarch was right. He glanced around the room. All of the gathered councilors averted their gazes except for Elaria. Colin sighed loudly. How was he supposed to accomplish anything if the councilors weren't even willing to look him in the eye? He had seen the armies turn on one another. He didn't know who or what had caused the storm—or the men to lose their wits—but he couldn't think of that right now. King Magnus was dead and they needed to take this time to declare Amaleah the rightful ruler of Lunameed.

"With King Magnus dead, the rightful ruler of Lunameed is the Princess—Queen—Amaleah," he corrected himself as he spoke. He met Elaria's gaze, "Have you heard anything from Dramadoon?" he asked.

"I have sent word to them of the king's demise," Elaria responded judiciously, "but am still waiting on a response."

"Do we trust the fae and the centaurs to recognize her?" he asked.

"They have always been our allies," Elaria responded.

Colin ground his teeth. Her response left much to be desired. He knew that they must all be calculating what the best course of action was. He was a foreign prince—one that their princess had denied marriage to—who belonged to a kingdom that they had warred with for centuries. There was no reason to believe that they would accept him as their commander now. He also knew they needed what remained of his troops and his experience commanding an army.

A knock came from the door. Colin nodded and a servant opened it wide enough to reveal a messenger. He proffered a letter sealed with the Lunameedian crest.

Colin accepted the letter with trembling hands. Starla had already told him what her uncle would do. She had provided intel about how the High Councilor had always coveted the throne and would see King Magnus's death as an opportunity to seize control of the kingdom.

The letter only confirmed what he already knew.

"What comes next, then?" Nylyla asked. Her voice shook.

Colin crumpled the letter in his fist before saying, "We keep fighting." He turned to Elaria, "We need to send out a search party to find Queen Amaleah."

The matriarch nodded, her face paling.

"Redbeard," Colin said, turning to face the older man, "I saw something during the battle." The flash of the red ax filled his mind, "I need you to lead an investigation." The older man grunted in response. It was all Colin needed.

"Starla," he continued, "I have a special mission for you, if you're up to it."

The assassin bowed her head for a moment, but then looked Colin straight in the eyes and nodded.

"Good," he responded. He looked around the room. "I know there is still a lot of confusion about what happened on the battlefield today. I can't promise you answers. All I can promise is that we will face every challenge that comes our way. Today was a great victory. The tyrant, King Magnus, is dead. The Lunameedian forces retreated against our significantly lesser numbers. The fae and the centaurs joined our cause."

Colin paused as he scanned the room. He had expected at least one of the attendants to exhibit exhileration at his words. Instead, none of them reacted. He sighed. "Queen Amaleah trusted me and I will not let that trust go to waste. She may be missing now, but we will find her. And," he continued, "we will deliver her throne to her."

To Colin's surprise, Kileigh rose from her seat at the head of the table.

"Thank you, Colin," she replied, her voice a purr. "These are precarious times." She stepped away from the table and began walking about the room. "After seeing what happened today, I have no doubt that there is something much more heinous threatening our lives than the rot found in the Lunameedian court. Our one hope is to find the Harbinger and bring her home again."

Colin gaped at Kileigh, but the elf didn't seem to notice. "I have read the signs. We all have. We know that the time for the Harbinger has come."

Colin smiled. He wasn't exactly sure what Kileigh meant by the Harbinger, but he was certain she was on board with seeking the princess out. Whatever her reasoning, her words had done the trick. Everyone in the room looked either at Colin or at the golden matriarch.

"So, let us begin," he said as the members of the council nodded in agreement.

Find the Other Works of S.A. McClure

The Search
Kilian
Keepers of the Light
Harbinger of the Light
The Last Siren

Explore the World of the Broken Prophecies at
https://www.samcclure.com/

Did you enjoy Destroyers of the Light?

Please consider leaving a review on Goodreads and Amazon!

About Me

I've been writing for as long as I can remember. It started off with silly short stories and poetry as a little girl and morphed into novels about love, loss, redemption, adventure and so much more. Storytelling has the ability to broaden our worldviews, help us understand ourselves and each other. It is a process. It is a journey.

I hope you enjoy my stories as much as I enjoyed writing them.

Made in the USA
Columbia, SC
10 June 2019